About the Authors

From as far back as she can remember, **Michelle Conder** dreamed of being a writer. She penned the first chapter of a romance novel just out of high school, but it took much study, many (varied) jobs, one ultra-understanding husband and three gorgeous children before she finally sat down to turn that dream into a reality. Michelle lives in Australia, and when she isn't busy plotting, she loves to read, ride horses, travel and practise yoga. Visit Michelle: michelleconder.com

Kate Hardy has been a bookworm since she was a toddler. When she isn't writing, Kate enjoys reading, theatre, live music, ballet and the gym. She lives with her husband, student children and their spaniel in Norwich, England. You can contact her via her website: katehardy.com

Maya Blake's writing dream started at age thirteen. She eventually realised her dream when she received 'The Call' in 2012. Maya lives in England with her husband, kids and an endless supply of books. Contact Maya: mayabauthor.blogspot.com, twitter.com/mayablake, facebook.com/maya.blake.94

Hidden Heirs

Hidden Heirs:

His One Night Heir

MICHELLE CONDER

KATE HARDY

MAYA BLAKE

MILLS & BOON

First Published in Great Britain 2023
by Mills & Boon, an imprint of HarperCollins*Publishers* Ltd,
1 London Bridge Street, London, SE1 9GF

www.harpercollins.co.uk

HarperCollins*Publishers*
Macken House, 39/40 Mayor Street Upper,
Dublin 1, D01 C9W8, Ireland

Hidden Heirs: His One Night Heir © 2023 Harlequin Enterprises ULC.

Prince Nadir's Secret Heir © 2015 Michelle Conder
Soldier Prince's Secret Baby Gift © 2019 Harlequin Enterprises ULC.
Claiming My Hidden Son © 2019 Maya Blake

Special thanks and acknowledgement are given to Kate Hardy for her contribution to the *A Crown by Christmas* series.

ISBN: 978-0-263-31931-6

This book is produced from independently certified FSC™ paper to ensure responsible forest management.

For more information visit: www.harpercollins.co.uk/green

Printed and Bound in the UK using 100% Renewable Electricity at CPI Group (UK) Ltd, Croydon, CR0 4YY

PRINCE NADIR'S
SECRET HEIR

MICHELLE CONDER

For Pam Austin, who planned the most wonderful holiday while I wrote this book. Meeting you on that train ride to Paris was one of life's little gifts.

And for Paul for always being there.

CHAPTER ONE

SOME DAYS STARTED out well and stayed that way. Others started out well and rapidly deteriorated.

This day, Nadir Zaman Al-Darkhan, Crown Prince of Bakaan, decided as he stared at a very large and very ugly statue squatting in the corner of his London office, was rapidly sliding towards the latter. 'What the hell is that?'

He glanced over his shoulder at his new PA, who blinked back at him like a newly hatched owl transfixed by a wicked wolf. She'd been recommended by his old PA, whose recently acquired husband had taken offence at the seventeen-hour work-days Nadir habitually kept, and he wasn't sure how she was going to work out.

In general people either treated him with deference or fear. According to his brother, it had something to do with the vibe he gave off. Apparently he emanated an aura of power and ruthless determination that didn't bode well for his personal relationships, which was why he didn't have many. Nadir had merely shrugged when Zach had delivered that piece of news. Personal relationships ranked well down below work, exercise, sex and sleep.

Not always, a sneaky voice whispered in his ear and he frowned as that voice conjured up an image of a woman he had once briefly dated over a year ago and had never seen since.

'I believe it's a golden stag, sir,' his PA all but stuttered, definitely falling into the fearful category.

Applying some of that ruthlessness his brother had mentioned, Nadir banished the image of the blonde dancer from his mind and turned back to the statue. He could see it was a stag and he only hoped it hadn't once been alive. 'I got that, Miss Fenton. What I should have said is—what the hell is it doing in my office?'

'It's a gift from the Sultan of Astiv.'

Ah, just what he needed—another gift from some world leader he didn't know, offering commiserations over the death of his father two weeks ago. He'd only been back in Europe a day since the funeral and he was, frankly, tired of the reminders which always brought up the fact that he felt nothing for the man who had sired him.

Annoyed, he strode across to his desk and sat down. His PA stopped in his doorway with her iPad clutched to her chest.

'Tell me, Miss Fenton. Should a person feel badly that their father has just passed away?'

His PA's eyes slowly widened as if he'd just raised a gun to her head. 'I couldn't quite say, sir.'

Meaning she didn't want to say. Which didn't surprise him. It wasn't as if he was known for seeking out the personal opinion of those who worked for him. Not on private matters anyway.

Still, he couldn't quite contain his frustration as his PA shuffled into his office and perched on the edge of an office chair. Between fear and awe he'd go with awe every time but his new PA looked as if she was waiting for him to attack her with a blunt instrument, which could have something to do with the whole host of unwanted emotions and memories his father's death had stirred up in him. He knew a shrink would tell him that was a good thing. As far as Nadir was concerned, long buried emotions and memories were long buried for a very good reason.

'What else have you got for me, Miss Fenton?'

She flashed him a relieved look that he had turned his mind to work. 'Miss Orla Kincaid left a message.'

Nadir already regretted calling up an old mistress to see if she was free for dinner. Earlier, when it had crossed his mind, he'd been bored by a group of business executives who couldn't give away a cold beer to a dying man in the desert let alone convince him to shell out millions to invest in a product they were trying to manufacture on the cheap. 'Let's have it.'

His PA shifted uncomfortably. 'She said—and I quote— "I'm only interested if he's going to take our relationship seriously this time"—unquote.'

Rolling his eyes, Nadir told her to strike that one. 'What else?'

'Your brother rang and wants you to call him ASAP.'

Maybe Zachim had received a giant stag as well. But more likely he wanted to know how Nadir was going with his plan to help haul their Arabic homeland into the twenty-first century. With a spaceship, Nadir thought wryly, or maybe a really big front-end loader. His father had ruled Bakaan with an iron fist and now that he was dead it was supposed to be Nadir's job to lead the country into the future. Something he had no intention of doing.

Years ago he had made a promise to his father that he would never return to rule Bakaan and Nadir always kept his promises. Fortunately, Zachim had been groomed in his stead and had agreed to take on the position as the next King of Bakaan. Poor bastard. 'Get him on the phone.'

'I have other messages,' she said, balancing her iPad with one hand.

'Email them to my palm pilot.'

Moments later his palm pilot beeped right after his land-line. His new PA was efficient; he'd give her that at least.

'If you're going to hassle me over the business proposal to reinvent the Bakaani banking system I'd like to

remind you that I do have an international business to run,'
Nadir grouched good-naturedly. Despite the fact that they
were only half-brothers, Zachim was the only person Nadir
would call a true friend and they caught up whenever their
work paths crossed.

'I wish it was only that.' His brother's tone was grim.
'You need to get back here right away.'

'Ten hours in that place was ten hours too long,' Nadir
drawled. Before that he hadn't been back to Bakaan for
twenty years and he'd be happy to make it another twenty.
The memories his homeland conjured up in him were better left buried and it had been more of a battle to keep them
at bay yesterday than he'd be willing to share with anyone.
In fact the only way he'd succeeded was to call up images
of that exotic dancer and he hadn't much liked thinking
about her either. Especially with the way things had ended
between them. And here he was thinking about her again.
He scrubbed a hand across his freshly shaven jaw.

'Yeah, well, you hotfooted it out of here before you
heard the news,' his brother said.

Nadir lounged in his seat with a relaxed feline grace
and propped his feet on his desk. 'What news?'

'Father named you the next in line to the throne. You're
to be King and you better get your sorry arse back here
quick smart. Some of the insurgent mountain tribes are
making moves to cause instability in the region and
Bakaan needs a show of leadership.'

'Hold up.' Nadir's chair slammed forward as his feet
dropped to the floor. 'Father named you the heir.'

'Verbally.' The frustration in Zach's voice was clear.
'It seems that doesn't hold much sway with the council.'

'That's ridiculous.'

'That's what happens when you die of a heart attack
without putting the paperwork in order.'

Nadir forced himself to relax and sucked in a deep

breath. 'You know it makes sense that you become the next Sultan. Not only do you run the army but you've lived there most of your life.'

He heard his brother's weary sigh and hoped another lecture wasn't coming about how Nadir was the oldest and how it was his birthright. They'd discussed this ad nauseam for years but it was only yesterday that he'd realised Zach had always believed that he'd one day return to Bakaan and take over. 'I think you're making a mistake but you'll need to officially renounce your position to the council.'

'Fine. I'll send them an email.'

'In person.'

Nadir swore. 'That's ridiculous. This is the twenty-first century.'

'And, as you know, Bakaan is labouring somewhere around the mid-nineteenth.'

Nadir ground his jaw and picked up the stress ball on his desk, tossing it through the basketball hoop set up beside the Matisse on his wall. His father might not have planned to die when he had but he would have known the succession protocol. Was this his way of trying to control him from the grave? If it was, it wouldn't work. Once, when Nadir was a child, they might have had a close relationship but that had ended when Nadir realised how manipulative and self-centred his father was. 'Set it up for tomorrow.'

'Will do.'

He rang off and stared into space. That was what you got for not tying up loose ends at the right time. Twenty years ago he'd left Bakaan after his father had refused to give his mother and twin sister a state funeral after a fatal car accident. They had shamed him, his father had said, when they had tried to flee the country to start a new life. It didn't matter to his father that they had not lived as man and wife for years or that his mother and sister were desperately unhappy with their exiled life in Bakaan. It only mattered that they continued to live where his father had placed them. When Nadir had stood up for their honour his father had basically said it was either his way or the highway.

So Nadir had chosen the highway and his father had disowned him. It was one of his old man's specialities—turning his back on anyone who displeased him—and Nadir had said *sayonara* and left to make his own way in the world. And it had been a relief because it helped him forget the role he'd inadvertently played in his mother and sister's deaths. It was also the last time he'd let his father manipulate him. Nadir had no doubt that not changing his will to reflect Zachim as the next leader had been a deliberate move on his father's part. But he wouldn't win.

Memories surged and Nadir cursed and rocked to his feet. He stared out of the window as a stream of sunlight broke through the clouds, casting a golden hue on the Houses of Parliament. The colour reminded him of Imogen Reid's long silky hair and his mood headed further south as he thought of her once more. She was another loose end he had yet to tie up, but at least with that one he had tried.

Frustrated with the way the day was turning out, Nadir thumbed through the messages his PA had sent to his palm pilot, his eyes snagging on one from his head of security.

A sixth sense—or more a *sick* sense—told him his day was not about to take an upward swing just yet.

'Bjorn.'

'Boss-man.' His head of security spoke in a soft Bostonian drawl. 'You know that woman you asked me to track down fourteen months ago?'

Damn, he'd been right and every muscle in his body tensed. 'Yes.'

'I'm pretty sure we found her. I've just sent through an image to your handheld for you to check.'

Gut churning, Nadir pulled the phone from his ear and watched as the face of the beautiful Australian dancer who had haunted his thoughts for fourteen long months materialised on the screen. Fifteen months ago he'd met her at the Moulin Rouge after he and Zach had found themselves in Paris at the same time.

His brother had claimed he could do with seeing something pretty so they'd headed to the famous dance hall as a lark. Nadir had taken one look at the statuesque dancer with hair the colour of wheat and eyes the colour of a freshly mown lawn on a summer day and four hours later he'd had her up against the wall in his Parisian apartment with her incredible legs tightly wrapped around his lean hips. Then he'd had her on his dining room table, under his shower, and eventually in his bed. Their affair had been as hot as the Bakaani sun in August. Passionate. Intense. *All-consuming.*

He'd never felt such a strong pull to a woman before and even though his brain had warned him to back away he'd still made four consecutive unscheduled weekend trips to Paris just to be with her. Right then he should have known that she was trouble. That their affair was unlikely to end well. Little had he known it would end with him finding out she was pregnant and her claiming the child was his. Little did he know that she would then disappear before he'd have a chance to do anything about it.

Likely she'd disappeared because she *hadn't* been carrying his baby at all but still, the thought that he had fathered a child somewhere out in the world and didn't know about it ate away at him. A flush of heat stole over him. He didn't know what her game had been back then but there was no question that she had played him. He just wanted to know how much—and why. 'That's her. Where is she?' he bit out harshly.

'Turns out she's in London. Been here the whole time.'

'Any sign of a child?'

'None. Should I ask? I'm sitting inside the café she works at now.'

'No.' A welcome shot of rage pumped through Nadir's bloodstream, priming his muscles. It looked as if today was the day he was being given a chance to rid himself of all the irritating issues in his life and now that he thought about it that could only be a positive thing. A faint smile twisted his lips. 'That pleasure will be mine. Text me your location.'

'That guy looking at you is giving me the creeps.'

Tired from lack of sleep due to her teething five-month-old daughter, Imogen stifled a yawn and didn't bother turning towards the back of the room even though she knew who Jenny was referring to. He was giving her the creeps as well and not just because of his hard looks. She recognised him from somewhere but couldn't think where.

She folded a paper napkin at her station at the bar and darted another quick glance outside the café window to see if her housemate Minh had turned up. Her shift had already ended but she'd stayed back to help tidy up until he arrived.

Jenny elbowed her. 'I think he wants to ask you out.'

'It's the blonde hair. He probably thinks I'm easy.' Fifteen months ago she'd had an equally imposing male think the same thing of her but he'd been wearing a three-thousand-dollar suit and had completely charmed her. He'd also been a billionaire playboy with the attention span of a single-celled amoeba. She wasn't so gullible when it came to men now. And, anyway, this guy looked as if he belonged to the secret service or something. Which only made her feel more uneasy. The little retro café where she waitressed didn't usually attract the kind of clientele who required personal security, and she knew that the playboy in the three-thousand-dollar suit used to have his own detail. Was that where she had seen this guy before? With Nadir? It seemed impossible but, before she could dart another quick glance his way, Jenny nudged her.

'No need to worry now. I think I spot your boyfriend outside.'

Heat shot through Imogen's face and her head came up as for a split second she thought Jenny was referring to the playboy she'd never be able to forget, no matter how much she tried.

When she caught sight of Minh waving to her through the café window a whoosh of air left her lungs in relief. Boy, but she was jittery all of a sudden.

'I've never seen him before,' Jenny continued. 'And he looks so gorgeous carrying your little girl in that sling.' She sighed. 'I wish I could meet a man who was a looker and also a caring dad.'

Heart still pumping, Imogen waved to her friend and infant daughter. She guessed Minh was a looker with his exotic Eurasian tanned features and he was certainly one of the nicest men she had ever met in her life but she'd never seen him as anything other than a friend. And not just because he was gay but because Prince Nadir Zaman Al-Darkhan had not only left her with a baby to take care of but he'd also left her with a phobia about falling in love.

Well, maybe not a phobia, exactly. More a deep resolve to never let a man take advantage of her again. Her own father had taken advantage of her mother's inherent goodness and it had devastated Imogen to watch her mother make excuse after excuse as to why her father hardly ever spent any time with them.

'*Your father works so hard, baby girl—he just needs time to relax, that's all.*'

Relaxing with another woman and eventually leaving his wife for her? Imogen would never let that happen to her. If she ever attempted another relationship in the future she'd do so with eyes wide open and it would be on her terms and her terms only. A picture of Nadir's handsome face materialised in her mind and she pushed it away.

'Unfortunately, he's not my boyfriend.' Or her baby's father.

She threw Jenny a smile and wished her a fab Friday night out on the town before heading towards the back of the bar to grab her handbag and head out to meet her makeshift family.

Minh had been a godsend in more ways than one this past year. When she'd discovered she was pregnant her roommate, Minh's sister, had told her that her big brother was heading to America for six months and was looking for someone to housesit. With the lease coming up on their flat in Paris anyway, it had seemed like an opportunity straight out of the heavens and she'd jumped at the opportunity to look after his swanky Knightsbridge pad. But then she probably would have gone to Siberia if it meant getting out of Paris at that time.

With no close family to fall back on in Australia, she'd anticipated having time in London to lie low and sort herself out before the baby arrived. Unfortunately she hadn't reckoned on being so sick she could barely move from Minh's sofa the whole time. When Minh had returned home he'd taken her under his wing and told her she could stay for as long as she needed. He'd even visited her in the hospital right after her precious daughter had come into the world, while no doubt her baby's father had been wining and dining some supermodel on a tropical island or some such.

Imogen grimaced. She'd known about Nadir's reputation as a handsome rebel bad boy from the start and as far as she was concerned you could add irresponsible bastard to that list of seedy qualities as well. And maybe add stupidity to her own because at the time she'd imagined she had fallen in love with him. *Fool*.

To say she owed Minh a lot was an understatement. She especially owed him a chance to have his boyfriend move in with him without her and Nadeena cramping their style and she gratefully accepted the tips the barman passed to her on her way out. In another week or two she should have enough to look for her own place but she knew Minh wouldn't push. He had a heart as big as a mountain.

'Hey, gorgeous,' he said, kissing her cheek. 'How was work?'

'Fine.' She grabbed her smiling daughter out of his arms and planted kisses all over her upturned face. Nadeena stared up at her with Nadir's striking blue-grey eyes and ebony lashes. His smooth olive complexion. 'What have you two been up to?'

'I took her to the park and the outdoor café. I hope she's not smelly,' Minh said as he untied the baby sling. 'It's like holding a hot brick against you in this weather. And they complain London summers are tepid.'

Imogen laughed. 'One twenty-eight-degree day and you English are ready to call it quits. The trouble is that you don't know how to handle the heat.'

Minh gave her a droll look. 'The trouble is we don't *want* to handle it.'

Grinning, Imogen took the sling and slid it over her shoulders and settled Nadeena against her, all her earlier feelings of unease completely gone. She linked her arm through Minh's. 'You know how much I appreciate your help, right? I mean I can't thank you enough for babysitting today. Yesterday.' She made a face. 'Last week.'

'She's a darling child and the dodgy film I'm editing is still in the can. Until they call me back I'm a free man.'

'Don't let David hear you say you're a free man,' she teased.

About to give her some spunky reply, Minh's jaw fell open and nearly hit the pavement. 'Hold that thought,' he breathed in a stage whisper. 'The archangel of heaven has just landed and he's wearing Armani and a terrific scowl.'

Laughing at the theatrics he picked up from working with film stars, Imogen turned and her jaw not only hit the pavement, it continued all the way to Australia.

The ruthless, heartless bastard who had left her pregnant and alone in Paris was heading towards her, his long, loose-limbed strides eating up the pavement and scattering startled pedestrians like a shark mowing down a school of tuna.

Imogen's arms instinctively came up to wrap around a sleepy Nadeena, her mind completely blank.

Nadir stopped directly in front of her. 'Hello, Imogen.' As tall as she was, she still had to tilt her head back to look into his eyes that were currently shielded by aviator sunglasses reflecting her own stunned expression back at her. 'Remember me?'

Imogen was in such a state of shock at seeing him after only just thinking about him so vividly all her addled brain could come up with was how impossibly good-looking he was in his black suit. How tousled his midnight hair looked—no doubt from where he had run his fingers through it a hundred times already. Her own immediately itched to do the same thing and she curled them into the soft fabric of Nadeena's sling, disconcerted by the immediate and compelling effect he still had on her.

'I...of course.'

She swallowed heavily as his eyes dropped to Nadeena. The glint from his sunglasses made him look like a steely-eyed predator eyeing succulent prey. 'You had the baby.'

Something in the way he said that in his deep, smooth baritone that defied geographical distinction made the hairs stand up on the back of Imogen's neck.

It was the underlying anger, she decided. Maybe even fury. And for the life of her she couldn't imagine why he should be so upset. *He* had left *her* fourteen months ago so didn't that mean she had the jump on anger right now? Unfortunately all she could conjure up was paralysed shock.

Sensing her unease, Minh shifted defensively beside her and Imogen took a deep breath, rallying her scattered senses. 'Yes.' She cleared her throat.

'That's nice.' Nadir's smile was all even white teeth and completely lethal. Then he slowly drew off his sunglasses and his shockingly beautiful blue-grey eyes drilled into hers with all the warmth of a glacier. 'Who's the father?'

CHAPTER TWO

WHO'S THE FATHER?

Imogen stared at Nadir, slowly digesting his snarled words. She'd only heard him use that tone once before and it was on the phone to some poor sod in his home country and the shock of it kick-started her brain into a usable gear. Steadying her trembling knees, she forced a smile to her lips and thought that of course he would want to know about the baby. Why wouldn't he? It was his doctor, after all, who had confirmed her pregnancy that fateful night in his Paris apartment all those months ago.

God, if she'd only left work five minutes earlier or later this whole situation might have been avoided. She swallowed heavily and forced herself to meet his hard stare, his raised eyebrow that could make him look either wickedly seductive or incredibly foreboding. Today it was definitely foreboding, which didn't help to explain the electrodes of excitement pulsing through her body, making her both shivery and hot at the same time.

No, not *excitement*, she corrected; it was *adrenaline*. Her fight or flight system was on overload; her reaction could hardly be considered excitement after the way he had treated her. The reminder of that helped calm her down and she gave him a tight smile, a deep sense of self-preservation warning her not to answer his question just yet. 'It's a surprise to see you like this.'

'I'm sure it is, *habibi*. Now answer my question.'

Swallowing heavily, she raised her chin. He used to whisper that term of endearment to her when he was about to seduce her and God, she wished it wasn't such an effort to hold those erotic memories of their fleeting time together at bay but it was. 'Why do you ask?'

'Don't play games with me, Imogen. I'm not in the mood.'

A ripple of unease slid down her spine and Minh, obviously sensing Nadir's ire as much as she could, half stepped in front of her. 'Ease up there, chief. There's no need to be aggressive.'

Nadir slowly turned his razor-sharp gaze to Minh and, although Minh didn't flinch, Imogen did. Unfortunately Minh had no idea that the infamous rebel prince was Nadeena's father. Imogen hadn't told anyone.

'And you are?' Nadir's question came out as if he'd just asked Minh if he had any last requests.

'Imogen's friend.'

'I suggest you back off, *Imogen's friend*.' Nadir's lip curled into a sneer. 'This is not your business.' Then he turned the full force of his attention back to her and Imogen really wished that he hadn't. 'Well?'

How could he make one word sound so powerful?

'Sorry, but I don't like your attitude, chief.' Minh puffed out his chest and Imogen groaned. 'You need to dial it down a little.'

'It's okay, Minh.' She gave his arm a squeeze, only just realising that her arm was still linked with his. 'I know him.'

Nadir pinned her with a patronising look. 'That's putting it mildly, *habibi*.'

His meaning was clear and Imogen felt a flush rise up her neck.

'I don't like him,' Minh said softly.

Neither did she but she drew on all her training as a performer and gave him a smile worthy of an award. 'It's okay. Really. Why don't you head home? I can take care of this.'

'You're sure?' Minh looked dubious.

'She just said she was, didn't she?'

Imogen only just managed to prevent Minh from trying to stand up to Nadir again and patted a sleepy Nadeena, who had grown restless. 'Go. Really. We'll be fine.'

'Call me if you need me,' Minh ordered, reluctantly heading towards Green Park tube station.

As soon as he was out of sight she let out a relieved breath. One hardcore male was better than two, wasn't it?

Reluctantly turning back, she calmed her breathing and faced Nadir. 'What's this about, Nadir?'

'What do you think?'

She tried to pull off a nonchalant shrug but her movements felt stiff and disjointed. He'd walked away from her fourteen months ago so she had no idea. 'If I knew I wouldn't ask,' she countered, slightly annoyed herself now.

His silvery gaze transmitted how unimpressed he was with her response. 'How old is she?'

'How do you know she's a she?' Imogen hedged.

'I don't think it's customary to dress a boy in a pink sunhat.'

'Maybe I'm just bucking the trend.'

His hissed breath held a wealth of reaching-the-end-of-his-tether impatience. 'How. Old. Is. She?'

Completely unprepared for both his anger and his relentless questioning, Imogen was at a loss as to how to follow the advice of her inner voice that warned her to tread cautiously and found herself blurting out the truth. 'Five months.'

He rocked back on his heels, his hands going to his waist and pushing his jacket back to reveal his broad chest. 'Then our affair did result in a child.'

Their affair? Talk about clarifying how he had felt about her back then... 'I didn't say that,' she retorted forcefully.

The words came out rushed and his eyebrows shot up. 'Then you *were* sleeping with someone else while we were together.' His voice held the tenor of a wounded bull, which didn't impress her at all.

'Trust you to take that line of thinking,' she said scathingly, remembering how he had basically accused her of the same thing their last night together in Paris. 'And it's none of your business.'

'If she's not mine then whose is she?' His gaze once again narrowed in on Nadeena.

'Mine,' she countered evenly.

Nadir's lips turned up into a snarl. 'Do you really think you can fob me off with semantics?'

Imogen felt a dull pain tweak behind her right eyebrow. After the way he had treated the news of her pregnancy, she wanted to know his current motivation before blurting out any more home truths. 'Look, Nadir—'

He said something in Arabic, cutting her off, and stepped closer to her, his wide shoulders blocking out all the natural light behind him. Imogen felt the cool glass of the shop window at her back and briefly closed her eyes to try and steady her racing heartbeat, only to snap them open again when Nadir's voice sounded way too close to her ear. 'Dammit, you're not going to faint, are you?'

Faint? Faint? She stared up at him and then darted her eyes to the side. No, she wasn't going to faint. But she did want to run. Fast.

'Uh-uh.' As if reading her thoughts, Nadir shook his head. 'You're not going to run again, Imogen, my sweet.'

Again? What was he talking about—*again?*

'I have no idea what you're talking about but I really need to go. I'm working another shift tonight.'

His eyes narrowed. 'Just so we're clear, *habibi*,' he

grated silkily, 'I have not searched for you for the past fourteen months to be given the runaround now.'

Imogen immediately felt hot and cold and then hot again and, just like the first time she had laid eyes on him, all the oxygen went out of the air—something that had almost been disastrous at the time as she'd been in the middle of performing the can-can in front of a full house. She'd noticed Nadir watching her almost straight away. He'd been sitting at a small front table with his brother—she'd later found out—but she had only had eyes for Nadir. And he for her, right up until the moment he'd found out she was *enceinte*.

As if sensing her distress, Nadeena stirred and shifted against her chest and Imogen tried to calm her nerves, if for no other reason than to keep Nadeena asleep.

Her first priority was to keep her daughter safe.

Secure.

Not that she expected Nadir to hurt her physically. No, what she feared was his power to hurt her emotionally, which was often much worse because most bruises healed while mental scars remained for ever. Imogen knew because she had spent many years trying, and failing, to win her father's love and she wasn't about to condemn Nadeena to the same fate.

A picture of the secret service type in the café came to her on a rush just as she caught sight of him standing a little way off to the side. Had Nadir been looking for her all this time? It seemed impossible.

Her troubled eyes flew to Nadir and her ripple of unease ratcheted up to dread. 'Fourteen months? What are you talking about?'

Noting the deep groove between Imogen's beautiful green eyes, Nadir instantly regretted his emotionally ragged outburst. What he needed to be right now was cool and controlled. Finding her with a child strapped to her body challenged that considerably. As did her evasive attitude, which implied that she had something to hide.

'We will not discuss this any further on the street,' he decided. Apart from the fact that Imogen looked uncomfortably hot, it was also far too public a place for this type of discussion. 'Come.'

'No.'

Haughty as ever, Nadir noted as he turned back to her. He'd been attracted to that regal aspect of her nature when they'd met. Now the trait annoyed him. As did her wide-eyed ingénue look.

Back when he'd first noticed her she'd seemed different from the other women who had adorned his life from time to time. Less artificial. More sincere. More genuine. Hell, he could laugh at that now. Imogen Reid had turned out to be as genuine as a whore with a hundred euros in her hand.

He glanced at the baby sleeping in her arms. Everything inside him said that she was his child and he wondered how much longer Imogen would have waited before turning up 'ta-da' style on his doorstep and demanding maintenance payments worthy of a queen. Not that it mattered. *He* had found *her* and that definitely gave him the upper hand.

And it mattered even less that her complexion had leached of all colour. These past months of not knowing if she had given birth to the child she had claimed was his, if she was okay, if the baby was okay, hell, if either one of them was even *alive* had eaten away at him. When she'd sent him a text telling him she had 'taken care of everything' he'd assumed she'd terminated the pregnancy. He'd felt sick at the thought but then knowing he'd got her pregnant in the first place hadn't exactly made him feel like dancing around a room.

Fatherhood wasn't something he'd ever contemplated before. Now it seemed that the fates had other ideas and if this woman had kept his child from him…deliberately… Callously…

He glanced at her. He didn't think he could like a person less if he tried.

'Nadir, please, if I…' She moistened her lips with the tip of her tongue. 'If I tell you that you're the father can we just leave it at that? Can we just…can we just part as friends?'

Nadir reeled. Was she serious? Because she couldn't possibly expect him to walk away from her after basically admitting the child was his with little more than *Have a nice life*. In fact, if he discovered that this child really was his then he wouldn't be walking away at all.

He stared down at her and noticed she had the look of a frightened mouse that had just been caught in a very large inescapable trap.

Apt, he thought—*very apt*. From the minute he'd laid eyes on her, his first instinct had been primal. He'd wanted to wrap her up and keep her. He'd wanted to brand her as his own. Disconcertingly, that urge was just as strong as ever.

He tugged on the collar of his shirt. Somehow, in the time between meeting her and now, he had lost his equilibrium and he wanted it back. Not even the thought of having to renounce the throne tomorrow affected him as deeply. Or maybe it was the combination of the two. 'I don't think you could have ever called us *friends*, Imogen.' Bed partners. Lovers. Now those fitted. Friends, not so much.

She looked up at him as if he'd just kicked a puppy. 'Good to know,' she said flatly, her ponytail swinging around her shoulders as she made to move past him. 'Frankly, I don't know why you're even here.'

It was supposed to be her parting shot but Nadir moved so that once again he was directly in front of her.

'Come now, *habibi*. I know you're smarter than that.'

'Look, Nadir, the stand-over tactics are very intimidating. Well done you. But you can't stop me from walking away.'

He blew out a frustrated breath. 'If you'd cooperate and tell me what I want to know I wouldn't need to use any *tactics*. Now, my car is waiting at the corner.' He arched his arm towards a low-slung black beast of a Mercedes. 'Shall we?'

'No,' she bit out, 'we shall not. Not until I understand what this is about.'

The line between her brows reappeared as she stared at him and a pulse point beat frantically in the base of her throat. A pulse point he still had an inexplicable urge to cover with his lips. His tongue.

He muttered an old Arabian curse and realised what he'd just done. What was it about this woman that made him unconsciously regress to his native language? *By Allah…* He cursed again. Jerked his eyes back to hers. 'What this is about,' he began with a calmness that belied the heated blood pounding through his veins, 'is that it looks very much like you had my child and didn't tell me.'

If possible, the line between her brows deepened and he had the stupidest notion to place the pad of his finger against it and smooth it away. 'What's her name?' he asked gruffly.

Emerald eyes darkened almost to black before dropping from his. 'This is pointless, Nadir.' Her soft, desperate plea fell between them as insignificant as one of her gauzy dance costumes and he savoured the defeat in it.

'Pointless for you, perhaps,' he agreed pleasantly.

A soft moan broke from her lips and his body registered it as one she used to make in bed and it appalled him that he could be so angry one minute and so aroused the next. It was those damned memories of having her spread out naked on his bed that were the problem.

During his more unguarded moments those memories

crept up on him like the flu and reminded him that once—
once—he had thought he'd found something special with
a woman.

A low growl filled the base of his throat. This, he would
have said, was not an unguarded moment and yet his control over his body felt tenuous, tangled up in the silken
awareness of the female in front of him, who was dressed
in nothing more provocative than denim jeans and a red
T-shirt.

'Please, Nadir...'

'Please what, Imogen?' he rasped, hating the sound of
his name on her treacherous lips and welcoming another
shot of anger as it jetted through him. 'Please forgive you
for keeping the birth of my child from me? Because she
is mine, isn't she?'

He didn't know if it was his words or his tone that
brought her chin up but her beautiful eyes glittered an-
grily. 'I did not keep her birth from you. You knew I was
pregnant and you didn't want anything to do with her.'

Her voice had grown shrill and a couple of shoppers
hesitated before passing them by.

'I don't think so. Now come.'

'You didn't even believe it was your baby. God,' she
exclaimed, 'can't you just forget that we ever saw each
other again?'

'Like you want to?'

She didn't answer, to her credit, which was just as well
because his control was heading in the same direction
as his day. 'Tell me,' he began silkily. 'Do you believe in
fate, Imogen?'

'No.'

'Then you'll just have to put this meeting down to luck,
won't you?'

She glared at him and pulled her bottom lip between
her teeth, which meant she was thinking hard. Not that it

mattered. He stepped closer to her, inhaling her wonderful, sweet scent that was somehow the same and yet different. He swallowed against a sudden rush of conscience. He had nothing to feel guilty about here. 'You're coming with me,' he said quietly. 'Even if I have to put you into that car myself.'

Her brows shot up at that. 'Not even you would do something so heinous.'

Nadir gave a sharp bark of laughter. If only she knew how close he was to doing *exactly* that.

'Then what are you afraid of, *habibi*?'

'I'm not afraid. I'm confused,' she said with bald honesty. 'What do you want?'

'To talk.' He had a lot of questions to clear up; not least of all was how she had hidden herself away so effectively his security team hadn't been able to find her until now. And then there was the small matter that he wanted to be a part of his child's life. A permanent part. But he had no doubt she'd welcome that. It would mean money and status and he hadn't met many people who wouldn't put that ahead of integrity and self-respect.

CHAPTER THREE

IMOGEN SLICKED HER tongue across her dry lips, her heart pounding towards a heart attack as Nadir led her towards the car.

To talk, he said. But was that really what he wanted? And why was he so angry with her about Nadeena?

Every instinct in her body warned her that she shouldn't go with him but really she wasn't afraid of Nadir. And, despite his hostile manner, it wasn't as if he would want to have anything to do with Nadeena in the long run.

In truth, he probably just wanted to make sure she wasn't going to go to the press with news of his indiscretion. Her stomach turned. That was the most likely scenario here. That and to ensure that she wasn't going to make any financial demands on him in the future. Maybe he'd even offer to set up a trust fund for Nadeena. If he did, she wouldn't take it. She would provide for her daughter herself. Nadeena need never know that her father hadn't loved her enough to want her in his life.

Unable to stop herself, her eyes ran over his face. He was still the most ruggedly attractive man she had ever laid eyes on, with thick black hair that fell in long layers, olive skin and an aquiline nose that perfectly offset a square jaw that always looked as if it was in need of a shave. And his mouth. Surely that had been fashioned by Ishtar because it could look either surly or sexy depending on his mood.

Currently, he wasn't in a good one. But okay, she would

be rational. Talk to him. Answer his banal questions. Reassure him that she wanted nothing from him. 'Fine. I can give you a few minutes.'

He didn't answer and warning bells clanged loudly inside her head again as the car door was smoothly opened by a burly chauffer. Then a waft of deliciously cool air hit her and she bent her head and manoeuvred inside as best she could with Nadeena still strapped to her chest.

'Wouldn't you be better taking that thing off?'

His gruff question came from the opposite seat and Imogen momentarily lost her train of thought as his masculine scent enveloped her. 'That *thing* is a sling and no, I can't. Not without waking her.'

'So wake her.'

'Not a good idea. Don't you know you should never wake a sleeping baby?'

His slight hesitation was loaded. 'How would I?'

Cold censure laced every word and she had to force her eyes to remain connected to his. Nadeena really did have his eyes, she thought absurdly. Lucky her. 'So I'm here.' She let out a pent-up breath. 'So talk.'

'This is not a conversation for a limousine.' Nadir made a motion with his hand and said something in rapid-fire... Italian? Greek? Before Imogen knew it, the car was in motion.

'Wait. Where are we going?'

Nadir's eyes snagged with hers and the heat from his gaze made her go still all over. His eyes drifted over her face with insolent slowness and sexual awareness turned her mouth as dry as dust.

Determined not to be so weakened by him again that she turned into a puppet on a string, she forced air in and out of her lungs in a steady stream. But the act took up every ounce of her concentration so when he informed her that they were going to his apartment it took longer than it should have for his words to take hold.

'Your apartment? No.' She shook her head. 'You've misunderstood me. I meant a few minutes *here*. In the car. And it's illegal to drive with an infant not strapped into a proper baby carrier.'

Nadir leaned forward and spoke to his driver again and instantly the big car slowed.

'My apartment is close by. And it is you who has misunderstood me, Imogen. We have to talk and a few minutes isn't even going to cover the first topic.'

Imogen narrowed her eyes. 'I don't see why. I did what you wanted fourteen months ago and disappeared from your sight so I don't understand what you want with me now.'

His sculptured lips thinned into a grim line. 'You did disappear, I'll give you that. And you still haven't told me her name.'

Her name? Imogen lowered her gaze to the safety of her daughter's head. No way could she reveal her name. No way did she want to see this man who had once meant so much to her mock her for her sentimentality. Maybe even pity her. At the time she'd named her she'd been feeling particularly sorry for herself and hopelessly alone. The three-day blues they called the come down from the emotional high some women experienced after giving birth. Now she wished she'd named her Meredith or Jessica—or any name other than the one she had.

Fortunately the car pulled up at the kerb before she had to answer and, feeling sick, she followed Nadir as he strode through the large foyer of his building with a bronzed water feature at one end and a smartly dressed concierge at the other.

'When did you move to London?' she asked, suddenly

wondering if they had been living in the same city the whole time.

'I didn't.' He stabbed at the button to call the lift and she remembered that of course he had apartments in most of the major financial centres in the world.

Casting a quick glance around his beautifully appointed living room, she inwardly shook her head at the absurd difference in their lifestyles. Of course she'd known that he was wealthy when she'd met him—her fellow dancers had informed her as to whom he was—but, apart from his outrageously divine apartment on the Île Saint-Louis, their time together had been incredibly normal. Nights in bed, mornings at the local patisserie, afternoons strolling or jogging along the Seine. More time in bed.

Shaking off the rush of memories, she headed straight for a set of plush sofas and laid Nadeena on one. Glancing back at Nadir, she asked him to hand her the baby bag he'd carried up and checked Nadeena's nappy while he stood beside her.

Of course Nadeena went quiet in that moment. Her big, curious eyes riveted to Nadir, as most other females were when they first clapped eyes on him. She blinked as if trying to clear her vision and a small frown formed between her round silvery-blue eyes.

'She has my eyes,' he said hoarsely.

The sense of awe in his voice was hard to miss and an unexpected swell of emotions surged inside Imogen's chest. Emotions that were so twisted together they were too difficult to define.

'Here you go, little one.' She lifted Nadeena into her arms and settled her back in the crook of her shoulder, silently willing her not to complain. Then she glanced at Nadir. 'I need to feed her.'

Nadir waved his hand negligently. 'Go ahead.'

Imogen moistened her lips. 'I'd like some privacy.'

He paused and Imogen was sure her cheeks turned scarlet.

'You breastfeed?'

Even though she had breastfed in cafés and parks and not blinked an eye before, this moment, in a quiet living room with a man she had once believed she had fallen in love with felt far too intimate. His continued perusal sent another frisson of unwelcome awareness zipping through her. 'Yes.'

She knew her voice sounded husky and when her eyes met his she couldn't hold his stare. What was she doing here in this room with him? More importantly, what was he doing in this room with her and Nadeena? She felt self-conscious and it was all too easy to remember how it felt to have him at her breast, drawing her aching nipple deep into his mouth. All too easy to recall the pleasure that had turned her into an incoherent puppet for him to master at his will.

When she continued to hesitate and Nadeena grew restless Nadir pivoted on his foot and stalked to the long windows overlooking some sort of dense green park that most likely belonged to him as well. Imogen quickly arranged her T-shirt and Nadeena latched on like a baby that had never fed before.

'When were you going to tell me I had fathered a child, Imogen?' His quiet question held a wealth of judgement and loathing behind it and Imogen felt as if someone had just dropped an icy blanket around her shoulders.

She didn't look at him. She couldn't because all of a sudden she felt horribly guilty about the fact that she had never intended to tell him. And hot on the heels of her unexpected guilt rode anger. Anger she welcomed with open arms. *He* was the one who had run away when he'd learned she was pregnant, not *her*. *He* was the one who had made it clear that he didn't want a baby in his life when she had felt such a rush of elation at the time she had almost grinned at him like a loon. Then she'd seen his stricken face and her world had fallen apart.

A sound like a low growl came from deep in Nadir's throat and he towered over her. 'Never? Is that the word that is at this moment stuck in your throat, *habibi*?'

'Don't call me that,' Imogen growled back, unable to contain her rioting emotions.

'It's preferable to what I want to call you, believe me.'

Imogen had never seen Nadir angry before and he was magnificent with it. Fierce and proud and so *powerful*.

She swallowed, hating that she still found him so utterly attractive. 'How dare you come over like the injured party in this scenario?' she snapped. She was the one who had been as sick as a dog carrying Nadeena. She was the one who had been all alone in the birthing suite as Nadeena had come into the world. She was the one who struggled day to day with the demands of motherhood and putting food in their mouths. And she had asked for nothing from him. Absolutely nothing. 'I have done very well for myself since you left my life,' she said, her body vibrating with tension. 'I have survived very well on my own. I've eked out a life for myself and Nadeena is healthy. She's happy and—'

'Nadeena?'

Imogen's eyes squeezed shut and her temper deflated when he repeated the baby's name. His irreverent tone somehow made her remember how lonely she had felt when Nadir had walked away from her. She'd felt lonely before, of course, but with Nadir she had felt as if she had got a glimpse—a *taste*—of paradise, only to have it snatched away when she was least prepared.

Powerful memories surged again and she couldn't look at him. 'Why am I here, Nadir?'

He didn't say anything, his eyes troubled as they made contact with her own. He leant against the cherry wood dining table, his gaze riveted to Nadeena, kneading her T-shirt like a contented cat, his silence drawing out the moment. Drawing out her nerves until they lay just beneath the fine layer of her skin like freshly tuned guitar strings. 'Why is there no public record of her birth?'

Bewildered by both the flat tenor of his voice and the unexpected question, Imogen frowned. 'There is.'

His gaze sharpened and she could see his agile mind turning. 'Under what name?'

Imogen stared at him. At the time of Nadeena's birth she had only put her own name down on the birth certificate. She hadn't known what to put in place of the father's and a kindly registrar had told her that it wasn't essential information. That she could fill that part out later. So far, that section was still blank because she'd been so busy and so tired learning how to care for an infant she hadn't even thought about putting Nadir's name on it. Sensing that this was a loaded question, she raised her chin. 'Mine.'

'Imogen Reid.'

His earlier words—*I have not searched for you for the past fourteen months to be given the runaround now'*—and his personal bodyguard waiting for his arrival came back to her and clicked into place in her mind and confused her even more. 'Benson.'

There was only the briefest of pauses before he roared, 'You gave me a false name!'

Imogen pressed back against the seat of the sofa. 'No.' Well, not intentionally. 'Reid was my mother's maiden name and...' She swallowed, hating herself for explaining but compelled to do so by the fury she read in his eyes. 'It wasn't deliberate. The girls suggested that I use a stage name because they sometimes had trouble with the clientele and you only asked me my name one time.' She took a quick breath. 'At the beginning.'

He stabbed a hand through his hair and paced across the

room like an animal trapped in a too-narrow cage. 'And your mobile phone number?'

'What about it?'

'You changed it.'

'I lost it…well, it was stolen my first day in London. I just use a pay-as-you-go now.'

He swore under his breath, a ferocious sound.

'What's this about, Nadir? As I recall you were the one who left town the morning after you found out I was pregnant. Are you now saying you tried to contact me?' She tried to stifle a small thrill inside, wondering if perhaps he had been worried about her. That perhaps he had cared for her after all… Another more skeptical voice reminded her of the horrible text he'd sent her but still some deeply buried hope wriggled its way to the surface.

'I had an emergency in New York and by the time I got back to Paris you had disappeared as if you'd never existed,' Nadir grated. 'The Ottoman Empire would have benefited from your stealth.'

Resenting his sarcasm, she stiffened. 'I did not disappear. I left.'

'Without a trace. No one had any idea where you had gone.'

That was most likely because the only person who knew had been Minh's sister, Caro, and she had been leaving to go travelling at the same time. Imogen had meant to keep in touch with some of the other girls but she hadn't counted on feeling sick and sorry for herself during her pregnancy and she hadn't had time since then.

'Nor did you give your employer a forwarding address or email.'

'I didn't?' She blinked. 'I wasn't exactly thinking straight at the time.' And since her pay went directly into her bank account, she hadn't even realised. 'I'm surprised you didn't check my bank records.'

His look said that he had. 'False names tend to hinder that kind of search.'

'I told you that wasn't deliberate.' She took a deep breath and tried to keep a lid on her emotions so she could think rationally. 'Why were you looking for me, anyway?'

'Because before you ran you were supposedly pregnant with my child.'

'I did not *run*,' she bit out tensely. 'Why would I when you had made it abundantly clear you didn't want anything to do with me any more?'

She heard the challenge in her voice and knew it was because some part of her was hoping he would refute her statement.

'I texted you from New York.'

Her top lip curled with distaste. That horrible text was still etched into her brain as if it had been carved there. 'Oh, please,' she scoffed, 'let's not talk about your lovely text.'

'Or your response,' he grated. 'Telling me that you had *taken care of everything*.'

Imogen tossed her ponytail over her shoulder, careful not to awaken Nadeena, who had dropped into another exhausted sleep. 'I did take care of it,' she said softly, her arms tightening around Nadeena.

'Yes, but not in the way I expected.'

Hoped, his tone seemed to imply. And there was the reason he'd been looking for her. He'd wanted to make sure she'd done what he expected.

Imogen felt that small spark of hope that she'd been wrong about him completely wither and die and she felt angry with herself for succumbing to it in the first place. Had she not learned anything from his treatment of her in the past?

Caro's words of warning came back to her. *'Be careful, Imogen. Any man who takes off like that without a word and accuses you of sleeping around is likely to insist on an abortion if he ever comes back.'* At the time Imogen had thought her friend had been overreacting. Now she knew that she hadn't been and she felt physically ill.

'And now you'll have to deal with the consequences,' he grated, staring at her as if she was somehow to blame for everything that was wrong in the world.

CHAPTER FOUR

IMOGEN LAPSED INTO a horrified silence, focusing on her daughter instead of the sick feeling swirling in the pit of her stomach.

Quite honestly she had never expected to see Nadir again and she really wished she hadn't. But at least he'd well and truly put paid to those times she'd wondered if she shouldn't contact him and let him know that his child had been born. Put paid to those silly girlish fantasies that he would one day ride in on a big white horse and offer her undying love.

Yeah, right. Probably she'd listened to way too many love songs while she had been incapacitated on Minh's sofa and possibly watched way too much day time TV.

But at least that whole time hadn't been a complete waste. She'd used it to plan out her and her baby's future and decided to follow a long-held dream and teach dance. She'd even taken a short online business course. She had a vision that when she had enough money she and Nadeena would move to a mid-sized town where she could open a studio. Nadeena would rush home after school and if she wanted to she could dance; if not, she could sit and do homework or read. Then they would go home together and chat while Imogen cooked dinner and at night…at night… she hadn't really thought about the nights. Her imagination had only gone so far as to envision her and Nadeena as a tight-knit unit.

The two of them happy and contented.

And when Nadeena asked about her father, as she surely would one day, Imogen hadn't quite worked out what she was going to tell her. She didn't want to lie to her but nor did she want Nadeena to know that her father had never wanted her. She glanced at Nadir standing by the window, his broad back to her as if he couldn't stand to look at her. Well, that was fine with her. She couldn't stand to look at him either.

Careful not to waken Nadeena, she eased herself off the sofa, not as easy as it looked since it was one of those squishy ones designed for long afternoons lazing about, and cradled Nadeena in her arms.

Hearing her, Nadir turned towards her and she hastily pulled her T-shirt back into place.

'Where do you think you're going?'

Imogen raised her chin at his surly tone. 'Home.'

'To that buffoon you were with earlier?'

It took her a beat to realise he was referring to Minh but she wasn't about to get into another lengthy discussion with him and, although it was illogical, her gut warned her that if she answered his question honestly he'd never let her leave. And that was exactly what she was about to do. 'You have no right to ask me that. But I am curious as to why you brought me up here. It seems like a waste of your time and mine.'

His eyes held hers and he continued as if she hadn't spoken. 'Is he your current lover?'

Chilled, Imogen cuddled Nadeena closer. 'You answer my questions and I'll answer yours.'

'I'm sorry.' Nadir's voice, his stance—heck, his very demeanour—had turned alert with predatory intent. 'Did you assume you were in a position to bargain with me?'

Imogen rubbed the space between her eyes, her arms starting to ache from holding Nadeena.

'What I assumed,' she said as she laid her daughter on the sofa and fixed cushions around her, 'was that you weren't interested in anything about me and what I do, or where I live.'

'You are the mother of my child,' he said as if that answered everything.

And then she remembered why she was here and could have laughed at her own stupidity. This wasn't about some romantic reunion of past lovers. This was about a man with self-preservation on his mind. 'We've already established that you don't care about that.'

'I care.'

Imogen curled her lip. What he meant was that he cared about how much cash she was going to hit him up for.

'I get it,' she said tonelessly. 'And while I think it's incredibly selfish of you not to want to provide for your own flesh and blood you'll no doubt be relieved to know that I don't want anything from you and I never will.'

'Excuse me?'

'Nor do I expect that you will want to see her and that's more than okay with me as well.'

He started to laugh and she felt even more disgusted with him. 'I don't see what's so amusing. It's a travesty if you really think about it too much. Which I try not to do.'

'You're serious.'

'I certainly don't think abandoning your own child is something to laugh about, but maybe that's just me.'

'Except I didn't abandon her—you took her.'

'Are we back to that again?'

His eyebrow rose. 'Did we ever leave it?'

'I want to go home, Nadir.'

'That's not possible,' he said briskly. 'I should have already left for Bakaan by now.'

His homeland?

'Please don't let me stop you.'

One corner of his mouth quirked in a parody of a smile. 'I don't intend to. But unfortunately we have run out of time to get things you might need from your house. If you write me a list I'll make sure you have everything on hand when we arrive. We shouldn't be gone long. A day at the most.'

Imogen blinked. 'We?'

'That's what I said.'

'You must be mad.'

He pulled his phone out of his pocket and started dialling as if he hadn't heard her.

'Nadir, what are you doing?'

He looked up at her. 'Claiming what is mine.'

Imogen waited a beat before responding. Waited for the punchline. When he stared back with all the confidence of a man used to getting his own way she felt dizzy.

'I am not yours and I never was!'

He raised an eyebrow. 'I meant Nadeena.'

Sanctimonious bastard.

Embarrassed at her gaffe, Imogen hauled the baby bag over her shoulder. 'Didn't you just hear me? I said I don't want anything from you.'

'I heard you.'

She shook her head. 'I'm going.'

Before she had time to reach Nadeena, Nadir abandoned his call and yanked the bag off her shoulder, spinning her around to face him. 'You've stolen the first five months of my daughter's life from me.' His voice seemed to harden with every word even though its tenor didn't change. 'You won't be stealing any more.'

Stolen? Imogen's knees started to shake and the sense of dread from earlier returned with force. 'I haven't stolen anything. And how do you know she's even really yours?'

A grim smile crooked the corner of his mouth. 'She has my eyes.'

'Lots of people have silvery-blue eyes,' she said on a rush. 'They're as common as mice.' Rats.

One dark eyebrow rose. 'You gave her an Arabic name.'

'Nadeena was a great-aunt of mine.'

'And you're proving to be a terrible liar. Which is in your favour.'

'I don't understand this at all.' She threw her arms up in front of her. 'You don't even want children. Why would you want us to go with you?'

He widened his stance and her eyes couldn't help but notice his strong legs and lean torso. God, did he have to be quite so damned virile?

'How do you know that?'

Gossip, mainly. She lifted her chin and focused on his hard face, which wasn't much better. 'Well, do you?' she asked coolly.

'I'd say that's a moot point now, wouldn't you?'

'No, I most definitely would not. I'd say it's very relevant considering the way you're behaving.'

'Sometimes, Imogen, life throws us curve balls but that doesn't mean we have to drop them. I don't need a DNA test to confirm that I have a child.'

Frustration made her voice sharper than usual. 'Of course you need to do a DNA test. What kind of crazy talk is that? No rich man in his right mind would take on a child as his own without doing a DNA test.'

Nadir laughed and this time it rang with genuine amusement. 'You always were just that little bit different from the pack, *habibi*.' His voice, so gentle and deep, brought a rush of memories back into her dizzy brain. 'But you need not worry. I plan to do my duty by her.'

His duty?

A sense of terror entered her heart. Was that what he meant by saying he'd be claiming what was his? She didn't want to know. Not right now. 'I don't need you to do the right thing by Nadeena.' She'd been looking out for herself for a long time now and she could look out for her child as well.

Nadir raked an impatient hand through his hair. 'Nevertheless, I will.' His striking eyes narrowed. 'Now quit arguing and give me a list of things you will need for our flight to Bakaan.'

Striving for calm, Imogen tried to slow down her heart that was banging away inside her chest so loudly he must surely be able to hear it. Right now she felt as if she was trying to survive a fierce gale that was corralling her towards the edge of a very high cliff. Then a horrible thought froze the blood inside her veins. 'I won't let you take my baby, Nadir.' She hated that her voice rang with fear. 'If that's your plan.' She'd never even considered it before but now that she had she couldn't push it from her mind.

He glanced at her impatiently. 'If I wanted that then you couldn't stop me.'

'I could. I'd…' Panic clawed inside her throat. 'I'll…'

'But I don't want that.' He made an impatient gesture with his hands. 'I am not so callous that I don't realise that a baby needs its mother. That is why I plan to marry you.'

Marry her!

She shook her head, biting back a rising sense of hysteria. She needed time to make sense of everything that was happening and she couldn't because her mind didn't know which way to turn.

'Breathe, Imogen.' Nadir went to put his hands on her shoulders and she jerked back, wondering how he had got so close to her without her being aware of it.

Imogen shook her head, fear spiking inside her like a flash of lightning. 'You're crazy to think that I'd marry you after the way you treated me.'

Nadir's mouth thinned and he stepped closer to her, contained anger emanating from every taut line of his body. 'I can assure you that I'm not. I've had a lot of time to review my options while you were in hiding and this is non-negotiable.'

Imogen tried to still the trembling inside her body. 'I was not hiding.'

'It's irrelevant now.'

She laughed. What else could she do? 'You can't just come back into my life and think you can do whatever you want.' Her father had behaved that way. Coming and going as he pleased with little concern for either her or her mother. As if she'd shackle her and her daughter to a man cut from the same cloth. 'I'll fight you.'

'What with?' She hadn't realised that her hands had balled into tight white fists until Nadir's mocking gaze drew hers to them. He reached out and raised them in front of her, enclosing them inside his much larger grip. 'With these, hmm? I have to confess that, as aggressive as you can be in bed, I didn't take you for the violent type.'

She wouldn't have before today either. 'Nadir, we had an affair,' she cried, throwing his earlier words back in his face and tugging at his implacable hold. 'We only had sex a…a…a couple of times.'

He resisted her feeble attempts to break free with embarrassing ease and hauled her closer. 'Let's see,' he said with a snarl. 'Four weekends, around three times a day, more at night.' His eyes dropped to her mouth and lingered before returning to hers. 'You don't have to be Einstein to know that comes to more than *a couple of times, habibi*. And it was good sex.'

His words and his tone combined to set off a wildfire reaction inside her body.

'It meant nothing,' she choked out, still trying to free her hands from within the prison of his. Wishing that his grip was hurting her to distract her from the riot of sensations being this close to him was setting off inside her.

She couldn't seem to focus her thoughts when she became enshrouded in his earthy male scent, the sensitive tips of her breasts rising against the lace of her bra and the deep achy feeling between her thighs reminding her of how it had once been between them.

'Nothing?' His soft question had a lethal undertone that had her raising her eyes to his, but she only reached his mouth, which seemed so close to her own that if she held still long enough she was sure she could feel his breath against her lips. 'Nothing, Imogen? I don't think so.'

'I'll get a lawyer,' she said breathlessly, yanking harder on her hands, only to find that they were now trapped against his hard chest.

He laughed. 'From what I know of your finances, you can't afford a decent babysitter.'

'Bastard!'

His eyes bored holes into hers. 'And what court of law is going to side with a mother who kept a child's existence from its father? Who leaves her baby with friends while she works?'

'Lots of mothers do that.'

'Yes, but lots of mothers do not have a child of royal blood. Nadeena is a Bakaani princess.'

'I don't think of her like that.'

'Right.'

'I don't!' she exclaimed at his cynical tone. 'She's just an innocent baby to me, not a commodity. And no court in the world would favour a father who thinks like that.'

Nadir arched a brow. 'You're not that naïve, surely.'

'Nadir, stop this, I beg you.'

'Do you?'

She flushed, remembering the last time she'd said those words to him. It might as well have been five minutes ago for the response of her body. The feeling of being help-less beneath him, her hands held above her head as he'd nudged her thighs wider with his knees, the feel of his silken hardness at that first moment he pushed himself inside her body, that feeling of her softness giving way to all that male strength in inexorable pleasure.

Her body clenched and mortification filled her. She tried to twist away from him now but somehow that only made her more aware of the press of his hips, forcing the hard ridge of his erection into her belly.

Erection!

Imogen's eyes flew to his. 'No.'

He gave a hollow laugh. 'Oh, yes, Imogen, you still turn me on,' he said thickly. 'Despite your treachery.'

His head descended towards hers and she shoved against his chest. She didn't want him—not again. He'd accused her of sleeping with someone else while seeing him—had probably done so himself while he was seeing her—he'd thought they were having an affair that he'd had no trouble ending while she had nearly died inside when he'd walked away from her. She didn't want him. She couldn't!

But she did and none of that mattered to her wounded heart when his lips touched hers in a searing kiss that narrowed the time they had been apart to nothing. Still, she attempted to resist him, clamping her lips into a straight line that, in the end, was no defence at all.

Certainly no defence against her own raging need to touch him and be touched by him and when he took advantage of her confusion and drove his tongue into her mouth Imogen was lost. He just felt too good, tasted too good, and it had been so long for her. So long since she had felt the press of a man's lips. The press of *his* lips.

All of a sudden she was no longer pushing him away, but drawing him closer. Her hands flattening over the hard muscles of his chest to snake up around his neck, her mouth moving beneath his in an age-old request for more.

And he gave it to her. Eagerly. Impatiently. Thrusting his tongue into her mouth and drinking in her very essence.

His other hand came up to cup her jaw, holding her steady. A low groan, more like the growl of a hungry wolf, worked its way out of his throat as he angled his mouth over hers and ravaged her lips as if he was as desperate for her as she was for him.

Nothing else seemed to matter in that moment. The room disappeared. The world. It was just the two of them. As it always had been when they'd come together. Like magic.

'Nadir,' she whispered, shuddering against him as his strong fingers followed the line of her spine, spanning her waist before dropping lower to cup her bottom and bring her even closer. Unbearably close. Imogen squirmed and forked her hands into his hair to anchor herself to him, one leg already rising to rest over his lean hip.

And then suddenly she was free and he had stepped back from her, reaching out to steady her as she stumbled without his body weight to hold her up. 'It seems I still turn you on as well, hmm, *habibi*?'

What?

Dazed, she blinked up at him and then his condescending words hit her and she was instantly appalled at her behaviour.

Had he just kissed her to prove a point? To prove how weak she was when it came to him? To prove how much power he still had over her? Her face flamed and she was so angry she wanted to punch him.

Realising just how close she was to hitting someone for the first time in her life, she lowered her bunched fists to her sides. 'Don't ever touch me again.' *Was she hyperventilating?* She placed a hand against her chest. It felt as if she was hyperventilating. 'I hate you, Nadir. I *really* hate you.'

'Don't be stupid about this, Imogen,' he rasped, pulling

his phone from his pocket again. 'You can't provide everything our daughter needs and I want her to grow up secure.'

'I want that too. Which is why I would *never* marry
you.'

From the stiffening of his spine she could see that he
didn't like that. 'Be serious,' she continued desperately,
trying to appeal to his rational side. 'You never *wanted*
Nadeena.'

'I may not have *planned* Nadeena.' His expression grew
fierce. 'But she is here and this is the best solution.'

Imogen's nostrils flared as if she was a lioness sensing
danger. Nadeena's emotional welfare was on the line and
Imogen had vowed a long time ago that she would rather
be a single mother than have her child raised by a parent
who didn't want her. Especially the autocratic tyrant Nadir
had turned into. But then maybe he had always been that
way. She had never challenged him before, had she? 'This
is the *worst* solution.'

Nadir put the phone to his ear. 'Bjorn, tell Vince we'll
be at the airport within the hour.'

He rang off and Imogen felt icy-cold with dread. 'You
selfish bastard,' she raged raggedly. 'You won't even consider my needs.'

'Actually, I would say I was considering them very well.'

'Ha!' she scorned. 'You're nothing but a bully.'

His eyes flashed a warning she was in no mood to heed.
'Careful, Imogen. I will only tolerate so much from you.'

'Like I care,' she fumed, restless energy making her
muscles vibrate. 'You can't do this, you know. I have
rights.'

She stared at him as if she really knew what she was
talking about but inside she was quaking. Not that she'd
let him see that. The stakes were far too high for him to
think that he had the upper hand. For him to assume that
she was a pushover.

'What you have,' he said in a carefully modulated tone, his face a cold mask, 'is my child.'

A discreet knock at the door interrupted the stark silence that followed that statement and Nadir turned to answer it.

'And Imogen?' She glanced at him, hoping he was about to tell her this had all been a joke. 'You *will* marry me.'

It was a great parting shot, she thought as she sagged against the arm of the sofa and speared wishful daggers into his broad back. But she would have the last word because she would never marry a man she didn't love.

CHAPTER FIVE

THE PLANE TOOK off into the air and Nadir wondered if he needed to have his head examined for bringing Imogen and Nadeena to Bakaan with him.

He could have easily had Bjorn or any one of his men watch her. And what was with the announcement that he was going to marry her?

He scowled. He hadn't intended to blurt it out like that but hell, that woman could make him do things he'd never intended to do. She always could.

Back in Paris it had been her coy smiles to get him to play tourist or to laze around reading the Sunday papers over brunch. Who had time for that, anyway? Not him. And the fact that he'd done it still rankled.

He'd been so overcome with lust back then he'd let her call the shots. He wouldn't do that again. Not that he was planning to be an asshole about it. He wasn't. But nor was he going to be hoodwinked by her nice girl persona either. Hoodwinked by her innocent sexuality.

No. She'd run once. He wouldn't give her the chance to do it again.

Still, he could have waited until he returned tomorrow afternoon before revealing his plan and he had no ready answer as to why he hadn't.

Probably he'd still been shocked from finding her with his child. That had to be it. He gulped down a mouthful of water from the bottle his staff had handed him upon boarding. He noticed that Imogen hadn't accepted one and he frowned.

She hadn't said boo to him since they'd left his apartment and that was fine with him. All except for the way she made him feel that she was being some sort of martyr in coming with him. And why would she be?

It didn't make sense. Was she still playing him in some way? Acting hard to get to whet his appetite? Not that it had worked. That kiss... He scrubbed a hand across his face, gulped down more water. He hadn't meant to kiss her before, let alone back her against the wall. And he didn't like to admit that he'd got lost in that kiss. Only the fact that she had as well had saved his pride.

Damn, but she tasted sweet. Exactly as he'd remembered. Even now his body throbbed with an inexplicable urge to have her. It was like a driving need. All-consuming. It had always bothered him. The extent of his need. Needing people led to emotional weakness, which led to mistakes being made. He knew that better than anyone and yet fifteen months ago he'd let himself be drawn into her silken web anyway.

Of its own accord, his mind returned to the Sunday afternoon he had found out she was pregnant—an extraordinary blue-sky summer day in Paris. Not wanting to think about his later flight home to New York, they had wandered around Paname—as the Parisians affectionately called their city. He had shown Imogen some of his favourite haunts and she'd dragged him around what felt like every flea market in the known universe. That was where he'd learned she adored Aubergine Provençal and that she was a hoarder of ancient postcards and scarves. The afternoon had ended with her vomiting over his toilet bowl and a doctor announcing her condition with a happy flourish that had floored him.

And okay, he hadn't taken the news that well. What contented bachelor would? So he'd flown back to New York and called his thousand-dollar-an-hour lawyer.

'First, establish the kid is yours.'

When Nadir had told him that was going to be a nine-month wait, his lawyer had shaken his head. 'Not so,' he'd said. 'Modern medicine has moved right along. There's a test, see. It's called some amnio thing. I had to arrange one for a client a few months back. Boy, was he relieved when the results came back negative. The lady had been sleeping around. Tried to pin him with someone else's kid.'

His lawyer had *tsk*ed in disgust and Nadir had murmured some agreement. Asking Imogen to take the test had made sense. So he'd texted her with the request. Perfectly reasonable in his view.

Finding her gone without a trace when he'd flown back to Paris hadn't been reasonable at all.

A dream he'd often had over the last fourteen months winged into his consciousness. It had always been about a child of indiscriminate gender. But the eyes had always been emerald-green and ringed with brown curly lashes. Usually the baby then became the woman, which was when he usually woke up. Usually sweating. Usually cursing.

He thought about her claim that she hadn't run away from him. The different surname. His gut tightened. Was he being played for a fool? And what was up with the buffoon who had tried to defend her? The one who had trod off like a trained seal at her bidding.

Seeing Imogen with her arm linked through his, that sweet smile on her face that could fell an army of warriors...another screw in his gut turned.

She lived with him. He knew that and the water turned sour in his mouth. He'd nearly decked the guy when he'd tried to keep him from her. As if he'd had a chance. On some level he knew his reaction wasn't logical, but logic had never been his firm friend when she was around.

He glanced over as she laughed at something Nadeena had done. He had always loved her laugh. Deep and throaty and redolent of all the pent-up passion of her personality. She had laughed a lot when they had been together. Laughed and teased him as no one else ever had. And she had done it right away, something he'd found as sexy as hell. As sexy as he found her now in faded denims and a simple cotton T-shirt. As sexy as he found her—

Breathing? a mocking voice in his head suggested.

No, Nadir silently snarled back.

And why was he even thinking like this? Brooding over things he couldn't change wouldn't make this whole situation any easier. It didn't matter that he had never met a woman who affected him as strongly—or as quickly—as Imogen. It didn't matter that she made him angry or frustrated or horny or hell—guilty. What mattered was that they get married and make the best of the situation.

What mattered was that he was a father.

A father.

Hell. The thought rocked him. But he knew it was true. He had known the minute the kid had looked up at him with his twin sister's soulful eyes staring back at him. His eyes. And Imogen had given her an Arabic name as if she'd been racked with guilt over knowing she was never going to tell him about his child. Anger rolled through his blood, thick and renewed, and he recalled how she'd called him a bully. Did she just expect him to give up on his daughter without a fight? Whether she liked it or not, he had a hundred options up his sleeve. And he didn't give a damn how Imogen felt about that because he wanted his daughter.

He had wanted Nadeena—truly wanted her—from the moment he had looked at her with her chubby hands fisted on Imogen's soft breast and her wide eyes staring up at him as if she was trying to learn everything about him, as if she was looking directly into his soul. He swallowed heavily. He'd taken one look at her and he'd been…he'd been smitten.

It had been the same the first time he had looked at Imogen and felt that his life would never be the same again.

Hell. What was he thinking?

His life hadn't changed when he'd first laid eyes on Imogen. They had only been having an affair.

No, his life had changed when she had become pregnant with his baby. And now hers was about to change and he had no doubt that she would acquiesce when she got down from her high horse and realised how much he could provide for her. He nearly laughed. As if she hadn't already thought of that.

But that was okay. He could live with her wanting him for his money. It would be a small price to pay to know that his daughter was safe and well.

He signalled the hostess waiting to serve them. This was going to be okay.

'Yes, sir.'

'Coffee, please and…' he glanced at Imogen '…food for Miss Reid—Benson. I haven't noticed her eating anything yet.'

'Miss Benson said she's not hungry, sir.'

Nadir checked out the thin outline of her once curvy body. 'Give her something anyway. Have the chef cook up Aubergine Provençal.'

'I'm sorry, sir. What was that?'

Yeah, what was *that?* He scowled. 'An omelette, then. Something. Anything. Just as long as it's vegetarian.'

'Of course, sir.'

Nadir flipped open his laptop, determined to focus on work for the rest of the trip. Once he renounced the throne tomorrow and married Imogen his life could get back to normal. Or as normal as it would be with a wife and a child and why didn't that notion bother him half as much as it had fourteen months ago?

Marriage?

The word clunked around in Imogen's brain for the millionth time like a giant-sized anvil and she hoped to God Nadir was at this very minute coming to his senses and seeing how ridiculous the idea was.

The best solution...

Of course there were other solutions, and she'd looked some up on her phone as she'd waited for his plane to take off. Not that she wanted to head down the shared custody route and she was sure—once he had calmed down and thought rationally—that neither would he. What rich playboy would? Especially once he learned how detrimental having a child would be to his bachelor lifestyle and she had every intention of pointing it out to him. Because, although she didn't think those things, she knew that once the reality of parenthood set in Nadir would never take his responsibilities seriously. Not with his reputation as a serial dater. No, he wasn't the faithful type and she'd been serious when she'd told him she wouldn't marry him.

And he couldn't force her. No one could do that in this day and age. The worst he could do was to take her to court and fight for custody of Nadeena. And that was... She swallowed heavily, her eyes darting across the aisle to where he was ensconced in work. Could he win? Would a court of law side with his sob story that she had run away with Nadeena?

Not that she had run; she'd simply taken charge of her life. Taken charge without him in it. And he hadn't wanted to be in it. Or at least that was the message she had taken from his acerbic text.

She still remembered with embarrassing clarity the

burst of happiness she had felt when it had pinged into her phone. It had sat there for a full five minutes before she had clicked on it and by then her heart had constructed a full-on fairy tale around what it would say. She had imagined that the text would confirm that he'd had time to think about things and he missed her. That he wanted her in his life. That he wanted their baby. In fact the foolishly sentimental organ in her body had imagined every possible thing he could have written except for what he had.

Imogen, there is a DNA test that can be done while the child is in utero. I have organised an appointment for you at a specialist. If the child is mine I will be in contact.

Devastated by his callousness and influenced by Caro's dire warnings, Imogen had left. And really, what had been the alternative? To write back to him and plead? *Are you sure you don't want our baby? Are you sure you don't want me?* She did have *some* pride.

A delicious smell wafted into the cabin and Imogen's stomach growled as a flight attendant stopped beside her.

'The chef has prepared an omelette for you, Miss Benson. It's vegetarian.'

'Oh.' How had the chef known she was vegetarian? 'I'm sorry. I didn't order this.'

'Prince Nadir ordered it for you.'

Imogen glanced across at the man she was trying hard to think about rationally. Objectively. Something that was almost impossible, given his startling demands and that kiss...

Kiss? She felt a blush heat her cheeks. That kiss had shattered her equilibrium. As had her response. Given his hateful, overbearing behaviour, she'd like to have been left cold when he had touched her. She'd like to have been able to say she was over her sexual infatuation for him and was completely unmoved. She'd also like to be able to say there was no poverty or no ugly wars in the world either.

She sighed and rubbed the back of her neck. It didn't make sense that he could still make her heart jump just by looking at her and her body throb for more with one touch. How could a man who was a veritable stranger and who totally disregarded her needs and desires still affect her so intensely?

He shouldn't be able to. That was the logical answer. Back in Paris, yes. Back then her mother had just died and her absent father had remarried a month later and Imogen had been looking for a change. She'd been looking for excitement and adventure. She'd been looking for passion.

She pulled a rueful face.

Maybe this was just a case of being careful what you wished for.

Because she'd got it, hadn't she. The excitement. The adventure. The *passion*. She'd got it in the form of a man who had awakened a hunger in her she hadn't even realised she'd possessed and who had given her a child. The child she loved. The child she could deal with. The man not so much. Especially not when he kissed her. When he touched her.

So she'd just have to be ready the next time and make sure he didn't get that close. And maybe he wouldn't try and touch her again because, although he had been as aroused as she had been, he hadn't wanted to desire her any more than she did him.

She watched her daughter stacking wooden blocks together on the floor in front of her and tried not to feel so anxious. She had to trust that even now Nadir was reconsidering his outrageous proposition—because surely no one would call 'You *will* marry me' a proposal. That even now he was trying to come up with a way to bow out of it gracefully.

And if he wasn't, well, Imogen had a plan. She would sit down with him over a cup of tea and she would go over all the information she had downloaded in a calm and rational manner. She'd point out, in the nicest possible way, that if his actions were motivated by some sort of guilt—or attack of conscience—then he could rest easy because she didn't need him in her life and she certainly didn't want to trap him.

She smiled. That word ought to put the fear of God into him. No man wanted to feel trapped, did they?

'Ma'am? Did you want the omelette?'

Yes, yes, she did. She just didn't want to have anything to do with the man who had ordered it for her. But that wasn't the hostess's fault and Imogen smiled up at her. 'Yes. Thank you.'

Her upbeat thoughts lasted right up until they landed and Imogen found herself in a small airport that made Tullamarine look like LAX. For some reason she'd thought Bakaan would be like Dubai—or the pictures she'd seen of Dubai. It wasn't. But, even so, it was immediately apparent from the few people milling around in traditional garments and the warm dry air that smelled faintly of vanilla and spice that she had entered an ancient realm full of mystique and promise. Much like her impression of Nadir had been that first night.

A shudder ran through her as the car raced through the night dark city and headed up an incline that led to an impressive well-lit palace that sat just above the ancient city like a golden mirage. As much as she hated to admit it, she was a little unsettled and a lot intimidated by the formality of the palace and the very real sense that she was the one who was trapped instead of Nadir.

'My Lord, it is so good to see you again.'

Imogen looked past Nadir to where a small white-haired servant in white robes knelt on the polished stone steps of the palace, his sombre tone increasing Imogen's sense of unease.

'Staph—' Nadir pulled the old servant to his feet '—I told you not to do that the other day.'

He'd been here recently?

The servant's mouth quirked but the solemn note didn't leave his voice. 'We are glad of your return, My Lord.'

'I wish I was.' He switched to Arabic then and the old man bowed at her feet and beamed at her, speaking in rapid-fire Bakaani. She smiled hesitantly, wondering what it was that Nadir had just told him.

'My Lord, Mistress Imogen, Princess Nadeena.'

Shocked at the label he had given her, Imogen shook her head. 'I am not his mistress,' she corrected a little more sharply than she'd intended. Had Nadir told him she was?

The little man dropped to his knees again and started spouting effusively in Bakaani but there was no smile this time.

Confused, Imogen shot Nadir a helpless glance and he sighed. 'Staph meant you no discourtesy, Imogen. The word does not mean the same in our country as it does in the West.'

'Oh, well...please tell him to get up. The ground must be really hard on his knees.'

She felt awful and smiled warmly at the man to show him she hadn't meant to hurt his feelings. 'I'm sorry, I—'

'Leave it, Imogen.'

Nadir's face softened as his eyes fell on his daughter, half asleep in her arms. 'Do you want me to take her?'

'No!' Nadir had offered to take her as they had boarded his plane earlier but she hadn't been ready for that. She still wasn't, even though her reluctance made her feel totally selfish. There was just too much unfinished business between them. 'No. I've got her.'

His eyes narrowed but he didn't push and she was grate-ful. 'Come then. I will show you to our suite.'

Their suite?

She hurried after him.

'I hope you know I'm not sleeping with you!'

Nadir turned halfway up the steps and the servant cast her a worried look.

Shaking his head, Nadir lowered his voice so he wouldn't be overheard. 'Bakaan is a conservative coun-try, Imogen, and Staph does understand some English. Please keep your discussions about our situation private.'

'I just want you to know that I'm not sleeping in the same bed as you in case you need to organise another room for us,' she half whispered.

'There are many bedrooms in the suite we will be using.'

'Well, good.' She felt her cheeks redden when she re-alised that he'd just confirmed her earlier suspicion that he didn't want to sleep with her any more than she wanted to sleep with him.

Or any more than she wanted to want to sleep with him, she amended to herself. 'At least we're on the same page about that.'

The look he gave her was a mixture of exasperation and something darker that she couldn't define. 'Imogen, I doubt at this point that we're even in the same book, let alone on the same page. But the steps of the Shomar Pal-ace are not the place to discuss it.'

Silently agreeing, Imogen followed him through a wide doorway into an atrium with high coved ceilings and deli-cate mosaic-covered walls. The champagne marble tiles that lined the floors and the ornate brickwork dated back to what she thought might be the Moorish period, the sur-rounding artwork and centuries-old statues recording a history that was both dark and wondrous.

'Has Prince Zachim been notified of our arrival?'

'Yes, My Lord. Will you be needing anything else?'

'Not tonight. Thank you, Staph.'

The man nodded. 'I will bid you goodnight then.' His English was stilted but Imogen appreciated the effort. 'And may I say congratulations, My Lady.'

This time Imogen waited for the servant to retreat before questioning Nadir. 'What is he congratulating me for, exactly?'

'Our marriage. This is your room.' He opened one of the doors inside and waited for her to precede him.

Imogen didn't move, incredulous that Nadir would say such a thing when she had not agreed. 'You told him we were getting married after I distinctly told you we wouldn't be?'

'Not exactly.'

'What does "not exactly" mean?'

'It means he believes we are already married.'

Imogen's brows rose to her hairline. 'I hope you relieved him of that erroneous view,' she said primly.

When he sighed she knew that he hadn't. 'As I said, Bakaan is a conservative nation.'

'You lied to him. That's why he bowed at my feet.'

'I didn't lie. He assumed we were married.'

'And you let him believe it.'

Nadir's eyes flashed his frustration. 'It was better than the alternative.'

'What? That I was your mistress and had your baby out of wedlock?'

A muscle ticked in his jaw. 'You might not care how Nadeena is perceived in the future, but I do.'

'Of course I care. You're just twisting my words to suit yourself but as soon as I see that man again I'm going to correct him.'

'No, you won't. I won't have Nadeena's name smeared because you can't see reason.'

'I can't see reason?' So much for her hope that he would use the time on the plane to reconsider his proposition.

He stopped directly in front of her. 'And, to all intents and purposes, we are married.'

Imogen coughed out a protest. 'We most certainly are not.'

'Signing a piece of paper isn't going to make it any more real, Imogen. You're going to have to get over whatever reservations you have and get used to it. But we can talk about this later, hmm? It is not a conversation we should be having in front of our daughter.'

'She doesn't understand,' Imogen snapped, fuming because she knew he was right and she should have thought of the same thing herself. Because, although Nadeena couldn't understand their words, she was soaking up the heightened emotions in the room and that wasn't good.

Sweeping past Nadir, she gasped as she entered a beautifully appointed bedroom with vast ceilings and long ornate keyhole-shaped windows lined with pale floaty curtains. Deep pink fabric was draped over the elaborate king-sized bed but, other than that, the furnishings wouldn't have been out of place in any five-star hotel. A freshly made up cot stood beside the bed.

'I thought you might like to keep Nadeena close.'

She hadn't expected him to show her that level of thoughtfulness.

'Thank you,' she said stiltedly, rubbing her arms against the chill in the air. 'Is it usually so cold?'

'Always.'

Startled by the gravity of his tone, Imogen stared across at him. His hands were shoved into his pockets and the hard planes of his face seemed even more austere, the grimness of his expression making her think he was talking about more than just the air temperature.

'I'll have the thermostat adjusted. Get some sleep. You look tired.'

Excellent. She looked exactly how she felt.

'I have organised clothing and baby-related items for you which should be through the dressing room. If there's anything the staff has missed just let me know.'

'How could you arrange this so quickly?'

'Bakaan might be somewhat of a backwater compared to the Western world, but it does have retail outlets. And Dubai is an hour away by plane. Anything we didn't have they would have.'

'It seems you've thought of everything.'

His eyes were shuttered as he looked at her. 'Let's hope so.'

With a brief glance at Nadeena, who was wide awake and taking in her new surroundings with open curiosity, Nadir left and closed the door softly behind him.

So civilised, she thought, feeling anything but civilised herself.

'Okay, baby girl. What now?'

Deciding to check out the items Nadir had supplied in the dressing room, she was shocked when she saw just how much he had bought.

She lay Nadeena on her tummy on the floor, watching as she slowly pulled herself towards a row of shoe boxes. Curious herself, Imogen lifted the lid on the first box and gasped at the sight of an exquisite pair of designer shoes nestled amongst the tissue paper. They were her size and she wondered how he had known and then she remembered the day he had taken her shopping in Paris. Did he still remember? Probably not. Probably, it had just been a good guess. He did know women, after all.

Not wanting to dwell on that disagreeable topic, she next checked the clothing hanging on the rack. Most of them were Western, with a few traditional-looking dresses amongst them.

There were more clothes on the hangers than in her own wardrobe and she felt uneasy at why he would have supplied so many. Not that she'd wear them. But she would need to change Nadeena and she couldn't suppress her delight at each of the baby outfits his staff had provided. Gorgeous soft cottons and silks, the like of which she hadn't been able to afford herself.

'All this for one day,' she said to Nadeena. 'The man has clearly never had to work to a realistic budget in his life.'

Nadeena answered with a litany of ga-ga noises and up-ended a box of shoes. Saving the shoes and confiscating the tissue paper, Imogen let her have the empty box, which she immediately started banging on the floor.

Feeling suddenly weary and lost, she changed Nadeena into a soft cotton sleeping suit and fed her. Then she laid her in the cot and grimaced when she saw how wired she was. Sleep looked like a long time coming. Deciding it would be a waste of energy to try to sing her to sleep, she rang Minh instead.

'I was beginning to get worried when I didn't hear from you after your brief text. How are you? How's our darling girl?' he asked.

'Nadeena is fine.' She'd particularly enjoyed Nadir's private jet. 'And I feel like I've been put through a spin dryer ten times. He wants to see her,' she added softly.

She heard Minh settle into his leather sofa and wished she was there with him with a nice bottle of red between them and a rom com on the TV.

'I've already guessed he's the father or you wouldn't be in Bakaan so you know, he does have a right to see her,' he said.

'I know that.' Imogen watched Nadeena stuff the ear of a soft teddy bear into her mouth and chew. 'At least logically I know that.' Emotionally, she wasn't ready to concede the parenting of Nadeena to anyone else but herself and a couple of trusted friends. 'I just never thought he'd be interested in her.'

'Well, he clearly is. And maybe that's a good thing.'

Imogen pulled a face. 'I don't see how.'

'He's a very powerful man. He can provide for her, you know.' Minh's voice grew soft down the end of the phone. 'And no doubt for you as well.'

'I don't want his money.'

'I know that. But you could use someone to take care of you.'

That had been her mother's mistake. It wouldn't be hers. 'And what about love?' She picked Nadeena up when she saw her yawn and laid her head on her shoulder.

'Are we talking about for Nadeena or for you?'

'Nadeena. The way he looked at me today...' She felt heaviness inside her chest and it was hard to get the words out. 'Believe me, there's no love lost between us.' And she would never want Nadir's love for herself again. She'd got over that unrealistic desire a long time ago.

'Try to look on the bright side,' he said. 'It might not be so bad.'

Imogen released a pent-up breath. Looking on the bright side wasn't exactly her forte. She was more a planning for the worst case scenario kind of girl. It was her safety blanket. It kept her from making mistakes—or being surprised by things. If her own mother had crossed every *t* and dotted every *i* maybe she wouldn't have been so shocked when her father had left them and never came back. Maybe she would have been more prepared.

'He left me when I needed him the most,' she said, wondering why that still had the capacity to hurt. She'd got over that as well, hadn't she? 'How could I ever trust him with Nadeena? With me?'

'That's definitely a black mark against him. But you have to think of what's best for Nadeena now.'

Imogen chewed on her lower lip so hard she tasted blood. '*I'm* what is best for Nadeena. He's nothing more than a playboy prince who comes and goes as he pleases and gets whatever he wants.' Imogen steeled her heart, more resolved than ever to resist him. 'I won't let Nadeena have my childhood and that's all Nadir can offer.'

They talked for a few minutes more, with Minh promising to call her boss and tell him that she wouldn't be in over the next couple of days, and then Imogen focused on getting Nadeena to sleep.

Her conversation with Minh had unsettled her. She'd wanted him to tell her that Nadir was a rat bastard but all he'd done was say things that had flashed across her own mind, which left her more conflicted than ever.

She knew giving in to his demand that she marry him would ultimately end in tears. Most likely Nadeena's. And quite possibly her own. In frustration, if nothing else!

CHAPTER SIX

IN THE END it took her an hour to put Nadeena to sleep and when she went looking for Nadir she wasn't expecting to find him barefoot and shirtless with a dark-haired woman bending over his lap.

The sight shocked her and suddenly a long-lost memory of her fifteen-year-old self flew into her mind. She'd been with a bunch of friends on a school excursion when they had come across her father in a passionate embrace with a woman who wasn't her mother. The woman's hands had been in her father's hair, his hand close to her breast, his mouth devouring hers. Imogen had been stunned. Sickened. The girls with her had giggled nervously and her father hadn't even looked contrite. He'd scowled at her and asked her why she wasn't in school. God, she hadn't remembered that in years.

The woman in the white *abaya* straightened and Imogen saw she was holding an empty silver tray and a tumbler of Scotch sat on the low table beside the sofa.

Imogen did a double-take when she realised that the woman was a servant who was now retreating from the room. Her mind had put two and two together and come up with ten. Maybe she was more tired than she'd realised…

'You must be Imogen?'

Whirling around at the sound of a deep male voice, Imogen saw a man bearing a striking resemblance to Nadir standing over by the keyhole windows. He looked tall and imposing in his traditional white robes and matching head-dress and Imogen knew that there was no way she would have missed him if she hadn't been so riveted by the sight of Nadir's impressive chest.

'Imogen, this is my brother, Zachim. Zach, this is Imogen.'

Zachim nodded, his eyes glinting amber-gold in the softly lit room as he regarded her. 'I remember you from the dance hall and it's a pleasure to finally meet you.'

Feeling trapped by her pent-up emotions and unsure what Nadir had told him, Imogen was uncertain as to how to proceed. It seemed highly improper to let rip with the frustration and angst clawing at the inside of her throat and yet she didn't want to wait till morning to discuss things with Nadir. It seemed important to do so now. 'I'm sorry; I didn't mean to interrupt. Perhaps you can let me know when you're free.'

'I thought you were going to bed?'

The easy familiarity with which Nadir spoke to her in front of his brother made her instantly defensive. 'Why—because you told me to?'

'No. Because you look like you're about to fall over with exhaustion.'

Imogen glared at Nadir and felt even worse when his brother cleared his throat discreetly from behind her. 'I think I should leave you both alone.'

'No, please.' She was horrified at what he must think of her. 'I didn't mean to interrupt you.'

Prince Zachim smiled but it was weary. 'You didn't. My brother is being his usual obstinate self. Maybe you can talk some sense into him. He won't listen to me.'

Imogen was about to say that Nadir didn't listen to her either when he rose from the sofa and the sight of all those hard muscles rippling across his abdomen as he moved made the words fly out of her head.

'I'm not going to change my mind, Zach.'

'It's your birthright.'

'If you're feeling guilty about taking something from me then don't. I don't want anything to do with Bakaan.'

'Nadir, I know you're still angry about the past but—'

Nadir made a motion with his hand that cut his brother off. 'Goodnight, Zach.'

Zachim scowled. 'All right, Nadir, You win this round.'

'Hallelujah.' Nadir's voice held no enthusiasm and Imogen wondered what it was Nadir was still angry about and what exactly Zach was taking from him.

'I have to fly to the mountains early tomorrow,' Zachim said as he turned to go. 'But I'll be back by noon.'

'I'll be waiting.'

Zachim gave her a weary smile. 'Lovely to meet you, Imogen. I'm not sure if I should congratulate you on your impending marriage to my brother or offer commiserations.' His smile held a touch of irony. 'But I definitely look forward to getting to know you and to meeting my niece over lunch tomorrow.'

Imogen smiled warmly. As handsome and dashing as he was, this brother didn't tie her insides up in knots like Nadir did. 'I look forward to it.'

Zach looked back at Nadir as if he wanted to say more but Nadir gave him a faint smile. 'Give it up, Zach. You're perfect for the role and you know it. And stop flirting with my fiancé.'

'Nadir!'

His name left her lips in an appalled reprimand but Zach just laughed heartily.

'You might not like being back in Bakaan, brother, but I like you being here'

Nadir watched his brother give him a mocking salute and stride out of the room and knew that he was doing the right thing in giving Zach the leadership role. They had different mothers and therefore vastly different experiences of their father and their homeland. And it wasn't just anger or resentment at the past that stopped Nadir wanting to be the next King; it was also the painful memories that haunted him every time he was here. It was the sense of guilt his brother would never understand because Nadir had never told him of the cowardly role he'd played in his mother and sister's deaths. The feelings of shame and ineptitude. A feeling of emptiness.

If he'd thought the people of Bakaan really needed him, if he thought he could add some value Zach couldn't as leader then he might do it. But the fact was Zach was a capable military leader and was perfect for the job.

'I apologise if I ruined your conversation with your brother. It wasn't my intention.'

He eyed Imogen still standing in the middle of the room and picked up his Scotch, hoping it would distract him from his bleak thoughts. He knew a way she could distract him as well but he didn't think she'd be as biddable as the Scotch. Unfortunately. 'You didn't; he was leaving anyway.'

She chewed the inside of her lower lip and he couldn't take his eyes off the little movement.

'Are you okay?'

Her soft question made him gulp a mouthful of the fiery liquid and he relished the burn of it down his throat. No, he wasn't okay. 'Concerned for my welfare, *habibi*? I'm touched.'

He saw her posture stiffen and regretted taking his frustration out on her. But hell, she was partly to blame. Sorting out the leadership issue would be over and done within a matter of hours. Sorting out the rest of his life with a wife and child… He didn't want to contemplate how long that would take. Particularly given the light of defiance burning hotly in Imogen's eyes. A defiance he had yet to fully understand.

'Don't be,' she responded smartly. 'It was an aberration that won't happen again.'

He smiled. He hadn't realised she was so feisty when they'd been together back in Paris. Back then she'd always been thrilled to see him, delight written all over her expressive face. And it had been catching. For those all too brief weekends he'd been happy too. Perhaps that had been her allure. That and the red-hot chemistry between them. 'Whatever you've got to say can wait until morning.'

'Really?' Her eyebrows arched skyward. 'Because you decreed it, *My Lord*?'

No, she definitely hadn't been this feisty in Paris but part of him—the part that turned caveman every time she was around—liked it a little too much for comfort. 'Yes. That and the dark circles under your eyes which suggest you need sleep more than conversation.'

'I'm sorry you don't approve of the way I look.' She dipped into a mocking curtsy. 'I'll try to do better next time, *My Lord*.'

'I wouldn't use that term too often,' he advised softly, tossing back another finger of Scotch. 'I might like it.'

She scowled at him but her eyes followed his hand as he rubbed it across his chest and his blood surged as he saw the breath catch in her throat. He'd forgotten Zach had interrupted his shower. Did the sight of him bother her? He'd sure as hell be bothered if she was standing before him half naked. Hell, he was bothered anyway and she still had on her crumpled clothes from earlier.

A spike of conscience needled him. She might still be as beautiful as ever but she really did look worn to the bone. His eyes scanned over her body and came to rest on her chest. And she was braless.

'So, anyway...' She cleared her throat and his eyes rose

from her round, full breasts to the pulse point beating like a small trapped bird inside her creamy throat. 'I've looked up some options I'd like to go through with you.'

With his instincts pulling at him to go to her and haul her up against him and tame that defiant look in her eyes until she softened and became once again pliant and wanton in his arms, Nadir forced his mind to recall her words. 'Options' was the only word that had stuck but he knew she wouldn't want to discuss the options he was presently interested in. 'Now is not a good time.'

'I disagree.'

Of course she did. 'You had ample opportunity to talk on the plane. You chose not to.'

She perched on the edge of the sectional sofa and faced him. 'Nadeena was awake the whole time. I didn't want her to realise how tense I was. At this age babies feel everything the mother feels.'

He gave a short laugh. 'If that's true you wouldn't have fooled her. Even a blind man could see you were about ready to snap in half.'

'And whose fault is that?'

'Mine, no doubt. Did she go to sleep easily?'

Her lips tightened. 'Yes, thank you.'

'Thank you?'

'For asking, I suppose.' Frustration flashed in her green eyes. 'I…can we just stay on topic?'

'By all means. But you can stop treating me like a stranger. I'm not.'

'You are.' She rubbed the back of her neck as if it ached and rolled her slender shoulders. 'But I didn't come out here to argue with you.'

Nadir took another swallow of Scotch. 'What did you come out here for?'

The air between them thickened and he nearly said to

hell with arguing; it was time to relieve some of the tension between them.

'To talk.'

'I've got a better idea.'

She frowned and he saw the moment the meaning behind his rough words became clear because her gorgeous eyes widened in shock. 'I hope you don't mean what I think you mean.'

'Oh, I definitely mean exactly what you think I mean.'

She gasped softly. 'How can you think about sex at a time like this?'

He thought about sex with her all the time. 'Too soon for you, *habibi*? That's okay. I'm a patient man. I can wait.'

'Look, Nadir—'

'Look, Imogen.' He scrubbed a weary hand across his face. 'I'm not in the mood for a discussion. We can talk tomorrow after one o'clock.'

'Why? What happens at one o'clock?'

At one o'clock one of his pesky loose ends would be resolved. 'It's not important.'

Her eyes narrowed. 'Does it have to do with what your brother was talking about before?'

'It doesn't matter.'

'It seemed to matter to him.'

'He'll get over it.'

Her lashes fluttered down to hide her frustrated gaze. 'Keep your secrets. I don't want to know them anyway.'

'It's not a secret. I have business to sort out in Bakaan that doesn't concern you.'

'Fine.' Her tone implied it was anything but fine. 'Let's stay on topic and discuss something that does concern me.'

'By all means let's stay on topic. Tomorrow.'

Imogen didn't like the way his gaze swept over her and wished she'd kept her bra on after Nadeena had gone to sleep because every time his eyes dropped to her chest her nipples peaked. She just hoped that the lighting from the lamps was low enough that he wouldn't notice. Not that she couldn't see every muscle shifting on his torso. He raised his hand to rub at the smattering of hair on his chest again and Imogen barely resisted the urge to fan herself. *Stay on topic yourself,* she admonished silently.

The last thing she needed right now was to think about the offer he'd just made. Which only reinforced his play-boy mentality.

I'm a patient man. I can wait.

So much for her earlier assumption that he didn't want to sleep with her. The man would obviously sleep with anyone but he'd be waiting a long time if he thought he could use her to slake his hunger for a night. Been there, done that and now had the baby to prove it! A baby who didn't need him.

Deciding that starting with that statement would be like waving a red flag at an irritated bull, she went straight to the second half of her plan instead.

'So.' She cleared her throat yet again. 'Given that you said that you wanted to be part of Nadeena's life, I looked up some alternative options for us that don't include marriage.'

'Good for you.'

His response was frosty but at least it cooled the air between them and she wouldn't let it put her off. She narrowed her eyes as he crossed his ankle over his knee and then she calmly folded her hands in her lap. 'So it's obviously not an in-depth analysis, but from what I can tell there's legal custody and physical custody and they're quite different from each other.'

'Are they?'

His laconic response reeked of disinterest and Imogen did her best to cap her irritation. 'Yes. They are. Legal custody is about who makes decisions for the child and can be sole or joint and physical custody is about seeing the child. Again, that can be either sole or joint and that breaks down into supervised and unsupervised and even virtual visits nowadays.' She took a deep breath and rushed on before he could interject. 'There's also the issue of how to split the time and it seems that the most popular is for the father to visit the child every second weekend and on public holidays. Unless you want to go the virtual route, of course.'

'Of course.'

Imogen waited for him to say more. When he just smiled and curved his hands behind his head she suspected he was toying with her. 'Well?' she prompted stiffly.

'I can see you've put quite a bit of effort into this.'

Imogen sucked in a litre of air and released it slowly. Perhaps she'd been wrong and he wasn't toying with her. Perhaps he was going to be cooperative and let her go. 'Not really.' She gave him a small smile that seemed to stretch her dry lips to the point of cracking. 'But it's a start.'

And, perversely, the possibility that he might agree with her didn't thrill her the way she had imagined it would. Instead, she felt unaccountably disappointed and realised just how much she still wished that their relationship in Paris could have progressed like so many other happy couples did. Couples like Minh and David, who loved each other so much they would do anything for the other person.

She sighed. What had her mother always said? *If wishes were horses, beggars would ride.* Such an old-fashioned saying, passed down through the generations. Would she pass it on to Nadeena with that same air of inevitability?

'Tell me,' he began conversationally, 'did the Internet mention the custody arrangements for a woman who kept her child's birth a secret from its father?'

No, he was not going to be cooperative and icy shivers tripped down her spine as she saw that she had angered him again 'No,' she bit out tersely.

'Then you're right—' his smile was even tighter than hers '—when you say that your analysis isn't very complete. And furthermore,' he drawled with icy control, 'while you might be happy sharing custody of our daughter, I am not.'

'I'm not either,' she replied hotly. 'But you're not giving me any other choice.'

'On the contrary; I've given you the best choice there is,' he drawled arrogantly.

'Marrying you?'

She could see instantly that he'd taken offence to her contemptuous tone from the stillness of his big body but dammit, he didn't love her. If he did…if he did then things might be different…

'This is all something you should have thought about before you ran away,' he bit out contemptuously.

'I did not run away,' she retorted. 'I left.'

He made a low noise in the base of his throat that startled her. 'I told you I would return and we'd talk about options.' His eyes glittered dangerously. 'You weren't there.'

'Like abortion?' she spat, remembering how cold she had felt reading his missive. How icy she had felt in his apartment when he had confirmed that yes, he'd have preferred not to be an expectant father.

'No, not that.'

He lost colour and tugged a hand through his hair as if the thought truly horrified him.

'Well, it probably would have happened if you had pushed for that horrible paternity test you told me I had to take.'

His brows drew together. 'A paternity test made sense.'

'Do you have any idea how dangerous those tests are?'

'No, I—'

'About one in three hundred amniocenteses end in miscarriage and I would have needed the earlier test. With the CVS you can double the chance of a miscarriage. But then that would have worked a lot better for you than this, wouldn't it?'

Nadir jumped to his feet, his movements lacking their usual grace. 'For the love of all things holy, Imogen, I would never have put you or our baby's life at risk. You must know that.'

Imogen wrapped her arms around her stomach, all the anger leaching out of her as he stood before her all ferocious and earnest as if he meant what he was saying.

Did he?

She didn't know. What she did know was that she didn't want to be forced to do something stupid that they would both later regret because Nadeena would be the one to pay the ultimate price when things turned bad. Still, a twinge of regret spiked inside her chest. The way he'd said 'our baby', as if he really felt something for Nadeena already. 'And you would have just accepted that I not take the test, I suppose,' she scoffed.

'Of course I would have accepted it.' He settled his hands on his hips. 'At what stage in our relationship did I ever show you that I was unreasonable?'

Imogen tapped her foot and wanted to say *all the time.* But the truth was that he had never been unreasonable towards her. Ever. He had always been thoughtful and kind. Loving. A lie she couldn't afford to be swayed by again. 'Now. You're being unreasonable now.'

'That's a matter of opinion.'

'Damn it, Nadir.' A flash of renewed irritation surged inside her. 'You can't keep me here against my will.'

'Actually, I can,' he said with all the arrogance of a man born to privilege. 'But I won't.' He paused, ran his hand across his stubbled jaw. 'I will, however, stop you from taking Nadeena away from me again.'

Imogen's insides seized and she knew her face went

pale, her breathing laboured. 'I hate you.' Because he'd just effectively narrowed her choices down to marriage to him or give up her child.

He nodded as if this was normal. As if she hadn't dreamt of him and wished in her darkest moments that he wouldn't come for her. Tell her that he missed her. Tell her that he loved her. Tell her that he couldn't live without her. Dreams not worth the sleep they had interrupted.

'A child deserves to be raised by both parents.' He regarded her steadily. 'Or are you going to argue with me about that too?'

'Only if both parents love and want her.'

'I agree.'

Imogen clamped her mouth mutinously closed and turned her attention to the intricate patterns on the Persian rug at her feet before she said something she'd truly regret.

Nadir sighed. 'Believe it or not, Imogen, I only have Nadeena's best interests at heart.'

'Do you?'

'Yes.' She heard a hardness enter his voice at her scepticism.

She looked at him and all the fight left her and a great sense of doom pervaded her limbs. 'And what if a marriage between us is the worst thing for her?'

He looked genuinely perplexed by her question. 'I don't see how it could be.'

'Because it would be nothing but a marriage of convenience.'

'I don't see it that way.'

She blew out a frustrated breath. 'How can you not?'

He stepped in front of her, breathing as hard as she was. 'Because there's nothing remotely convenient about marriage and ours will be real.'

Real? Imogen swallowed heavily and lost her breath. 'I hope you don't mean what I think you mean.'

'We will be man and wife in every sense of the word, *habibi,'* he said softly with the same confidence she had once loved.

Imogen's chin jutted forward. 'I didn't think you were into force.'

She knew that if she revealed just how badly he affected her it would be akin to lying down and waving a white flag. So she held her breath as his eyes ran over her face and down over her throat and willed herself not to move, silently urging her racing heartbeat to slow to a moderate gallop.

As if he couldn't help himself, he raised his hand and brushed his thumb across her lips in a whisper-soft caress that made every one of her nerve endings tingle. For a long moment they just stared at each other and then he ruined the moment by speaking. 'Force, *habibi*?'

The gentle words mocked her and she jerked back and stepped away from him, doing her best to ignore the way the blood pounded heavily through her body and highlighted her inability to control her attraction to him. No man had ever affected her so deeply that she forgot who she was and where she was and she refused to give him that kind of power over her again. It made her feel helpless to follow her own will. It made her hungry to taste him. It made her willing to risk everything. Almost...

Forcing herself to take another slow step backwards, she banked her confused emotions as best she could and reached down deep for reason. 'Be serious, Nadir. A child will completely cramp your lifestyle. They're inconvenient and messy and exhausting and...and...' *Wonderful and joyous and funny and loving...* She swallowed. 'And smelly. Really smelly at times.'

Nadir paced away from her and then turned sharply on his heel. 'I don't understand you. Most women would be jumping for joy at the prospect of having a rich man take care of her and her child.'

'Except I'm not most women and I *know* this is a mistake. My parents married because my mother was pregnant with me and it was a miserable affair for everyone. They stayed together even though my father was seeing another woman because my mother believed a child should be raised by two parents. My father resented being tied to us and after a while I stopped wishing he would pay me attention.'

'I won't resent you.'

Embarrassed at having revealed her deepest wounds to him, Imogen scoffed. 'How can you say that? You have a reputation of being the unobtainable playboy that spans continents.'

His lips thinned into a flat line. 'People see what they want to see. But if you think love is some sort of guarantee of a happy union, it isn't. My parents were the poster children for that particular misconception and they didn't last.'

Imogen frowned. 'I find that hard to believe if it was true love,' she said huskily.

'Believe it. They separated when my father took a second wife and—'

'Took a second wife!'

'Yes, it is the custom that men in Bakaan can take more than one wife.'

'You can definitely forget marriage then.'

He smiled wearily. 'Don't worry. I am not a masochist.'

'Is that supposed to be funny? I think it's appalling that men are allowed to have more than one wife. I bet the women aren't allowed more than one husband.'

'No. And it bothered my mother just as much. In the end they hated each other so much there was never any joy in visiting either one of them. My mother was always trying to get us to prove our love by feeding her information about our father and our father was constantly derogatory about her and wanting to know what she was up to behind his back. It was as if they couldn't let each other go and frankly it was exhausting.'

And no doubt emotionally crippling, Imogen thought. Which was so unlike the picture she had formed in her mind about his childhood. For some reason she had assumed that his life had been full of opulence and fun and the security of belonging to an ancient dynasty. It seemed she had been wrong. At least about the fun and security.

Curiosity made her pause and she wanted to ask him more but he got in first.

'Forget it.' His flinty gaze seemed to penetrate deep into her mind. 'And forget shared custody, Imogen.'

At the reminder of their earlier argument Imogen's spine straightened. 'You're impossible to reason with.'

'That's because you know I'm right.'

Shaking her head, she would have turned away from him then—anything to put some distance between herself and his half-naked body that seemed to beckon her to reach out and touch it—but his hands came down on her shoulders and held her immobile.

Imogen trembled and knew he felt it by the satisfied gleam that seemed to soften his gaze. 'I've never stopped wanting you, Imogen, and that kiss back in my apartment proves we share an incredibly strong chemistry. Why fight it?'

Realising with a pang that she was held captive under his unwanted spell, Imogen wrenched herself out of his hold and swung away from him. Embarrassed at how easily she became enthralled by him, how easily she succumbed to his words, his touch, she let anger at him, at herself, at the whole world take hold. 'You want to know why?' She squared off in front of him. 'Because, no matter what happens, I have no intention of marrying you and because, despite what you believe, a marriage based on sex will always be weak.'

'Perhaps. But you're a smart girl and you must realise that a marriage based on mutual chemistry and shared interests has strength.'

Imogen didn't feel very smart right now. She felt wrung out and beaten. 'And what do you think that we *share*, Nadir?' she all but spat at him, desperate to lash out at him in any way that she could. Desperate to alleviate the giant ball of emotion welling up inside her and threatening to burst right out of her. 'That could possibly hold a marriage between us together?'

She slapped her hands on her hips and waited for his response but she should have known that he'd have an answer poised on his lips that would floor her. She should have known that a man whose negotiation skills in the business world were second to none would have something up his sleeve to make her feel as big as a thimble.

'Nadeena.' He paused to let his words sink in. 'We have Nadeena.'

CHAPTER SEVEN

After waiting for Zach inside the council chambers for nearly an hour it was safe to say that Nadir was now extremely irritated. Yes, he'd managed to field a few important work calls while he waited but there was only so much he could get done from a country with limited Internet resources.

He also needed to sort things out with Imogen but she'd steadfastly avoided him all morning and frankly he hadn't tried that hard to challenge her on it. Last night's discussion—hell, argument—had played heavily on his mind and made sleep impossible.

Before picking her up yesterday he'd expected to find that she'd aborted his baby, mainly, it had to be said, because she hadn't approached him for a truckload of money and for a while yesterday he'd continued to think that maybe she was somehow playing him for a fool. He'd continued to believe that she had run from him because she'd had something to hide.

He didn't think that now. She was too earnest in her attempts to get him to change his mind about their marriage. Too earnest in her belief that he had been the one to do the wrong thing by her and not the other way around.

He recalled her fierce expression when she'd mentioned his text. At the time he hadn't contemplated the possibility that she would be upset by it. He hadn't contemplated the possibility that she would feel abandoned by his return to New York and feel as if she had to deal with her pregnancy alone. Guilt knifed through him.

He supposed, if he was honest, he'd been mostly to blame because he hadn't communicated his feelings to her, but how the hell was he supposed to have done that when he didn't know how he had been feeling?

Dealing with emotions had never been his strong suit, even before his mother and sister had died.

He remembered his mother encouraging him to embrace that side of his nature and his father telling him it was dangerous and it had been his father who had been proved right.

Nadir sighed. He'd never seen the benefit of rehashing the past and he still didn't. A man either took action or he bowed out of the game. Nadir had no intention of bowing out. Not with Imogen at any rate.

He glanced at the admiral's chair his father used to occupy at the end of the room during council meetings. As heir to the throne he had always been encouraged to sit in on those meetings and he'd loved them. He'd loved listening to his father taking charge and issuing orders. Watching him handle political issues.

His father had openly shared this side of himself and it wasn't until Nadir had left Bakaan that he'd realised how isolated and increasingly paranoid his father had become. How only a select few were ever allowed into his inner sanctum and then only if those select few agreed with him. From the age of twelve Nadir had started to do that less and less and that was when the rot had set in. That was when his father had started trying to keep him from his mother and sister, explaining that the ties he found the hardest to cut were the ones that needed to be cut most of all.

He rubbed a hand across his face. One of the issues between him and Imogen was that she was, at heart, an emotional and sensual woman who didn't hold back. It was both a draw and a deterrent—although right now he was honest enough to admit that the draw side was definitely winning out. Probably it had been too long since he'd had a woman. It wasn't natural for a healthy male to go without sex for fourteen months.

Hell.

Did he owe Imogen an apology for his behaviour back then? It wasn't a position he had found himself in for years and the last two people he'd needed to apologise to were dead.

Out of the corner of his eye he noticed one of his father's senior council members break away from the group and, like a drowning man grasping for a life raft, he welcomed the interruption to his thoughts.

Old and set in his ways, Omar had never been on Nadir's list of favourite people but he was knowledgeable and, as far as he was aware, loyal to a fault.

'Well?'

'We don't know where he is, Your Highness. He's not answering his phone.'

Nadir gritted his teeth. His brother had said he needed to go into the mountains on some business or other. He'd flown the helicopter himself. Now he was nowhere to be seen and the helicopter was still at the airfield. There was no sign of foul play or anything amiss. 'Fine—we'll proceed without him.'

'I'm afraid that's not possible, Your Highness.'

'Why not?'

'In order for you to renounce your position as King, we need to have your successor present.'

'Well, he's not here and I have a business to run.'

'The council understand, Your Highness,' he said in a way that let Nadir know they didn't understand at all. 'But you are still our acting King and there is a UAE dinner tonight that has been planned for months. It is too late to cancel. Many of the heads of state have already flown into Bakaan. It was quite a coup for Prince Zachim to arrange it. Many will be staying all week on official business.'

'Then Zachim should be here to run it,' Nadir bit out.

'Indeed, Your Highness.' Omar nodded deferentially.

Aware that he was being manipulated but knowing that he was boxed in until Zachim returned, Nadir muttered a curse. 'Okay, I'll do it.

'Very good, Your Highness. And shall I set a place for your wife?'

Nadir's gaze sharpened on the older man. 'Why would you do that?'

'Because spouses have been invited to the dinner. As everyone has heard about your wife, they will expect to see her there.'

Nadir had a good idea how Imogen was going to take that news. 'Try calling my brother again.'

'Of course, Your Highness.'

Nadir paced again while Omar dialled his phone. Most likely it wouldn't work, given the rudimentary telecom system his father had installed in the country. That was another possible reason why no one could reach Zachim. Either that or his brother was hiding out in some attempt to get him to step into the role as leader.

Nadir stilled. Was that it? Was Zach forcing his hand? He frowned as the idea sprouted roots and leaves. As a child, Zachim had often run away and hidden when he was in trouble, waiting for their father's wrath to subside before coming out again. By then Nadir had usually copped Zach's share of the punishment as well as his own so it wasn't a bad strategy—one Nadir had been too proud to ever try himself—but it was quite possible that Zach was right now holed up somewhere with a woman and a case of wine. If he was…Nadir shook his head. If he was, he'd beat him to a pulp when he returned.

'No luck, Your Highness.'

'Fine. Set a place for Imogen.' Nadir turned to leave the room, already thinking about what needed to be done before the evening dinner when Omar's next words stopped him cold.

'And your wedding?'

'Excuse me?'

'Your wedding? You may have forgotten but a Western marriage is not recognised as legal for a member of the royal family. It would be best, Your Highness, if you formalised the marriage in a traditional ceremony as soon as possible.'

Hoping that the issue of his legal ties to Imogen wouldn't have arisen in the small amount of time he was supposed to be in Bakaan, Nadir sighed. 'I suppose you have a perfect date available, Omar?'

'As soon as possible, Your Highness. There is some unrest in the northern part of the country and some who would wish to destabilise the throne. It is important that the people observe their crown prince behaving in a way befitting the leadership.'

'You know I do not intend to become the next leader of Bakaan, Omar, so the timing doesn't matter,' Nadir said tightly.

'As you wish, Your Highness.'

Realising that he was being obstinate and the council members had no idea why he didn't want the damned leadership role, Nadir softened his position. 'I know you're worried, Omar, but don't be. Zachim will most likely be back before the evening meal is served. In the meantime, if you think that formalising my marriage is absolutely necessary then organise the ceremony for a week from today.'

That would give Zach plenty of time to stop playing his

games—if he was actually staying away on purpose—and get back here. And on the off-chance he was still holding out on him in a week then they would marry. It wasn't any big deal because it was going to happen, one way or another.

'I'm sorry—who did you say you were?'

Imogen placed Nadeena in the baby recliner beside the beautifully paved swimming pool and fastened the safety catch, the fronds of the palm trees overhead keeping the scorching sun from burning her. When she was done she turned to the two women standing in the open doorway. One was young and striking-looking in the traditional cream-coloured outfit that denoted the palace servants and the other woman was much older and dressed in faded black garments. And her eyes were transfixed by Nadeena.

'My name is Tasnim and this is Maab,' the younger one said with a wide smile 'We are your servants, My Lady.'

'Oh.' Imogen smiled kindly. Used to fending for herself and preferring it that way, she had no need for servants. 'Thank you, but—'

Before she could say anything, Maab had moved closer to Nadeena and was crooning something in Arabic. As if sensing Imogen's regard, she turned and bowed her head, speaking in rapid Bakaani.

'I'm sorry,' Imogen said, 'I don't understand.'

'Please excuse Maab, My Lady. She does not speak very much English but she is excellent with babies and helped raise the royal siblings when they were little. She is asking if she might approach the little princess.'

'Well, of course she can.' Imogen smiled encouragingly and the old woman knelt down in front of Nadeena and gasped in surprise. She started spouting the name Sheena and smiling broadly.

Confused, Imogen turned to Tasnim for clarification.

'Maab says that the little princess looks just like Sheena.'

'Sheena?'

'The King's sister, My Lady.'

'Oh, Nadir's aunt? That's nice.'

Tasnim gave her a funny look. 'No, My Lady, she means King Nadir's sister.'

Imogen was silent for a moment as she processed that piece of information. She'd never heard of Nadir having a sister but that wasn't surprising, really. Their short relationship in Paris hadn't progressed past the intensely sexual phase and, whether by accident or design, neither of them had wasted their time talking about family or personal history. For Imogen that had been deliberate. She hadn't wanted to talk about her mother's recent death and her father's remarriage a month later. Had Nadir chosen not to speak about his past because he was upset by it as well?

'The King has asked me to help you prepare for the evening ahead. Would you like to do that now, My Lady?'

The evening ahead? Feeling as if her life was once again spinning out of her control and not wanting to look like a complete dill, Imogen kept her expression bland. 'By King you mean…Nadir?'

'*Na'am*, My Lady. Yes.'

A sudden sense of unease fluttered up from her stomach. Nadir couldn't be King because if he was that would mean they were going to be here for a *little* longer than a day, but if he wasn't then why were these women even here?

'I think there must be some mistake,' she began slowly and then Zach's words jumped into her head from the night before.

It's your birthright.

Was Nadir here to discuss some sort of succession planning? She hadn't contemplated that and perhaps he would expect her to meet his father. She nearly grimaced. It was one thing to meet his brother but if his father was anything like her own then he was unlikely to approve of her.

Maab started saying something again in Arabic and there was a hint of pride in her voice.

'Maab says that we are delighted that he has come back, My Lady. That King Nadir will be a great king because he was a great boy. Kind and loyal and very strong.'

Imogen had no doubt that Nadir had been strong but she wasn't so sure about the kind and loyal part. *Ruthless and self-serving?* Now that she would have believed in an instant and she wasn't sure how she felt hearing this woman's hero worship of a man she was convinced was set on doing the right thing because of a *guilty* conscience rather than a *good* one.

'That's lovely,' she murmured.

Tasnim nodded. 'She was very sad to think that Nadir would not return after the death of his father.'

'The death of his father?'

Tasnim gave her another funny look and Imogen's pride kicked in. 'Oh, yes, the death of his father.'

What the heck was going on here?

'It has been a troubling two weeks for those of us working in the palace,' Tasnim continued. 'And not knowing what would happen…but I'm sorry, My Lady, you don't want to hear all this.'

Not want to hear it? Imogen wanted to hear that and more. She could hardly believe what Tasnim had said so far. Had Nadir's father truly died two weeks ago? And what did that mean? Was Nadir going to be King? Did he expect Imogen to move to Bakaan? The whole concept was totally implausible and she could feel panic threatening. She needed to speak to Nadir to sort this out. Right now.

Giving Tasnim what she hoped was a benign smile,

she said, 'Thank you, Tasnim. Would you mind telling *my husband* that I don't need any help and I'd really like to see him?'

'Your wish is my command, *habibi.*'

Swinging around at the sound of Nadir's voice, Imogen's jaw nearly hit the floor at the sight of him dressed in flowing black robes that made him look like a pirate. Absurd excitement gripped her and rational thought was whisked away on the light, hot breeze.

And she wasn't the only female affected by the sight of him because Maab rushed to her feet with the agility of a woman half her age and threw herself on the ground in front of him.

'Maab.' Nadir raised the woman and hugged her tightly, speaking to her in his native language, his tone warm and deep. Tears sparkled in the old woman's eyes and, seeing it, Imogen felt tears as well; her emotions much closer to the surface since her daughter had been born.

She wasn't sure what Nadir had said to the women but moments later they had bowed low to them both and disappeared as quickly as they had arrived.

Nadir's gaze swept over her and a small frown of disapproval immediately knitted his brow. 'Why aren't you wearing the clothing I provided?'

Tense and uncertain after what she'd just heard, Imogen was in no mood to talk about fashion. 'Forget the clothing. Why did you lie to me?'

'I did not lie to you. I have never lied to you.'

'You told me we would be leaving today and I've just heard that I'm supposed to be attending a dinner. And that you're the King.' She peered at him, looking for signs that something had changed. 'You're not really the King, are you?'

'No, I'm not the King,' he said in a way that didn't convince her at all.

'Then why do those two women call you the King?'

'Because they believe that I soon will be, I suppose.'

'But why would they think that?'

His face turned grim and Imogen felt worry spike inside her. 'A glitch.'

'A glitch?'

'Nobody is King until the coronation but in the meantime the country needs someone to lead it. I am acting head of state until Zachim returns.'

'So, it's true that your father died recently.'

He shoved his hands into the pockets of his robe. 'It's true.'

Imogen didn't know what to say in the face of his implacable regard. 'I'm sorry for your loss.'

'Don't be.' He drew a weary hand across his jaw. 'The whole purpose of my return to Bakaan was not to take over the throne but to cede it to Zachim.'

'Oh.' Didn't he want to be King? And if not, why not? 'I suppose, given that women aren't allowed multiple husbands in Bakaan, your sister isn't allowed to take over the throne instead.'

'My sister?' A muscle flickered in his jaw. Once. Twice. 'Who told you about my sister?'

Not wanting to get the young servant into trouble, Imogen hesitated. 'Tasnim. But don't blame her. I pushed for the information.'

'Then you didn't push hard enough.' His expression made her feel chilled. 'My sister is no longer alive either.'

'Oh, God, I'm so sorry.' Imogen felt stricken as she saw a mask of pain briefly cross his face. 'Did she die with your father?'

'No.' Nadir expelled a harsh breath, his emotions hidden behind the screen of his impossibly long eyelashes. 'But you are right. She would not have been allowed to be a sheikha.' His lashes raised and she could see that his emotions were now firmly under control. 'Now, since Zachim has disappeared for the moment, I must attend a state dinner tonight and I need you to accompany me.'

'But what about our return to London?'

'It has been delayed.'

'It can't be delayed. I have a job I need to get back to and we're really short-staffed at the café.'

Nadir gave her a dry look. 'You will no longer need that job, Imogen, so you might as well quit.'

Imogen shoved her hands onto her hips. 'I will not quit.'

Nadir let out a long sigh. 'I hope to Allah that not every conversation we have is going to feel like I'm pulling out hen's teeth. If you go into your dressing room you will find an evening gown for the dinner and Tasnim will help you prepare. If you need anything else—'

'Nadir, every conversation feels like a struggle because you won't listen. And I'm not going anywhere with you tonight when nothing has been resolved between us.'

'Of course it has. We resolved everything last night.'

As far as Imogen was concerned, they had resolved nothing last night. 'When?'

'When we talked.'

She shook her head, frustrated that he could be so obtuse. 'You might have resolved something last night but I didn't.'

His sigh was one of aggravated patience. 'Okay, tell me what you need to make this work for you.'

Was he serious? 'Time.' *For one thing.* 'You listening to what I want would help.'

Nadir pulled a wry face. 'I promise to try and listen to you but unfortunately I can't do anything about your first request because time is something I seem to be in short supply of right now. And I have never seen the point in stalling when the outcome is not in question.'

His high-handedness was one of the things that had attracted her to him so she really only had herself to blame. 'I take it you mean the outcome of us marrying and if you do then the outcome is only not in question for you.'

'For us.'

'This is what I would call not listening,' she said with exasperation. 'Because at this point there is no us. There is you and me and a baby. I mean—what about where we're going to live? What about what school Nadeena will go to? What about her emotional well-being?'

His crooked grin made her breath catch and she wondered if that wasn't exactly the outcome he'd been trying to achieve. 'You will live where I live. Nadeena will go to a good school and we both want what is best for her.'

'You're simplifying.'

'And you're making it complicated.' It was he who sounded exasperated now.

'It *is* complicated.'

'It doesn't have to be.'

Imogen's eyes shot to his as the tenor in his voice roughened and, just like that, sex was in the room again. Or at least in her thoughts. 'Be serious, Nadir—we don't even like each other any more.'

'I like you.'

About to tell him that what he thought of her was inconsequential anyway, she found the words dissolving on her tongue as she watched him hunker down and start trickling water over Nadeena's feet. Nadeena reached forward and grabbed one of his thick fingers in her chubby hand. Imogen closed her eyes and then opened them again when Nadeena giggled and splashed the water with her feet.

Nadir smiled. That smile that had melted a thousand hearts, including her own.

They looked so beautiful together. Her daughter and the man who had once made her so impossibly happy she'd thought she would burst. Both dark-haired and with goofy smiles. Nadir started saying something softly to Nadeena in Arabic and Imogen felt that strange tug in her chest she knew was a type of longing. A type of longing that she really didn't want to feel again.

'Don't you want more?' The words were out of her mouth before she knew she was even about to say them and when Nadir looked up her heart stuttered at how incredibly virile he looked.

His eyes skimmed over her and if she wasn't mistaken lingered on her lips. Heat suffused her cheeks. 'More what?'

Imogen didn't want to say it but it was as if someone else was directing her mouth. 'Love. Don't you want to marry for love?'

His grimace spoke volumes. 'Love is for greeting cards and grandmothers, not for marriage.'

'Which shows you how wrong we are for each other because I only want to marry for love.'

'I already told you my parents married for love. It caused nothing but grief.'

She could tell by his tone that he was deadly serious. 'You really believe that, don't you?'

'No, I know it. Otherwise you would not still be arguing with me and resisting this marriage. You would be embracing the fact that I can give you a life few others can.' His mouth tilted mockingly at the corners. 'Including your *friend* back in London.'

Ignoring his last comment, Imogen was shocked by his view. 'You would prefer that I marry you for your money? That's so cold and…empty.'

'It's honest.' He gave a frustrated shake of his head, keeping his face soft for Nadeena's sake. 'And tonight is important, Imogen. Or I wouldn't ask.'

She swallowed and lifted her eyes to his. 'Why?' she

asked bleakly. 'I got the impression that Bakaan doesn't mean anything to you.'

'That's complicated too.'

'How?'

His face closed down and she knew he wouldn't answer her.

'Let's just say that it is and leave it at that.'

'So much for listening,' she muttered.

He looked at her. 'I have answered every question you've asked.'

'You think?'

He rubbed a hand across his jaw. He needed a shave, she thought absently, and how was it possible for his mouth to be such a perfect bow? He caught her staring and awareness pulsed between them.

The kiss they had shared the day before jumped into her mind and by the way his eyes had now dropped to her own mouth she suspected it had jumped into his as well.

His silent scrutiny unnerved her and she moved sideways to get around him and hoped to heaven that he didn't touch her because she wasn't sure how she'd react if he did. Or at least she *was* sure but she didn't want to have that reaction. She had a horrible way of mixing sex up with love when it came to this man and given his miserable views on love it would be emotional suicide for her to risk her heart—and Nadeena's—on him again.

'My country suffered a great deal because of my father's reign. I will not worsen that by ignoring my current duties. Now, as much as I *enjoy* arguing with you, we are out of time. Will you come with me tonight?'

It wasn't really a question. 'Do you always have to be so pushy?' she complained.

A cloud came across his face and, just like that, he was a stranger again. 'I will watch Nadeena while you get ready.'

Frustrated at the way he just seemed to corral her into

a corner as if she was a rogue horse, she tried to think of some way out. 'She needs a bath.'

'Then I will give her one.'

'By yourself?'

'Don't look so surprised. I doubt it's rocket science but if it makes you feel better I will have Maab present so that Nadeena can bond with her.'

Outdone by his logic, Imogen gnashed her teeth. 'It will be a mistake taking me.'

'Why do you say that?'

Because she had no experience of dealing with world leaders and dignitaries and she'd likely embarrass them both. 'I'm a dancer. I danced at the Moulin Rouge. Surely everyone will think I'm unsuitable to be the wife of a king.'

'No doubt some will.'

That stung and his ready agreement was like the flick of a knife across a wound that hadn't quite healed.

He glanced at her impatiently. 'But I won't be King so it doesn't matter.'

'Why not? Too much responsibility for you?'

He shoved his hand through his hair and turned it into a sexy mess. 'Are you trying to annoy me to get me to change my mind about our union?'

'Would it work?'

'No.' His brow quirked with a mixture of frustration and humour. 'Now, stop with the delaying tactics. Nadeena will be fine and, as beautiful as you undoubtedly are, yesterday's jeans and T-shirt aren't going to work tonight.'

'I hate you,' she said, but the words lacked the heat they had carried the day before and by the way he smiled he knew it.

'I got that memo last night. Now, let's get this duty over and done with, hmm?'

Yes, Nadir was all about duty but Imogen knew that

duty was a poor motivator that led to anger and neglect and resentment unless it was backed up by something deeper and she feared that was exactly where they were headed if she conceded to his demands.

CHAPTER EIGHT

'KID, THAT'S SOME pitching arm you've got on you.' Nadir leant down and picked up the ball Nadeena had lobbed from her high chair for the millionth time. It was a game she never seemed to tire of. 'I can see you being a softball star when you're older.'

She babbled gleefully when he placed the soft fabric ball back in front of her but, instead of throwing it straight away, she reached towards him with a big grin and tried to grab his *keffiyeh*. 'Not that.' He grinned down at her and pushed his headdress back over his shoulder. 'I've explained that it doesn't look so good scrunched up by grubby baby hands.' Redirecting her attention to the ball, he checked his Rolex again and spied the empty doorway.

If Imogen didn't show up soon they wouldn't have time to stop for him to give her the ring that was burning a hole in his pocket and he didn't want her facing a room full of dignitaries and gossips without it. And somehow it seemed important to solidify things between them. Important to re-mind her that she was with him now and always would be.

Their earlier conversation and her look of surprise when she'd asked him if he wanted more—and he'd said no—re-played in his head. For a moment she'd looked so vulner-able that he'd wanted to snatch the words back but there had been enough misunderstanding between them and he didn't want there to be any more. But he supposed he should have realised that she was a romantic. That she would want love. It still irked him that she had said she didn't want to marry without it because clearly she didn't love him and he didn't love her.

Which did not mean that their marriage was doomed. He had feelings for her and she might not think great sex was any reason to get married but it was a start and he knew she wasn't as immune to him as she tried to pretend to be. Hell, that kiss had been proof enough of that, as was the way she held herself so carefully whenever he got close to her.

Nadeena clapped her chubby hands together with delight when he returned the ball to her yet again. 'If only your mother was so easily pleased,' he said softly.

She blew him a raspberry and he stroked his hand over her silky head. His daughter was a revelation to him—as was the depth of his feelings for her. Which only made him more determined to forge ahead with this marriage. Nadeena would not suffer the division of two parents' expectations for her the way he and his sister had.

As she babbled at the ball again as if she might direct it from sheer will alone, Nadir grinned and felt his heart clench at her trusting gaze. He dropped a kiss on top of her head, turning when he heard the swish of fabric behind him.

Only to have his heart clench all over again.

Imogen stood framed in the doorway wearing a blue silk floor-length gown that on the hanger had looked beautiful. On her it looked extraordinary. Her slender dancer's arms and the graceful line of her neck was exposed to his gaze, her hair a soft fall of golden waves around her shoulders. She looked every bit a royal princess. Every bit a woman any man would want on his arm. In his bed.

'I think this is going to be too much for Nadeena. She didn't sleep well last night.'

Nadir couldn't take his eyes off her. 'Do you mean you didn't?'

Imogen's mouth tightened. Her face looked pale and he could see the pulse in her throat going crazy. It bobbed as she swallowed and he couldn't control the wave of tenderness that overcame him in that moment. Imogen—fearless Imogen who took him on at every turn—seemed truly daunted by the prospect of the evening ahead. Or was it something else? Him, perhaps?

It annoyed him that she was so set on ignoring the chemistry between them that pulled tight every time they were together. As far as he was concerned, that was the *only* thing really working for them right now and he'd happily embrace it if she would.

'I've never left Nadeena with a stranger before.' She gripped her hands together tightly. 'She's always had the neighbour across the street or Minh.'

The mention of her ex-lover seemed to wipe any rational thought from his brain. In fact imagining her with any other man did that... 'She will be fine.'

'My daughter *needs* me.'

'*Our* daughter,' he said impatiently. 'And she's just had two hours to get used to Maab and she seems genuinely happy with her.'

'Two hours! It takes more than that to feel comfortable with someone.'

It hadn't taken him five minutes to feel comfortable with her. 'The grand ballroom is in the west wing, only a few minutes from here.'

'I think I feel sick.'

Sympathy replaced irritation. This was all new for her; he had to remember that. 'I will be by your side, *habibi*.'

She threw him a pithy glance. 'Is that supposed to be of comfort?'

Yes, it had been. 'Should I have told you that you will

be on your own and if you make a mistake you'll receive a thousand lashes?'

'I might have believed that.'

Her dry sense of humour had drawn him from the start and right now he wanted to laugh, shake her and kiss her all at the same time. 'Come.'

She stood stock-still. 'I am not a dog, Nadir.'

'No, you are a stunning woman who is trying her best to rile me,' he said softly. 'Fortunately for you, I have infinite control.' Usually, he amended. Usually, when she wasn't in the room, shredding it. He watched her wide, kohl-lined green eyes sparkle and then drop behind a veil of ebony lashes. Did she have any idea how incredibly beautiful she was to him? How much he wanted to possess her? How much he wanted to haul her into his arms and eat that pink gloss right off her lips? Having his old nanny and his daughter in the same room helped prevent it. But only just. 'We need to go.'

If possible, she angled her chin higher. 'To London?'

'Not quite. But I admire your humour.' He opened the door and beckoned for her to precede him.

She walked over to kiss their daughter before speaking to Maab. 'If she cries at all then you'll come and get me?'

'*Na'am*, My Lady.'

'Immediately?'

'*Na'am*, My Lady.'

Her gaze looked troubled when she neared him. 'I notice they say that a lot,' she whispered. 'Can I trust her?'

God, she was breathtaking. 'Nothing will happen to Nadeena. Relax.'

Relax? Impossible. She was too acutely aware of the way Nadir's regal robes brushed against the skirt of the amazing dress he had provided for her and the sense of power he effortlessly exuded. Walking beside him, it was hard to remember that none of this was real and that she didn't want it to be real.

Or did she?

The moment Nadir had leant forward and kissed the top of Nadeena's head as he played with her jumped into her consciousness and her heart lurched inside her chest. It had been identical to the thousands of kisses she had deposited on her daughter's head herself—an instinctive and unconscious gesture of love. Was it possible she was wrong about Nadir? Was it possible he might one day love their daughter as deeply as she did?

Feeling confused and out of her depth, her steps faltered as they entered a grand atrium with exquisite inlaid arabesque carvings on the ceilings and walls and highly polished bronze flooring. Six elaborately dressed Bakaani guards stood to attention with guns strapped to their hips. One of the men glanced briefly at Nadir and stepped forward, his hand poised on a gilt-edged doorknob.

Imogen swallowed heavily, aware that she had no experience of this kind of thing, and insecurity and a deep sense of inadequacy fought it out for top position in her mind.

Stopping beside her, Nadir delved into a hidden pocket in his robe, muttering something about 'earlier' under his breath. Then he turned towards her and held out a ring with a stone the size of a small grapefruit—an oval-shaped diamond grapefruit that was exquisitely hand-crafted and the most divine piece of jewellery Imogen had ever seen. Both her heart and her mind did a double-take.

'Before we go in you'll need to put this on.'

Momentarily blank, she stared at it.

'It's an engagement ring.'

She knew what it was. Sometimes as a young girl she had imagined receiving one from a man she loved. She and her friends had even gone engagement ring shopping once when they had been bored after school. They had then dreamed up elaborate ways their future beaus might pop what had felt like the biggest question of their lives back then. At no time had any of them come up with the man of their dreams saying, 'You'll need to put this on.'

And how many times was she going to get her hopes up over this man only to have them dashed by the reality that he was here because she was the mother of his baby and for no other reason?

'That's not necessary,' she said huskily, instinctively snatching her hands behind her back.

A frown drew down his brows as if her reluctance hadn't occurred to him. 'Of course it is. Many of the guests at the dinner are Western. They will expect to see you wearing my ring.'

A sickening sense of inevitability crept over Imogen and made her feel incredibly vulnerable. Incredibly exposed. 'I can say I lost it if anyone asks.'

His frown turned into a scowl. 'If it's the fact that you didn't choose it yourself that's the problem you can swap it at a later date.'

That wasn't the problem. The problem was that she didn't want to swap it. The problem was that the ring was exactly what she would have chosen had he given her the choice. But he never would. The ruthless way he kept sweeping aside her insistence that she would not marry him as if it was nothing more than an empty spider's web dangling in a doorway was evidence of that alone.

'You have no idea, do you?' she tossed at him, wanting to somehow hurt him the way he was currently hurting her. 'I don't want to wear your ring because it will ruin it when someone who really loves me wants to give me one.'

Swearing under his breath, Nadir's expression grew stormy. 'Damn it, Imogen, there won't be anyone else putting a ring on your finger. So you can get that out of your mind right now.'

She shook her head, aware that they were studiously *not* being watched by the guards who stood to attention around them. As if sensing her discomfort, or uncomfortable himself, Nadir drew her to the side of the room in what probably looked like a loving gesture.

'I thought I had explained how important tonight was.'

'You don't explain things, Nadir, you talk until you get what you want.'

'I *have* explained.' His tone was marked with frustration. 'I was supposed to renounce the throne today but Zach didn't show up. Now I have to host a dinner.'

'But why don't you want to be King? Zach said it was your birthright.'

He shut down. She saw it instantly in the set of his jaw. 'The why is not important. It's the intention that counts. I don't want the job. Zach does. I suppose you intend to be difficult about this as well.'

Hurt by the implication that she was being difficult just for the sake of it, she flinched. 'I'd like to understand it.'

'Do you want to be Queen—is that it?'

'No, that's not it. I didn't even think about that until just then.'

He looked at her.

'I didn't. Why would I when I haven't even agreed to marry you?'

She'd be flattered at his insistence on marrying her if she thought there was any deep sentiment behind it. Basically, it was because of Nadeena with great sex thrown in as a side order.

Without warning, Nadir reached out and raised her chin so that her eyes met his. Instead of looking fierce and commanding he looked frustrated and weary and her heart lurched.

'I need you to cut me some slack here, Imogen. I feel like I'm holding on by a thread.'

The raw words and his pained expression gave her pause but she was loath to let her heart soften towards him because he'd likely trample on it without even noticing.

Of course the traitorous organ didn't listen to her head. It never did when he was around. When he was this close to her that his scent wound its way inside her and made her ache to lean in and press her face into his neck.

'What is it, Imogen?' His thumb drew light circles across her chin, the gesture more comforting than sexual. 'What are you thinking?'

The width of his broad shoulders blocking the soldiers from her view established a feeling of intense intimacy between them and it was as if the dinner guests on the other side of the large doorway didn't exist. 'Honestly, Nadir, I don't know what to think.' She looked up at him and knew that her expression was troubled. 'I don't know what to feel or what to do any more. This is all so confusing and unexpected. One minute I'm alone with Nadeena and then... And what we had in Paris.' She swallowed heavily and his frown deepened. 'It was so...so...' She couldn't say it. She couldn't say that it was so special. That she had counted the minutes from Monday to Friday during that month they had been together and prayed that he would fly in and rap on her front door and kiss her even before he said hello. 'And now I'm scared because everything feels so broken.'

Broken like her own home life had been. Like her heart had been after he had left Paris and like she feared it would be again if she let her guard down and agreed to marry him.

Nadir cupped her face, gently smoothing his fingers along her jaw line, stroking the velvety skin beneath her earlobes.

'Imogen, look at me.' The whispered words were fierce and oh, so close to her ear she could feel his warm breath stirring her hair. She could feel the tips of her breasts pressed lightly against the front of his robes. She stopped breathing as his voice washed over her in deep, melodic waves, her eyes riveted to his as her emotions surged to the surface. 'Do not be scared. I promise you that I will take care of everything. You...Nadeena. I will protect you and provide for you.' He tilted her chin up with the tip of his finger when her eyes fell away from his. 'You will want for nothing, *habibi*. Not clothing or food or shelter.' He searched her face. 'Not diamonds or holidays or palaces. Whatever your heart desires I will give to you. What more is there?'

Love, Imogen thought achingly. Trust. Companionship. *Friendship*. And while she could see that he meant what he said, she knew that he was unlikely to feel those things for her and she was so afraid that she already did for him.

Imogen looked up and found that his silvery-blue eyes had turned stormy with emotion, dark with desire. His nostrils flared. She felt the change in the taut lines of his body and an answering response immediately swept through her own and made her feel soft and weak.

Force majeure, the French dancers had called him and they weren't wrong. He was an irresistible power, a force of nature, and Imogen was like a house of straw caught up in the devastating storm of his masculinity. The devastating storm of his self-assurance.

The hand at her hip moved to the small of her back, pressing her so close it was bordering on indecent. Her gaze shifted to his mouth. His lips parted and hers did the same. Would he kiss her? Here? Now?

'What do you say, Imogen? Will you give us a chance? For Nadeena.'

Imogen felt as if a lead weight had landed inside her chest. He wanted this for their daughter, who bound them together and divided them at the same time. She knew that if she continued to say no it would be beyond selfish because Minh had been right. Nadir did have a right to their daughter and she could either dwell on the past or try to embrace the future.

Feeling as if she was standing on the edge of a precipice with no clear landing over the side, she held out her left hand. 'Okay, Nadir.' She swallowed heavily. 'For Nadeena.'

With only the briefest of hesitations, Nadir took her hand in his and slid the ring into place. Imogen stared at it, cold and heavy on her finger, and willed her heart to stay uninvolved this time.

CHAPTER NINE

NADIR DISMISSED MAAB after she gave him a full report on
Nadeena's well-being at the end of the evening and circled the living room waiting for Imogen to return from
checking on her.

In many ways they were just like any other couple returning home at the end of an evening out. One saw to the
sitter, the other checked on the baby.

He glanced towards the drinks cabinet and thought
about pouring them a glass of brandy. If they really were
just like any other couple they would take advantage of the
fact that the baby was sleeping and maybe have a nightcap before falling all over each other as soon as possible.

Nadir's eyes tracked down over Imogen as she stepped
into the room, the evening gown flowing around her svelte
frame and clinging to her hips. Images of her in his king-
sized bed fogged his brain. Her long, toned, flexible legs
wrapped around his hips, her supple back arched in passion as she rode him, her small, high breasts jutting forward, begging for his mouth. If they were just like any
other couple he'd have her in that position pronto.

And why not? She had agreed to marry him. Or, rather,
she had acquiesced—because that was what her strained
little *For Nadeena* had sounded like to his ears. Even so,
he should be feeling relieved right now to have that sorted.
Triumphant, even. But he didn't. If anything, he felt as if it
was a Pyrrhic victory because, while he might have gained

her agreement, he could see by the wall she had erected between them that he had gained very little else.

And right now he wanted to tear that wall down. Right now he wanted more from her than shy, covert glances that only served to heighten his awareness of her as a woman. His awareness of her as *his* woman.

All night she'd been giving them to him as she worked the room like a pro. At first he'd thought her nervousness stemmed from some sort of insecurity but he'd soon discounted that. She'd handled herself beautifully. Talking to the Sultan of Astiv about his love of antique glassware while those around him nearly fainted with boredom and then recounting war stories about the trials and tribulations of competitive waterskiing with the Prince of Mana.

He'd hated the prince knowing something about her that he hadn't had a clue about and he'd liked even less the way the Prince had looked at her. But then he pretty much didn't like the way any man looked at her and that possessive feeling wasn't something he'd ever had to deal with before.

She gripped her hands together as if she didn't know what to do with them. 'Nadeena is asleep.'

'Good. Maab said she had most of the milk you expressed at eleven o clock.'

'Oh, okay. In that case I'm glad I didn't wake her to change her nappy because she should sleep for a few more hours now.'

'Good.' Nadir wondered how it was he could stand in the middle of the room having a stilted conversation about Nadeena when all he wanted to do was strip Imogen naked and bury himself deep inside her lush body. 'How long do you think we've got before she wakes up?'

He watched her eyes widen as comprehension dawned and thought, *Oh, yes, my sweet, I have exactly that in mind.*

If he was going to be breaking down walls tonight he didn't plan on doing it with a sledgehammer.

'Not long.'

He smiled. Her 'no' couldn't have been more transparent.

Realising that he still wore his *keffiyeh,* he reached up and yanked it from his head, ruffling his hair. He felt her eyes on him but when he glanced over her gaze flitted away and she shifted like a mare scenting the approach of an overly randy stallion.

She cleared her throat and lifted her chin and he knew she was about to try and call an end to the evening. 'Well, I hope the night was okay from your point of view but—'

'The night was excellent. You were brilliant.'

'Oh. Well, thank you.'

He studied her. 'Why were you nervous tonight?'

'Who said I was nervous?'

He felt a small smile touch his lips. 'I could tell. But I don't know why.'

'Because I knew everyone would be looking at me.'

'But you're a dancer—you must be used to being on show in front of people.'

'Being in a performance is totally different from being myself.'

So he'd been right about the insecurity. He frowned, wanting to reassure her. 'People like you. You're a natural. And a waterskier, I understand. How was it that the Prince of Mana knew that you had once won the Australian championships and I had no idea?'

'Maybe because he asked and you didn't.'

Nadir scowled. 'I'm asking now.'

She shrugged. 'It wasn't that big a deal. My mother was into waterskiing, which is how I came to do it, but when I was sixteen my ballet teacher told me that I needed to give up all dangerous sports if I was to take the dance seriously and I stopped.'

'But you loved it,' he guessed.

Her eyes glowed with an inner light that made them sparkle. 'The speed was pretty exhilarating.'

He grinned. 'Something we have in common.'

In Paris he'd been too obsessed with touching her to get to know her properly. Now he realised he wanted both. 'Have a nightcap with me.'

'I don't think that's a good idea.'

Nadir walked over to the wet bar and smiled. 'Have one anyway.'

Imogen knew that smile. He'd used it often when they'd been out and he'd come up and wrap his arms around her and tell her something, like how tired his feet were from walking or how cold he was and how he really thought they should head indoors. What he'd meant was that they should be in bed. Usually she'd melt against him at that point and he'd hail a cab, her need for him just as overpowering as his was for her.

Even that first night her need for him had eradicated her natural cautiousness around men and overshadowed her commonsense. She closed her eyes in the vain hope that the memories would go away but instead she felt as if she was back in Paris inside his elegant apartment.

The only reason they'd even shut the main door that first night was so he could crush her up against it. After her show he had prowled into the backstage area, his eyes hot with intent. Imogen had quivered with raw excitement, a deep feminine instinct having already warned her that he would come for her. And he had. He'd told her his name and asked her how long it would take her to change. When she'd told him ten minutes to scrub off the stage make-up he'd said, 'I'll wait.'

He'd made it sound as if he'd wait for ever. One of the other girls had rushed to lend her a short black dress since she'd only brought her jeans and a T-shirt to change back into and had sighed as if she wished she'd been the chosen one. Heels had materialised and the girls had tittered around her and told her who he was. Imogen hadn't really taken any notice, her mind buzzing with a sexual excitement she'd never felt before. He had taken her to one of Paris's exclusive supper clubs in his black Ferrari and been the perfect gentleman while they ate.

Not that she remembered much of the food. Or the conversation, for that matter, but she remembered how his hands had cradled his glass of Scotch as he'd watched her then he'd led her back to his car, his hand hot on the small of her back. He'd asked if she would like to go to his place for coffee. She'd said yes even though she hated coffee; a fact they had laughed at the following morning.

Imogen remembered feeling immeasurably shy and nervous seeing as how it was her first time going home with a man. Her only other lover had been a self-centred dancer who had come on to her after a sweaty but exhilarating rehearsal in her late teens and the rehearsal had been so much better.

Not that she'd told Nadir any of that. She hadn't known how. To tell him in the car ride to his apartment that she was pretty new to all this would have seemed presumptuous in the extreme and then when they had taken the lift— the very tiny and interminably slow lift—to his floor he hadn't touched her. He hadn't said a word to her in fact and nor had she to him, but her body had hummed with a life of its own and a hollow ache had risen up between her thighs with every floor that flashed past.

Finally they'd arrived. Nadir had pushed the door open, Imogen had made to move past him and accidently brushed her bare arm against his. That was all it had taken. One touch of his skin against hers and she had been lost. Gone up in a fireball of heat and need and powerful yearnings that had driven out all sense and caution. She remembered that the door had slammed shut and then thankfully she was up against it as her body had grown too heavy for her legs to hold her up.

Nadir had groaned against her neck, told her how much he wanted her. He'd cupped her face and pushed her hair behind her shoulders. Then he'd taken her mouth with his, ran his hands all over her body, pulled up her too-short dress and ripped her silky panties away. Awestruck, Imogen had been unable to do anything but grab onto his broad shoulders and kiss him back as he'd filled her. His body hot and hard and so powerful as he'd thrust into her. She'd had a moment's discomfort, which he'd sensed because he'd slowed and the change in pace had pushed her over the edge embarrassingly quickly. She'd cried out. He'd cried out and then they had been meshed together, both panting in the silent, dark hallway. He'd given a self-deprecating laugh, told her it had never been like that for him before and carried her into the bedroom. Ran the tub. Made love to her what felt like a hundred times more throughout the night.

'What are you thinking about, *habibi*?' His deep voice broke into her reverie and she started, her hands pleating the sides of her dress.

She took a deep careful breath in and eased it out. She wasn't stupid, she knew what he'd been suggesting before and she knew she wasn't emotionally ready to take that step. Not after a night of having his focus on her as if she was the most important person in the world to him. 'Nothing.'

He stepped in front of her. His eyes were dark and intense on hers. She wanted to look away because she knew her own must mirror the hunger she saw there but she couldn't. She was trapped by a desire that was becoming harder and harder to ignore the more time they spent together.

His eyes slid down her body, warming her from the inside out until they stopped on her hands.

'Where's your ring?'

All night he'd been at her about the ring, telling her not to fidget with it because then everyone would know that it was new.

'Everyone would be right,' she had whispered irritably at the start of the night. 'And it feels wrong on my finger.'

Of course he'd been annoyed by that. 'Before you know it you'll forget it's even there.'

Just as he would one day forget her and Nadeena were even there? 'What did you do with it?' he asked now.

'I took it off,' she said with a touch more defiance than she'd meant.

A muscle ticked in his jaw. 'So you can keep pretending this is not happening, *habibi*?'

When she didn't answer, because yes, in some way it was easier to pretend this wasn't happening, he stalked past her and straight through the doorway into her bedroom.

'Nadir!'

Worried that he would wake the baby, she ran after him and nearly collided with him in the doorway. Grim-faced, he reached for her left hand and jammed the ring back on her finger. 'That stays on.'

Supremely irritated with his overbearing attitude, Imogen wrestled with the ring, not sure what she intended to do with it once she got it off, but Nadir grabbed her hands and shoved them behind her back, bringing her body into full contact with his own.

Time seemed to stop as they stared at each other, both breathing hard. She wanted to tell him to let her go and perversely to hold her tighter at the same time.

She stared up at him, slightly dazed. Perhaps she was losing her mind…

'Dammit, Imogen, you would try the patience of a saint and I'm definitely not a saint.'

She'd had every intention of resisting his kiss but every moment seemed to converge with her wanting his mouth on her. His hands. It was madness. It was glorious and when his mouth came down over hers and his hand rose to palm her breast Imogen moaned and gave herself over to the mindless pleasure of being close to him again. This—touching him, tasting him—was thrilling and she wasn't sure how far she would have gone or when she would have called a halt to things when fate stepped in—or was it luck?—and they both broke apart as the high-pitched wail of a baby's cry rent the air.

Panting and shocked at the sheer wantonness of her own response, Imogen nearly fell out of Nadir's arms in her haste to put some space between them, her mind spinning, her body sluggish with arousal.

Nadir stared at her, his own chest heaving, and beneath his heated gaze and Nadeena's sharp cries her breasts started to tingle and leak milk all over the front of the exquisite silk dress. Mortified, she cupped her hands over her breasts and fled next door to her daughter.

Trying to slow her breathing, she reached for the baby and cradled her against her chest before easing into the corner chair to feed her. 'It's okay, angel. Mummy's here.' She closed her eyes, her face hot with embarrassment at how easily she had slipped back into Nadir's arms without thought or care of the consequences. Yesterday she had been trying to convince him that marriage was a mistake and now she had agreed to it. She had his ring on her finger and she still wasn't sure she wasn't about to make the biggest mistake of her life.

As if conjured by her thoughts, Nadir materialised in

the doorway, his hair askew where her fingers had tangled in it, his features drawn tight with unfulfilled desire.

'Do you need anything?' His deep voice rumbled through her and momentarily distracted Nadeena. She glanced down to find her daughter's eyes open and staring, trying to find her father and feed at the same time.

'I'm fine.' Imogen stroked her hand over Nadeena's head, settling her. She wasn't fine, of course—she was flustered, confused, *unsatisfied*.

'Water? Can I get you water?' For the first time he looked out of his depth and her heart clenched. 'I read that breastfeeding mothers need to drink lots of water.'

He had? Her surprise must have shown on her face because he ran a hand through his hair and his jaw set hard.

'Water would be nice,' she said softly, her mind struggling to adapt to the return to normality between them. She shook her head at that. It struggled to adapt to what passed as normality between them since Nadir had stepped back into her life. A normality that was still defined by past hurts and an uncertain future.

'Here.'

She blinked as a glass of water was thrust in front of her.

'Thank you.'

'You're welcome.' He nodded and took it back when she'd drained the glass. 'Can I get you anything else?'

'No, no.' She placed Nadeena on her shoulder to burp her. 'No, everything should be—oh!' Imogen squirmed as she felt warm baby spew slide down over her bare shoulder and the top half of her dress. 'Oh.'

She heard Nadir chuckle. '"Oh" is right.'

The look on his face made her suddenly feel like laughing and groaning at the same time with embarrassment. Then Nadeena grew fussy and started crying, jamming her tiny fists into her mouth.

'What's wrong with her?'

'I suspect it's her teeth.' She touched her hand to Nadeena's forehead. 'She's not overly hot so...' She scrunched her brow. 'It could be that she's just tired and out of sorts because it's late. It's hard to figure out what's wrong with babies sometimes.'

'Not just babies.'

His rueful comment hung between them and just when she might have asked what he meant by it he held out his arms. 'Here, give her to me.'

'No, no...it's fine, I can—'

'I know you can, Imogen,' he agreed flatly. 'But you need to go clean up and I can settle her while you do it.'

'Oh, right.' Clean up. She'd completely forgotten about the sour milk on her shoulder and dress. She handed Nadeena to him and watched as he confidently tucked her into the crook of his muscular arms. 'Come on, *habibti*,' he crooned, 'let's get you settled.'

Again Imogen was momentarily struck dumb by the sight of them together but unfortunately Nadeena didn't stop crying and it made her hurry into the shower, where she quickly rinsed her hair and washed herself.

Pulling on the oversized T-shirt she had used the night before, she hurried back to her room to find Nadir pacing back and forth and singing what sounded like an Arabic lullaby in his soft baritone.

'She's nearly asleep. Should I put her in the cot?'

'I need to change her first.'

'I've done it already.'

Imogen stared at him. 'You have?'

'I'm not completely useless, Imogen. I can change a baby's nappy.'

Given that Nadir was the most capable man she had ever met, she didn't know why she had ever doubted he could. Maybe because her father had never shown much interest in his duties as a parent. It made her realise just how low her expectations had been on the night that Nadir had walked out after discovering that she was pregnant. Maybe they had been low all along.

The thought stunned her.

Had she been waiting for him to disappoint her? Fail her? Because he had. Spectacularly so. Which didn't fit with why he was being so helpful now. Was it to garner her cooperation with his dogged plan for them to marry or because he genuinely cared?

Too many questions and too few answers but Imogen suspected that maybe he wouldn't change his mind about marrying her and, worse, part of her didn't want him to. This…she swallowed back a ball of emotion rising inside her chest…this was nice. Sharing the care of Nadeena with him, working together as a team. It was every woman's wish to have her lover—her partner—around to talk with and iron out the kinks of parenthood. To journey through life hand in hand with someone there to help field the knocks it inevitably handed out. Someone who would care.

But Nadir wasn't her lover or her partner at this point and her mother's dating advice had been to warn her that a man could put on a good show for thirty, even forty, days before the cracks started appearing. If you added up their time together in Paris and the last couple of days, Nadir fell smack bang in the middle of her mother's bell curve. Would he revert to his playboy ways after that and start ignoring them both?

'Imogen?'

Realising she had spaced out and that she was extremely tired after all the emotion of the last couple of days, she glanced up at him holding Nadeena. She looked so tiny and perfect in his arms.

'Just…' She had no idea what she was going to say. 'She might need a top-up.'

'A top-up?'

'A bit more milk.' Her face flooded with colour as he understood and she thought how ridiculous that she should be embarrassed after all they had shared but she was. 'I'll do it in bed. It's sometimes easier.'

'But is it safe? What if you fall asleep?'

'Of course it's safe,' Imogen said sharply. 'I wouldn't put her at risk, Nadir.'

'I wasn't questioning your mothering skills, Imogen, I…oh, hell.' He rubbed his jaw. 'This is all new to me. I want you to be safe.'

Imogen's heart gave a little leap. *Not you*, she derided the foolish muscle in her chest; he means he wants Nadeena to be safe. 'I won't fall asleep,' she said wearily. 'You can go.'

Their eyes connected in the dim light and Imogen saw a look come over his face that she couldn't quite define. If she had to guess she'd say it was as if he was trying to work something out but, whatever it was, it seemed to elude him.

She lay on the bed and waited almost breathlessly as he leant over and laid Nadeena in the crook of her arm, sleepiness invading her limbs as her daughter latched onto her nipple once again.

'Your hair is wet,' he said gruffly.

'I know.' Imogen lifted her hand to smooth the damp, irritating strands away from her shoulder and tried not to show her surprise when Nadir's hands took over the task, smoothing the long strands out on the pillow behind her.

'It's fine,' she said, her breaths shallow and hurried at the intimacy of the moment. 'You don't have to do that.'

'Stop trying to shut me out, Imogen. If you leave your hair like this it will be all tangled in the morning.'

He continued working out the kinks and Imogen decided it was better if she just let him do it. And it felt good. So good.

'Go to sleep,' he said gruffly as he perched on the bed behind her. 'I'll transfer Nadeena to the cot when she's finished.'

'I can…' Imogen yawned. She wanted to say she could do it but she didn't. Instead she did something she hadn't done for months. She fell into a contented sleep before her baby had fully settled.

CHAPTER TEN

NADIR LOOKED DOWN at the woman sleeping on the bed so soundly, her deep breaths even and relaxed. He remembered that she had always slept like the dead and he had often teased her about how hard he'd had to work to wake her through the night. Sometimes he'd even been in the process of kissing her soft body, teasing her awake with caresses that had tortured him and woken her panting. Always when she came awake like that she had wrapped her arms and legs around him and pulled him closer. Always she had moved with him and he'd angled his body in such a way that he knew would bring her to orgasm in no time. She'd groan in his ear, clasp him tighter, urge him on and then afterwards she'd sigh and curl herself around him, pretty much like she was doing to their daughter right now, and Nadir had the strongest urge to get into bed behind them and do the same thing.

Only he didn't.

They both looked too peaceful. His heart clenched and he took a step back. He wondered how life had brought him to this point. To this woman and child. Fate?

It certainly wasn't planned. All his adult life he'd assumed he'd walk his path alone and he'd been okay with that. After the rigid childhood he'd had where his father's word was law he had made sure that he had plenty of choices in life that had all been about taking care of himself. It was a selfish existence for sure but it was also safe because he didn't need anyone and no one needed him in return.

But that had changed now. Now he had a child and a woman he was responsible for and he was determined that they would make a better family unit than his had been. Nothing would make him turn away from them.

Careful not to wake either female, he carefully lifted Nadeena into his arms and marvelled at how small and how fragile she was. He nuzzled her downy dark hair and breathed in her sweet baby smell.

A smile curved his lips as he recalled how Imogen had tried to put him off marrying her by telling him that babies were smelly. They were but in a good way.

They were also a lot cuter than he'd ever noticed before and he grinned when he placed Nadeena into the cot and she promptly sprawled onto her back with her arms flung out to the sides, her tiny mouth moving as she resettled into sleep.

Feeling comfortable that she wasn't about to wake up, he turned towards Imogen. She had shifted more onto her stomach, her leg hitched high on the bed. If he'd been lying beside her that leg would have been draped over his hips and his groin hardened predictably. He wanted her and he didn't mind admitting it. Sex was normal. Healthy. But deep down he knew what he felt for her went beyond sex. For once he didn't try and stop his mind from drifting back to the way things had been between them in Paris. Carefree and passionate. Relaxed and somehow contented. *Contented?*

His mind processed the thought. Had he really been contented when he'd been with her in Paris? When they'd been strolling together arm in arm around the city just like any other couple in the world? He remembered ignoring those feelings at the time and putting them down to sex. Lust. Passion. But, looking back, he could see that he'd felt completely at ease in her company. Relaxed and, yes, contented. And then another startling thought gripped him. He didn't want her to endure their marriage. He wanted her to want it. He wanted her to want to make it work as much as he did. He wanted her to want him.

He rubbed his eyes and for the first time he wondered if he was doing the right thing by forcing this marriage onto her. But what else could he do?

She made a sound, almost as if she was having a bad dream, and called out his name. Nadir stilled. In his mind's eye he saw her rising from the bed, her short T-shirt riding high on those shapely legs before she reached him and wound her arms around his neck and pulled his mouth down to hers as she had done so many times in the past.

Naturally enough, she didn't do that but she did call out again and Nadir found himself crossing the floor to her side.

'Imogen?' He reached down and placed his hand lightly on her shoulder. 'You're dreaming, *habibi*.'

He thought he'd spoken softly enough not to really disturb her but her eyes flew open and she blinked and the little frown line appeared as she stared up at him.

'Where am I?'

Despite the warning in his head telling him she was tired and needed sleep, he didn't stop himself from reaching down and placing his finger against the frown line. 'It's okay. You're in Bakaan.'

She made a small sound and pushed up into a sitting position. She wasn't wearing a bra and he couldn't keep his eyes off the gentle sway of her breasts. 'Imogen.' Her name was more like a groan on his lips when he caught her staring at his mouth.

By Allah, he wanted her. Wanted her more than he'd wanted any other woman in his life. More than he'd wanted anything at all for a long time and, as if in slow motion, he reached out and took hold of her hand and tugged her up onto her knees.

She rose to him, all sleepy and pliant, and his mouth swooped down to capture hers in a sweet, lingering kiss. He felt her hands flutter close to his jaw and snag on the stubble of his beard growth. He'd need a shave if he was going to stop himself from marring her pale skin but more than that he needed her and for the first time ever he didn't feel concerned by that driving need.

Something had been slowly changing within him since he'd found her again. He didn't know what it was but it was almost as if a piece of his life had slotted into place. Impossible really, given how out of synch his life was right now but still...the feeling persisted.

Not wanting to disturb Nadeena, he broke their kiss and tugged her towards him. When she clung to his shoulders he swept her into his arms and strode out of the bedroom.

'Nadir?' She wriggled and he let her slide down the length of his body until she found her feet. But he didn't immediately let her go.

'I want to make love to you, Imogen. I want to take you to my bed and show you how well this can work between us. How good it can be again.'

The words were raw, his voice almost hoarse with need. Her eyes widened and even in the low-lit hallway he could see colour rising high on her lovely cheekbones.

She swallowed and pushed the tumble of her hair back from her face and he just wanted to bury his hands in it. He just wanted to kiss her. So he did.

As soon as his mouth touched hers, Imogen felt her body catch fire and soften against him and all thoughts of the past and the future dissolved. How was it possible to feel so much for one person? To want so much from one person? And then she couldn't think any more. Just feel—her heart ruling her actions.

Moaning, she gripped his hair in her hands, letting her body melt against his. This was what she had craved for so long. This aching pleasure only he could give her. And like this they were equals with no past and no future. Just the present.

Pressing closer, she felt Nadir fall against the wall, his laugh husky as his hungry mouth worked its way down her throat. Imogen arched and rose onto tiptoe, her lower body aching to join with his.

Driven by a deep yearning, she clawed at the yards of fabric that made up his robe and felt him turn them both and press her against the wall, his hands pushing up the hem of her T-shirt and hastily dragging her panties down her legs and then finally, blissfully she felt him cup her and she almost dissolved as he parted her slick flesh and delved between her legs, his fingers and thumb gliding over her and into her and stroking her in all the right places.

'Nadir, you—'

'Imogen, *habibi*, you drive me—'

She shifted and he grunted, wedging his knee between her thighs to hold her upright while he parted his robes singlehandedly.

Imogen tried to bring her hands down to help him but he effortlessly held her high against the wall, his upper body powerfully hard beneath her fingertips and then he brought her down over the top of him and she heard a loud keening sound as his smooth, thick hardness opened her up and penetrated deep inside her body.

He swore. Maybe she did too and for a minute they were both completely still, suspended between two worlds, both adjusting to the exquisite sensation of being joined together.

Then he tangled one hand in her hair and tugged until

her dazed eyes met his. The skin on his face was pulled tight, his eyes glittering with a hunger that sent shivers racing down her spine. Those eyes said that this time together would not be gentle or slow. That it would be fierce and urgent and uncontrolled. That she would feel him plunge into her with every fibre of her being and her body pulsed in anticipation.

'Is this okay?' His question was a panting growl and tinged with desperation as if he was having trouble holding himself back. 'I mean you had a baby not long ago and—'

Imogen wound her legs around his waist and hugged him tight. Now that she had given herself over to this it was all she could do not to let the fire inside burn her up. 'It's fine. Please, Nadir—'

He crashed his mouth down over hers again, his tongue thrusting deep as he gave her what she craved and moved powerfully inside her. In no time at all Imogen felt her orgasm building and writhed against him, forcing him to press one hand against the wall to hold them both upright and then she was there, on the pinnacle of that exquisite release she had only ever experienced in his arms, their mouths fused together as if their lives depended on it. Imogen opened her eyes at that moment to find him watching her and the connection was so elemental it hurtled her over the edge into a place filled with bright lights and dizzying heights. And then it was all too much and she threw her head back and let her release rush through her on long exquisite pulses. Seconds later Nadir's grip on her hips tightened to the point of pain and his thrusts grew brutal just before he threw his own head back and bellowed her name into the still night air.

The comedown from the desperate rush to orgasm was slow and noisy, both of them panting hard to catch their breaths.

Nadir raised his head from where it was now buried against her neck. 'Are you okay?'

'Yes. Out of shape, but good.'

Nadir gripped the underside of her thighs and hoisted her legs higher around his waist while he remained buried deep inside her. 'You're not out of shape, *habibi*. You're perfect.'

'Where are we going?' she asked quickly as he carried her down the hall.

'My bed.'

'What about Nadeena?'

'I'll leave the door open.' He strode inside the room and didn't even bother with the light as he collapsed with her onto the bed.

Imogen tilted her head back and felt the silky fabric of the comforter against the sensitised skin of her back. Part of her knew that she should get up but her body felt as if it was on fire, renewed desire coiling through every cell, and all she wanted to do was wrap herself around Nadir and not think about anything right now. Not the future that seemed so insurmountable and not the past which was tinged with the bittersweet memories of first love and then the utter despair of rejection. Right now her body just wanted his, *needed* his, and she was powerless to resist.

Not that Nadir was exactly giving her time to question his demands as he kissed and licked his way down over her collarbone towards her breasts.

Before she could object, he raised her T-shirt over her head and tossed it onto the floor.

'This time we do it a little slower,' he said gruffly. 'And I might even throw in a little finesse for good measure.'

Imogen laughed at his playful words and then suddenly felt self-conscious as she realised where his mouth was headed. 'Nadir, stop. My breasts aren't the same any more and I'm feeding.'

He batted her hands away and rose up on one powerful arm to peer down at her, his other hand drawing lazy circles around the outer swells of each breast before cupping each one in turn. She felt her nipples peak and rise up eagerly for his touch. 'I don't care. You're beautiful, Imogen.' He lowered his head and laved one nipple lightly with his tongue, making her gasp with pleasure. Nadir grinned. 'I love that you can feed our child. I love that your nipples are slightly darker than before.' His head bent again and he blew across one straining tip. 'I love your taste. The way you feel.'

Lost in his words and his touch, Imogen's arms rose up again to mould his sinewy shoulders and cling to the taut wall of muscle at his back. It was that untamed, unrefined side of him, encapsulated within sleek, sophisticated masculinity that had always drawn her to him. Had always drawn every woman to him.

Forgetting about the past, she inhaled, pulling the wonderful scent of sweat and man deep into her body. 'I love the way you taste too. Take off your robe. I want to feel you against me.'

Nadir didn't need any further urging and within seconds he had come down over the top of her again. Naked. A gloriously prowling male in his prime. Imogen's breath caught at the sight of his thick length jutting hard up against his ridged abdomen. He was so potently virile. So unselfconsciously male he took her breath away.

'Like what you see, *habibi*?' he drawled lazily.

'Comme ci, comme ça.' She pretended to yawn.

He growled at her cheekiness and pushed her thighs wider with his knees. 'I'll give you *comme ci, comme ça*,' he whispered roughly, reaching beneath her to angle her bottom up better for his penetration.

He groaned as he sank into her warm, willing flesh. 'I was going to take this slow but now...' he thrust forward and Imogen clung to his arms, her fingernails digging into his hard biceps to anchor herself against him '…now I just want to plough into you and make you scream. How's that for finesse?'

'Finesse is so terribly overrated.' She gasped out each word as he did exactly what he said.

He grunted his pleasure, his gaze hungry as it raked over her face. 'Tell me if I'm too rough?'

Imogen shook her head and brought her hands up to cup the hard planes of his face, her fingers stroking over the rough bristle on his jaw. 'No. Give me more. I want more.'

'Ah, hell, Imogen. *Habibi.*' His words of praise became more urgent and mixed with Arabic as he drove into her over and over and over until they both fell apart with the extent of another mind-blowing orgasm.

Finally sated, Nadir bent down and kissed her sweetly on the mouth. Then he rolled onto his back and took her with him, tucking her head into the crook of his shoulder and it was as if no time had passed at all. She could almost hear the sounds of Parisians dining and chatting and going about their business from the open window of his apartment. But time had passed and it had created a chasm and her chest tightened as she thought about getting up and going back to her own room. If only she wasn't feeling so weak, ripples of her release still coursing through her lax body.

'What?' he asked as if he sensed her tension.

'I should go back to Nadeena.'

He gently tugged her still damp hair out from under his arm and stroked it back against the pillow. 'Stay. I've missed holding you like this.'

His admission startled her and set off a warm glow as if a cluster of fireflies had set up house inside her chest. 'Me too.'

She felt him place a light kiss against her hair and turned her face into his throat.

'Then sleep. I'll check on Nadeena in a minute.'

She wanted to protest, she wanted to say that she needed to do it because she always had and Nadeena's safety was her responsibility but Nadir rolled her onto her side and spooned her, his big body swamping hers and cocooning her in the most delicious warmth and a deep lassitude invaded her already weakened limbs and turned her limp. It was blissful, this feeling of being utterly taken care of, and no doubt—if she let it—highly addictive.

CHAPTER ELEVEN

OR IT COULD have been highly addictive if it had continued. But of course it had not, Imogen thought glumly as she stretched to place her nose against her knee, her groin muscles protesting the once effortless stretch.

They had made love twice more during the night, once fast and another time slow and indulgent, his fingers drifting and stroking over every inch of her body as if he couldn't get enough of her and then in the morning she'd woken up to find him gone.

At first she'd not minded, stretching her overused muscles and indulging in sensual recall. Then she'd realised that she couldn't hear anything and that she'd overslept for the first time since she'd become pregnant and had raced out of bed, pulling on her T-shirt that had been wedged half under his giant bed and set off down the hallway to find Nadeena's cot empty.

Slightly panicked, she'd then rushed into the living area to find Tasnim and Maab taking care of Nadeena at the outdoor table. Relieved, she'd pulled up, taken her smiling daughter into her arms and hugged her, the rush of relief bringing with it the subtle aches and pains in her body that brought her awareness back to how well loved she had been the night before. Then she'd glanced around for Nadir. Tasnim said that he had given Nadeena the small amount of milk left over from when Imogen had expressed the night before and told them not to wake her unless it was absolutely necessary.

As if on cue, her breasts had tingled and she'd sat in a shaded lounge chair and fed her daughter. And waited for Nadir to return.

She'd sat there with a secret smile on her face and thought that maybe she'd been wrong to leave Paris so hastily fourteen months ago. That maybe she'd been wrong not to have realised that he would want what was best for her and the baby.

That had been yesterday morning's thoughts. Now, another day and a half later, Imogen was wishing that she had run further fourteen months ago and that he'd never found her because, apart from a note sent to inform her that he would be in late last night, she hadn't seen or heard from him since.

It would have been the classical wham-bam-thank-you-ma'am scenario except for the fact that she still had an enormous ring on her finger that she was sure someone would hack off to obtain if she ever ventured out into a public place with it on.

She glanced at it now, wondering why she still wore it.

It wasn't because she was under any illusion that the man who had given it to her genuinely cared about her. And it definitely wasn't because she thought he craved her company as much as she stupidly craved his. Not that he'd ever know that was how she felt. No, she might have felt her heart crack open a little when he was touching her, kissing her, *making love to her,* but his behaviour over the last two days had sealed it back up with more precision than a blowtorch. And to think she'd imagined that she was falling for him all over again. Thank goodness she'd disabused herself of that errant notion.

And yes, on some level she knew she was being unfair to him because of his current issues in Bakaan but she knew he had a reputation for working hard. Working hard and playing hard. So she knew this was just a sign of her life to come and she didn't like it. He made her feel like an afterthought while she found herself wanting so much more from their relationship. More than he clearly did.

The realisation was emotionally debilitating and if he thought that giving her a couple of extraordinary orgasms would be enough to make her comply with his every wish then he had another thing coming. Especially since she'd had at least a day now to stew over the news that they were to be married at the end of the week.

She doubted she would have taken the news that well if it had come from Nadir, but since it had come from Tasnim asking what style of dress she would like to wear she felt like telling Nadir to go to hell. That she'd been right all along and this was nothing but an enormous mistake they would both live to regret.

A slight noise from behind her had her hackles rising as she recognised the subtle shift in the air that told her it was him. Pride kicked in and fortified her spine. There was no way she would let him know that his actions had hurt her. Determined to be cool and dignified despite her racing heartbeat, she finished off a leisurely stretch and then stood up as if she didn't have a care in the world.

He walked towards her, his eyes raking over the casual clothing she had found in amongst the clothes he had provided for her. She hadn't wanted to wear them but then she hadn't really had any choice. Nadir was garbed in traditional white robes that emphasised his regal bearing and sun-bronzed skin. How a man could make robes look sexy was beyond her, but unfortunately they only seemed to enhance Nadir's physical perfection rather than detract from it.

He ran a hand through his hair and she realised that he looked tired beneath his natural tan. 'Where's Nadeena?'

Of course he would ask after their daughter first. It was why she was even here after all. Stupidly, it hurt.

'Having a late afternoon nap.'

He nodded. 'Has she been okay?'

'Great.'

'Okay then it's you.' His eyes narrowed. 'What's wrong?'

She kept her expression bland. 'What could possibly be wrong?'

Nadir didn't know, but something was. He'd spent the last two days meeting with members of the UAE to determine Bakaan's future membership into the federation and he was exhausted. It had been a frustrating endeavour because his father had never been interested in political or economic alliances and instead had treated Bakaan as a lone wolf. Naturally enough that made some of the members of the federation highly suspicious of what Bakaan's intentions were and what the benefit was in including them into the federation at all. When he had explained his and Zach's vision of the future—drawn up and refined over many years and many lagers—he'd had a breakthrough and all but one had signed the new treaty.

Reform would be slow, he knew, and arduous but intensely satisfying once it started to take effect. And it was also supposed to be Zach's job—not his. Zach, who had still not returned any of his phone calls.

Now Nadir was supposed to travel to Sur, a Northern city, and present the terms of the agreement to the outer tribal elders who still held a lot of influence in certain sectors of Bakaan.

First, though, he'd wanted to stop off and see Imogen and Nadeena. He'd been frustrated the past two days that he hadn't been able to see them at all but the federation members had been due to leave and Nadir had needed to strike while the iron was hot. When he'd returned to his suite late last night, even though he'd sent a note telling Imogen when he would finish up, he'd been disappointed to find her already in bed. And not his. After their love-making two nights ago he'd assumed that things between them would improve. Seeing the look on her face now, he knew that had been an erroneous assumption.

He stepped closer to her and she stepped back. His smile turned wry and he deliberately kept his gaze above her neck or he knew he wouldn't give a damn about find-ing out what was wrong and fix it in his own way. 'I don't know, Imogen. But something is.'

She shrugged and he gritted his teeth. The wall was back up between them and she'd added a couple of bricks for good measure. Did she really find the idea of being tied to him so hateful? Or was it something else? Her London lover, perhaps?

He tried to cap his instant irritation at the thought of them living together and reminded himself that the buf-foon was part of her past and she was as entitled to one as much as he was. Unfortunately, it didn't help. 'Did you get my message last night?'

She tossed her head in a feminine challenge and her wheat-blonde braid swished over her shoulder like the tail of an angry cat. 'I did.'

'But you ignored it.'

'I was tired.'

Not much he could say to that since the reason she was most likely tired was because he'd kept her up most of the previous night making love to her.

'And what would have been the point in waiting up anyway?'

Now there was a lot he could say to that and he barely resisted the urge to just pull her into his arms and show her. 'I would have thought after the night we spent together you wouldn't need to ask that.'

She shrugged again. 'We were two people letting off steam. It meant—'

'Do not say *nothing*, Imogen.' His jaw clenched tight. 'Not unless you want me to set about proving just how much it did mean.'

Her eyes flashed and it looked like she bit her tongue. 'Did you come here for a reason? Has your brother returned?'

He drew his hand across his lower jaw. 'No. Unfortunately not. And something about his lack of contact no longer rings true. I've sent a convoy out to check on his whereabouts. In the meantime I have to convince our tribal leaders in the north that this union will be for the good of Bakaan.'

'Sounds busy. You'd better go.'

A muscle ticked in his jaw.

Imogen turned dismissively as if she had a hundred better things to do and Nadir's frustration and tiredness tripped over into anger. 'You could show a little more interest than that.'

She seemed unconcerned by his outburst. 'What would you like me to say?' She was formal, polite. *Reserved.* The warmth from their lovemaking had gone as if it had never existed. 'Break a leg?'

It took three steps to reach her and when he clamped his hands around her slender arms she went as rigid as a poker. He gentled his touch. 'What's wrong, *habibi*? Has someone upset you?'

She tried to shake him off. 'You don't talk to me about anything—why should I talk to you? I'm just an additional problem you don't want. Nadeena and I both.'

'That's not true. I don't have a lot of time right now.'

'When will you?' She lifted her chin. 'Never, that's when. If this marriage goes ahead—'

'It will.'

'So I heard.' She lifted her chin. 'In five days' time, *apparently*. It would have been nice of you to tell me. What if I wanted to invite some of my friends for support?'

'Invite whomever you want.' His brow furrowed. 'And I thought I had told you. It's been decreed by the council.'

'I don't care if it's been decreed by the Queen of England. The last thing I want is a husband who is off having a good time without his family. I tell you, Nadir, if Nadeena ever hears of any affairs you've had I will unman you.'

'There will be no affairs.'

'Right.' Her green eyes flashed sceptically. 'All that travel and long hours at work…I know how it goes.'

'I do not operate that way and I never have.'

'And if you fall in love one day?' Her delicate brows arched in challenge. 'What then?'

Nadir gritted his teeth. 'That won't happen.'

Instead of being relieved by his reassuring words, she looked achingly vulnerable and he was beyond frustrated because he had no idea how to please her. No idea how to win her over.

'Go away, Nadir. I understand you have important people waiting for you.'

Her words stuck in his head. There was no doubt the emirs waiting for him were important. But so was she and he didn't want to spend another night away from her. 'Actually, I don't. I've cancelled all my other obligations.'

Her eyes narrowed warily. 'You have?'

No, but he would. It was only a white lie and what was he doing telling white lies anyway? He hated lies and liars and had never seen any excuse for those who did so. And yet here he was, telling one because he knew if he didn't he'd somehow hurt her again.

Anyway, Omar could travel north with the emirs. He was equipped for the job and Nadir could use the time to take stock of all that was happening in Bakaan. Take stock of the fact that he'd relished the challenge of the last couple of days. And why wouldn't he? It was what he did for a living after all. Bought companies experts said were dogs and turned them into cash cows.

If it was part of Zach's plan to disappear so that he'd have no choice but to get involved in Bakaani business then it had worked. To a degree because he still wouldn't take on the leadership role, no matter how sly Zach was. But right now all that was second to putting things right with Imogen.

He felt her try to pull away again but he slid his hands down her arms and felt goose bumps rise up on her flesh. His muscles hardened as he registered what the shiver beneath her skin betrayed and the need to stamp his claim on her became paramount. Forcing his hold to remain gentle, he sipped at her lips, took her bottom lip between his teeth and suckled it rhythmically until he heard the small hitch in her breath that said she was his. That little sound always undid him and he drew her closer and groaned as her soft curves yielded to his hardness.

'And I'm taking you out for dinner,' he found himself saying. 'There's a dance troupe in the city showcasing some of Bakaan's tribal dances. They're performing tonight.' He was sure he'd seen it on the list of possible excursions for the emirs because he'd immediately thought of her. 'There might be some other leaders present but I booked a private table.' Another white lie that would only be so until he got onto Staph.

CHAPTER TWELVE

NADIR WAITED FOR Imogen to return from the restaurant bathroom and thought that if one more person stopped at their table to suck up to him he'd have them locked up for making a nuisance of themselves.

Of course it wasn't just him they were interested in. With her blonde hair and natural grace, Imogen would no doubt become the Jackie Kennedy of Bakaan if he were to become King. Something everyone assumed was already the case.

He sighed and was thankfully distracted from heading down that line of thought as Imogen wove her way through the crowd, Bjorn keeping a discreet but alert distance. She'd chosen to wear a traditional *abaya* for their night out and the thoughtfulness of the gesture wasn't lost on him. She could just as easily have worn something shockingly skimpy to embarrass him but it wasn't in her nature. He didn't know why he hadn't seen from the start that she wasn't manipulative or two-faced, as many of the other women he had dated in the past had turned out to be. Women who would simper and preen and bend any which way he asked them to. He smiled as his memories of the other night came back on a rush. He was already looking forward to the end of this evening and bending Imogen to his will again.

'Wow—this looks delicious.'

Nadir followed her gaze to the table. He'd forgotten all about the food.

'I hope you didn't wait for me to start.'

'Of course I did.'

'Oh, thanks.' She leant forward and sniffed apprecia-tively. Her eyes closed and a look of total bliss swept across her face and he very nearly called for his car.

'Is that cardamom and cinnamon I can smell?'

'And vanilla and honey,' he said roughly. Like her skin. 'What's this dish?'

Shelving his sexual appetites for now, Nadir turned his attention to the food. For the next hour they ate and talked and when it was time for the music to start the tables were cleared to make room for the dancers to take the floor. Of course he and Imogen were given a central position and moments later a lute started playing. Then a flute joined in along with a *riqq*. Imogen started swaying in time with the music.

She leant closer to him so that she could be heard above the music and revelry of the excited audience, her lips so close to his ear he could feel her warm breath. 'What's that instrument?'

Nadir turned his head, his gaze snagging with hers, their mouths inches apart. He thought about kissing her but knew he couldn't. Public displays of affection were currently considered a crime in Bakaan. Instead he in-haled her fragrance and reminded himself that he was a man reputed to have wonderful self-control. 'Which one?'

She swivelled her head and pointed towards a group of musicians and he breathed in her tantalising scent.

'The one across that man's lap that looks like a harp.'

'A *qanun*.'

She smiled up at him. 'It's beautiful.'

No, she was beautiful and he wondered how it was pos-sible for his heart to feel so light when Zach's continued lack of contact was starting to worry him and insurgents were right now threatening to disrupt industry in the north.

She tapped her feet in time with the music and the lead dancer noticed. With a smile on her face she headed their way and Nadir knew what was coming.

'Would the new Sheikha like to join in the line-up?'

Imogen's face lit up and she said, *'Shukran,'* which impressed everyone within earshot, and joined them.

The audience cheered when they realised what was going on and the female dancers surrounded Imogen, much to Bjorn's consternation, and wound shimmering skeins of fabric around her to match their own costumes.

She stood with her feet together, toes turned out and he grinned as he remembered the time he had teased her about looking like a duck. She'd quacked and told him that after years of dancing she couldn't help it. He'd kissed her and told her he loved it. He still did.

Missing a step, she laughed and delighted the other dancers with her unaffected nature and he tensed as he wondered how any man looking at her could fail to want her as much as he did. Immediately following that thought was the one that said he should bundle her up right now and take her back to the palace. Back to his bed.

Only the dance had started and he couldn't turn away from her as she mastered the routine. His gut tightened and then the dance changed and the men joined in.

They looked at him with an air of hope rather than expectancy because, of course, his father had never mixed with his people like this, preferring to rule from the lofty heights of the palace walls. If he were to take the job he wouldn't rule that way and neither would Zach.

And then he realised what dance they were about to perform. It was the dance a man did when he was courting a woman and his instinct was to beg off but then he caught Imogen's eyes, her swaying figure. To hell with it. He moved to stand opposite her. He had never performed it before but he had seen it done many times as a boy. She looked up at him with a shy expression. Did she know what this performance represented? That it signified undying love?

His steps faltered as he circled her. Was that what he was feeling? Love? He immediately discarded the idea. He'd never wanted to find love in his life because—as he'd learned from first-hand experience—deep emotion brought even deeper mistakes and he liked his mind clear and sharp. Not that it was exactly clear or sharp right now but that was just lust and lust could be sated.

Imogen's words about how she only wanted to marry for love came back to him. What would it be like to have hers? Something tightened in his chest. He didn't want that from her. It was enough that they were compatible in bed. That they enjoyed each other's company. He stepped closer to her than he should have. 'Let's get out of here,' he growled in her ear.

She looked up at him with big eyes and he thought to hell with it and kissed her before dragging her off the dance floor amidst the shocked gasps of his countrymen. Things would be changing soon enough in Bakaan. He'd just add PDAs to that long list of improvements.

Imogen could feel the tension radiating from Nadir's big body in the car and desire made her blood grow sluggish in her veins. That dance they had performed back at the restaurant had been highly erotic even though they'd never actually touched. And Nadir had performed it like a professional. She'd guessed that it was some sort of mating ritual and she wondered if Nadir had ever danced it with another woman before. She wanted to ask, but she wouldn't.

Instead she thought about how much his people had loved it when he'd joined in and she wondered yet again why he didn't want to be King. He would be exceptional in the role. Was it because of his father? His sister who she didn't feel comfortable enough asking him about? And when would she start to feel comfortable enough with him to be able to freely discuss what was on her mind?

'Did you have a good time?'

'Yes.'

His eyes narrowed. 'You're biting your bottom lip. What's wrong?'

Imogen glanced at the driver of the car. 'Nothing.'

'By now I understand that *nothing* inevitably meant *something*.'

'You're not that clever,' she said, smiling in spite of her misgivings. But he was and it was a bit disconcerting to think that he knew her so well already.

Fortunately he let it drop as the car swung through the palace gates and stopped at the front steps. They both got out and Nadir didn't try to talk to her until he'd closed the door to his suite.

After finding out Nadeena was okay, Imogen once again found herself standing awkwardly before Nadir when what she'd love to do was go up to him and wrap her arms around his neck and kiss him.

With masculine grace he moved to lounge on the sectional sofa. 'You want to talk about nothing yet?'

Imogen sighed. 'Okay, fine. I was wondering why it is you don't want to be the next leader of Bakaan.'

She saw the minute the shutters came down over his eyes and shook her head. 'And why it is that as soon as I ask you something personal you refuse to talk.'

'I run a large organisation that is already showing the strains of my absence. I don't have time to run Bakaan as well.'

'You told me once that you love to take companies that are on the verge of collapse and turn them into something wonderful and, from what I can tell, Bakaan is in an identical situation.' She studied the way he rigidly held himself.

'If it helps, you are clearly a natural born leader, Nadir, and the people love you. You could do this job with your eyes closed.'

'It's not a question of capability. It's...' He sprang from the sofa as if he had too much energy coursing through his system. 'I never expected to do it. And what about you? That would make you my queen. Given that you're struggling with the whole concept of wife I can't imagine you'd be thrilled with the role.'

Surprised that he was even asking for her opinion, Imogen thought carefully before answering. 'I honestly don't know. I always thought I would one day open a dance studio and teach dance and...women seem to be very much held back here.'

'In some ways, yes, but equal opportunity for women is one of the key reforms Zach and I have discussed, along with better social infrastructure that would turn Bakaan into a competitive and vibrant place people would want to visit and invest in.' He stopped as if he realised how impassioned he sounded. 'Zach will make a great leader. And you should definitely open a studio. You're a beautiful dancer.'

Was he serious?

'You'd accept having a wife who danced for a living?'

'Why not?'

'I don't know...' Imogen felt at a loss. 'Maybe because you're a prince who has a Harvard education and speaks nine languages.'

The way he studied her unnerved her. 'Why should that matter?'

'I don't know but it does.'

'Not to me.' He frowned. 'Who made you feel bad about your profession? About yourself? Was it your father?'

His shrewd comment startled her. 'Why would you say that?'

'My head of security spoke with him when I was trying to find you and, as far as I'm concerned, a man who doesn't know the whereabouts of his daughter can't be much of a father.'

'He wasn't. And no, he never approved of my occupation. He was quite tyrannical at times and really remote at others. It was very confusing when I was little.'

'Ah, don't tell me—his affection was conditional on how well you toed the line.'

'Your father too?'

Nadir raised an eyebrow. 'My father's idea of giving someone a choice was to tell them how he wanted it.' A shadow came across his face as clear as a puff of smoke being brought in on the breeze. 'I left home at fifteen and headed to the Caribbean, where I took up bartending at a strip club.'

Her eyes widened with shock. 'You did not!'

He laughed. 'I can mix a Slow, Comfortable Screw with the best of them, I promise.'

'Nadir!' Imogen covered her mouth to stop a giggle from breaking out. 'Seriously?'

'It wasn't the most salubrious establishment on the street. After that I joined a building crew in the States and made money playing online poker.'

'I...I'm shocked.' And he made her Moulin Rouge career look like Disney. 'I take it you and your father weren't close,' she said ruefully.

'Actually, we were in the beginning. I was the heir. The golden child. As far as my father was concerned I could do no wrong.' He paused and stared into the middle distance for so long she started to think he'd finished but he hadn't. 'And then I did.'

His blue-grey gaze fixed on hers as if challenging her to ask him what he'd done that was so bad he'd lost the position as the favourite son, his face a mask of dark shadows.

The moment seemed distinctly brittle compared to their earlier camaraderie and she didn't know what to say. Ever since he'd come back into her life she'd wanted him to open up to her like this and share more of himself but now she felt that it would be invasive to ask him to continue because it was obvious these memories were incredibly painful.

He regarded her from beneath his long lashes, a look of self-disgust etched across his face. 'You don't want to know what I did?'

The quietly spoken question was savage and underscored by deep pain. Imogen swallowed heavily. She wanted to go to him and offer comfort but she had no idea how he'd respond to that kind of overture other than to disconnect from her again and it pained her to feel so awkward at a time when she felt he needed her the most. 'Only if you want to tell me,' she said, deciding that the decision had to be his alone without any real prompting from her.

He scrubbed a hand across his face in a gesture she knew meant that he was stressed and her heart went out to him.

'If we stay here for any length of time you'll find out anyway.' The words were toneless, as if he'd locked all emotion about what he was about to reveal in a place he could no longer access. 'When I was fifteen my mother and twin sister were killed in a car accident because my father's soldiers were chasing after them.'

His twin sister?

'Oh, Nadir, that's horrible.' She knew words were inadequate in the face of losing someone special because she still remembered how it had felt to lose her mother but she said it anyway because she wanted him to know that she was there for him. 'Why would they do that?'

'My sister suffered from Tourette's syndrome and my father never accepted her condition.' His tone was layered with resentment and contempt. 'As she got older my mother saw how detrimental life was for her in Bakaan and she wanted to move to somewhere in Europe.' His expression hardened. 'My father refused her request even though they were divorced and so she decided to do it in secret. I was supposed to go with them but I knew my father would be angry and I didn't trust what he would do once he found out.'

Almost afraid to ask the obvious question, she did anyway. 'And did you? Go with them?'

He walked away from her towards the windows and leant his arms against the frame as he gazed out at the darkness. 'No.'

If Imogen had ever heard a more bleak word she couldn't remember it and she waited for him to continue, suspecting that whatever he revealed next cut right to the core of who he was as a man. 'Selfishly, I didn't want them to leave either and so I told my father the plan.' He gave a brittle laugh. 'He set his men onto them; my mother panicked during the chase and rolled the car down a steep incline. They died instantly, so I was told. A small comfort, wouldn't you say?'

Imogen sat so perfectly still she wasn't even breathing—she didn't know what to say. It was clear that he blamed himself for their accident and she wasn't sure words alone would be sufficient to ever relieve his guilt. And in a way she understood how he felt because she was sure if their situations were reversed she'd feel just as awful as he did about it. But she also knew that he had to deal with his guilt and let it go because it really hadn't been his fault.

She remembered what he'd said to her on her first night at the palace about how his parents had dragged him and his sister through their marital problems and suddenly she saw him as the eldest child who had been torn between his love and loyalty to both parents and who was damned if he did and damned if he didn't. At least in her own situation she'd had her mother's unconditional love. Nadir had only had his brother…and his sister, who he no doubt felt he had to protect and whose life he felt he had cut short, and she could only imagine how horrible he must feel.

Wanting to at least close the physical distance between them, she went to stand beside him. She stared at his austere profile and she knew she had tears in her eyes because she just felt for him so much and wanted to rip the pain from his body with her bare hands.

'Afterwards my father refused to give either one of them an honourable funeral.'

Imogen's brow scrunched as she absorbed that piece of information. She shook her head. 'Why not?'

Nadir sucked in a deep breath and she knew he was containing his emotions and locking them down tight. 'He said that they had dishonoured and disrespected him and so to this day they don't have headstones on their graves.'

Without thinking, she reached out and covered the hand he rested on the windowsill with her own. His was much larger than hers and sprinkled with dark hair that stroked across her senses. It also felt cold. 'Was that why you left Bakaan when you were fifteen?'

'Yes.' He watched her fingers lightly stroke over the back of his knuckles. 'We argued about it and because I had challenged him once too often he disowned me so I left.'

And closed himself off from everyone ever since. 'Nadir, you know you can't blame yourself for what happened. You were only a child.'

He carefully shifted his hand out from underneath hers. 'I was fifteen. Old enough to know better,' he said bitterly.

'No, not old enough to know better,' she denied hotly and she knew that first-hand because at fifteen she had witnessed her father's affair with another woman and she'd had no idea what to do about it. In the end she hadn't told her mother because she'd known it would break her heart but her father assumed that she had and it had led to him leaving anyway.

He moved away from her and she heard the give of the cushions as he dropped back onto the sofa.

'I don't even know why I told you any of that so please if you're going to patronise me by trying to make me feel better then don't. Nothing will ever do that.'

Imogen crossed to stand behind the opposite sofa and gripped the backrest. 'I'm not being patronising, Nadir, but it's not rational to think that you caused their deaths.'

'I was a selfish idiot.'

'You were a *normal* teenager who was trying to keep his world intact.'

'Imogen—'

'No, I'm serious. I know you're hurting over this but how long are you going to punish yourself for the actions of a man who was an adult and should have behaved better?'

'You don't understand—I knew he would go after them.' His voice sounded as if it was wrenched from a place that was deep and dark.

Rounding the sofa, Imogen stopped directly in front of him. 'Nadir, you loved them and it sounds like your loyalty was completely divided. That's not a nice thing for parents to do to kids of any age.'

'There's no excuse for selfishness.'

'Maybe it wasn't you who was the selfish one. Maybe it was your parents.'

He looked at her as if he'd never contemplated that before and she knew that was probably because instead of processing what had happened he'd just tried to completely forget about it. 'Did you happen to get counselling at all?'

Her question brought a surprised bark of laughter. 'Sure I did. The place was called The Painted Pony.'

Imogen put her hands on her hips and felt the air between them become charged as his gaze drifted over her. 'I'm not talking about the strip place you worked at, although I'm sure there were many ladies ready to offer you a shoulder to cry on.'

'Unfortunately, I don't cry.'

'What a surprise. But, seriously, Nadir. I hate to think that you still blame yourself for something that really wasn't your fault.'

'And I hate to think that we're going to waste a whole evening while Nadeena is asleep rehashing an event that is best forgotten.'

Deciding to ignore that, she continued as if he hadn't spoken. 'Tell me this,' she began quietly. 'If this was Nadeena and she had made a mistake like the one you feel you made would you want her to punish herself for it for ever?'

He pushed himself up from the sofa and paced away from her, holding himself rigid. 'That's unfair.'

The fact that he'd even shared this side of himself with her made Imogen glow. It meant that he trusted her. And maybe it was time for her to start trusting him a little as well. 'Maybe you're the one who is being unfair. To yourself.'

Without thinking too much about it, she went to him and wrapped her arms around his broad back.

He stiffened but didn't move away from her and she could feel the heat of his body through the thin cotton of his *dish-dasha*. 'I think your mother and sister want you to be happy, don't you?'

He made a low sound in his throat that sounded like it came from a wounded animal and her heart felt as if it had been squeezed by a giant fist.

Acting purely on instinct, she ran her hands across his

broad shoulders and pressed herself closer. He didn't move a muscle but she knew she'd got to him because his breathing quickened just a little. Circling around, she stopped directly in front of him and smoothed her hands over his chest.

Emboldened by the fierce glitter in his eyes, she reached up and pulled his head down to hers. He yielded but she knew his mind was still in another place. A bad place.

About to pull back and give him time, she groaned with pleasure as he plunged his hands into her hair and took her mouth in a hungry kiss that completely immobilised her. Dazed at the swift rise of arousal, she pulled at his robe and moaned in frustration when she could find no way into it. 'These things are not fashioned for easy access, are they?' she complained.

Nadir growled and reefed the garment over his head and she heard one of the seams give in his haste to get it off.

Trembling with excitement, Imogen dug her fingers into the waistband of the cotton pants he habitually wore beneath the *dish-dasha* but his hands shoved hers out of the way so he could pull at her own clothing.

Hampered by the delicate *khaleeji abaya* she had chosen, he cursed in Arabic and she gasped when he grabbed hold of the neckline and ripped it clean down the middle. With her breasts bared to his gaze and his hands, Imogen felt her nipples peak as he bent his head to take one into his mouth. She threaded her fingers through his hair to hold him tight and felt his own skim down over her quivering belly, sucking in a deep breath as he ran the tips of his fingers around the lace between her legs.

'So wet,' he murmured. Imogen moved against him but his hands drifted to her thighs, gripping her hips as he dropped to his knees and kissed a line down her belly.

'Nadir, I—'

She didn't finish her sentence because he hooked his

fingers inside her panties to remove them and widened her stance with one hand while he delved between her legs with the other. Almost sobbing with need, Imogen placed her hands on his shoulders and watched as he pressed his face between her legs and stroked her with his tongue. She cried out as he pleasured her, her long hair swinging around them like a curtain as she almost bent double when her orgasm hit.

'Imogen.' Nadir lifted his head and scattered kisses across her pelvis. 'Your taste drives me wild.'

Gazing down at him with his knees spread wide on the carpet and his chest bare, Imogen swooned. 'I want to taste you too.'

She dropped to her knees as he rose before her and shoved the soft cotton pants down his legs. As always the sight of him aroused and erect gave her pause because he was just so big and imposing, so lethally male.

'Touch me, *habibi*,' he urged in a raw voice husky with need, his hands tangled in her hair, his warm strong fingers massaging her scalp. So she did. Flicking her tongue out to wrap around the head of his shaft as her hands slid rhythmically up and down. He let her have her way with him for what seemed like only seconds before he took over, groaning about self-control and need as he pushed her to the floor. Then he was above her and the only sounds that broke the silence were the mingling of their own harsh breaths.

'Look at me, *habibi*,' he commanded. 'I love to watch your eyes as I come inside you.'

'Nadir, please—' Imogen threw back her head as he shifted his weight and then drove deeply into her slick heat. She couldn't have said if her eyes were open or closed because she was in another world and when he brought his mouth down on hers in a demanding kiss she could hold nothing back as her world coalesced into this moment and then splintered into a trillion tiny pieces. He swore and

Imogen held his head in her hands and wound her tongue around his as her orgasm continued to roll through her.

Unable to contain his own climax, Nadir threw back his head and roared his own relief and Imogen knew she would do anything for this man. That she would follow him anywhere. That she loved him completely and utterly.

God, did she? Had she really fallen for him all over again? No, she hadn't fallen all over again because she'd never stopped loving him. She groaned and didn't realise she'd made the sound out loud until Nadir swiftly rolled to the side so he was no longer covering her. 'Are you okay?'

Cold replaced his slick warm skin and she shivered. *Was she okay? Would she ever be again?*

'Imogen, did I hurt you?'

No, not yet. 'No.' She cleared her throat and shifted on the silk Persian carpet beneath her. 'I'm fine.' At least she hoped she was.

He leaned over and cradled her cheek in the palm of his hand. 'You're sure? I wasn't too rough?'

God, he was divine. Beautifully rugged and so elementally male. Would he hurt her? Or did knowing that he would never love her mean that he didn't have that power any more? Because it was the hope before that had made the crash-landing so disastrous, wasn't it?

'Imogen, you're scaring me.'

'I'm sorry. I'm fine. I was just thinking…I was thinking that this thing…'

She fluttered her hands between them and he smiled. 'It only gets better. Stronger.'

Was he feeling it too? Was it possible he had fallen for her as well? 'Yes,' she whispered, her heart lodged somewhere near her throat and constricted her breathing. 'I…'

'Yes,' he agreed and pushed her hair back from her face. 'Every time we make love I want you more. I wouldn't have said that was possible. It's certainly never happened to me before.'

'Possible...' And then his meaning became clear and she felt quite ill. 'Sex?' He was talking about sex...

'Not just sex.' His eyebrow rose in a sexy slant. 'Hot sex.' He kissed her. 'Great sex.' Another kiss. '*Phenomenal* sex.' His smile was sinful and Imogen buried her face against his neck.

God, she had nearly made an utter fool of herself by blurting out what was in her heart and he was talking about sex!

'I've made you blush.'

She forced herself to laugh softly because what else could she do?

'You feel the same.' There was a deep satisfaction in his voice and Imogen pushed her feelings aside. She raised a small smile because she knew this wasn't a love match and to his credit he had never pretended it was. And what would telling him how she felt achieve anyway? It would only make her feel awkward around him and probably him around her as well.

No, it was better if this was her secret to deal with alone.

CHAPTER THIRTEEN

IMOGEN CAME AWAKE slowly and felt the sun on her face before she opened her eyes. She felt blissfully relaxed right up until she realised that she was alone in Nadir's bedroom; the only sound she could hear was a hawk calling periodically outside her window.

Nadir had gone again. He'd woken early and left her. Still unused to having help with Nadeena, she sprinted out of bed and only paused long enough to pull on a robe behind the door on her way out. It was Nadir's robe, of course, and it smelt of his special blend of male and spice. Trying to ignore the way his scent made her tingle all over, she padded quickly down the marble hallway and into the living room.

When that was empty she headed for the outdoor terrace.

Expecting that she would find the same scene as she had the last time, Imogen heard the sound of Nadeena's infectious giggles. She waited for the sight of the devoted Maab playing peekaboo with Nadeena when her heart all but flew into her mouth as she discovered that it wasn't Maab or Tasnim entertaining her daughter, but Nadir— in the pool. The sight of his bronzed torso stopped her in her tracks and she drooled at the way the sun glinted off his skin and turned it to burnished copper.

Pausing in the doorway and half hidden by a massive potted palm, Imogen watched Nadir throwing Nadeena up in the air and catching her just as her toes flittered across the top of the water, his biceps stretching and bulging in a fascinating display while Nadeena squealed with delight and clung to his neck.

She watched quietly for a moment, completely unnoticed as father and daughter frolicked in the sunshine. It seemed impossible that only a few days ago he had been a single-minded playboy who worked and played to excess and she could hardly fathom that he could be just as at home presiding over a boardroom full of world leaders as he was blowing raspberries on a baby's stomach.

His handling of Nadeena as he turned her onto her stomach and floated her across the top of the water, speaking to her softly in his native tongue was gentle and tender. But then she'd always known he had the capacity for that because she'd experienced it herself fifteen months ago in Paris.

And after last night she knew he was a man who felt things deeply and she felt awful. Awful for the tragedy he had endured and for the fact that he believed he had created it and awful because she had kept Nadeena's birth from him and had never planned to tell him. In her defence, she had believed that she was acting in the best interests of her daughter but watching the two of them together over the past few days had shown her that she had been wrong.

It seemed bizarre that a week ago she would have said that he was not father material and yet her own father had been held up as a wonderful family man in the community and she didn't have one memory of him holding her and playing with her as Nadir was doing with their baby now.

A lump formed in her throat. Yes, Minh had played with Nadeena and there was no doubt he was a wonderful male figure whom she hoped would stay in their lives for ever but he wasn't Nadeena's flesh and blood and why would she want to substitute that when Nadir obviously cared for their baby so much already? Yes, he could change his mind one day; yes, he could walk away, but maybe he wouldn't either.

'Imogen! *Habibi*.'

Catching sight of her, Nadir moved towards the edge of the pool and Nadeena bounced in his arms with excitement as she smiled and stepped outside. 'I've been teaching the kid to swim and she's a natural.'

Imogen grinned as he called her *the kid*. 'She's five months old—you can't possibly tell.'

'I can tell. And I read that the earlier you get a child used to water the better they are and she loves it.'

She also loved him, by the look of glee on her chubby face, and it only drove her feeling of guilt deeper. 'Does she need feeding?'

'Maybe.' His gaze swept over her and she realised how dishevelled she looked. 'You come straight from bed, *habibi*?'

The way he said *bed* made her blush and she was constantly surprised by her visceral reaction to this man. All he had to do was look at her like he was now and she would happily let him do whatever he wanted as frequently as he wanted. Was it any wonder she had fallen for him again? She knew she'd been a fool to think that she could spend time with someone so utterly virile and not crave more.

'Are you hungry?' he said, climbing out of the pool with Nadeena lifted high against his shoulder. 'There's pastries and fresh fruit on the table and also a pot of tea, although it might need reheating.'

'Thanks.' About to take Nadeena from him, she was startled when he dropped a sweet lingering kiss on her lips. '*Sabah el kheer*. Good morning, beautiful,' he said with a sexy grin.

Imogen swallowed the lump that hadn't quite disappeared from her throat. 'Good morning to you too.'

She settled into an outdoor chair and put Nadeena to her

breast while Nadir sat beside them and fielded calls on his phone. He hadn't bothered to put anything else on in the heat and she couldn't take her eyes off his long lean form in black swimming trunks and nothing else.

When Nadeena had finished he made a joke about her burping technique and walked Nadeena around until her stomach had settled.

Knowing there was no easy way to say what needed to be said, Imogen decided to just bite the bullet. 'Nadir, I'm sorry I didn't try to contact you when she was born. It was wrong of me. I see that now.'

Nadir stilled as if he hadn't been expecting her apology and why would he? It was only this morning she'd really understood how wrong she had been.

He looked at her. 'I wasn't exactly at my best at the time I found out you were pregnant.' He rubbed his stubbled jaw and gave her a crooked grin. 'And I don't blame you at all for running when you did. Hell, I probably would have as well.'

Imogen hated that he still thought she had run from him but then she realised with a flash of insight that that was exactly what she had done.

She had run.

She had done what she had so often begged her mother to do when she'd found her crying over her father yet again.

'That's nice of you but in hindsight I should have hung around to have at least talked to you.'

'But I wasn't there, *habibi*, and I didn't tell you when I'd be coming back.'

She sighed. 'I know, but…'

He moved closer to her and slipped the arm not holding their daughter around her waist. 'It's I who owe you an apology, Imogen. I was the one who failed you in your time of need.'

'No…' She shook her head and he leaned in and kissed

her. Nadeena clapped her hands and Imogen's smile turned watery.

'Yes.' His voice was rough with emotion. 'I should not have walked out on you. It was cowardly.'

'You were in shock.'

'So must you have been.'

Imogen bit her lip and studied him. 'You don't think I did it deliberately, do you? You don't think I tried to trap you?'

He shook his head. 'At first I thought all types of things like that. But I don't any more. I know you would never do something like that.'

Imogen smiled, wondering how it was that she felt better when she'd wanted to make him feel that way.

'What was her birth like?'

His gruff question surprised her and it took her mind back to what might just be the best and toughest day of her life. 'It was hard,' she admitted. 'I was in labour for twenty-four hours and…well, you've probably heard women talk about pushing out a watermelon?'

Nadir nodded.

'Try a beach ball.' She laughed and picked up a bottle of water from the table and took a gulp. 'A very large and very hard beach ball.' Her eyes misted over. 'And then it was over and she was on my chest and honestly I…' Her throat clogged as she remembered that she had looked around the stark, empty hospital room and wished that Nadir was there. She could feel the heat of his gaze on her and her eyes caught his. 'The midwife said that during the birth I called your name.'

In the process of laying Nadeena on a shaded rug, he stilled and looked at her. Imogen instantly felt self-conscious revealing so much and would have taken another quick gulp of water but Nadir was there and pulling her in against his chest. 'I'm so sorry I let you down.' He drew back and stared into her eyes. Rubbed his thumb gently over the drop of water that clung to her lower lip. 'I'm so sorry you had to go through that alone.'

'I wasn't completely alone.' She sniffed back a rush of tears. 'Minh visited and took care of us afterwards.'

'Great.' The word came out on a snarl. 'Remind me to thank him next time I see him.'

Wondering what was up with him, she frowned. 'He's com—'

Nadir placed a finger over her lips. 'I don't want to talk about him.' His voice was low and fierce. 'You won't ever need him or any other man again, do you understand, Imogen?' He was as intense as he had been when he'd told her he was taking her to Bakaan and wouldn't accept any arguments and Imogen was riveted. 'And if we have more children you will never have to go through that without me again. I promise.'

More children? She hadn't given any thought to more children but they hadn't used contraception the whole time they had been in Bakaan. Silly, but she hadn't even thought of it. Her hand went to her belly and she tried to make sense of the jumbled emotions that assailed her. Happiness, disbelief, anxiety...

'What is it, *habibi?* Don't you want more children?'

Yes, oh, yes. She loved being a mother. 'Yes. Do you?'

His smile was the sweetest thing Imogen had ever seen. 'Many.'

A giddy thrill rushed through her. The only thing that would make this moment more special was if he said that he loved her.

She let out a shaky breath. Oh, what she would give to hear those sweet words come out of his mouth.

'I never thought you wanted children,' she said softly.

He gave a short laugh. 'I didn't. I guess things change. People change.'

Imogen thought about her father and wondered if he had changed. If he was nicer to his new family. Had it just been her and her mother he couldn't love?

'What is it, *habibi*?'

Imogen bit the inside of her lip. She smiled up at him and shook her head. 'Nothing.' Why ruin the moment by thinking about the past? Nadir cared about her, she could see that much in his eyes, and he wanted her. Physically, their relationship was as good as she could wish for. As good as she remembered. She rested her head against his shoulder and tried not to give in to the gremlins inside her head that said this bubble of happiness couldn't last.

'Come—I have organised a surprise.'

'What is it?'

'Sand-boarding.'

Having expected him to say something like spa, or oasis, or beach, Imogen was completely flummoxed when he named something she'd never heard of before and which sounded like something builders did to houses when they repaired them. 'What is it?'

'You'll love it, *habibi*. Trust me. It's just like water-skiing.'

'I trusted you,' she groaned as she stretched her over-worked hamstrings. 'And sand-boarding is nothing like waterskiing.'

Nadir lounged in the doorway to her bedroom and grinned. 'It isn't?'

Imogen glared at him. Sand-boarding had been just part of the surprise he had organised. He'd also taken them to an oasis and taken delicious advantage of their time alone together every time Nadeena went down for a nap. They had existed in a blissful bubble and then she'd ruined it by trying to sand-board down a dune as big as a mountain. 'You know it isn't. It's completely insane to throw yourself down a one hundred foot sand dune in the middle of the blazing sun.'

'Ah, but that was your mistake, *habibi*—throwing yourself down. The trick is to actually stay on the board.'

Imogen rubbed her sore bottom she'd used to skate down when the steep incline had petrified her. 'Thanks for the tip.'

'But I was very impressed that you even tried it. I don't know another woman who would.'

Imogen rolled her eyes because she'd slid most of the way down on her bottom. 'Pride,' she said ruefully. 'They say it always comes before a fall and I fell so often my butt is still stinging.

Nadir straightened away from the door and came towards her. 'I can kiss it better if you'd like?' He leaned in and kissed her and Imogen wrapped her arms around his neck. Finally when he drew back he left his arms around her waist and she gazed up at him. 'I've had a wonderful couple of days. Thank you.'

'My pleasure. I hope you enjoyed the oasis. It's one of my favourite spots.'

'It was extraordinary and I don't know why it isn't already on everyone's top ten tourist destinations. Really, Nadir, your ideas for turning it into an eco-resort are second to none.'

'You are second to none, *habibi*. Now, please tell me you have changed your mind about us spending the night before our wedding alone.'

Imogen pulled back and made a face. 'I haven't. You know it's a tradition for the bride and groom to spend the evening apart and I want to start our marriage off on the right foot.' And usually the bride spent it with her friends but Caro and Minh hadn't been able to fly in until tomorrow so it was just going to be her and Nadeena once Nadir left. 'But what about Zachim? I know you're really worried about him now and if you want to postpone the wedding we can.'

'No.' He shook his head. 'The council have turned it into a big deal so it's important that our wedding goes ahead. I'll find Zach.'

'And if you don't?'

'I will.'

He was always so confident. So sure.

'Tell me, are you happy, *habibi*?'

Imogen hesitated. Would she jinx herself by saying yes? Because she was happy. Happier than she had been in a long time. Deciding that was a silly superstition anyway, she nodded. 'Yes, I am.'

He kissed the tip of her nose and went to the cot to kiss his daughter, who lay sprawled asleep on her back, and Imogen wrapped her arms around herself and wondered if she had a right to feel so contented.

'Goodnight.'

Nadir gave her a searing kiss that nearly had her changing her mind about tradition but then he pulled away, briefly rested his forehead against hers and left.

Imogen closed the door behind him and leant against it, which was when she realised that she was still wearing his *keffiyah*.

Pulling it from her head, she clutched it to her chest as she remembered him winding it around her head to keep the sun from burning her. She sighed. Already she felt lonely without him and she told herself it was dangerous to want him so much. Dangerous to rely on him so much. But, try as she might, she couldn't remove the grin from her face.

Her phone beeped a text message and she smiled when she saw it was from Minh, telling her they would be arriving tomorrow around noon. Since the wedding wasn't until the afternoon, that would give them time to catch up beforehand.

When she had invited them she had been feeling as if her world was crashing down around her and she'd desperately needed their support.

It had only been a couple of days ago that she'd felt that way and yet so much had happened since then it felt like months. Now she was glad they were coming, not so much for the support and friendship they would offer but because they would be sharing in what was going to be one of the happiest days of her life.

Nerves fluttered in her stomach but she steadfastly refused to give into them and headed towards the shower.

CHAPTER FOURTEEN

NADIR HAD NEVER been one to suffer from nerves and yet today, his wedding day, he was as jumpy as a stock trader facing his first day on the floor.

Maybe it had something to do with the overcast sky when normally it was true blue and cloudless this time of year. He gazed at the gathering cloud cover. The wind hadn't picked up enough to trigger a sandstorm so that was something at least. Especially since the convoy Nadir had sent out to find Zach had located the four-wheel drive he had been using overturned and buried in the sand. He hadn't told Imogen but he felt slightly sick at the thought that something sinister had happened to his brother. Fortunately no body had been recovered, which meant that he hadn't been buried along with the vehicle.

He knew he should probably call off the wedding until he knew what had happened but for some reason he couldn't bring himself to do it. He didn't think he'd properly relax until Imogen was truly his, which was ridiculous because she'd already agreed to marry him and she seemed happy about it. Or was she just making the best of a bad situation?

He frowned, recalling her slight hesitation the night before when he'd asked her if she was happy. She'd said yes and he had no reason to believe she was lying but that hesitation... Telling himself he was being paranoid, he counted off the other thing bothering him. The leadership position. For days now his mind had been vacillating over what to do about it and for a man who was used to making quick decisions that was just damned annoying.

His daughter bounced excitedly in his arms and he refocused his attention on the one area of his life he felt he had a handle on.

He had taken her early so that Imogen could relax in a deep scented bath and be prepared for him like so many brides had been prepared for their men in times gone by. He'd looked at her seriously and told her it was a tradition she couldn't refuse. She had laughed and said she was a girl and not only would she not refuse, but she'd revel in it while she was there.

That had set off all sorts of images in his head about her naked and wet and smelling like the sweetest flower. Tasting like the sweetest flower.

Nadeena pointed to something over his shoulder and started babbling. 'What is it, *habibti*?' he asked before his mind wandered any further down the sex route. One night away from Imogen and he felt as randy as a teenager who'd just been given the green light to go all the way.

He turned in the direction of Nadeena's chubby finger and saw a young stable hand grooming a mare outside the stables.

'Hisaan,' he told her. 'Horse.'

He strode over to it and stroked its arched neck. His sister had loved horses and suddenly a picture of her materialised in his mind and guilt assailed him, as it always did when he thought of her. As it usually did when he felt happy.

'If this was Nadeena and she had made a mistake like the one you feel you made would you want her to punish herself for it for ever?'

She was smart, his Imogen, smart to strike right at the

heart of the issue because of course he wouldn't want that for her. So why did he want it for himself?

He shook his head. As awful as that time had been, perhaps it was time he dealt with it and put it behind him. Of course he would change it if he could but he couldn't. But what he could do was take care of his own family. He could do what was right by them. Do what was right by Imogen.

He watched as his daughter gathered her confidence and reached out to place her hand against the horse's soft muzzle. The horse snorted a breath and she drew back, her wide eyes flying to his for reassurance. He gave it to her. Smiling and putting his hand back on the horse, encouraging her to do the same. 'It's okay, *habibti*. Nothing will happen to you while I have you.' His heart clenched as she followed his lead and then the skin on the back of his neck prickled. He glanced back towards the palace and saw Imogen watching them from the balcony of the temporary suite she had occupied the night before. Time seemed to stop and he couldn't take his eyes off her.

Her hair had been swept into an elaborate updo in preparation for the afternoon ceremony and her eyes were rimmed with kohl, her lips a deep pink. The honking of a car horn reminded him that stately cars had been coming and going all morning, delivering guests who would witness his joining with this woman he cherished above all others.

Cherished?

Loved.

He went dead still.

Was that really what was going on here? His heart pounded inside his chest as the words took root in his mind. He nearly laughed. Of course he loved her. It was as clear as crystal all of a sudden. His obsession with finding her, his uninterest in considering shared custody—and yes, he had strong views about that and he never wanted

Nadeena to suffer as he had—but Nadeena wasn't him and neither he nor Imogen would do that to her.

He wiped a smudge of dirt from Nadeena's cheek. The simple fact was that Imogen completed him. Waking up beside her, holding her in his arms at night, listening to her talk about her dreams, her hopes…wanting to see her fulfil her true potential.

Last night she'd turned him away because she had wanted to start their wedding off on the right foot. Now he wanted to do the same thing. Because he knew she only wanted to marry for love and he wanted to tell her how he felt before the ceremony. He didn't want her going into this wedding thinking that this was nothing but a marriage of convenience for him. Or inconvenience, as he had arrogantly claimed a week ago. He gave his daughter a wry smile. 'Your papa can be an ass.'

She looked at him solemnly and babbled something as if she was in complete agreement.

Laughing, he glanced up at the balcony again only to find it empty. A sudden feeling of vulnerability gripped him hard. What would she say when he told her how he felt? And was now really the right time? Perhaps he should wait, sound her out a little before he dived straight in with the *I love you*s? Hell, how did a man even start a conversation like that?

Deep in thought as he strode into the palace, he didn't see his brother until he almost ran straight into him.

Relief was followed swiftly by absolute fury. 'Where the hell have you been? You have a lot of explaining to do.' He took in Zach's dishevelled state—his wrinkled clothes that were covered in dust and dirt, his beard growth that looked to be at least a week old.

'*I* do?' Zach raised a dust-covered eyebrow. 'Thanks for the concern and the belated rescue team.'

Nadir frowned. 'You look like hell. What happened?'

'The short version is that I had an unfortunate run-in with one of the less welcoming tribes in the mountains.'

'Hell. For a while I thought you were holed up with a woman.'

Zach laughed. 'I suppose technically you could say that I was but it wasn't by choice and she's more like a spitting she-cat than a woman. One who is currently locked in the old harem. Not the most convenient situation on your wedding day, but then I didn't know it was your wedding day until about an hour ago.'

Nadir stared at him. 'You have a woman locked in the harem?'

'Farah Hajjar, to be exact,' he growled, his words laced with disgust.

'Mohamed Hajjar's daughter!'

'One and the same.'

Nadir swore. 'Hajjar will have your head for that.'

Zach's gaze turned wry. 'They both very nearly did.'

'For the love of...' Nadir's gaze narrowed. 'You didn't compromise her, did you?'

His brother gave a sharp bark of laughter. 'A wild boar couldn't compromise that woman and nor would it want to.' His gaze fell on Nadeena. 'I take it this is my niece.'

'You're changing the subject.'

'I am.' He smiled at Nadeena. 'She's beautiful.'

'I know.' Nadir wanted to ask his brother what the hell had happened but there'd be time for that later. It was enough that he was back and in one piece. 'I don't have time to get the details now but you're okay.'

'No thanks to you,' he said without rancour.

'Ever heard of the boy who cried wolf? That will teach you for playing so many tricks as a kid.'

Zach grinned. 'Come chat while I get cleaned up.'

'I can't.'

'Why not? The wedding isn't for hours yet.'

'No, but...' Nadir shook his head. He wanted to see Imogen and it was all he could think about. 'Here, take your niece and get acquainted.'

He handed his daughter over and was surprised when Zach took her so easily.

'Hey, don't look so surprised. I'm okay with babies. They're like women and horses. Handle them with the utmost care and don't do anything to rub them up the wrong way. Isn't that right, *habibti*?'

Waiting just long enough to make sure his daughter wasn't going to start bellowing in protest, Nadir smiled when a little frown line materialised between her eyebrows as she reached up to touch Zach's beard. 'Don't let her cut herself on that and if she cries take her to Maab.'

'Where will you be?'

'With Imogen.'

'Ah.' His brother cocked his head and gave a knowing grin and Nadir took the stairs to Imogen's suite two at a time.

This time Imogen made sure she kept well away from the balcony doors. She shouldn't have gone out there before but the time since she had woken until now had been interminable. And she still had another four hours until the wedding.

Butterflies danced in her stomach and her lips felt dry again. At this rate she would go through the whole tube of Rose Delight Tasnim had given her before the ceremony even started.

She wasn't in her dress yet, just a silk robe that was part of a dowry Nadir had ordered for her. It was gorgeous Parisian silk, as was the underwear she had on. The dress too was beautiful. It had been sewn by twenty local ladies and Tasnim had told her they had worked around the clock to create a dress fit for a queen. Which reminded her that she wanted to pay for her own dowry and she headed back inside and wrote a quick note to herself. It was only a small thing but she had started to wear the clothes Nadir had bought for her and she didn't want him providing everything she needed.

She sighed and tried to find something else to distract herself with because none of her old performance tricks seemed to do anything to settle her pesky nerves.

Or was it anxiety? Was it because everything had turned out so perfectly in the end? Or nearly perfectly. Nadir had not told her that he loved her but he cared for her and she believed that he would always do the right thing by her and their children.

Imogen pressed her hand to her belly. Could they have created another life together this week?

A knock on the door startled her and she knew it was Nadir. She hadn't missed that searing look he had given her from the courtyard or what it had meant. The butterflies in her stomach flexed their wings. He wanted her, that much was obvious, but still a little gremlin of doubt managed to insinuate itself into her mind. *What if he'd changed his mind…? What if—?*

Mentally slapping the negative thoughts away, she marched over to the door. Even though she knew she shouldn't see him again before the ceremony, she didn't care. She needed the reassurance of his touch.

'Minh!'

Imogen burst into tears the minute she opened the door and saw her friend standing on the threshold dressed in a bespoke suit and tie, which he'd always said he would never wear.

'Imogen—' Minh stopped smiling and strode inside '—what's wrong?'

All the pent-up emotion of the last week spilled over

and, even though she told herself not to cry because it would ruin her make-up, she couldn't seem to stop.

'Imogen, tell me what's wrong. If that bastard hurt you I'll deck him.' Minh took her into his arms and she shook her head to say that she was fine and buried her face against his chest. It was stupid to cry like this and she gave a hiccup and lifted her head, her smile tremulous. 'I'm sorry…I don't know what came over me. I've been waiting for you to get here and…oh, Minh, I'm just so—'

'Happy?'

Hearing Nadir's deep voice behind her, Imogen reared back from Minh and stared at Nadir. His face was closed. Hard. He raised an eyebrow. 'Ecstatic, even?'

Well, yes. She wiped beneath her eyes and her fingertips came away black. Oh, she must look a fright! 'I didn't hear you knock.' It was a stupid thing to say but the tone of his voice had thrown her mind into a spin.

'You left the door open.' His steely gaze scared her and then he cut his eyes to Minh. 'I need to speak with Imogen. Alone.'

'What have you done to her now?'

'Minh, don't.' Imogen had a sense of *déjà vu* but she knew by the expression on Nadir's face that something was very wrong. Had he received bad news about Zachim?

'I don't like this, Im. I told you—'

'Please, Minh. I'm sure this won't take a minute.'

Minh's reluctance to leave was as palpable as it had been back in London.

He threw Nadir a warning glare. 'I'll be right outside.'

Imogen breathed out when he closed the door behind him. She turned back to find Nadir by the arched windows, staring out. 'Nadir, what's wrong? Has something happened? Nadeena—'

'She's fine. I left her with Zach.'

'Oh, then he's back!'

'Yes.'

'That's wonderful news. I thought maybe, but…' She took a deep breath. Started again. 'Is he okay?'

'He's fine.'

She hesitated. 'So that's good. Isn't it?'

'It's very good.'

He turned and stuck his hands in the pockets of his jeans and stared at her.

'You're starting to scare me, Nadir.' She gave a soft laugh as if to alleviate the tension in the room but it just ratcheted it up even more.

'I'm sorry. I don't mean to.' He cleared his throat. 'But we need to clarify some things before the wedding.'

His voice was so devoid of emotion it made Imogen's stomach roil. 'Like?'

'Like the fact that you wouldn't be here if it wasn't for Nadeena.'

Her lashes came down to shield the hurt in her eyes. They both knew that was why he had brought her here. It wasn't news. So why was he mentioning it? Was he afraid she had twisted the reasons for their marriage into something it wasn't? Was he afraid she had fallen in love with him? Taking a deep breath, she tried to tell herself that everything was going to be okay. 'I know that.'

He nodded. 'And the fact that you never wanted this marriage.'

Imogen frowned. She half expected to see a gavel in his hand. 'No. I…' She hesitated, wondering how to answer when he jumped in first.

'Wanted to marry for love? Is that what you were going to say?'

She nodded and then shook her head. No, she hadn't been going to say that; she'd been going to say that in the beginning she had wanted that but now—

'Yes or no, Imogen?'

'Yes, I wanted to marry for love but...' She swallowed, her eyes searching his face for some clue as to what he was thinking or feeling. But this was the stranger Nadir—the man who had picked her up a week ago. The man who had walked out on her in Paris. A terrible premonition raised goose bumps along her arms but she pushed aside her apprehension and answered honestly. 'I've come to terms with that now.'

As if he'd somehow been waiting for that exact answer, he slowly raised guarded eyes to hers. 'Then you're free to go.'

'I'm sorry?'

'I said you're free to go.' He moved towards the door.

'Nadir...wait. I don't understand what you're saying.'

'I'm saying that I agree with you. A marriage of convenience is not a good enough reason to tie two people together for ever. Even for the sake of a child.'

'Hold on.' Imogen felt as if she had to fight to get every word out of her mouth. 'You're saying that you no longer want to marry me?'

'I'm saying you're free. You can leave.'

The room tilted and Imogen put her hand out to grip the back of a chair. Tears of disbelief spiked behind her eyelashes but she refused to let them fall. 'What about Nadeena?'

'My lawyers will be in touch about visitation rights—isn't that what they're called?'

Isn't that what they're called?

He was so cool and remote she wanted to scream. 'I meant—what about your desire to be part of her life? *Permanently.*'

Her body started shaking. This couldn't be happening. It just couldn't be happening.

'I still plan to be in her life. I just...' He looked away

as if it was too difficult to look at her. 'I have reconsidered my position.'

He had reconsidered his position? As if they were nothing more than a piece of furniture he had decided he no longer wanted.

'Oh, my God!'

'I still want her,' he rasped harshly. 'But not this way.'

Stunned, Imogen could only stare at him, his words barely registering as her heartbeat raced out of control and her thoughts went along for the ride. All she could think was that he had changed his mind. 'I told you this would happen.' Suddenly she was fifteen again and her father was standing in the doorway and her mother was crying on the sofa. Thank God Nadeena wasn't old enough to witness her own humiliation at the hands of this man. She lifted her chin. 'Where's Nadeena now?'

'I told you she's with Zach.' He swiped a hand across his face but Imogen barely noticed.

'Damn it, Imogen. I thought you'd be happy.'

Imogen felt bile rise up in her throat but she held it back by sheer force of will, determined that he would not see how much he had hurt her again. How much she had *let* him hurt her again. God, she was an *idiot* of the most astonishing proportions. 'I am.'

He nodded. 'Then there's nothing left to say.'

'Nothing,' she assured him and sailed into the en suite bathroom before he saw the utter despair in her eyes.

Nadir sat behind his father's old desk, staring at his computer screen. When the door banged open he looked up and found his brother dressed in celebratory robes with a scowl on his face.

Zach didn't waste any time on niceties. 'What are you doing?'

'Working. You look better.'

'It's amazing what a shower and a shave will do.' Zach parked himself in the chair opposite the desk. 'Why are you working? You're getting married in less than two hours.'

Nadir focused on the email he'd been trying to read. 'Not any more. I've instructed Staph to send the guests home.'

'I know. He came to me.'

'Well, it's good that you're here. We need to discuss who will lead Bakaan and I've reconsidered my position. If you don't want the position then I'll be the next King.'

'Big turnaround.'

Nadir grimaced. 'It's amazing what can happen in a week.'

He'd found his ex-lover and his daughter, he'd fallen in love with them both and he'd lost them both. And taking on the role of leading Bakaan into the twenty-first century would keep him busy enough so that he wouldn't think of any of it.

'Nadir, bro…?' Zach used the kind of placatory tone he might if he was facing a band of militants with only a soup spoon to defend himself. 'I'm not sure that's the most important thing to discuss right now. What's going on?'

Nadir thought of the scene he had interrupted in Imogen's room. Her ex-lover holding her tightly in his arms.

At first he'd been furious, his instinct to grab hold of the smarmy buffoon and pull him off her and beat him to a pulp for daring to touch what was his. Then he'd registered that Imogen wasn't resisting. That she was snuggled against him and that she was weeping. Sobbing, almost.

Those tears had torn at his heart and he'd realised in a flash of unwelcome insight that he was behaving exactly as his father had done in stealing his mother from her tribal village in a fit of passion and then forcing her to bend to his will when he had taken another wife. Of course his circumstances were different from his parents, he knew that, but he also knew that the common denominator wasn't. He was a tyrant who hadn't given her a choice. He now had and she'd very definitely exercised it.

He forcibly shut his emotions down. He knew it had been a mistake to let them out. They had confused things. Made him think that sex was love when the truth was that he and Imogen shared a phenomenal chemistry and a child and he cared enough about her that he couldn't force her to do something she didn't want to do. 'Nothing is going on.'

Zach looked at him. 'Pull the other one—it has bells on it.'

Nadir cut him a brooding glare. 'Fine. I found Imogen in the arms of her ex-lover.'

'Naked!'

'No—' he heaved a sigh '—she was crying.'

Zach frowned. 'Why?'

'Because she wants to marry him, not me.' Nadir surged to his feet in irritation and turned towards the windows. 'How the hell should I know? Suffice it to say, she invited her ex-lover to our wedding and now they're together.'

Zach blew out a breath. 'That's rough. Why'd she do it?'

'I assume because she loves him.'

Zach nodded as if he fully agreed and then started shaking his head. 'No, I meant why did she agree to marry you when she's still in love with someone else?'

'Does it matter?' he asked briskly. 'The fact is she was living with this guy in London and now she's free to go back to him.'

Zach nodded again. 'Which she wants.'

'Right. Now, there's a lot to sort out. I'm hoping you want to stay on in Bakaan if you don't take the leadership role because I'm going to need a right hand and I want that to be you.'

'So, to be clear,' Zach began, completely ignoring his

attempt to change the subject, 'she actually said that she preferred this other guy to your face.'

Nadir swiped a hand across his jaw. 'Can we just forget Imogen?' A muscle knotted in his jaw. 'She's not relevant to this discussion.'

'Sure.' Zach eased back in his chair. 'If you're happy with her bonking another guy then who am I to argue?'

Nadir slammed his portable mouse down on the desktop. 'I told you to forget her.'

'I will if you will.'

'Already done.'

'Nope.' Zach glanced at his feet. 'Must have left the bells in my rooms.'

'Dammit, Zach, I gave her a choice and she chose him. You want to rub my nose in it, you can go to hell.'

'Hang on a minute, buddy.' Zach surged forward in his seat. 'I'm not rubbing your nose in anything. I'm saying you might be wrong.'

'I'm not.'

'Then let me ask you this. Are you currently sleeping with her?'

Nadir stared at him, hard. 'You continue down this line of thinking and I can tell you it won't end well.'

'Just hear me out.' Zach threw up his hands defensively. 'I'm not trying to get a blow-by-blow description of your love life, I'm trying to say that I know women.'

Nadir scoffed.

'Scoff all you like, but I do, and I don't know many that would sleep with one guy while they were in love with another.'

Nadir eyed him coolly. 'They're out there.'

'Okay, sure, so what you're saying is that Imogen is one of those—'

'No, she's not. She would never play with people's emotions like that.'

'Right. So stop being a horse's arse.'

'Look, Zach, I know you're trying to make me feel better but you don't have to concern yourself. I'm good.'

'Bro, I'm not trying to make you feel better; I'm trying to talk you down off a ledge.'

'I'm not on a ledge.' Nadir's jaw hardened. 'The fact is I had no choice but to let her go. I forced her to come here. I forced the idea of marriage onto her and I wouldn't take no for an answer.'

'Like the old man.'

'Yeah.' Nadir blew out a rough breath. 'Just like the old man. Hell.' He stared at Zach bleakly. 'When did I turn into him?'

'You didn't.' Zach frowned. 'Admittedly, you're stubborn and a little on the arrogant side but you don't take advantage of people and you'd never step on someone else for your own gain.'

'That's where you're wrong.' Nadir stared at him bleakly. 'I stepped all over Imogen.'

Zach shook his head. 'I doubt that's true but if you did then go apologise and make nice. Tell her how you feel. See what happens.'

The thought of that made Nadir's gut pitch. He never told anyone how he felt. It was easier and no one got hurt that way. Least of all him. 'Hell. I love her.'

'You think?'

Nadir shook his head. 'I know you think you're pretty clever but frankly I wouldn't wish this sick feeling in my gut on anyone.'

'I would love to care for a woman as much as you do yours. Instead, I have to figure out how to stop myself from being shackled to a living, breathing fire-eater who would as soon run me through with a *kanjhar* than look at me.'

Nadir had forgotten all about Farah Hajjar. 'I doubt her father will push it. He hates our family.'

'It's fine. I can deal with Farah and her insane old man. You just do us both a favour and go get your woman.'

'Prince Zachim!' Both men looked up as Staph knocked and shot through the door like a rocket, his breath heaving. 'You need to come quick. The woman you put in the harem has disappeared.'

'Disappeared?' Zach frowned. 'That's impossible. I've put an experienced guard on the door.'

'Yes, My Lord. He can't find her.'

Zachim rattled off a string of curse words Nadir hadn't heard in a long while. He smiled and came around the desk. 'I'd love to stay and help but...'

His words faded as Zach, his mind already on the disaster that awaited him, strode out of the room.

Nadir headed for the door himself and stopped. 'Staph?'

'Yes, My Lord?'

'What did you tell the wedding guests who have already arrived?'

'Nothing, My Lord.'

Nadir gave him a faint smile. 'You're a sly old dog, Staph. I hope your faith in me isn't misplaced.'

'I would say not, My Lord.'

'And Imogen and my daughter?' He cleared his throat. 'Where are they?'

'In your suite.'

Imogen sorted out what she would need for Nadeena for the plane trip back to London and searched around for some sort of bag to put it into. Nadir had luggage in his dressing room but no way was she going back into his bedroom ever again.

What he had said to her before...she still couldn't digest it because it felt as if he'd ripped a hole in her heart and inserted a stick of dynamite for good measure.

The only thing she was thankful for was that her daughter would never know how it felt to have an absent father because she would be used to having him part-time in her life and Imogen only hoped he would be good to her when he had her. That he wouldn't have a string of stick-thin models parading through his house who— Oh, God. Imogen felt her stomach heave and leant against a chest of drawers to steady herself.

It was so ridiculous to feel like this because she had known all along that once the reality of marriage and parenthood set in then he would run a mile and she'd been proven right. And the prize? She shook her head at her reflection in the mirror. Her prize was a broken heart the size of Asia.

'Imogen? *Habibi*? Are you all right?'

Imogen swung around at the sound of his voice, fire pouring out of her eyes. 'What are you doing here?'

He stopped short and she was thankful that she had wiped all her make-up off after her initial crying fit and dressed in her T-shirt and jeans. She intended to go home exactly the way she had arrived. Well, almost.

'I needed to see you.'

To make sure she was all right? She couldn't fault his manners. 'Well, now you've seen me, please go.'

'*Habibi*, I—'

'Do not call me *habibi*.'

'Okay—fine.' He held up his hands as if she were a wild thing about to pounce on him and maul him to death. What a pity, she thought, that shape-shifting was pure fantasy. 'I know I'm the reason you're upset and I just want to talk.'

'No.' Imogen shook her head for emphasis. 'No more talking. I'm done here, Nadir.'

He looked around the room and frowned when he saw the minuscule amount of clothing on the bed. The empty cot. 'Where's Nadeena? Isn't she due for a sleep?'

'Yes, but since we're leaving, Minh is trying to keep her

awake so that she'll sleep on the—oh, this is not important. Could you please just go?' The last thing she wanted to do was break down and sob in front of him and the longer he stayed the more likely that was to happen. It was too painful to see him. Too painful to be near him.

He cleared his throat and shoved his hands into his pockets. 'It's probably good that we talk about him and get it out of the way.'

'Talk about whom?'

'Your friend, Minh.'

'What about him?'

He looked at her and his throat worked as he swallowed. 'Do you love him?'

Did she love him? 'Why are you asking me that?'

'Because I need to make sure I've done the right thing in letting you go.'

'Letting me go?' She shot him a fulminating look. 'You told me to go. You've reconsidered, remember—you don't want to marry me.'

'Of course I still want to marry you. I only reconsidered the reason for our marriage.'

Imogen shook her head. 'You're not making any sense. You cancelled the ceremony.'

'Yes, but I didn't want to.'

'Then why do it?'

'Because you told me the reason you were marrying me was because we had Nadeena and I wanted more.'

'More?'

'Hell.' He swiped a hand across his face. 'I need to start again. What I'm trying to tell you is that I love you.'

'You love me?'

Her shock must have registered on her face because his expression turned grim. 'Yes, but if you prefer Minh then I'll walk away.'

'Nadir, Minh is gay.'

'Gay!' The look on his face was priceless and Imogen would have laughed if she hadn't felt so ill. Had he seriously thought that Minh was her lover? Looking back, she supposed he might have got that impression initially but... 'How could you think that I could be in love with him and make love to you?' she demanded hotly.

'As I explained to our daughter this morning, I'm an ass. Particularly where you're concerned. I can't seem to keep my head on straight when you're in the room and every male who looks at you sideways is a threat.'

'Are you serious?'

'Yes. If you knew how many ways I wanted to hurt them—'

'No.' She gazed up at him, not really daring to believe this was happening. 'The part about loving me.'

Nadir cupped her chin in his hand and kissed her deeply. Imogen moaned and pulled back. 'Stop that—it will only confuse things.'

'On the contrary, our physical relationship is the only thing that's not confused. Imogen, *habibi*, can you ever forgive me for being so stupid this afternoon? My only excuse is that when I saw you crying in the arms of your... friend I assumed it was because you didn't want to marry me and I couldn't bear the thought of hurting you.'

'But why would you think I didn't want to marry you?'

'Because I realised today that I'm more like my father than I would like to think I am and that I was forcing you to bend to my will and I couldn't do it. I wanted to set you free, to give you a choice.'

Imogen dashed at the tears on her face. 'I thought you had decided that you didn't want me. That I wasn't enough for you.'

'Oh, *habibi*, you're too much for me. You're too wonderful, too beautiful, too giving. I'm pretty sure I fell in love with you the minute I saw you in Paris because I haven't been able to stop thinking about you since, only I didn't want to see it because I was so afraid of getting hurt.'

Imogen sniffed back more tears. 'I'm guilty of the same thing and oh, Nadir, I feel exactly the same way. I fell in love with you the minute I saw you and I've never stopped. I love you so much it hurts.' Elation rushed through her until she thought she might burst. 'Pinch me—I can't quite believe this is happening.'

'Believe it,' he growled, pulling her in close against him. 'And mark my words when I tell you that there will be no more misunderstandings between us. No more worrying about how the other person feels. You know that I love you. That I will always love you and whatever children we have. Tell me you believe me.'

'I believe you.' She grinned up at him. 'And not just because you command it to be so.' And then she turned serious because she knew she had to be just as open with him. 'I think part of the blame for today lies with me, though, because in my own way I saw what I expected to see and I didn't fight for you. I didn't fight for us. I won't do that again. I won't doubt either one of us again.'

'And I will never give you a reason to. Now, please, *habibi*, if you wouldn't mind giving me this?' He took her ring from her finger.

Then he got down on bended knee and Imogen didn't think she could love him more but, before he could ask her the question she knew he was about to, there was a noise in the doorway and she looked up to find Minh standing there with Nadeena, his eyes as big as saucers as he took in the scene.

'Ah, I think we'll come back.'

'No.' Nadir rose and swiftly crossed the room. 'I know we haven't formally met but I am Nadir Zaman Al-Darkhan and I would like my daughter, please.'

'Oh, right.' Minh blinked up at Nadir and Imogen thought he might swoon.

Then Nadir was in front of her again and taking up all her attention. He handed her Nadeena and then got down on one knee again. 'I'm glad our daughter is here because I want her to witness how a man should behave when he's in love with a woman so she will be in no doubt as to what to expect from a man in the future.'

'Oh, Nadir—' Imogen's nose tingled as tears formed in her eyes '—I love you so much.'

Nadeena clapped her hands and tried to reach for the ring Nadir held up but he shook his head. 'Sorry, *habibti*, this is for your mother.' Then he lifted his blue-grey gaze to hers. 'Imogen Reid Benson, will you please do me the honour of becoming my wife later this afternoon?'

'This afternoon!'

'Yes. Apparently there is a room full of guests waiting for us.'

'But I'm not ready!'

Nadir gave her a wry smile. 'Can I take that as a yes?'

'Yes, oh, yes. Most definitely yes!' She pulled him to his feet and stepped into his arms, where Nadeena promptly laid her head against his broad chest. Seeing it, Imogen did the same and Nadir cupped the nape of her neck and lifted her mouth to his.

'I think I need a tissue.'

Having forgotten all about Minh in the doorway, Imogen beamed him a wide smile. 'I'm getting married.'

Nadir brought her mouth back to his for one last searing kiss. 'Yes, you are. In an hour. And you should know that I've told Zach that I intend to become King if he doesn't want the position.'

Imogen smiled and finally felt that everything was as it should be in the world. 'He won't. You were born to be King, Nadir.' She reached up and ran her hand across his stubbled jaw, her eyes full of the love she felt for him. The love she would always feel for him. 'You were born to be *my* King.'

Nadir's smile was slow and sexy. 'A king who will be at your service. Always.'

* * * * *

SOLDIER PRINCE'S
SECRET BABY GIFT

KATE HARDY

For Cara Colter and Nina Milne – it was such fun
working with you!

PROLOGUE

May

TEN MINUTES UNTIL MIDNIGHT.

Ten minutes until the charity gala was over and the guests were due to leave, and then another three-quarters of an hour to finish clearing up.

And then Tia could go home to bed.

She was exhausted. She'd already done her usual full shift at the café that day, and Saturdays were always a rushed-off-your-feet day. When she'd got home, all she'd wanted to do was to have a long bath and then curl up on the sofa with her mum to watch a movie. But her old school friend Sadie was managing a charity gala tonight and Tia had promised that she'd help out, serving canapés and clearing glasses, and Tia never went back on her promises. Particularly as the cause—supporting children who'd been bereaved—was so close to her heart; she knew first-hand how it felt to lose a member of your family in the armed forces.

Twice.

Their neighbour, Becky, was keeping an eye out for her mum—as she always did on the few occasions that Grace Phillips managed to persuade her daughter to go out somewhere. In less than an hour, Tia could go home.

And tomorrow was late opening, being Sunday, so her shift didn't start until ten. It wasn't so bad. She'd had tougher days.

Though she couldn't shake the feeling that someone was staring at her.

She turned round and caught the eye of a tall, dark-haired man across the room.

There was something very familiar about him. Then again, half the people at the charity gala were house-hold names: everyone from musicians to movie stars to models. All the men were wearing tuxedos, and all the women were wearing the kind of posh frocks and designer shoes Tia would never have been able to afford in a million years. This was another world, one where she was supposed to be invisible—the anonymous waitress who smiled as she served canapés and cleared glasses quickly and efficiently. The guy across the room shouldn't even be noticing her.

As she went out onto the hotel balcony to collect glasses from the abandoned tables, still thinking about him, she realised who he was.

Antonio Valenti.

Prince Antonio of Casavalle, to be precise.

The man who had been her older brother Nathan's best friend, who'd served with him as his team commander in an alliance of international armed forces.

The man who'd broken her heart, and her mum's, four months ago, when he'd brought the news that Nathan had been killed in action. Antonio had delivered the news coldly and calmly: a stoic man in a military uniform who didn't even blink as he told them that Nathan's vehicle had hit a land mine on his last mission and he'd been killed instantly. Tia had been too shocked to say anything, but her mother had collapsed at the news that she'd lost her son the same way as she'd lost her husband, so Tia had had to damp down her own grief to support her mother.

Prince Antonio had clearly cared so little about Nathan that he hadn't even stuck around to comfort Grace Phillips or check that she was all right. He'd left almost as soon as he'd delivered the news. He hadn't even stayed for a cup of tea, let alone turned up at the funeral; and, apart from a formal embossed condolence card which he'd scrawled his name across, he hadn't been in contact with them since.

OK, sure, the man was a prince and he had important official duties as well as being in the army. Tia wasn't stupid. She understood that. But would it have hurt him to spend a few minutes with Grace after delivering the news, just to share some memories of her beloved son with her? Or show his face at Nathan's funeral? Or later, perhaps, he could've sent Grace a photograph or a private note via the Palace press office. It wasn't as if her mother was going to rush to the media and try to get money for it, or sell it online. All Grace had needed was a little gesture to let her know that Nathan had *mattered*.

But there had been nothing from Prince Antonio but silence.

Prince Charming? More like Prince Cold and Uncaring, Tia thought, curling her lip. How on earth had her brother been close friends with someone who was so cold and starchy?

And he was probably only here at the gala because he was attending in an official capacity; a man like him certainly wasn't warm enough to care about the work of the charity, or about the children who'd lost their parents or siblings in war. He certainly wouldn't be there rattling a collecting bucket along with the rest of the volunteer fundraisers or schmoozing people into buying tombola tickets.

She put him resolutely out of her mind and continued stacking glasses on a tray ready to carry through to the kitchens.

Tia Phillips looked absolutely exhausted.

Guilt balled in a hard lump in Antonio's throat.

He'd been there when his second-in-command's vehicle, the one in the convoy in front of his, had been blown up by a land mine. Mercifully, death had been instant, so he knew Nathan hadn't suffered; but Antonio had been shattered by the loss. During his years in the army, his team had become like a family to him. Nathan had been his best friend as well as his second-in-command.

But Antonio had been brought up not to show any emotion in public; as a prince of Casavalle, he was expected to be cool and calm in every situation. He and his elder brother Luca had been brought up knowing their duty always came first. And you never, ever said or did anything that made you look as if you'd lost control of your emotions. That had been reinforced by his military training, so Antonio knew he'd been calm and reserved when he broke the news to Nathan's family.

Too calm and reserved, perhaps, in their eyes.

Antonio knew how much Nathan had loved his family. He knew that Grace Phillips was poorly and that Nathan and his little sister Tia had spent their childhood as her carers rather than having the freedom to be children; and he'd promised Nathan silently by the side of his coffin that he'd keep an eye on Grace and Tia.

But he'd been called away almost immediately on another mission, so he hadn't even been able to attend Nathan's memorial service. He'd written a personal note and asked Miles to post it for him—but he knew that a note wasn't the same as actually being there. It had felt horribly like a weak excuse.

And then the fallout from his own father's death had kept him on special leave from the army. For the last four months, Antonio Valenti had been kept busy supporting Luca as his brother took over the reins of ruling Casavalle. He'd also been helping with the preparations for both the coronation and Luca's upcoming wedding to Princess Meribel, the oldest daughter of King Jorge of the house of Asturias in the neighbouring kingdom of Aguilarez. He'd barely had a minute to himself since returning to Casavalle, so he'd let his unspoken promise to Nathan slide.

Though Antonio knew he should've *made* the time. Especially as he knew how bad Nathan had felt, leaving his sister to care for their mother while he'd joined the army at the age of sixteen so he could send money home to help them financially. He should've done more to help support his best friend's family. Been there for them, because he knew they had nobody else.

Tia had glanced back at him before going out on the balcony with an empty tray, presumably to collect glasses, but he had no idea whether or not she'd recognised him.

Then again, she was clearly working and her boss wouldn't be happy if she stood around chatting to guests at the charity gala when she was supposed to be clearing up. Given her family's circumstances, Antonio knew that Tia needed her job. It wouldn't be fair to risk her losing the job and having that added financial pressure, just to salve his own guilty conscience.

But he couldn't just leave things. Not now he'd seen her again. Surely she could spare him two minutes?

'Please excuse me. I'm expected to mingle,' he said to the guests he was with. As the patron of the charity, he was supposed to talk to every guest and thank them for their support; but he was pretty sure he'd already done that. So his conscience was clear as he headed towards the balcony where Tia had gone.

She was standing on the other side of the door as he opened it, and almost dropped her tray.

'Sorry,' he said. 'Tia. It's good to see you.'

'Thank you, Your Royal Highness,' she said coolly. 'I would curtsey, but I'd rather avoid the risk of dropping my tray.'

He winced, knowing he deserved the rebuke. 'You don't need to curtsey, and it's Antonio to you. Your brother was my friend.'

'Yes, Your Royal Highness.'

Which put him very much in his place. He'd been a stranger and he deserved to be treated like one, despite his current attempt to be friendly with her. Given how he'd behaved, the last time they'd met, maybe it wasn't so surprising that she preferred to keep a barrier of formality against him. OK. He'd stick to formality.

'Ms Phillips,' he said. 'I appreciate that you're working right now, but perhaps we could talk when you've finished?'

'I really shouldn't be taking up guests' time, Your Royal Highness,' she said.

Which was a polite way of telling him he shouldn't be taking up her time, either. Another deserved rebuke, he thought. 'After your shift,' he said, glancing quickly at his watch. 'The gala finishes in five minutes.'

When it looked as if she was going to think up an excuse, he said softly, 'Please. It'd be so good to talk to someone who knew Nathan.'

For a moment, his brown eyes were filled with pain, before his expression returned to its former careful neutrality. So maybe the Prince wasn't quite as cold and uncaring as he'd seemed. That glimpse of pain just now told her that the Prince really *had* cared about her brother. Maybe she should cut the man some slack. Be kind to her brother's friend. Even though part of her still felt he should've made more of an effort, for her mum's sake.

'All right,' she said. 'I'll meet you when I'm done here. But I'm working tomorrow. I can't stay long.'

'Just a few minutes. Thank you.' He paused. 'I'm staying in the penthouse suite. I can of course arrange for a chaperone, if you prefer.'

'That won't be necessary, Your Royal Highness.' Like her brother, Prince Antonio was a man of honour. Tia knew without having to ask that his behaviour towards her would be respectful. 'The penthouse suite,' she echoed.

'My security team will let you in,' he said. 'Forgive me for being rude, but I'd better go back to the guests. I'm the patron of the charity.'

Meaning that he was here on official duties? Though the Prince had been so cold and starchy when he'd come to tell Tia and her mum the news about Nathan, she wasn't convinced he really cared about bereaved children, the way the patron would normally have a personal interest in the cause they supported. Though maybe losing his friend had taught him a little more empathy.

To her surprise, he held the door for her so she didn't have to struggle with her tray of glasses.

This was surreal.

She'd just made an assignation with a prince. In his penthouse suite.

A prince who'd been her brother's best friend, though because Nathan had kept his work and his family separate this was only the second time she'd ever met Prince Antonio. They didn't really know each other. The only thing they had in common was Nathan and the hole his death had left in their lives.

But maybe she should hear what he had to say. Maybe he'd give her some crumb of comfort she could give to her mum. That would be worth her feeling even more tired tomorrow morning.

The next few minutes passed in a blur of clearing tables and attending to the last-minute needs of guests, but finally she was done.

Sadie hugged her. 'Thanks so much for helping tonight, Tia. I owe you.'

'That's what friends are for,' Tia said with a smile. 'And you know it's a cause close to my heart.' She'd been in exactly the same position as the children that the charity helped.

'Get a taxi home. I'll pick up the bill,' Sadie said.

Tia shook her head. 'It's fine. I'll get the night tube. The walk will give me a chance to wind down.' After she'd met Prince Antonio. Not that she planned to tell her friend about *that*.

'Then I'm buying you dinner, some time this week. No arguments,' Sadie said.

'That would be good. Depending on how Mum is,' Tia added swiftly. No way was she going out if her mum was having a tough health day. Family came first.

'Or maybe I could bring dinner round for the three of us,' Sadie suggested.

'That might be nicer, if you don't mind. Mum would really like that.' And the company would help to brighten her mum's day.

'Then we'll do it. Check your diary tomorrow and text me with your free dates,' Sadie said.

I'm free every day, Tia thought, but didn't say it. She was just grateful that one of her old school friends actually understood her situation enough to make the effort to stay in touch. Grace had encouraged her to make a life for herself; even though her grades hadn't been good enough for her to train as a teacher, Grace had suggested other ways into the classroom. Tia could work as a classroom assistant or at a playgroup, perhaps, or maybe she could do a foundation course at university and then do her degree and train as a teacher. But Tia hadn't wanted to leave her mum, knowing that Grace's health really wasn't good. Being away from home would've left her worrying that her mum was struggling, and eventually Tia had convinced her mother that she was much happier staying where she was.

'I will,' she promised.

Instead of leaving the hotel, Tia took the lift up to the penthouse suite. A man in a very ordinary suit leaned casually against the wall opposite the lifts as the doors opened, but Tia wasn't fooled; it was obvious that he was the Prince's security officer.

'Ms Phillips.' It was a statement, not a question. He clearly knew who she was and was expecting her. 'Would you like to come with me?'

It was a polite enough question, but she knew there wasn't a real choice. It was accompany him or go straight back down in the lift.

'Thank you,' she said.

He ushered her over to the door of the penthouse suite, and knocked. 'Your guest has arrived, sir.'

Not 'Your Royal Highness'? Or maybe he was from the Casavallian military.

'Thank you, Giacomo,' Antonio said as he opened the door. 'Please come in, Ms Phillips.'

The carpet was the sort that you sank into when you walked on it. One wall of the sitting room was pure glass, looking out over the Thames; it was late enough that the lights from the bridge and the buildings on the other bank were reflected on the dark water of the river.

'Thank you for coming. May I offer you a drink? Champagne?'

This was her cue to refuse politely and ask him to just get on with it and see what he had to say. But since he had offered refreshment and she'd been on her feet all day and all evening…

'Actually, Your Royal Highness, I could really do with a cup of tea.'

'Of course.' He smiled then. 'You're very like your brother. At the end of the day, most of the team would relax with a cold beer. But Nathan said nothing could refresh you like a cup of tea.'

She could almost hear her brother's voice saying the words, and it put a lump in her throat.

'Strong enough to stand a spoon up in. One sugar. A dash of milk. And in a mug, not a cup,' he added.

That was when she knew for sure that he really had been close to Nathan. Because it was exactly what her brother would've said. And all of a sudden she felt a bit less wary of him.

'I remember,' she said, her breath catching.

'Do you take yours the same way?' he asked.

Normally she was just grateful if her tea was hot. 'Yes. Thank you, Your Royal Highness.'

And he actually made the mug of tea for her himself. No calling room service, no pretensions. Were princes supposed to be like this?

And, she noticed, he joined her in drinking tea. He didn't take sugar in his, though.

'Cheers,' he said, lifting his mug in a toast. 'To Nathan.'

She lifted her own mug. 'To Nathan.'

'You must miss him terribly. As do I.' He looked at her. 'I'm sorry I haven't kept in touch, Miss Phillips. Life is a little bit complicated at the moment.'

'Complicated?'

He shrugged. 'My father died not long after Nathan was killed. Obviously my older brother will be the one to succeed him, but there's a lot of political stuff to sort out.'

She'd had no idea that he'd lost his father, too. 'My condolences on the loss of your father, Your Royal Highness,' she said formally.

'Thank you. I know you've been in that situation.'

'Except I was ten when Dad died,' she said. 'He was killed in action, too.'

'That's tough for you,' he said. 'Losing your father and your brother the same way.'

'It's one of the reasons why I worked here tonight,' she said. 'I wanted to do my bit to help the charity.' To support children who'd been bereaved the way she had, because she knew what it felt like.

'You were a volunteer tonight?' He sounded surprised.

'Yes. Though, actually, my day job's in a café.' A proper Italian café, run by a middle-aged couple from Naples who'd taken her to their hearts and who always sent her home after her shift with treats for her mum.

'It's good of you to help. Thank you.' He paused. 'How is your mother?'

'Fine.' It wasn't strictly true, although thankfully this week Grace was having a good patch where she was fully mobile and not quite as exhausted. Chronic fatigue syndrome was the kind of illness that had peaks and troughs, and Tia knew that a good week like this would be balanced out by one where her mother could barely get out of bed and would need a lot more help with day-to-day things.

'I'm sorry. I should've kept in touch.'

'Or come to his funeral.' The rebuke tumbled out before she could stop it.

He inclined his head. 'My apologies. I intended to be there. But I was called away on a mission, and it wasn't one that I could delegate to someone else.'

That hadn't occurred to her. It was a valid excuse, she supposed, though she still thought he could've sent her mother a personal note.

As if he'd guessed at what she was thinking, he said, 'I did write a letter to apologise for my absence.'

'Mum didn't get any letter from you.'

He frowned. 'I'm sorry it didn't arrive. I promise you, I did write.'

'It must've got lost in the post. That's not your fault.' Though he hadn't followed up on his note after his mission. Surely he could've found the time to at least call her mother?

He took a deep breath. 'What can I do to help?'

'Nothing,' she said immediately. They didn't need to lean on anyone. She and Grace were doing just fine on their own. They had their routines and they had good friends to support them. They didn't need a prince throwing money at them to salve his conscience.

'Nathan said you were proud and independent,' Antonio said gently. 'Which is a good thing. But your brother was part of my team. My friend. And, despite what you must think, my team are like family to me. If I can help to make life easier, Miss Phillips, please let me know. Nathan wouldn't have wanted you to struggle.'

He was offering her a financial handout? She kept her temper with difficulty and said politely, 'Thank you, Your Royal Highness, but we're managing just fine as we are.'

'I didn't intend to offend you,' he said. 'Just...' For a

moment, he looked racked with guilt. 'I couldn't do anything to save your brother.'

'It wasn't your fault that he was killed. And Nathan knew the risks of the job before he signed up for it.' She knew her brother had wanted to follow in their father's footsteps.

'I know. But it doesn't stop me missing him.'

Then he looked shocked, as if he hadn't meant to say that out loud.

And again that bleakness was back in his eyes for a moment before he managed to hide it again.

Prince Antonio, despite his privileged upbringing, seemed lonely, deep inside. Right now she'd been given a glimpse of the man behind the cool, collected mask. And she could almost hear her brother's voice echoing in her head: *He could do with a hug.*

Which would be way outside official protocol. Then again, some things were more important than protocol. So Tia put her mug on the coffee table, walked over to Prince Antonio, put his mug on the coffee table next to hers, and wrapped her arms around him.

For a long, long time, he just stood there, unmoving; but then, just as she was about to apologise and take a step backwards, he wrapped his arms around her and held her back, warm and comforting.

She really, really had intended it as comfort. *Just* comfort. Sharing their grief.

But one of them—she wasn't sure which of them—moved, and his cheek was pressed against hers. Her skin tingled where it touched his. Another tiny movement—hers? His?—and the corners of their mouths were touching.

The tingle spread.

Another infinitesimally small shift, and then his mouth was brushing against hers.

She shouldn't be doing this.

He was a prince and she was a waitress. Their lives were so far apart, it was untrue. Neither of them was in a position to start any kind of relationship. He had official duties and she was busy working and looking after her mother. Nothing could possibly come of this.

But the temptation to take comfort from him and to comfort him in turn was so strong.

Maybe this was something they both needed. Just for one night. No strings.

Because, just as Antonio had shown no emotion when he'd come to tell them the news about Nathan, Tia had locked her own tears away because she'd needed to be strong for her mother.

When he broke the kiss and looked into her eyes, she could see the tears glittering there, the emotion he was trying so hard to repress.

Maybe tonight they could cry together. Find a release together. Comfort each other. *Heal* each other.

Just for tonight.

'Stay with me, Tia?' he whispered.

Common sense said that she should leave. She was due at work tomorrow morning. And there was her mother to think about.

But Becky was only next door if she was needed. Tia could drink coffee tomorrow rather than tea to get her through her shift. Right now, Antonio needed her—and she needed him.

She laid her palm against his cheek. 'Yes.'

He kissed her again, scooped her into his arms and carried her to his bed.

CHAPTER ONE

November

THERE WAS NO other way round it, Tia thought, curving a protective hand around her bump.

Miles Montague, the palace secretary, had been perfectly polite to her just now. But, just as he'd done with every single one of her previous calls, he'd rebuffed her, refusing to put her through to Antonio. She'd begged him to pass on a message, asking Antonio to call her. She'd told Miles that she knew the Prince, and it was really important that she speak to him.

But Miles had left her with the impression that, as an eligible bachelor, Prince Antonio had hundreds of women calling, claiming they 'knew' him because they had shaken his hand once or attended an event where he was on the guest list. The palace secretary clearly thought she was just another in a long line of unwanted callers, and he wasn't going to put her through.

Miles had been kind enough. He'd asked her if he could help. He'd asked her to tell him what the problem was.

But how could she let news like *this* go through a third party, no matter how discreet he seemed or how well she knew Antonio? This was something she needed to tell the Prince herself. That their one night together, the night that was supposed to give them both comfort and never be referred to again, had had consequences.

She'd tried to explain that Antonio knew her brother; but Miles had asked in that kind but immovable way exactly *how* Antonio knew her brother, and she'd ended up in tears of frustration.

How could the palace secretary not even know the names of the people who were on Antonio's team in the international alliance? Surely he'd know information like that?

Frustrated and miserable, she'd ended the call.

She'd tried a dozen times now to talk to Antonio, to tell him about the baby.

And failed a dozen times, too.

She didn't have his email address, and even if she did she suspected that someone else—probably Miles Montague, or one of his team—would check through the messages before they reached Antonio, weeding out the ones they judged unimportant or inappropriate, which would definitely include hers. The same would go for letters. Any message she left would be blocked just as effectively as her phone calls had been blocked.

It left her with no other alternative. She'd have to go to Casavalle herself to tell him about the baby. Face to face.

If she sat on Antonio's doorstep and refused to budge, they'd have to let her talk to him. And she could tell him the news—well, as she was six months pregnant, he'd be able to see that quite well enough for himself, she thought wryly—and then leave.

Originally, she hadn't intended to tell him at all. She hadn't realised for a couple of months that she was pregnant; then, when she'd finally realised her period was a lot later than usual and did a test, she'd seen the centre spread in the celebrity magazine she'd bought for her mum as a

treat. A story about Prince Antonio of Casavalle, speculating which of the four women who'd graced his arm that
month might be his future bride.

How ironic. Tia had thought she'd had a glimpse of the
real Prince, the man her brother had been friends with—
but maybe he was exactly what the media said he was.
He hadn't really needed her to comfort him, that night,
because he had strings of women ready to comfort him.
And she'd been so angry at herself for being a fool that it
had taken her mum another month to talk her round into
telling Antonio about her pregnancy.

Six weeks later, she still hadn't told him—though not
for the want of trying.

She grimaced. She didn't expect anything from him,
either for herself or for the baby, and she certainly wasn't
looking for a cash handout or anything like that. Antonio
had been her brother's friend, and she owed it to him to
tell him that the baby existed. And that was the limit of
their obligations to each other, because their lives were
too different for anything else to happen.

She flicked into the Internet. The cheapest flight to
Casavalle would get her in at about half-past eight tomorrow evening. She had no idea how far it was from
the airport to the palace, but even though she wouldn't
have to wait to collect her luggage she would still have
to go through airport security and customs. Maybe she'd
get to the palace at ten p.m.—which was way too late for
anyone to be admitted to the palace offices.

To get there for the early afternoon… She scanned the
flight schedules. She'd have to leave London really early
in the morning and change planes at Rome, and she'd
have a two-hour layover in between. Plus the flight was
a lot more expensive. It was money she could really do
with elsewhere in her budget; but if she got the cheaper

flight and stayed at a hotel overnight, it would cost even more, and she couldn't waste money that she needed to spend on the baby.

She stroked her bump. 'Hopefully we'll find somewhere quiet to sit at the airport, and we'll get a taxi from the airport to the palace.' She'd ask to speak to Miles Montague. And as soon as he saw her he'd realise exactly why it was so important for her to talk to Antonio. Then she could deliver her message—and go home.

Wednesday. 'Hump day', they called it in civilian jobs. The middle of the week.

Except you didn't get a day off from being a prince, Antonio thought.

And you particularly didn't get a day off when you had a long-lost older sister who was very probably going to be the one taking their father's place as the ruler of the kingdom, and an older brother whose fiancée had told him on the eve of their wedding that she was pregnant with her true love's baby, resulting in the royal wedding that the whole country had been looking forward to being cancelled at the last minute. The Asturias family were just as keen as the Valentis to minimise the scandal, so they'd issued a joint statement to the media that the wedding had been cancelled due to 'irreconcilable differences' between the bride and groom.

Luca, wanting to get away from the palace, had gone to meet their long-lost half-sister Gabriella in Canada; which meant that, instead of their original plan of Antonio being the one to go over and meet Gabriella, he was stuck here.

In charge of the country.

Something he'd never really expected to happen, despite being third in line to the throne. He'd thought his father would go on for ever, and then Luca would take over, and then Luca and Princess Meribel would have children who would be next in line.

But, this last year, their lives had been turned upside down. Everything he'd thought he knew turned out not to be true.

Life at the palace was turning out to be much more stressful than taking part in dangerous missions in the army. At least as a soldier Antonio had known what he was doing. He'd had a strategy. He'd had a team he could rely on. They were all working on the same side; his team listened to him, as their leader, and he'd had a brilliant second-in-command in Nathan. In Casavalle, things were nowhere near as clear cut. It was so easy to misinterpret words and put the wrong spin on things; the most innocent comment could swiftly turn into a political nightmare.

Just one day, he thought wistfully. He'd love to have just one single day where he could have the time to gather his thoughts instead of constantly firefighting and dealing with political situations. Had it been like that for their father? Was that why King Vincenzo had always been so remote and distant, even from his sons, because he'd simply been worn out from watching every single word or expression or gesture?

At the rap on his open door, Antonio looked up to see the palace secretary standing there.

'Good afternoon, Miles. What can I do for you?' he asked, forcing a smile and hoping that whatever the secretary wanted from him wasn't going to mean yet more politics and media attention.

'Sir,' Miles began.

The palace secretary was usually unflappable. Right now he looked distinctly nervous and Antonio's heart sank. Was the palace about to be hit with yet another scandal? They said things came in threes, and a long-lost princess and a broken engagement because the bride was pregnant by someone else definitely counted as two...

This felt like living in a television soap opera. And Antonio wasn't enjoying the drama one little bit. Yet again, he wished he was back in the army. Back in the job he was really good at.

'What is it?' he asked.

'I have someone asking to see you.'

Why would Miles be worried about that? 'Who?' he asked, narrowing his eyes.

'A young lady. Tia Phillips. She said she knows you.'

Tia was here?

Antonio shook himself mentally and damped down that little frisson of desire. Their one night together wasn't going to be repeated. They'd both made it clear that it was for comfort, it was for one night only, and neither of them had any expectations of the other. And Miles didn't need to know anything about that. He just needed to know that Tia was telling the truth. 'Yes, she knows me. I served with her brother.'

Guilt flooded through Antonio. In a way, he'd abandoned Tia twice, now—the first time after he'd told her that her brother had been killed, because he hadn't known how to deal with it; then he'd been called back to work, and after that his father had died and he'd been busy with official duties. The second time had been that night in London following the charity gala, when they'd ended up comforting each other in bed. Tia had vanished early the next morning before he'd awoken, leaving him a note explaining that she was due at work.

Which had pretty much let him off the hook.

Part of him had felt relieved, because it meant he didn't have to unpick his feelings and deal with them; but part of him had felt guilty about sleeping with his best friend's little sister. It had been mutual comfort, but he still felt responsible. And he'd planned to call her to see if there was anything he could do to help her mother. He wasn't that much of a cad, no matter that the media liked to call him a playboy who would never settle down. The only true bit about the media's claims was that he didn't want to settle down; he kept his love affairs short and very discreet. And he always made it very clear that he wasn't offering his girlfriends a future. That the relationship was just for now, not for ever.

But, as he'd been about to call Tia, that morning, his mother had called him with the news about Gabriella and her potential claim to the throne. Queen Maria had needed her youngest son to come home to discuss the situation with her and help her to plan what they should do next; and it would all have to be done confidentially because she hadn't wanted to put the extra pressure on Luca, who they both thought had quite enough on his plate ruling the country. All thoughts of Tia had flown out of his head and he'd gone straight back to Casavalle without getting in touch with her.

Antonio and the Queen had been close to working out how to deal with the situation about Gabriella when Princess Meribel dropped her bombshell and Luca's wedding was cancelled. Everything had gone haywire after that, and in the last month Antonio felt as if he'd barely had a moment to breathe.

'She's telephoned the palace a few times,' Miles said, 'but I didn't expect her to turn up here.'

Tia had called a few times? Why? 'Why didn't you put her through?' Antonio asked.

Miles winced. 'I didn't want to repeat the mistake I made with Gabriella's letter to Queen Maria.'

Gabriella's letter. The bombshell that had made it

through to the Queen because it was marked 'Personal and Confidential'. Luca had been quite hard on the palace secretary about it, and Miles had been extremely vigilant about which messages made it through to the family ever since.

But Antonio was the youngest child, and he was pretty sure he was more approachable than his father had been—or even his elder brother. And surely Miles had known him for long enough to realise that Antonio wouldn't go all cold and icy on him if he made a mistake? Things happened unexpectedly; you just had to deal with them efficiently and effectively as they came up.

'And now she's here, wanting to see you,' Miles continued.

Antonio smiled, wanting to reassure the secretary. 'That's fine. As I said, I worked with her brother. He was a good friend. I can spare a few minutes to talk to her. Where is she?'

'In my office,' Miles said. 'But, sir, before you go to meet her, you need to know that she's making some quite outlandish claims. She says she's six months pregnant—and she says the baby is yours.'

'She *what*?' Antonio felt as if someone had just winded him.

'She's pregnant. Very pregnant.' Miles winced. 'You can see the baby moving in her stomach.'

Antonio counted back in his head. May. They'd slept together in May.

And now it was November.

Six months.

Antonio was pretty sure that this wasn't a situation like his brother's, where Princess Meribel had been at the point of possibly passing off another man's baby as Luca's. Nathan had been proud of his little sister, proud

of her independence and her loyalty and her resourceful-
ness. Antonio believed that Tia wouldn't lie about something like this.

Plus the timing fitted exactly.

'But of course the baby can't be yours,' Miles said.

Oh, yes, it could.

Six months.

Tia must've known she was pregnant for at least three
of those months, probably more. Why on earth hadn't she
said anything to him before?

Then again, Miles had said she'd called a few times
but he hadn't put her through. Clearly Tia *had* tried to
talk to him and she'd been gently put aside by the palace secretary.

'How long has she been trying to get in touch with
me?' Antonio asked.

'A few weeks,' Miles admitted.

So she must've tried to tell him almost as soon as she
knew about the baby, then. If Miles had been stonewall-
ing her for weeks, coming here must've been the last resort for her because she'd had no other way to get in touch
with him—apart from going to the media and causing his
family maximum embarrassment, and that just didn't fit
with what he knew of Nathan's little sister.

'I spoke to Prince Luca about it,' Miles continued, 'and
he agreed it was most likely she'd seen your photograph in
a magazine, decided she was in love with you and made
up a story to—'

'Hang on. *Luca* knew about this?' Antonio cut in.

'That she'd called you. Not about the baby.' Miles
squirmed. 'I only found out about that today, when I saw
her. The bump is, um, quite noticeable.'

Antonio groaned. 'We'll discuss this later. Luca, too.
But I need to see her. Now.'

'You mean she's telling the truth, sir?'

'Yes,' Antonio said grimly, the guilt he felt at sleeping with his friend's little sister intensifying by the second. Not only had he slept with her, he'd made her pregnant. 'The timing matches up, so I'm pretty sure the baby's mine.' And he sprinted out of the room towards Miles's office.

Tia felt sick—and it was nothing to do with her pregnancy and everything to do with the situation. What *had* she been thinking, coming here? Now Miles Montague had left her in his office, her surroundings sank in. She was in a palace—a *palace*, for pity's sake. People like her didn't go to palaces, not unless they were visiting a stately home or museum while on holiday. This was surreal.

And just how was Antonio going to react to the news? With shock? Dismay? Horror? She'd told herself all the way here that his reaction didn't matter, that she'd deliver the news and walk away—but it *did* matter, now she was here. And a tiny, very foolish part of her couldn't help hoping that he'd be thrilled to see her and would sweep her into his arms…

Of course that wasn't going to happen. She was six months pregnant, and he certainly wouldn't try to lift her. And this was his territory. He'd be every inch the cold, snooty Prince who'd told her that her brother had been killed.

Right on cue, Antonio strolled into the room, all cool and calm and unruffled. He didn't even bat an eyelash or look remotely shocked; just as she'd guessed, he was totally cold. And that tiny, daft bit of her that had been hoping for the impossible simply shrivelled and died.

Worst of all, the flare of attraction she'd felt towards him was still there. Stronger, if anything, now she knew what it felt like to spend the night in his arms. Even seeing him made her heart feel as if it was doing a somersault.

How stupid was she? He was a prince and she was a waitress. The stories about Cinderella, Snow White, and Beauty and the Beast were just that: fairy stories to entertain children. This was real life; and her life was about as opposite from Antonio's as it was possible to get. They didn't have a future together.

'Good to see you, Tia,' he said.

Was it? His face was so unreadable, she didn't have a clue.

'I trust Miles has offered you some refreshment?' he asked.

'Yes.' And she'd refused. All she'd wanted was to see Antonio, deliver her message and leave so she could catch her plane home. Now she was here, she *really* wanted to leave.

He looked at the clear desk in front of her and frowned. 'I'll organise some tea. That is, assuming you can drink tea?'

She knew what he was referring to; but she was well past the morning sickness stage. 'Thank you, but no thank you. I'm not staying.'

He said nothing, simply tipped his head slightly to one side to indicate that he was listening to whatever she had to say. He looked every inch a prince, and incredibly remote and forbidding.

She lifted her chin. 'I just came to let you know the situation.'

'That you're six months pregnant, according to Miles. You could have—'

Told him? OK, so she'd waited a month, not wanting to talk to the Playboy Prince. But for the six weeks since her mother had persuaded her to talk to him, she'd been trying, and it stung that he was making her feel as if *she* was the bad guy. 'I tried,' she cut in quietly. 'I rang the palace. More than once, actually. But I didn't want to leave a message about this. I wanted to tell you myself. Mr Montague wouldn't put me through to you when I called. In case you'd lost my number, I left it again. But, as you didn't call me back, I assumed he didn't tell you that I'd called.'

She didn't have a clue about how he was reacting to this. Was he shocked, angry, horrified? This man had inscrutability down to a fine art.

'It meant that coming to tell you in person was my only option. So now you know.'

He hadn't made a single move towards her. That night in London… Well, obviously Antonio had drawn a line under that, a long time ago. They both had. Neither of them had expected consequences. Although she'd left him that note, and a tiny bit of her had hoped that he'd call her, she hadn't really expected him to do anything. That night was what it was. A one-night stand.

Then the reality of it hit her. She'd assumed that Miles Montague hadn't passed on the message. Maybe he *had* given Prince Antonio the message, but the Prince simply hadn't wanted to return her call. How could she have been so stupid?

She clearly wasn't wanted here, and neither was the baby.

Though she'd expected Antonio not to want to know, she'd had time to get used to the idea of being a single mum. She'd cope. Coping was what she'd done every day since Nathan had left to join the army and she'd become her mother's sole carer at the age of thirteen. She'd find a way to juggle motherhood, a job and continuing to care for her mum. Giovanni and Vittoria, her bosses at the café, were kind and sympathetic. It would be fine.

She suppressed the memories that had rushed into her head when Antonio had walked into the room—the surge of desire, the memory of the way his skin had felt against hers, his strength combined with surprising gentleness. Although this man was the father of her baby, she had to remember that first and foremost he was a prince—and her feelings towards him were completely inappropriate, as well as completely unwanted by him.

She didn't even know what to call him.

Your Royal Highness? Prince Antonio?

Considering that they'd spent the night together...

It was all too much for her. She didn't want to stay in this cold, formal palace a minute longer than she had to. She wanted to leave. *Now.* 'Excuse me. I have a flight to catch.' She stood up, gathered her coat under her arm and turned away.

Antonio reached out and touched her shoulder, gently making her turn to face him again. 'Tia. Please stay. We need to talk.'

Even though there was soft cotton between his skin and hers, the contact was enough to stir up old memories, making her skin tingle. Which was completely inappropriate, and it made her feel so out of sorts that she snapped, 'There's nothing to talk about.'

His gaze flicked down to her bump and up to her face again. 'I rather think there is.'

'Look, I'm not expecting anything from you. I haven't come here looking for financial support or anything like that. I'm not planning to sell an exclusive to the gossip columns. I just thought you had a right to know about the baby's existence, that's all.'

'Thank you for telling me. And I'm sorry that the palace made it difficult for you to get in touch with me.'

So was she. But, when she thought about it, she could

kind of understand it. 'You're a prince. For all they knew, I could've been some crazed stalker.'

'You're the sister of my best friend,' Antonio said.

And the mother of his child. Though he hadn't said as much.

'And yet again I owe you an apology. I seem to be making a habit of not contacting you.'

He could say that again.

He'd done it twice now. She wasn't setting herself up for a third mistake, where Antonio Valenti was concerned. How did the saying go? Fool me once, shame on you. Fool me twice, shame on me.

She'd been quite enough of a fool. Though at least he wasn't offering some flimsy excuse. On the other hand, a simple 'sorry' might have been nice. He'd said he owed her an apology, but he hadn't actually given her an apology, had he?

'Tia, please stay. I'm still in the middle of processing the fact that I'm going to be a father,' he said. 'And we have a lot to talk about. But, first, I'm going to organise that cup of tea. And you've come all the way from London, so I'm guessing you haven't had anything to eat.'

'I had a sandwich on the plane.' Half a sandwich. It had made her feel sick. Or maybe that had been nerves at the idea of coming here to tell Antonio about the baby.

'Airline food,' Antonio said, 'isn't the most wonderful.'

'I don't want to bother your kitchen staff.'

He smiled. 'You won't be bothering them. Come to my apartment. I'll make you a mug of tea and a sandwich myself. Or pasta.' He spread his hands. 'Or whatever it is you'd like to eat.'

She blinked at him, trying to take it in. He was offering to make her some food? Seriously? 'But princes don't cook.'

'They do if they're in the army,' he said. 'If they want their team to respect them, they take their turn doing everything. And I mean everything. I've done my share of cleaning duties, too.'

'Oh.' She really hadn't expected that. Even though he'd made her a mug of tea himself, that night in London.

'Come with me,' he said. 'And I'll carry your bags.'

'I don't have any luggage. I have a seat on the late flight back to London via Rome, tonight,' she said. 'I only came to tell you about the baby. I wasn't planning to stay.'

'Don't go. Please.' He blew out a breath. 'We really do have a lot to talk about. I don't know if you've followed the news about Casavalle, but an awful lot has been going on here. It's wall-to-wall scandal sheet stuff. The media is going to take one look at you, rub their hands with glee and start digging for more scandal.'

She hadn't thought of that. 'But they don't know why I'm here.'

'They'll speculate. It doesn't matter whether it's true or not. They'll suggest whatever gives them the most readers. They'll talk to anyone who knows you and dredge up any hint of scandal. Your mother is going to be a sitting target for them. From now until at least when the baby's born, you're all going to need my protection,' he continued. 'Which includes the help of Miles Montague. And, as you know, almost nothing gets through Miles. Even when sometimes it should.'

There was a rap on the office door.

'Yes,' Antonio said.

The palace secretary himself opened the door to his office. 'Sir? Miss Phillips? Is everything all right?' he asked, looking concerned.

'It will be,' Antonio said. 'Miles, I'll brief you properly later. But for now this isn't to be discussed anywhere or with anyone—and that includes my mother, Luca and Gabriella.'

There was a slight note of warning in his tone, and the older man flushed as he walked over to his desk. 'Of course, sir.'

Antonio sighed. 'I'll talk to them when I'm ready,' he said, and this time his voice was a little gentler. 'If anyone needs me urgently in the next hour or so, we'll be in my apartment. But I'd appreciate it if you could stall anyone if possible, Miles. Tia and I really need to talk in private and without interruptions.'

'Of course. If you need anything…'

Antonio patted his shoulder. 'You're there. I know. And I'm grateful for that.'

Miles nodded, then looked at Tia, his expression awkward. 'I apologise, Miss Phillips, for earlier. When you called the office, and when you first came here.'

It had upset her, but she could understand why he'd acted that way. 'You were doing your job,' she said. 'Protecting the Prince.'

'And Tia's going to be under your protection now, too,' Antonio said. 'I'll brief you shortly. Tia, come with me.' He looked at her and added swiftly, 'Please.'

Good. Because she wasn't Antonio's subject or his employee, and she wasn't going to let him order her about.

The palace had seemed daunting enough from the outside: a massive white stone building with towers and turrets and spires and huge windows; a long driveway lined with enormous Norway spruces covered alternately with blue and white lights; and huge entrance doors at the top of the sweeping granite steps. Tia had found the interior even more daunting, with the enormous foyer that felt more like a cathedral space, with a Christmas tree that had to be a good forty feet tall; the angel on top was close to touching the ceiling, and it was beautifully decorated with what looked like priceless one-of-a-kind baubles, one of which seemed to be in a special display. Crowds actually came in to the palace to see the tree, which was how Tia had managed to slip in and ask to see the palace secretary in the first place.

It was magnificent. But it was also very formal, and it didn't leave her with the warmth she felt with their own Christmas tree back in London, with its decorations that had been collected year after year by her mother and every single one of them had meaning and memories. Their rather threadbare artificial Christmas tree didn't go up until the week before Christmas; here, it was early November and already everything was in its place. Then again, she supposed, things were different with the public rooms of a palace; visitors would expect to see decorations on display this early.

Behind the beautiful garlands of fir and pine on the mantels and staircases, the rooms were richly decorated, with cream walls and lots of gold everywhere. There were huge windows, large mirrors that reflected the light back from the windows and the crystal and gold chandeliers and made the rooms seem even more massive, ceilings covered with priceless paintings, Christmas trees in every room whose decorations she suspected had been put in place with a ruler measuring the precise distance between each one, enormous exotic poinsettias gracing side tables, sweeping staircases leading into long corridors, luxurious carpets you literally sank into as you walked on them…

It was another world, one where the likes of Tia could never fit in.

And it was overwhelming.

Tia was aware that Antonio was talking to her as he ushered her up the sweeping staircase to his first-floor apartment, but she couldn't concentrate on what he was saying. All she could see was the regal magnificence of their surroundings, and it left her feeling more and more out of place.

Finally he opened a door and indicated to her to enter.

His sitting room was much more ordinary than the rest of the palace. The furniture here didn't look too antique and too priceless to touch, let alone sit on, and to her relief there was much less gold in evidence. There were photographs on the mantelpiece in what looked like solid gold frames, mainly of what she assumed was Antonio's family; but there were also photographs of Antonio's team in the army, and tears pricked her eyelids when she recognised her brother among them.

'Let me get you that tea,' Antonio said, ushering her into the kitchen—a sizeable room by normal standards, but thankfully smaller than the rooms she'd seen so far in the palace.

'Thank you. That would be nice.'

'What would you like to eat?'

She shook her head. 'Thank you, but I'm not really hungry.'

He gave her a speaking look. 'You're pregnant. You need to eat.'

She didn't reply but, a couple of minutes later, she found herself sitting at his kitchen table with a mug of tea made just how she liked it and a chicken salad sandwich.

'I really didn't expect you to—' she began.

'Eat,' he cut in. 'Then we'll talk.'

It left her with no choice but to follow his instructions. And she had to admit that the sandwich and the mug of tea did make her feel better. He didn't say a word until she'd finished, simply sipped his tea.

And then he looked at her. 'OK. So, first off,' he said gently, 'how are you?'

'I'm fine.'

'*Really* fine? Because I know some women have a tough time in pregnancy.'

She shrugged. 'I had a bit of morning sickness in the early weeks. Nothing out of the usual.' She opened her handbag, took out a photograph and handed it to him. 'I wanted to give you this.'

'Thank you,' he said politely.

'It's our baby. From the twenty-week scan, last month.'

'Our baby,' he echoed.

She still had absolutely no idea what he was thinking, what he was feeling. His voice and his face were completely expressionless as he looked at the photograph. On the surface he was all urbane charm, just as a prince should be. But was he shocked? Horrified? Secretly pleased? She didn't have a clue. Who was the real man behind the royal facade?

'So,' he said. 'I'll ask you the difficult question first. Do you plan to keep the baby?'

'It's way too late for a termination.' Not that she'd wanted that, in any case.

'I didn't mean that. Were you planning to give the baby up for adoption after the birth?'

'No.'

'So you're keeping him. Or her.'

Not 'it'. She was grateful that at least he hadn't said *that*. 'Yes.'

'Then I have financial responsibilities towards you.'

'That isn't why I came. I can manage.' It would be a struggle, but she was used to that. She'd muddle through, the way she always had, working whatever hours she could fit in around the baby and her mum.

'Tia, this is a Valenti baby,' he said. 'There are expectations. If nothing else, this baby…' He sucked in a breath. 'The way things stand, this baby could be fourth in line to the throne.'

She looked at him in shock. 'What? How?'

'It's been a bit complicated around here. Which is why I didn't get in touch with you after…London.'

The night they'd spent together.

The night that clearly hadn't meant anything to him.

The night that had resulted in their baby.

'Uh-huh,' she said, in an attempt to be as cool and calm and collected as he seemed, though inside she wanted to yell at him.

'You left me that note and I fully intended to call you later that day, after your shift,' Antonio said. 'But, that morning, my mother called me to tell me about Gabriella—my father's daughter from his first marriage, except none of us had any idea she even existed until quite recently. My mother needed to talk to me about it and help her decide how to deal with the situation. She wanted to talk to me because Luca already had enough on his plate, ruling the country and preparing to be King. I had to come straight back to Casavalle, because my family needed me.'

Tia could understand that. It was the same for her and for Nathan: they'd been there for their mother because she was their family and she needed them.

'And I'm afraid my mind was so focused on the situation at home, I didn't think to contact you. I'm sorry.'

Tia had been hurt when Antonio hadn't been in touch after the charity gala, even though she knew she was being ridiculous about it: of course a prince wasn't going to fall for a mere waitress. Of course he wanted nothing more from her than their night of passion. It had been a one-off thing. But now she was seeing things from a different perspective. Antonio was part of a much bigger picture.

'At the moment we're waiting for DNA results, but my mother, Luca and I all think it's very probable that Gabriella is indeed the oldest child of our father, which means she's entitled to accede to the throne and rule Casavalle. She has no children, which makes my brother Luca her heir and puts him second in line to the throne. Luca also has no children; although Princess Meribel, his former fiancée, is pregnant, the baby isn't Luca's. So that makes me Luca's heir and third in line to the throne; and that means our baby is my heir and fourth in line to the throne.' He shrugged. 'Though if we're wrong about the DNA test or Gabriella decides not to accede to the throne, then everything shifts up one place and our baby will be third in line.'

It hadn't really hit home until that moment, but Tia realised right then that her baby was of royal blood.

A baby in line for a crown.

'I...' She tailed off, hardly able to take in the enormity of the situation.

'As I said,' Antonio continued quietly, 'it's been a little complicated around here. Luca's wedding to Meribel has been planned for a very long time. But Meribel told Luca on the eve of their wedding that she was in love with someone else and was pregnant with his baby, so she couldn't go through with marrying him. We agreed with her family that we'd say the wedding was cancelled due to irreconcilable differences, though the people of Aguilarez—Meribel's kingdom, on the other side of the mountains—assumed that meant Luca had practically jilted her at the altar, and they blamed him for the wedding not happening.

'It was politically...' He grimaced. 'Let's just say it was

a bit sensitive. If we didn't tell the truth, it could lead to a great deal of discord between our countries. Yet if we told the truth—that Meribel was the one to have the affair—then it would be putting the blame on her, and that would be dishonourable.'

Tia didn't quite understand that. 'How could it be dishonourable when *she* was the one who had the affair?'

'It's still dishonourable,' Antonio insisted.

'So whatever you did, you'd lose,' Tia said slowly.

'Something like that. Except then someone leaked the truth of the matter. Not from our side,' he was quick to clarify. 'Meribel is in hiding right now, and it feels as if the media has put Casavalle under a microscope, scrutinising every move any of us makes and spotting every potential scandal.' He looked at her. 'Someone in the palace will have noticed you, and they will have heard you ask to speak to Miles. They will definitely have noticed your bump. So people will be asking questions about you—who are you, and why did you want to speak to the palace secretary? Whose baby are you carrying? They'll be watching for you to leave the palace.

'And the paparazzi don't play nice, Tia. They'll strike up a conversation at the airport and you'll think you're simply chatting to another passenger to pass the time. They'll ask all kinds of questions and pump you for information without you even knowing what they're doing, and the next thing you know it'll be all over the media. They'll dig on the Internet and they'll know everything about you before you get back to London—where you live, where you work, all about your mother's health. They'll follow you and they'll doorstep you.'

'Doorstep me?' She didn't understand.

'They'll wait outside your front door in a gaggle. The back door, too. There's no escape from them. The second you open any door, the flashbulbs will go off and they'll be yelling your name and asking you questions. If you've ever seen it happen in a film, I can assure you that it's been romanticised. In real life, it's much harsher. You have to push your way through the mob, and all the time there will be microphones shoved in your face and flashbulbs going off and people yelling.

'If you say anything, it'll be spun to suit their agenda. If you say nothing, then they'll speculate, and they'll do it with the nastiest implications—and you won't be able to protest because they'll claim they're asking questions, not making a statement. Your life won't be your own.'

That hadn't occurred to her. She'd simply thought to let Antonio know that their night together had had consequences, then quietly go back to London. 'I... Look, if there's a way you can get me from the palace to the airport without them seeing me, then I promise not to talk to a single person until I'm back home with my mum.'

He shook his head. 'It's already too late for that. As I said, things have been complicated around here lately.'

And she'd just added another complication to his life. An illegitimate baby.

Her misery must've shown in her expression, because he took her hand. 'Tia. I know neither of us planned this. But you have my support now and you definitely need my protection. I think we both need to get our heads round the situation, and the middle of a royal palace isn't the best place to do that. I know somewhere quiet we can go for a few days that will give us a chance to think things through and talk about the future.'

'But I wasn't planning to stay here, not even for a night. I don't have even a toothbrush with me, let alone any clean clothes,' Tia protested. 'And my mum's expecting me back home tonight.'

'Then call her. Tell her that you're staying here for a little while.' He paused. 'Give me three days, Tia.'

'Three *days*?' Tia was horrified. 'What if Mum needs me?'

'Do you have a neighbour or a friend nearby who can keep an eye out for her?' Antonio asked. 'Or I can arrange for a nurse to come in and help her, if you prefer.' He looked at her. 'I apologise. Nathan didn't tell me much about your mother's condition, other than that she'd been poorly since you were small. And I was brought up not to ask personal questions. So I'm afraid I don't know how ill she is.'

'Mum has chronic fatigue syndrome,' Tia said. 'It used to be called ME—myalgic encephalomyelitis.'

When Antonio looked blank, she continued, 'After Dad was killed in action, Mum went down with a virus, and we think that's what triggered the CFS because she never really recovered. It's a bit like having the flu, with joint pains and a headache you simply can't shift, and absolute exhaustion—but it doesn't go away after a couple of weeks, like the flu does. She has it all the time. So she needs to rest a lot.

'It's a variable condition; some days she's fine and to look at her you'd never know she was ill, and other days she can barely get out of bed. And she's *not* lazy or stupid. It's not like when you're feeling just a bit tired after a busy day—she gets absolutely exhausted and physically can't do anything. If she has a day when she's feeling really well and overdoes things, then she'll really pay for it for a few days afterwards. She has to be careful.'

'And you look after her?'

'Yes, and I don't begrudge a second of it. I love her. She's my mum.' Growing up, Tia had had days when she'd wished her life had been more like that of her friends, where she'd had time to do homework and hang out with her friends and meet boys, instead of struggling to keep up with her studies and worrying that her mum's condition was getting worse, and never starting a relationship because she knew it couldn't go anywhere. But she'd done her best to hide it from her mother, because she loved Grace and didn't want her mother to feel as if she was a burden.

Grace had encouraged her to go out with her friends, but Tia didn't like leaving her mum, except when she went to work and she was only just round the corner and could rush back if there was an emergency.

'Tia,' he said gently, 'we're going to need to talk about the best way to support your mother when you have a small baby to look after as well. Because you're not going to be able to do everything.'

Oh, yes, she could. She always had. 'It'll be fine.' She lifted her chin. 'I'll manage. We always do.'

Meaning that she'd struggle and drive herself into the ground.

Antonio was shocked by the sheer protectiveness he felt towards her. And it wasn't just because she was his best friend's little sister. There was something about Tia Phillips. She was brave and strong and independent, not looking for the easy way out—she'd been very explicit that she expected nothing from him. He admired her courage; yet, at the same time, he wanted to take some of those burdens away. What she'd just told him, in addition to the little that Nathan had let slip, made him realise that she must've spent most of her life looking after her mother. She'd never really had a normal childhood.

Well, she didn't have to struggle any more. He could support her. Though he was pretty sure that her pride would get in the way and she'd refuse any help. So he needed to gain her trust, first. And that meant being specific rather than vague.

'Come with me to my house in the mountains for three days,' he said. 'Let's give ourselves a bit of time to adjust to the situation, and then we can talk about the baby.'

She looked torn. 'It depends on how Mum is.'

'Call her,' he said. 'Talk to her. See what she thinks. I'll give you some space. I'll be in the sitting room when you're ready.'

'Thank you,' she said.

He left her to it, and went into his sitting room. Babies. This was the third baby shock in a row for the palace: first Gabriella's mother being pregnant and never telling her ex-husband, King Vincenzo, about the baby and running away without telling him; then Princess Meribel's affair ending in her being pregnant by another man; and now Tia expecting a baby after their one night together.

The media would have a field day. And, although he had the resources to ride out the storm, Tia was vulnerable.

There was only one solution to this.

But he didn't think it was going to be an easy solution. He was going to have to tread very carefully indeed.

Grace Phillips answered on the third ring.

'How are you, Mum?' Tia asked.

'I'm fine,' Grace said, a little too quickly for Tia's liking. 'Did you get to see Prince Antonio?'

'I did.' She sighed. 'Mum, he wants me to stay for a few days—three days, he said. He wants to talk things over.'

'That's a good idea,' Grace said.

'But I don't want to leave you on your own.'

'I'm fine, love. Really. Becky's next door if I need anything.'

'But that was just for today. I can't ask her to keep an eye out for you for three whole days.'

'You don't have to. I'll ask her,' Grace said. 'And I'm not overdoing things, before you start worrying. I can manage.'

Tia wasn't so sure. 'But what if you have a bad day tomorrow?'

'Then Becky will help,' Grace said. 'You need to talk to Prince Antonio, for the baby's sake. And for yours.'

'Mum, I…'

'I know he's from a different world,' Grace said gently, 'but Nathan always said he was a good man. Listen to what he has to say.'

'But I can't stay here. I haven't got any clean clothes with me, or even a toothbrush.' This was ridiculous. Tia was used to being independent, sorting things out. Their financial circumstances had taught her to be resourceful. So why did she suddenly feel like bursting into tears?

Maybe that fish-out-of-water feeling showed in her voice, because Grace said, 'I'm sure someone at the palace will be able to lend you something to wear, and you can ask them to launder what you're wearing right now. They must have guests all the time. I'm sure they'll have a spare toothbrush and toiletries, at the very least.'

'I don't want to have to ask. I don't want to be depend—' Then she remembered who she was talking to. Someone who also didn't want to be dependent on others, but who didn't have a choice because of her health.

'Darling, sometimes you have to lean on others,' Grace said, as if guessing what Tia was thinking. 'Don't worry about me. I'll be absolutely fine.'

'And you'll let me know how you are?'

'I'll text you every day while you're away,' Grace said. 'Or I'll call you. But right now you need to put yourself first.'

Something Tia had never done, and it didn't feel right for her to do that now.

As if Grace guessed, she added, 'And the baby.'

Tia thought about it.

OK. She could do this. But only for the baby's sake. And so her mother wouldn't worry.

'All right,' she said. 'But I want you to promise me you'll let me know if you need me, Mum. I mean *really* promise. Otherwise I'm going to worry myself sick about you.'

'I promise,' Grace said. 'Love you, Tia.'

'Love you, too, Mum.'

After Tia ended the call, she went in search of Antonio. He seemed to be checking something on his phone; he looked up when she walked in. 'How's your mother?'

'She's fine.' It was Tia's stock answer.

'So you'll stay here with me for a while?'

'Three days,' she said, 'until we've talked.' But she needed to make it very clear it wasn't for her own sake. 'For the baby's sake.'

'Good.' He smiled at her, and Tia was unnerved to realise that it was the first genuine smile she'd seen from him since she'd been in Casavalle. A smile that actually reached his eyes.

Antonio Valenti was absolutely gorgeous when he smiled. Tall, with melting brown eyes and dark hair that was just a shade longer than it should be for the military.

Not that she should be noticing how attractive he was, or remembering how good it had felt when he'd kissed her and touched her. They didn't have a future. All they needed to do was to talk about the baby and arrange access—if he wanted it, and she had no idea at all what he was thinking.

'And I need to let my bosses know that I'm staying here for longer than I expected,' she added. 'They'll need to arrange cover for me in my absence.'

'Of course. Call them. Then, when you're ready, we'll go to the mountains,' he said. 'My family has a house in a quiet village there—a bolt-hole, if you like. It's where I go when I need some space.'

Because, as a member of the Casavallian royal family, Antonio must live his life virtually in a goldfish bowl. He was always on public view.

'Is there any way we can stop at a shop on the way?' she asked. 'Just... I don't have anything with me. No toiletries, no pyjamas, no clean clothes.' Even if Antonio happened to have a whole wardrobe of things that his previous girlfriends or guests had left behind, it was pretty unlikely that any of them would fit a six-months-pregnant woman.

'Give me a list of everything you need and your clothing size,' he said, 'and I'll arrange things.'

He was probably used to ordering clothes from high-end designers, whereas she bought hers second-hand from charity shops. And her toiletries were supermarket own-brand basics, not from expensive Parisian perfume houses. She couldn't afford to waste money on luxuries. 'That's very kind of you,' she said carefully, 'but I'm not sure your budget would fit mine.'

He sighed. 'Look, it's my fault that you have to stay here for a few days in the first place. So please, Tia, let me buy you a few basics.'

'As long as they *are* basics,' she said. The idea of having to accept things from him made her feel awkward, even though she understood that a prince couldn't exactly go browsing in a charity shop or a supermarket. 'One change of clothes—and I assume I can have access to a washing machine and a tumble-dryer at this house in the mountains?'

'Yes. Give me a list of what you'd like,' Antonio said. 'And then we'll go to Picco Innevato.'

Snowy Peak, she translated mentally. He was taking her to a place called Snowy Peak. Well, he'd said his house was in the mountains, and it was late November. Winter. The name probably suited the place perfectly.

'OK,' she said. 'I assume we'll drive there?'

'No. We'll fly,' he said. 'I have a private jet.'

She blinked at him. 'Of course you do.' A private jet. Something far, far beyond the reach of normal mortals. She hadn't flown very often, and when she had—like today—it was always economy class. It was yet another reminder of the huge gulf between them.

'Tia, it makes sense to fly. Otherwise we'll be driving on difficult roads in the dark,' he said. 'We'll drive to the airport from here and fly over to the mountains, then drive to Picco Innevato from there. And hopefully that will mean the media won't work out where we are—or at least not until we've worked out how to manage the situation.'

Manage the situation. What a horrible way to describe a baby. OK, so she wasn't the only woman in the world who'd had an unplanned pregnancy, but right at that moment she felt more alone and miserable than she ever had before. Every nerve in her body was telling her to run back to London, where she had family and friends. What was the point of staying here to talk to Antonio? He'd made it pretty clear he wasn't interested. She was pretty sure she knew how this was going to end: with her and the baby living anonymously in London. And her baby would be very much loved; whereas here in the palace the baby would be seen as a 'situation'. If only Antonio would let her go back to London now. She'd sign any bit of paper he wanted her to, releasing him from any obligations towards herself or the baby and promising never to talk to the press. Anything. She just wanted to get out of here, be some place where she didn't feel like something people had to scrape off their shoe.

'As you wish,' she said, only just resisting the urge to add 'Your Royal Highness' and tug at her forelock, and concentrated on jotting down her list. The sooner this was over with, the better.

CHAPTER TWO

WHEN TIA HAD given Antonio her list and called her bosses to arrange an extension of her leave, Antonio's driver took them to the airport. Giacomo, one of Antonio's security officer whom she'd met in London on the evening of the charity gala, accompanied them. And it was nothing like Tia's previous experience of the airport. This time, she didn't have to wait in a queue to show her passport to the border officials, or go through any kind of security—presumably because she was travelling with a member of Casavalle's royal family. And the plane itself…

It was quite a bit smaller than the plane she'd flown on from Rome, but the interior wasn't the crammed-in rows of seats she'd experienced. This felt more like an office or a living room than an aeroplane, with deep carpeting, four massive and very comfortable-looking seats, and masses of leg room. There were tables, too, so there was plenty of room for working.

'This is how you fly all the time?' Tia asked, feeling slightly overawed by it all.

'I would normally pilot the plane myself,' Antonio said, 'but I thought you might prefer some company.'

'You can fly a plane?' She regretted the question instantly. How stupid and naive of her. Of course a man like Antonio Valenti would be able to fly a plane.

Antonio shrugged. 'I learned a few years ago.'

'And this is how you travel with your family?'

'Sort of. We don't tend to go to the same events,' he said. 'And we don't travel together. When we were young, Luca and I would travel with our nanny and our security team, not our parents.'

It hadn't occurred to her before, but now she realised that if a disaster happened in the air or on the road, it would mean the ruler and his immediate successors would all be involved. For their country's sake, of course they would have to travel separately.

'Sorry,' she mumbled.

'I'm used to it,' he said gently. 'It's how things are for me. But I realise it's not how normal families are.'

She could barely remember flying anywhere with her parents and Nathan; since her father's death, either her mother hadn't been well enough to travel, or a holiday abroad had been way out of their budget. The most they'd managed in the last three or four years was the occasional day trip to Brighton, and the effort had exhausted her mother for days afterwards.

'Tell me about Picco Innevato,' she said, wanting to change the subject.

'It means "snowy peak".'

She wondered if she should tell him that she'd learned to speak Italian over the years she'd been working for Giovanni and Vittoria, but decided maybe not just yet.

'It's a very pretty village,' he said. 'In winter it serves the ski resort nearby, and in summer people go there for hiking. My family has a house on the outskirts. The villagers are good to me when I visit; they don't ask questions and they treat me as just another neighbour.'

'I guess it must be like living in a goldfish bowl when you're at the palace,' she said.

'The media are keen to know my every movement,' he admitted. 'But in Picco Innevato I can be myself. I spent quite a few summers there as a child, so I made friends with the local children. We played football and ran around in the park together.'

Things she'd taken very much for granted as a child, going to the park with her mother and Nathan and playing on the swings and slide. It had never occurred to her that other children would have a different kind of upbringing, one where they had to watch everything they did and everything they said. 'That's nice,' she said.

'It was. And I think it kept me in touch with our people better than if I'd grown up only at the palace,' he said.

For a moment, he looked sad, but she didn't want to pry. Because then he might ask her awkward questions, too—things she didn't want to answer.

'May I offer you some refreshment?' he asked. 'The flight will take about twenty minutes.'

She would've liked a cup of tea, but as the flight was so short she could wait. 'I'm fine, thank you,' she said.

They made small talk for the rest of the journey, the kind of thing she was very good at from her job at the café, but both of them skirted round the difficult questions they'd need to discuss later. The baby. What Antonio expected from her. Whether he'd let her just go quietly back to London and disappear—which was her preferred option.

Once they'd landed, they were met by another car; this time, Antonio drove them himself, with Tia in the passenger seat next to him and Giacomo in the back of the car.

It wasn't long before they'd gone from the smooth wide roads around the airport to a narrow pass going through the mountains; the scenery was incredibly pretty, with pine trees and a dusting of snow, but the road was full of hairpin bends and there was a sharp drop straight down the mountain on one side of the car. Not wanting to distract Antonio from driving, Tia remained silent and just tried to enjoy the scenery, even though she felt as if she'd stepped into a completely different world. A magical world, like the ones her mother had read stories about when she was small—where the girl was by the side of the handsome prince and there was a happy-ever-after.

She knew it was unrealistic to expect a happy-ever-after. Her world was so different from Antonio's that she would never be able to fit in. Plus she was six months pregnant—something else you never saw in fairy tales. Of course they didn't have a future together.

Yet, out here, with the mountains and snow and fir trees all around, a tiny bit of her began to hope. Maybe they could find a way to work something out. Maybe he could be part of the baby's life. Maybe he could even be part of *her* life, too. Perhaps it was a fantasy and she'd come crashing back down to earth with a bump: but she'd definitely felt a connection with Antonio, the night they'd spent together. Something more than just sex. Something more than physical attraction. Something that made her understand the glances she'd seen between her parents as a child, that sparkle in her mother's eyes and the special smile her father had reserved for her mother. And when Antonio had kissed her, when he'd carried her to his bed, there had been something special and cherishing about his touch…

She shook herself and concentrated on her surroundings. The village of Picco Innevato was incredibly pretty. Honey-coloured stone houses with terracotta tiled roofs nestled together in the main street, and there was a church with a spire. There was a pretty square in the middle of the village with a fountain and, given that she could see people on ladders hanging Christmas lights, a space for what Tia guessed would be an amazing Christmas tree. It was a picture-postcard village—the sort she'd dreamed about when she was growing up, longing for the space of the countryside rather than being stuck in a cramped flat in a dingy part of London.

Antonio stopped at some gates at the far end of the village and tapped in a code. When the gates swung open, he drove down the long driveway and then parked in front of a large honey-coloured stone house. 'Welcome to my bolt-hole,' he said. 'Let me show you around.'

A bolt-hole to Tia meant somewhere small. This house was huge, especially in comparison with the tiny two-bedroomed flat she shared with her mother.

Feeling slightly intimidated, she followed him up the steps to the house.

Downstairs, there was a massive kitchen that was as big as their entire flat. The counter tops were all polished granite, the cupboards and drawers were solid wood and the sort she recognised from magazines as soft-closing, and the floor was terracotta tiles.

Antonio looked in the large American-style fridge and smiled. 'Excellent. Gina's stocked up for us.'

'Gina?'

'Our housekeeper,' he said. 'She lives in the village, rather than here, but I asked her to do some shopping for me.'

It made sense for Antonio's family to have someone looking after the house, as they didn't live here all the time, but Tia was finding it hard to get her head round the idea of having staff. In her world, people *were* staff. Her previous job before the café had been as a cleaner.

'I'll cook for us tonight,' he said.

Clearly he was trying to make her feel more comfortable, and make her feel as if he was an ordinary man rather than a prince.

Except he wasn't.

He was the father of her baby.

He'd asked her to come here with him so they could talk.

And she didn't have a clue about his feelings. Or her own. The whole thing was a muddle. She couldn't afford to fall in love with someone so out of reach, even if he was the father of her baby. But, if she ignored her practical side... Being in the same room as him made her pulse skitter. It was nothing like the way she'd felt when she'd been on dates in the past. This was something that made her catch her breath, made her feel as if fireworks were going off all around her and lighting up the sky.

And she didn't know what to do about it.

Was it possible that he felt the same? This whole mixed-up yearning and wishing and wondering? Or was she just kidding herself and setting herself up for disappointment?

She forced herself to smile. 'Thank you. And I will do the washing up.'

'We'll share the washing up,' he said.

A prince, doing the washing up?

Then again, he'd told her that in the army he'd done exactly the same tasks as everyone else in his team, including cleaning. And he'd told her that this place was his bolt-hole. So maybe being a prince wasn't the lifestyle he would've chosen for himself.

He showed her around the rest of the ground floor. There was an office, a dining room with a table that seated twelve, and two large sitting rooms, both with plenty of room for several comfortable sofas and armchairs. One had a state-of-the-art television, and the other had a piano and a wall full of books. And finally there was an enormous conservatory with a view over a large and very neat garden, with the mountains looming behind.

'We're lucky here. We can see the sun setting behind the mountains in the evening, and then at sunrise, when the mountains are covered in snow, it looks all pink,' he said.

'That's lovely,' she said, but her voice must've shown that this kind of luxury and space made her feel out of place.

'Tia,' he said gently, 'it's all relative. I know this is a bit big for a normal person's bolt-hole, but please remember it isn't just my house. It belongs to my family. And our security team needs a bedroom and a bathroom each, plus sometimes we have guests to stay.'

'Uh-huh,' she said.

Upstairs, there were eight enormous bedrooms, all with their own bathrooms.

'I thought you might like this room, because it has a view over the mountains,' he said, showing her to one bedroom. It was a fairy-tale suite; the king-sized brass bedstead had deep pillows, a thick duvet and pretty floral bedlinen. The beautifully carved dressing table had an ornate mirror; to one side of the room there were doors that she assumed opened to a built-in wardrobe. There was a comfortable armchair by the window; the small coffee table next to it had a vase of beautiful pink and white roses and copies of the latest glossy women's magazines—in English, she noted, so had they been bought with her in mind?

The bathroom was huge, too: a marble floor and marble walls, a deep bathtub, a shower cubicle with an enormous shower head and what looked like jets coming out of the walls, a gilt mirror above the sink, and a shelf that was already stocked with toiletries and a new toothbrush still in its packaging. She recognised the brands as ones that she couldn't even afford as special presents when they were discounted in the post-Christmas sales. This was sheer unadulterated luxury, and a whole world away from her normal life.

'I hope these are OK,' he said, gesturing to the shelf.

'I… Thank you.' She'd work out later how to replace the toiletries for him. It would put quite a hole in her budget, but she'd always been good at juggling.

'Gina bought a couple of changes of clothes for you,' he said, 'and she put them away in the wardrobe and the dressing table. Though if you'd prefer a different room, I can move everything for you.'

He'd managed to arrange clothes for her already? She stared at him in surprise. 'But I only gave you that list an hour ago!'

He shrugged. 'Picco Innevato might look small, but there are a few shops here. As I said, the village is used as a ski resort in winter, and people come for the hiking in the summer.'

If it was a touristy place, then the clothes sold here would be by expensive designer boutiques rather than cheap and cheerful chain stores or supermarkets, she thought.

As if he was guessing what she was thinking, he said gently, 'It's my fault that you're here as my guest, so I'm simply providing you with a couple of changes of clothes, just as any of my family would do for a guest staying here. The same goes for the toiletries. There are no strings, Tia, and I'll be very offended if you offer to pay for them.'

Although Tia wanted to argue and tell him that she could manage to buy her own clothes, thank you very much, she had the baby to think about—and the fact that she'd be on maternity leave in a couple of months, reducing her budget even further. Which meant she'd have to swallow her pride and accept his kindness. 'Thank you,' she said, feeling miserable and selfish and totally mixed up. She had never relied on anyone in her life, and she didn't want to start now. But, for the sake of the baby and her mother, she might have to.

It would help if she had a better idea of what *he* wanted. The man, not the Prince. But how could she ask without sounding ungrateful? She was stuck.

'Take your time settling in,' he said. 'If you want to take a bath or shower to freshen up, or have a nap, that's fine. We're not on palace time. And call your mother to let her know you're here safely. I'll be downstairs when you're ready.'

'Thank you.'

He left her to look over the clothes. And they were utterly gorgeous—a couple of long-sleeved silky maternity tops, a pair of maternity trousers, a soft cashmere cardigan, a smart black skirt and a pretty floral tunic dress. There was underwear, too, and maternity tights. Three pairs of pyjamas, with soft jersey trousers and lace-trimmed matching camisole tops.

Tia's eyes filled with tears. They were so pretty. And this was so kind of his housekeeper, to do this for a complete stranger.

Antonio made himself a coffee, but he didn't feel as relaxed as he usually did here in his bolt-hole.

What was he going to do about Tia Phillips?

He saw her through a haze of guilt: his best friend's little sister. The woman he should've supported after her brother's death, but he'd let her down. The woman he'd let comfort him. The woman he'd made pregnant—albeit unknowingly—and abandoned.

The woman, if he was honest with himself, who made him feel different—as if he was more than just the younger Prince of Casavalle or a team commander. She made him feel as if she saw right through the pomp and the public face to the man behind it. Just like that night they'd spent together, when she'd comforted him and let him comfort her: he had no idea why, but she'd broken through all his barriers. Though he didn't want to examine it too closely and work out why she was the only one who'd made him feel that way. Emotional stuff made him antsy because he'd never really learned how to deal with it—and he didn't want to deal with it now. Duty was much, much easier than emotion.

Just put it down to sexual attraction, he told himself, and move on.

Because his duty to Casavalle had to come first. He had to think about the baby and what it would mean for his country. And then he would do the right thing.

Miles would be discreet, Antonio knew. So he had a breathing space before he had to tell his family the truth about the 'personal matters to attend to' he'd texted them about. And he had absolutely no idea how they would react to the news of the baby. His mother would be furious. His brother—although Luca knew that Tia had tried to contact Antonio, he didn't know why, so he would be shocked. Gabriella… She was an 'unexpected' baby herself, so she might have a different viewpoint.

But he knew they'd all be disappointed in him.

What he'd done had been very far from honourable, even though it was completely unintentional. And he needed to fix the situation. Now.

He'd never thought he'd settle down and have children. When they'd been growing up, it was always assumed that Luca—as the eldest son—would take over from their father, and Luca would be the one who had to marry someone suitable and produce the next heir to the throne. The arrangement with Princess Meribel had happened years ago, so Antonio had had the freedom to join the army, travelling the world and taking on dangerous missions. He'd loved every second of his job and he'd relished his freedom. He'd been planning to go back to the army once Luca was settled as the King of Casavalle—or Gabriella as the new Queen. Either way, his time in Casavalle had been temporary.

Now… Now it was different. He was going to be a father. Going back to the army and putting himself in danger was less of an option now. He had responsibilities: emotional as well as financial.

And that was the problem.

Emotional stuff. The thing he found difficult.

Growing up, he remembered both of his parents being very formal and his father had been distant. Antonio couldn't remember his father ever hugging him, or saying he loved his younger son, or saying that he was proud of him. He'd worked hard in the army and he'd earned his promotions through merit, not through his connections; but King Vincenzo had never acknowledged that or made any comment about how hard his son had worked. Queen Maria was warmer but, like his father, she'd always encouraged him to put his civic duty before his feelings.

And, although Antonio had dated plenty of women, he'd never felt a real connection with any of them. He'd enjoyed their company, but had always made it clear right from the start that the relationship was strictly short term.

Except for Tia, a little voice said in his head.

Tia Phillips, with her soft brown eyes, her tumble of black curls, and her petite frame that hid amazing inner strength. When he had seen her again today in the palace, he'd felt that leap of his pulse, the slow burn of pleasure that was more intense than he'd ever experienced with anyone else. If he was honest with himself, she was the only person he'd ever really felt connected to. That night in London when they'd shared their grief over losing her brother and held each other tightly. That night when she'd broken through all his barriers. The night when they'd made a baby...

The baby.

Antonio took the photograph she'd given him from his wallet. The baby was lying on his back, knees up, and one arm was raised so Antonio could see a tiny hand. Fingers.

Their baby.

He dragged in a breath. It was miraculous and terrifying at the same time.

And Tia had been dealing with this alone.

The more he thought about it, the more he knew he had to do the right thing by her. Marry her, make their child legitimate, support her. And she'd looked so worried when she'd sat in the palace secretary's office, waiting to tell him the news. Guilt squeezed his insides again as he thought about it. Did she really think he'd abandon her for a third time?

Then again, he hadn't given her any reason to think he'd do anything else. He'd abandoned her and her mother after breaking the news of Nathan's death, and he hadn't got in touch again after the charity gala. Where Tia was concerned, he had a really terrible track record.

So when she came downstairs, he'd reassure her. Tell her they would get married.

On the other hand, he knew that Tia was an independent woman. Extremely independent, according to Nathan; she'd spent her life being their mother's carer, putting her own dreams aside. Dreams of travelling the world and becoming a primary school teacher, so Nathan had said.

In that case, would she even agree to marry him, even though it was the right thing for the baby?

But Antonio knew it was the right thing to do. If they got married, he could fulfil his duties as the baby's father, and he could help Tia with her mother. He could bring Grace Phillips over to Casavalle, where the climate might be better for her health and she'd have access to much more support than she had in London. Then Tia would be able to be Grace's daughter rather than her carer; and, although Tia would need to support him in his royal duties so she wouldn't have the time to become a primary school teacher, she would at least be able to travel the world with him.

And maybe Luca—or Gabriella, whichever of them was crowned—would allow him to have some kind of special responsibilities for education, so Tia could fulfil her dreams that way, working with him.

He had the whole thing sorted perfectly in his head by the time Tia came downstairs.

'Is everything all right? Is there anything you need?' he asked.

'Thank you, everything's lovely. I'm fine.'

He noticed there was a slight disconnect between her words and her expression; although she was smiling, it didn't reach her eyes. He wasn't quite sure what was wrong, but she definitely wasn't fine. 'Tea?' he asked.

'No, thank you.'

Or maybe she was worrying about his reaction to the baby. Maybe she needed reassurance. He could sort that out right now.

'Let's go into the conservatory,' he said.

Giacomo had tactfully gone to his own room, giving Antonio and Tia the space they needed to talk.

Tia let the Prince usher her through to the conservatory and settle her on one of the comfortable sofas.

'I've been thinking,' he said. 'There's a very simple solution to this. We'll get married.'

Married?

Just like that?

Tia stared at him in disbelief.

Of course Prince Antonio didn't want to marry her. He didn't love her. He clearly didn't feel anything towards her except a sense of duty and honour. He hadn't hugged her, he hadn't told her he'd missed her—in fact, he'd barely even touched her other than to support her elbow as she'd climbed the steps to the plane, which she was fairly sure he'd do for any female he accompanied because it was a very regal and very polite thing to do. And, even though her skin had tingled when his hand had accidentally brushed against hers, she was pretty sure it hadn't been the same for him.

Prince Antonio of the House of Valenti was an unemotional *machine*.

Yes, he could put people at their ease—because that was what royals were trained to do. It was all about duty, where he was concerned. He hadn't brought her here to his bolt-hole because he wanted to spend time with her, but because he needed to get her away from the media and protect his family's privacy.

His suggestion of marriage was utterly ridiculous. She hadn't come here to demand he do the old-fashioned 'right thing' by her; her sole intention had been to let him know about the baby's existence and then leave. She'd managed the six months of her pregnancy so far perfectly well without him, and she'd manage the birth and their child's life in exactly the same way.

She'd been born to a couple who hadn't been married but who had loved each other deeply and who'd adored their children. OK, so maybe it had turned out that her dad was wrong about marriage being just a bit of paper; but she understood where he was coming from. You should be with someone because you loved them and the world felt like a better place because they were in it, not because you were bound by a contract.

No way was Tia getting married to a man who didn't want her and who saw their baby as a burden and a duty. That was the complete opposite of what her parents had had. It wasn't what she wanted. At all. Yes, it was honourable of him to suggest the marriage, and she appreciated that: but marriage would be completely the wrong thing for both of them.

'No,' she said.

Antonio looked taken aback.

Which wasn't so surprising: she very much doubted he'd ever heard the word 'no' when he was growing up. Everyone around him was more likely to have said, 'Yes, Your Royal Highness,' bowed deeply and done exactly what the little imperious Prince had demanded.

'No?' he asked, clearly expecting her to say she'd made a mistake and of course she would marry him.

'No,' she said.

'Why?'

Because you're an automaton who has no real emotions.

Not that it would be tactful to say so. But she could still tell him the rest of the truth.

'Because,' she said, 'you don't love me. You're asking me to marry you because of the baby. Because you think it's the honourable thing to do.' Hadn't he talked about honour before, about not letting Princess Meribel take the blame for her own actions even though she'd been the one to behave badly? 'That isn't what I want. So I'm not going to marry you.'

He blew out a breath. 'Tia, this baby is fourth in line to the throne.'

'Not if I don't marry you, he isn't.'

Antonio's eyes widened. 'The baby's definitely a boy?'

'I don't know. They can't always tell on a scan, and I chose not to find out. But I don't want to call the baby "it"; he's a person, not a thing.'

'Fair enough.' Antonio looked at her. 'But I don't understand how you can say that my child isn't in line to the throne.'

'Because surely any heir to the throne has to be legitimate?' she asked. 'Which means we have a very obvious solution to the problem. If you don't marry me, then the baby isn't legitimate and therefore won't be your heir—and that means you have no legal obligations to either of us.'

'It's a matter of honour,' he said stiffly.

Just what she'd thought. This was all about honour, not love. 'My parents loved each other deeply,' she said quietly, 'and I'm not settling for anything less than that. My answer's still no. I won't marry you.'

He frowned. 'Tia, I know I've let you down twice now, and I apologise deeply for that. But I won't make that mistake a third time.'

No, he wouldn't—because she wasn't giving him the chance to do that. She spread her hands. 'I'm not making any demands on you whatsoever. I've already explained to you that I told you about the baby purely out of courtesy. Because I thought you ought to know. Not because I expected anything from you. Marriage isn't an option.'

He raked a hand through his hair, and the slight disarray made him look more human. Touchable. Not the cold, emotionless Prince who'd greeted her at the palace, but Antonio the man.

Oh, help. She needed to get a grip.

Touching really wasn't what she should be thinking about right now.

Touching was what had got her into this situation in the first place. Holding him, because she'd felt sorry for him and thought that a hug would comfort both of them. Except hugging had turned to kissing, which had turned to him carrying her to his bed, which had turned out to be the most amazing night of her life…

Antonio Valenti wasn't the only man she'd slept with, but he was the only one she'd felt a real connection to. He'd made her feel different. Special, as if she was really important to him. The differences between their social positions hadn't mattered; it had been just the two of them, and that night she'd felt as if the Prince had seen her for who she really was, not just the cheerful waitress with a complicated home life. She'd responded to him on a deeper level than she had to anyone else before; it was a fact that scared her and thrilled her in equal measure. She didn't want to be emotionally dependent on a man who kept his emotions in check all the time. She definitely didn't want to fall in love with someone who couldn't love her back.

But between them that night they'd managed to make a baby.

Now she was facing the consequences.

What should she do now?

Antonio was gorgeous. A total fairy-tale prince, except he was real. And that weird feeling she got when she looked at him—it wasn't the baby kicking. It felt more as if her heart was doing some kind of weird somersault, something that wasn't even anatomically possible.

But how could he ever be really hers? He had responsibilities towards his country, so if he ever settled down with someone it'd have to be for dynastic reasons. His wife would probably have to be at least the daughter of a duke, if not an actual princess.

Which meant there was no real future in any relationship between Antonio and herself, despite the baby and his offer of marriage just now. He probably shouldn't even have asked her to marry him without checking with the palace first. If she let herself act on the pull she felt towards him, she'd just be making a fool of herself, and it wouldn't help either of them. She needed to be cool-headed and calm. And utterly, utterly sensible. He didn't love her. And her own feelings towards him were so muddled that she couldn't make sense of them.

'I am *not* marrying you,' she repeated.

Antonio really hadn't expected this.

Tia had refused his proposal of marriage because she wanted to get married for love?

But that was something that just didn't happen in his family. King Vincenzo had learned the hard way from his first marriage, to Sophia Ross. He'd married for love, and look how that had turned out. Sophia hadn't been able to cope with a royal lifestyle. She'd left Vincenzo to go back home to Canada; she hadn't told him that she was expecting a baby, and Gabriella had grown up completely unaware of who she really was.

Then it occurred to him that Tia at least hadn't done what Sophia had done. She hadn't kept the baby secret.

He thought about it some more. His parents' own marriage had been arranged and it had been successful; his father had grown to love his mother, even though he hadn't shown any affection outwardly. But the arranged marriage between his older brother and Princess Meribel had gone badly wrong, because Meribel had been rash and chasing after true love instead of being sensible and joining their two countries' dynasties. Arranged marriages meant that you had to make compromises, but that went with the territory of being a royal. You had to put your country's needs before your own desires. Luca and Imogen had fallen in love and got engaged; maybe his elder brother was just lucky, Antonio thought. Because, on the whole, his own family's experience had taught him that relationships based on love tended to end up in a mess.

Why couldn't Tia see that you couldn't rely on love? That honour and duty was a better solution?

His head was spinning.

Right now he didn't know what to think. He was filled with guilt for the way he'd treated Tia; he was still trying to get his head round the changes in his own family; he missed his best friend and he missed his father, at the same time as he wished that things had maybe been different and he'd been able to make Vincenzo as proud of him as of his elder brother Luca.

And now there was the baby to think about. He was still trying to process the fact that he was going to be a father. Duty said the right thing to do would be to marry Tia and give the baby his name. But there was more to being a parent than just creating a baby. Would he be any good at it? Would he be able to give his child more than his parents had given him—the kind of warmth his best friend had exuded when he'd talked about his parents? Was Tia right and she'd be better off as a single mum, without him bumbling around and making a mess of things because he didn't really know how to do emotional stuff?

He couldn't find the right words to say to her.

And clearly she wasn't impressed by his silence, because she added, 'And that's an end to the matter.'

Oh, no, it wasn't.

They needed to talk about this properly and work things through. Together.

Tia was having *his* baby. And he could give her and the baby the security they needed. His best friend would never be able to follow his dreams, thanks to the land mine that had blown up his armoured car; but perhaps Antonio could give Tia the chance to follow her dreams.

He just had to persuade her to give him a chance, too.

'Tia—'

'It's not up for discussion,' she said. 'We are *not* getting married.'

Nathan had been proud of his little sister's independence, but right now Antonio was starting to get a bit annoyed by her stubbornness. He wanted her to help him here. Be reasonable.

But he realised that demanding that she marry him wasn't going to convince her that marriage was the right thing to do. He needed to persuade her. Turn on a charm offensive, maybe. He needed to take the emotion out of it, the way he always did. Make it a military operation and treat it as clear-headedly as he treated his work: Operation Persuade Tia.

So for now he'd make a tactical retreat. 'OK.'

She looked slightly shocked, as if she hadn't expected him to agree so quickly. So what did she want? Had she wanted him to fight for her affections?

Love and affection wasn't something he'd thought to have. He wasn't entirely sure that he wanted them; he'd seen what a mess they could cause. Yet, on the other hand, he knew there was something missing from his life. Something he rather thought might be important. All the short-term relationships with no promises, no future: if he was honest with himself, they'd stopped being fun a long time ago. But he'd never met anyone who'd made him think that there could be something more. Not until Tia.

'But,' he said, 'we do need to talk.'

'About what?'

'Everything we didn't say at the palace. But now we've got the space and time to talk properly. Let me make that cup of tea, first,' he prevaricated. The English solution to everything, he thought wryly.

At least she didn't argue about *that*.

He left her in the conservatory, swiftly busied himself in the kitchen, and made two mugs of tea.

'Thank you,' she said when he returned and handed her a mug.

'So when did you realise that you were pregnant?' he asked.

'A couple of months after—' She stopped, and blushed.

After they'd comforted each other and it had turned into lovemaking. Yeah. He didn't want to say that out loud, either. He didn't want to unpick the feelings he'd ignored since then.

'I was busy, I lost track of the time, and it didn't occur to me that my period was late.' She sipped her tea and looked away. 'When I finally realised that my period was late, I did a test.' She paused. 'I probably should've tried to tell you about it back then.'

Why hadn't she?

Clearly she anticipated his question—that, or it was written all over his face—because she continued, 'It took me a while to come to terms with being pregnant and think about what I wanted. Especially when—' She stopped.

'When what?'

'You're photographed with a *lot* of women. The celeb magazines talk about you and your dates all the time. They say that you're a playboy.'

Which wasn't what she wanted from her baby's father? He could understand that. And it wasn't who he was. He grimaced. 'I don't sleep with every woman I date. And I have to show my face at a lot of events where I'm expected to bring a plus one. The media try to spin stories when there isn't really anything to say. I'm not a playboy.'

He hadn't been in a relationship with Tia; but maybe he hadn't been as honest with her as he had been with his usual dates. And even though he hadn't been dating Tia so technically he hadn't cheated on her, he'd been out with other women while Tia was pregnant with his baby—which felt like cheating. Even though he hadn't known about the baby at the time. And it made him feel really, really guilty.

Uncomfortable with the direction his thoughts were taking, he turned the subject back to the baby. 'And you want to keep the baby.'

She nodded. 'What happened… It's not the baby's fault.'

'No.' And it hadn't even occurred to Antonio that there might be consequences from that night. He hadn't thought of anything at all recently except his family's situation. They were all still getting used to the new order of things, following his father's death. Trying to support their people and their country, not letting their personal feelings show. He'd kept busy, but inside he'd felt lost and empty, missing his father and missing his best friend, unable to talk to anyone about how he felt.

The only person he'd come close to confiding in was Tia, the night of the charity gala, when they'd turned to each other for comfort. Having her here, close to him again, made him antsy. Part of him wanted that closeness back; yet, at the same time, that closeness had led them to this tricky situation.

Right now, he thought grimly, he could do with the equivalent of an armoured car so he could lock his heart safely away in it.

So what were they going to do?

He'd used a condom when he'd made love with Tia, but clearly the protection had failed. Or maybe it had happened the second time they'd made love, when they'd both been half-asleep and seeking comfort from each other. He wasn't entirely sure he'd used a condom then so, actually, this whole thing was his fault. He should've been the one who'd been responsible. He should've kept himself under control.

'I'm sorry,' he said.

'It is as it is,' she said with a shrug. 'Mum and I manage. And my bosses have been great. Vittoria, my boss, fusses over me a bit and makes sure I sit down between the really busy periods.'

Then it occurred to him what her job was. She was a waitress in a coffee shop. Which meant that she'd be on her feet all the time, taking orders, ferrying drinks and snacks to the customers, clearing tables and rushing about—because, from what Antonio had learned from her brother, Tia Phillips wasn't the sort to slack off and expect other people to shoulder her duties. 'Is that good for you and the baby, being on your feet all day?' he asked.

Within seconds he knew he'd asked the wrong question. She had that stubborn, independent set to her jaw he was beginning to realise meant trouble. 'Women have managed to stay on their feet and work while they're pregnant for hundreds of years, Antonio.'

'Yes. Of course. I apologise.'

Though at least she'd used his given name, rather than calling him 'Your Royal Highness' or awkwardly not calling him anything at all. Funny how that made him feel warm inside; and it made him feel wrong-footed at the same time.

He wasn't used to women making him feel in a spin.

What was it about Tia Phillips that was so different? And how could he get everything back under his control, the way it usually was?

'I eat properly and I rest properly, before you ask,' she said.

He didn't quite believe her on the 'resting' bit. He knew that she was still caring for her mother, meaning that she must be doing the majority of looking after the house and preparing meals when her mother wasn't well, plus she was handling the demands of her job.

'And, as soon as I realised I was pregnant, I started taking folic acid. I know it was a bit late, but it was better than nothing. Mum makes sure I take a vitamin tablet for pregnant women every morning,' she said.

'That's good,' he said, not knowing what else to say.

He was good in social situations. He'd been good at leading his team in the army, he'd been diplomatic with Meribel's family, and he'd helped Gabriella to feel more at ease in the palace, knowing from his experiences in the army how overwhelming the life of a royal could seem to someone who hadn't been brought up in it.

But with Tia, right now, he was all at sixes and sevens. She wasn't reacting the way he expected her to react. Plus, if he was honest with himself, she made him feel things he'd never felt before. A kind of yearning, mixed with

something he couldn't quite put his finger on. Not nervousness, exactly, and not the adrenalin rush he was used
to at work. This was deeper, tangled up with his emotions,
so he couldn't compartmentalise it, and it unsettled him.

'You've had regular appointments with the hospital?'
he asked, trying to bring things back to facts. Unemotional facts that he could deal with.

'Only the dating scan and the twenty-week scan—the
one where they gave me the photograph. The rest of my
appointments are with the community midwife. And, yes,
I've gone to every single one.'

There was a slight edge to her tone. 'I wasn't accus-
ing you of putting the baby at risk,' he said quietly. 'I'm
concerned about *you*.'

Colour flared into her face. 'Sorry. I didn't mean to
snap. I guess...' She grimaced. 'Blame it on the hor-
mones?'

The situation couldn't be easy for her, either. He inclined his head. 'Of course. So your plan after telling me
the news was to go back home, have the baby, and then
someone would look after the baby while you work?'

'I have a friend who's expecting a baby and she's also
a waitress,' Tia explained. 'We were going to try to work
out some kind of arrangement, so while one of us was
working the other would look after both the babies. That
way neither of us would have to pay for childcare, and
we'd both be able to spend time with our babies. Although
I don't know how realistic that would be.'

But doing that would also mean that Tia would be
working fewer hours, which in turn meant she'd be earn-
ing less than she did now. Money would be really, really
tight. Especially as Nathan was no longer able to help
out financially.

Antonio had to find a way around her pride.

And the best way to do that was to persuade her to marry him.

If she insisted on marrying for love… Then somehow he had to make her fall in love with him, and make her believe that he'd fallen in love with her. And then finally she'd let him help her.

'I can see you've thought everything through,' he said.

She narrowed her eyes at him. 'Are you being sarcastic with me?'

'No. Actually, I think your ability to work out a strategy to manage any situation is every bit as good as any general I've worked with,' he said.

She went slightly pink. 'Oh. Thank you.'

'And I appreciate you coming here with me. I didn't bring you here because I'm ashamed of you—or of what we did.'

Her blush deepened. 'Uh-huh.'

Interesting. So maybe she wasn't completely immune to him.

He wasn't immune to her, either.

Not that he was going to let his emotions cloud things. Emotions just made things messy. If the idea of love made it easier for her to accept his proposal of marriage, then fair enough. But he was keeping his mind clear. He wasn't letting his heart rule his head.

'I brought you here,' he continued, 'because I wanted us to have the space to talk, without any pressure. Because what *you* want is important.' And hopefully he could persuade her to want what he wanted, too.

'So you're not going to railroad me into anything?'

'No.' He was going to charm her into doing what he felt was best for them all. And there was a difference. He wasn't a bully. He wanted to look after her and the baby properly, and he wanted her to accept his help willingly.

'These three days are all about us getting to know each other a bit better. Understanding each other.'

'That works for me,' she said. 'Thank you.'

'So perhaps you'll agree to have dinner with me this evening,' he said. 'I'll cook.'

She frowned. 'I don't expect you to wait on me.'

'I thought that maybe we could prepare dinner together,' he said. Doing things together might help. Working as a team. It might show her that they could be good together, despite being near-strangers.

And then she might agree to marry him—and all the fuss and confusion could stop.

CHAPTER THREE

TOGETHER, THEY WATCHED the sun set over the mountains, the sky striped in shades of pink and blue and gold against the snow-capped peaks.

'It's beautiful here,' Tia said. 'I can see why you come here when you need a bolt-hole. But you said the media follows you everywhere. Does that mean they follow you here?'

'Not as much as they'd like to,' Antonio said. 'The villagers are fairly protective of me, probably because they remember me coming here as a child and some of them remember playing with Luca and me when we were young. They're fairly good at misdirection when it comes to the media. And I'm very grateful for it.'

'It must be hard, having to be in the public eye so much.'

'It's one of the reasons why I appreciate being in the army,' he said. 'Obviously the media don't cover me at work, because they know that would be putting me and my team at risk. But, yes, one's position as a royal can be tricky. It's the way things are so easily misinterpreted, the way people look for hidden meanings that just aren't there.' He shrugged. 'But it is what it is. Shall we go and find something for dinner?'

'That'd be nice,' she said.

He ushered her into the kitchen.

'So what do you like to eat?' he asked.

'I eat practically anything. I'm not fussy.'

He coughed. 'Even *I* know that there are things women need to avoid eating in pregnancy, and things that they need to eat for the baby's sake.'

'I'm just going into the third trimester,' she said, 'so I need lots of calcium.'

'So that's milk and cheese, right?'

'As long as it's pasteurised. And lots of dark green leafy veg, dried apricots, sardines and that sort of thing.' She grimaced. 'Though not too much spice, please, as I've discovered that garlic and very spicy foods give me heartburn.'

He looked through the vegetable drawers in the fridge. 'We have spinach and kale, and Gina's bought chicken, but I'll get some sardines ordered in for tomorrow, if you like.' He looked in the cupboards. 'We have dried apricots and couscous, so I could make you a sort of chicken tagine, with spinach and kale stirred in, and I'll keep the spices mild.'

She was surprised. 'You can actually cook a tagine?'

'I learned while I was in the army. With a team assembled from many different countries, you get to learn about other people's cultures and ideas. Thanks to that, I've learned quite a bit about food, and making stews over a fire. And in return I taught my team how to make a really good tomato sauce for pasta, and how not to overcook pasta.' He rolled his eyes. 'My team-mates only ever served me soggy spaghetti once. And don't get me started on pasta in a tin with that orange stuff claiming to be *sauce*.'

This was a side of him she hadn't really seen. She could understand now why her brother had been friends with him: there was a slight bite to his humour. This side of Prince Antonio, the more human side that he clearly didn't let show very often, was one she rather liked. A man whose company she could enjoy—much more than the formal, slightly stuffy royal personage who bossed her about and irritated her.

'You miss the army, don't you?' she asked.

'I do,' he admitted. 'Yes, there are days when I see terrible things that no human should ever have to see, but it's a job where my team and I can make a real difference. Where we can help people.'

'Will you go back to it?'

'If my father had still been alive, I would've been back with my team now,' he said. 'But at the moment my brother, my mother and my new sister need me.'

She could understand that—and she liked the fact that family was important to him.

'So can you take a sabbatical until things settle down, or will you have to leave the army?'

'I'm on special leave for now, but I'll do what it takes to support my family and my country.'

She wasn't entirely sure whether that meant he put his duty first or his family first. Or maybe they were one and the same for someone in a royal family. 'So you'd be happy to stay at the palace?'

He looked at her, as if weighing it up. 'This stays between you and me?'

'Of course,' she said. 'I have no intention of running to the media and gossiping.'

'I was thinking less of the media and more of my family,' he said dryly. 'But OK. Thank you. The palace I can handle. But the politics drives me insane.' He rolled his eyes. 'The senseless squabbles and point-scoring between people. I want to bang their heads together and tell them to stop behaving like pompous kindergarteners boasting "My dad's more important than yours" because there are so many more important problems in the world that need solving, and you solve things much more effectively if you work together as a team.'

She grinned. 'I guess you'd get into a lot of trouble if you did that.'

'Yes. I don't know how my brother copes with it.' He wrinkled his nose. 'Well, I do. He was brought up knowing that he'd serve our country. He's trained for the job.'

'What about your half-sister?' The woman who might end up being Queen.

'She didn't even know who she was until this year,' Antonio said. 'Her mother, Sophia, never told her about her heritage—and Sophia died when Gabriella was three, so Gabriella was brought up by her aunt and uncle. She ran a bookshop in Canada. She certainly wasn't brought up the way Luca and I were. And then she found a letter from her mother while she was clearing out. She contacted my mother to find out the truth of it—and obviously as she's older than Luca that would make her my father's heir. The DNA test will prove things beyond doubt.'

'Do you think she's your father's daughter?'

'Yes. I look at her and I can see my father,' Antonio said. 'A softer, warmer version.'

So his childhood hadn't been idyllic? If his father had been formal and cold, it would explain why Antonio suppressed his emotions. Why he didn't seem to believe in love.

'Is she nice?'

'I like her,' Antonio said. 'She's sensible. I think she's a lot like Luca.'

'It must be hard, suddenly discovering you're not who

you think you are,' Tia said. 'And having to do it in the public eye.'

'She's strong. She'll cope. Plus,' Antonio added, 'there is the palace library. Hundreds and hundreds of rare volumes. I think that will be her bolt-hole. A place where she'll be surrounded by books.'

Antonio's bolt-hole meant that he was surrounded by mountains. Was he trying to tell her something? Or was she reading too much into it?

He let her prepare the vegetables and the couscous while he sizzled the chicken and made the sauce for the stew, and soon the kitchen was filled with a delicious scent.

'I'll just go and see if Giacomo wants to eat with us,' Antonio said. 'I'll be back in a minute or two.'

Tia sat down and sipped a glass of water, reflecting on what she'd learned about Antonio. It sounded as if his childhood had been lonely; although his family was wealthy, it didn't seem as if he had the same close bond that she and Nathan had had with their parents before their father died. And because everything was so formal at the palace, it would explain why he'd seemed so reserved and emotionless there.

Maybe he wasn't really like that, inside. And hadn't he said something about the media making up a story when there was nothing to tell? Maybe he'd grown up not trusting himself to show any feelings, in case they were misreported and it made waves for his family.

Poor little rich boy.

If she'd had to choose between her own impoverished childhood filled with love and his wealthy childhood filled with rules and regulations, it would've been an easy choice. She'd pick love, all the way.

Could Antonio learn to love? Could he be a real father

to their baby and a partner to her? Could they actually make this work?

Or would it be kinder to all of them if she just disappeared quietly back to London?

Antonio came back into the kitchen. 'Giacomo says he's going to have something later, in his room.'

'Does that mean he's speaking from experience and he knows your cooking doesn't taste as good as it smells?' she asked.

Instead of looking slightly affronted, he surprised her by laughing. 'No. But he's probably going to taste this, pull a face and add a lot of garlic and chilli.'

And now she felt guilty. She'd been the one to ask him not to use garlic or spices. Antonio, too, would probably find the meal tasteless. She could put up with the indigestion. All she'd have to do was sit upright for most of the night and take frequent sips of water. 'Sorry. Please don't think about what I said. Add the garlic and chi—'

'It's fine, Tia,' he cut in. 'I'm happy to eat the same as you. Shall we eat in the dining room?'

'Could we eat here in the kitchen?' she asked. 'Otherwise the two of us are going to be a bit lost, sitting at a table big enough for twelve.'

'Sure.'

She laid the table while Antonio dished up. And he was surprised by how nice it felt, eating in the kitchen with her: how cosy and domestic. It was a world he'd never really experienced. It had never occurred to him before that this existed: this feeling of being settled, of belonging, of being close to someone.

Home.

He'd never yearned for domesticity before. He'd enjoyed travelling the world and the adrenalin rush of his job, knowing that he was making a difference. But settling down... Now he was beginning to see what it could be like. And he was shocked to discover how much he wanted this.

'This is good,' she said when she tasted the tagine.

'Not too garlicky or spicy?' he checked.

'It's perfect,' she said. 'Thank you for accommodating me.'

'My pleasure.' Though he was uneasy about behaving like polite strangers to each other when they'd been so much more than that. Her very obvious baby bump was proof of what they'd been to each other, for that one night. And, even though it made him antsy thinking about the way she'd made him feel, at the same time he wanted that closeness back. Here, in the one place he could remember having fun as a child and where he felt free of the restrictions of the palace, he wanted to keep her talking to him. Maybe starting with a neutral topic would help. 'So what do you think of Casavalle?'

'The village here and the mountains are beautiful. And your palace is a bit like a fairy-tale castle, all pure white stone and turrets,' she said.

He'd never really thought about it like that before. 'I suppose so.'

'And that Christmas tree in the palace foyer is amazing,' she said. 'It must've taken ages to decorate.'

'We have a team in charge of decorating the palace,' he said.

She smiled. 'I guess you can't have the King of Casavalle climbing up a ladder and reaching across the branches.'

'We use scaffolding for a tree of that height, actually, but you're right.' He looked at her, suddenly curious. She'd focused on the tree. Christmas for him was a time of duty, but had it been different for her? 'What were Christmases like when you were young?'

'We'd put the tree up as soon as Dad came home on leave, the week before Christmas,' she said. 'We'd go and choose one together, as a family—a real one that smelled lovely. And then Dad would put the lights on, and Mum would get out the box of decorations and we'd all take turns in putting an ornament on the tree. Each year Nathan and I would choose a new one in the shop, and we'd have one each that we'd made at nursery or school.' She smiled. 'Yogurt pots we'd painted and covered in glitter and decorated with a tinsel loop so they looked like a bell, or a star we'd cut out and glued pasta on and spray-painted gold, and an angel made out of a cardboard tube, a ping-pong ball, scraps of fabric and wool. Mum kept every single one of the ones we made; even though they're too worn to go on the tree nowadays, she can't bear to throw them away.'

A small family Christmas, with decorations on the tree that had meaning and had been made with love, rather than being bought *en masse* from a retailer, or priceless baubles that had been part of the family for decades but were never allowed to be played with. So very different from his own. What would it have been like to grow up in a warm, close family like that?

'And every year on Christmas Eve we'd hang our stockings at the foot of the bed. Mum made them herself—she's amazing with a needle—and she embroidered our names and stars on them with silver thread so they sparkled. We'd set out a glass of milk and a chocolate biscuit for Father Christmas, and a carrot for his reindeer; and every year we'd come down to find an empty glass, a plate with just crumbs on it, and a half-eaten carrot.'

His family had never had traditions like that. He

couldn't even remember when he'd stopped believing in Father Christmas.

'When we were little, our stockings would be filled with sweets and a couple of tangerines, a colouring book and crayons, maybe a toy car for Nathan and a bottle of bubbles with a wand for me.' She smiled. 'Even after Dad died and money was a bit tight, Mum would still fill a stocking for us. She used to buy a little something every couple of weeks and she'd hide the gifts away in a box at the top of her wardrobe so we wouldn't find them. On Christmas Eve, we'd go to midnight mass with Mum in the church round the corner and sing carols, then come home to have hot chocolate and marshmallows before going to bed.

'Even when we stopped believing in Father Christmas, we still put our stockings out. Nathan and I used to make a stocking for Mum, too. We'd save our pocket money and buy her nice bath stuff from the market and make her photo frames, that sort of thing. She cried the first year we did it, and we were so worried we'd upset her, but she told us how special the stocking was and how much she loved us.'

Love. A word that was never really used in the palace. Their father had always been distant, even here; although their mother was warmer, Queen Maria was very practical and didn't tend to talk about emotional things. And, although Antonio loved his brother and looked up to him, he wasn't sure he'd ever actually told Luca he loved him, and Luca certainly hadn't said it to him. They just didn't do that sort of thing.

And now he was beginning to wonder if he'd missed out. If his childhood had been so structured and full of regulations that there hadn't been room for love. Grace Phillips had clearly done her best to give her children as much of their dreams as she could afford, but the main thing had been that those gifts, however much she'd spent, had been chosen with love.

'What about Christmas with you? Do you have traditions?' Tia asked.

'You've seen the tree in the foyer. That's one of our traditions,' he said. 'Each of the decorations is a special one designed for us by Buschetta—that's a family of jewellers in Casavalle, a bit like Fabergé. The tradition has been going on for more than a century, and there's a secret compartment in each one. Every year, there's a special ceremony to unveil that year's ornament.'

It was about as close as he could get to the special decorations chosen by Tia and her brother each year. Just on a different scale.

'We have Mass in the palace cathedral, and the day after Christmas we open the palace to all the citizens. There's a buffet, with mulled wine and hot chocolate; the palace kitchens bake for days beforehand. Then Luca and I stand at the palace doors with our parents and greet everyone.' Except this year would be different. The first one without his father. The first year with the new King— or Queen. He pushed the thoughts aside. 'There are ice sculptures in the fountain area, and the hedge maze is all lit up for the children to explore. We make sure we give our people a magnificent, beautiful Christmas.'

'I get that you need to do something for your people—like the Queen of England at Sandringham, going to church with her family on Christmas morning and greeting everyone who's queued up outside to see them,' she said. 'But I didn't mean the public stuff. I meant your *private* family Christmas. What about traditions for you? Did you have stockings or anything like that?'

No, they hadn't. Not in the way she meant. 'As royal

children,' he said, 'Luca and I had masses of gifts from other royal families and from around the world. To the point where we needed people to help us open them and we didn't always know what people had bought us.'

She frowned. 'You didn't have special things just for you, Luca, your mum and your dad? Not a special story they always read to you, or a film you always watched together?'

'No.'

'That,' she said softly, 'is a shame. Because Christmas isn't about the gifts. It's about love. It's about spending time with your family. Playing games—we'd play everything from snap to charades to snakes and ladders, and I think the best year ever was the year Nathan bought me this game with kazoos where we had to play whatever song was on the card we picked up. We were all terrible at it, Mum and Dad and Nathan and me, and we laughed so much our sides hurt.'

That was something he'd definitely never done with his family. It was more like the sort of thing he'd done with his army friends. 'That sounds like fun,' he said carefully.

'It was. And I'm sorry you didn't get to share something like that with your family.'

'We had our duties to perform,' he said. Though, now she'd said it, he was sorry, too. He wished he'd been able to share that sort of fun with his parents and his brother.

Would it be different for his baby? If he could persuade Tia to marry him, would she change things at the palace? Would she institute new, more personal, traditions? Would *he* change, too?

The ground felt as if it was shifting under him.

'So did you always want to be in the army?' she asked.

'I'm the younger son, so there weren't quite the same expectations for me as there were for Luca. I had a lot more freedom. And I liked the idea of travelling the world, of being able to make a positive difference for people.'

'Like Nathan,' she said. 'Like our dad.'

'What about you?' he asked.

'I'm fine as I am.'

'No, I mean, what were your dreams when you were young?' He already knew the answer, but he wanted to hear it from her.

'I didn't want to join the army, but I did want to travel,' she said. 'I would've liked to be a primary school teacher, but my grades at school weren't good enough.'

Nathan had always talked about his sister being bright, and Antonio had seen that for himself when he talked to her. He guessed that, as her mother's carer, she'd been too busy to concentrate on her studies at school. 'You could,' he said carefully, 'train as a teacher now. Be a mature student.'

She shook her head. 'Mum suggested that, but I don't want to leave her. And I'm happy as I am. I like my job. My bosses are lovely, and we have regular customers who tell us all kinds of stories of London in the past.'

He had the strongest feeling that Tia was the sort who'd manage to find happiness in any situation: she was one of those incredibly positive people. And she was also incredibly proud and independent. He needed to back off before he upset her. 'OK.'

Once they'd finished dinner, Tia insisted on helping him to wash up, and then they headed back to the conservatory to watch the stars. Rather than switching on the overhead light, guessing that she'd prefer something softer, Antonio lit the scented pillar candles in their wrought iron and glass lanterns.

'This smells like Christmas,' she said. 'Cinnamon and cloves and orange.'

'I'm glad you like it,' he said. 'Would you like some music?'

'That'd be nice.'

'What do you like?' He knew so little about her.

'Anything.'

'You don't have to be polite,' he said. 'What do you really like listening to? Pop? Classical?'

'This time of year,' she said, 'I really like Christmas music—carols as well as all the old pop songs.'

It didn't take him long to find a medley of Christmas music on a streaming service.

'This is lovely,' she said with a smile. 'All that's missing is the Christmas tree.'

He remembered how her face had lit up when she'd talked to him about the Christmases of her childhood, with her family. Maybe this was a way of getting closer to her. Although he could simply buy everything and have it all shipped in while he took her out for the day tomorrow, he had a feeling that she'd find that much too impersonal—hadn't she said that Christmas for her was all about love and spending time with your family? She'd talked about decorating the tree *together*. So maybe that was what they should do.

'We could have a tree, if you'd like one,' he said. 'Perhaps we can choose one together tomorrow.' He looked at her. 'And maybe we can choose a special decoration for our baby. Together.'

'We're not going to be together, though,' she said softly. 'We come from different worlds.'

'But the baby's part of both of us,' he pointed out. 'The baby's where our worlds combine.'

'I guess,' she said, and there was a hint of sadness in her face.

He wanted to make her feel better. And the only way

he could think of was to go and sit beside her on the sofa, and hold both her hands in his. 'It's all going to be OK,' he said.

'I know. I just wish…' She blew out a breath. 'Nathan would've made such a good uncle. Such a good dad. I wish he'd had the chance. But he never talked about anyone special. I'm guessing it was because he felt responsible for Mum and me so he didn't let himself get close to anyone.'

Antonio thought that was a shrewd assessment. But it was only part of the truth. 'He loved you both,' Antonio told her. 'He didn't see either of you as a burden. He was so proud of you.'

'I was proud of him. So was Mum. And I wish Dad could've seen him grow up past the age of thirteen—and me past the age of ten.' She looked at him. 'I'm sorry. This must be hard for you, too, right now. Your first Christmas without your father.'

He nodded. 'It's…a little strange.'

Her fingers tightened around his, giving him comfort. 'The firsts are hard. Your first birthday without him, his birthday, Christmas, the first anniversary of his death. But he's still in your heart. Always. That never changes.'

But Antonio's relationship with his family was very different from hers. Duty came before everything else. And, like the rest of his family, he didn't allow himself to think about feelings.

Right now, here in the cosy warmth of the room, with Christmas music playing in the background, the view of the mountains lit by moonlight, and the soft glow of the candles illuminating her face, he felt different. As if something was unfurling inside him and spreading through him, something that made him feel warm and mushy and very mixed-up, all at the same time. And he didn't know how to tell her how he felt, just in case he was making a fool of himself and she didn't feel the same. After all, this was the woman who'd refused to marry him—even though she was pregnant with his child. Instead, he said, 'Will you dance with me?'

She blinked. 'Dance with you? I...'

Of course she didn't want that. He was expecting way too much from her. 'Sorry. I shouldn't have asked.' He let her hands go.

'It's not that. Just...' She looked wistful. 'Dancing isn't really something I've done very much.'

No, because when she wasn't working she was looking after her mum. She probably wouldn't have gone out to discos at school, or nightclubs, or the kind of glitzy social events he went to. But if her not knowing how to dance was the only barrier between them, he could fix that. Right here, right now. The words spilled out before he could stop them. 'I can teach you.'

'Teach me?'

And suddenly it was as if there was a kind of electricity in the air. Something that made it hard to breathe.

Would she let him closer? Or would she make an excuse and back away?

Waiting for her answer made time seem to slow down; every second felt ten times as long as usual, as if he was watching a film in slow motion.

But then she nodded. 'OK.'

He drew her to her feet. In bare feet, she was more than six inches shorter than he was, and it made him feel even more protective of her.

'OK. Follow my lead.'

Michael Bublé crooned 'Have Yourself a Merry Little Christmas' as Antonio swayed with Tia in the candlelight. And he rested his cheek against her hair, feeling the softness against his skin and breathing in her light floral scent.

* * *

With Antonio's arms wrapped protectively round her, Tia felt safer than she'd felt for a long, long time. It was amazing to be dancing in his arms by candlelight, to the kind of Christmas music she loved most. It felt as if the room was lit by a thousand stars, and she'd always thought herself a bit clumsy, but right now she was dancing effortlessly in his arms, not putting a foot wrong because he was guiding her.

Just for a moment, she could let herself believe this was real. That he was holding her, not because he was being polite and doing his duty but because he really wanted her—her and their baby. That he *cared*.

But then the music changed and a choir began to sing 'Silent Night'.

Her mother's favourite.

Homesickness washed over her. She missed her mum; she worried about Grace constantly. And Antonio had hit the nail very firmly on the head earlier. Just how was she going to cope with working part time, looking after their baby and looking after her mum? Right at that moment the future felt filled with anxiety.

As if Antonio sensed her tension, he pulled back. 'Everything's going to be OK, Tia,' he said softly.

It was, oh, so easy to say; and much less easy to be sure that it was true. 'Uh-huh,' she said, not wanting him to think she was feeble and weak, or that she wanted to give up and let him sort everything out for her. Because that wasn't who she was. She managed. She always had.

'You've had a very long day and you've done a lot of travelling,' he said. 'Let me run you a bath and make you some hot chocolate.'

Tia was perfectly capable of running her own bath.

But, at the same time, she was bone-deep tired. And

he was right: she'd had a long day and a lot of travelling. She'd been on three planes, two cars and a train. And she was six months pregnant. She had more than herself to think about: there was the baby, too. Just this once, maybe it wouldn't hurt to let him look after her. Right now she was his guest, and you looked after your guests, didn't you? 'Thank you. That'd be really kind.' She gave him a grateful smile.

Antonio was almost surprised that she'd given in so easily. Then again, she was six months pregnant and it had been a long day. He wasn't going to make a big deal about this, and then hopefully it would soften her stance and she would let him do more to help.

Though he had no idea what kind of form that help could take. Tia Phillips was independent to a fault.

Again and again, the only thing he could come back to was that they should get married. She was expecting his baby. A baby who was fourth in line to the throne of Casavalle. It was the honourable thing to do. The right solution. He could look after her, look after the baby, and look after her mother.

Though she'd made it clear that she'd only get married for love.

Did he love her?

They hardly knew each other. He wasn't even sure that he believed in love, let alone love at first sight; how did you even know how love felt? How did you know someone was 'the one'? How did you know it would last?

As a prince, he couldn't afford to risk a relationship that might go wrong and make things awkward for his family. Duty always came first.

And yet… There was something about Tia that drew him. He liked her. He enjoyed her company. He was definitely attracted to her. So that was a start. Somehow, over the next three days, he needed to make her happy and show her that this could work out. That they could have a proper partnership. Work as a team. Learn to love each other, if that was what she wanted.

Once she was back downstairs, clad in pyjamas and with her hair wrapped in a towel, he settled her on the sofa in the living room with a mug of hot milk and a fleecy blanket. 'It must've been hard for you growing up, losing your dad and with your mum ill.'

'We managed,' Tia said. 'Mum took in sewing and mending and she worked from home, so she could rest when she needed to.'

And he'd just bet that Tia had picked up the slack. Now he thought about it, Nathan had been good with a needle, too. No doubt he'd also helped with their mother's work.

'Nathan got a job at the corner shop working weekends, and I had a paper round,' Tia explained. 'I took over at the shop when he joined the army. The manager was brilliant—she knew the situation with Mum, so she'd let me nip home to check on Mum if she was having a bad day. Between us, Nathan and I sorted the housework when Mum couldn't do it.'

Meaning that Tia had had to do it all on her own after her brother joined the army. It was so far away from Antonio's own life of privilege, and he really admired Tia's strength. And Nathan's, too; although his friend had never confided much about his past, he'd had amazing strength of character.

'It must've been tough, though. What about school?'

She shrugged. 'I got by.'

But not, he thought, with the kind of grades her brother thought she was capable of. Even if you were bright, if you were caring for someone else you simply wouldn't have time to keep up with your schoolwork and your grades would suffer. He could see how Tia's dreams of travelling and becoming a primary school teacher just hadn't been possible.

'Don't judge my mum,' she said softly. 'If the authorities had known how ill Mum was and how much help we needed to give her, they might've taken us away from her and put us in care—and they probably would have made Nathan and me live with different families. That happened to someone in my class and I was terrified that it would happen to me. I didn't want to be taken away from Mum and Nathan, and he didn't want to leave Mum and me, either. So we just got on with things and made sure the teachers and everyone didn't really know how ill Mum was. It was fine, because we had each other and we were together.'

This was so much worse than Antonio had realised, and his heart ached for Nathan and his equally brave little sister. 'You didn't have any family who could help? Any grandparents?'

'Mum was an only child, and her parents died before I was born,' Tia said. 'And Dad's family didn't like my mum. There was a big row when they first got together, and they never made it up. Nathan wrote to them after Dad died, but they never replied. But it's OK.' She spread her hands and smiled. 'You don't miss what you've never had. And my mum's brilliant. Even when she's having a really bad day, she never complains. She's the kindest, most loving mum anyone could ask for and I'm really grateful I have her.'

Guilt flooded through him. 'I'm sorry I haven't been there to support you both since Nathan died.'

'*Support* us? Mum and I don't need your money, Your Royal Highness,' she said crisply. 'We're not a charity case.'

He looked at her, horrified to realise she thought that

he'd meant money. 'Of course you're not, and I wouldn't insult you by treating you that way.' He knew she was proud. Offering her money would be the quickest way to put a barrier up between them.

'I'm sorry,' she said, and bit her lip. 'I shouldn't have snapped at you. Just… I guess I've learned that rich people tend to think about everything in terms of money.'

'And, as a prince, I'm from a very wealthy background, so it figures you'd think I'd be even more that way,' he said grimly. 'Though I didn't mean money. I meant I should've come back and given you some emotional support—you *and* your mother. And instead I disappeared and just left you to it.'

'You told me you weren't at Nathan's funeral because you had to go on another mission, and then your dad died so you had responsibilities in your own family. Of course you didn't have time to come and support us. And I apologise. I didn't mean to insult you just now by implying…' She grimaced. 'I suppose it sounded as if I thought that you were trying to buy my silence.'

'But you must've felt that I'd abandoned you when I didn't come back and see you.'

'Not so much me—I was angry with you for my mum's sake,' Tia admitted. 'I thought it wouldn't have been that much of a sacrifice for you just to spend a few minutes with her, sharing your memories of my brother. Or send her a photograph or a personal note or something. Just so she knew he mattered.'

'He did matter. He mattered a lot.' Antonio raked a hand through his hair. 'And you're right, I should have made the time to do that. I handled it badly when I came to see you. I'm sorry I got it so wrong.'

'And I'm sorry for going off at the deep end,' she said, and the sweetness in her smile ripped his heart in two.

'I think,' he said, 'we could both do with an early night. In separate rooms,' he added hastily. 'There are no strings to you staying here.'

'I'm a bit tired,' she admitted.

'We'll talk again in the morning,' he said. And, just so she'd know he didn't make promises lightly, he added, 'And then we can go and get that tree.'

'OK,' she said.

He took her empty mug from her and washed up before heading to bed, but he lay awake for a long time before he finally fell asleep.

Would Tia trust him enough to let her support him?

And, if not, how could he teach her to trust him?

He really needed to think things through properly before tomorrow. He couldn't afford to get this wrong.

CHAPTER FOUR

THE NEXT MORNING, when Tia woke, she felt slightly disoriented. It was strange not to hear the low hum of traffic that she was used to, and even stranger to be lying in a wide bed instead of her narrow single bed. She glanced at her watch, and realised it was a quarter past seven; normally she'd have been up for nearly an hour, getting ready to help her mum and then go to work.

Then again, London was an hour behind Casavalle, so this was pretty much the normal time for her to wake and she wasn't late. Though maybe, given the time zone difference, it was a little too early to ring her mother in London and see how she was.

Tia climbed out of bed and looked out of the window. The sky was streaked with pink and gold. As she watched, the snow on the mountains gradually turned pink. So pretty, and such a lovely way to start the day.

But this wasn't how her life was going to be, so she wasn't going to let herself get used to it.

She showered swiftly and dressed in one of the silky long-sleeved tops and the maternity trousers Antonio's housekeeper had bought for her. The fabric was so soft against her skin and felt so nice.

Tears pricked at her eyelids, and she grew cross with

herself. It was utterly ridiculous, starting to cry over a complete stranger being so kind to her.

'Get a grip,' she told herself. 'You're here for three days and you need to sort out a compromise with the Prince.'

There was no sound in the house, so she crept quietly down the stairs and into the kitchen to make herself a mug of tea. She thought about making a mug of tea for Antonio, but that would mean taking the mug into his room and she felt too shy to do that. How ridiculous that was, given that she was carrying his baby; but he was almost a complete stranger. They were worlds apart. She was a waitress, living in a tiny flat in a very ordinary part of London, and he was a prince who lived in an enormous fairy-tale palace in the middle of the Mediterranean. He wouldn't fit into her life and she wouldn't fit into his.

The problem was she'd felt so close to him last night, when she'd told him about Christmases in the past with her family. It was her favourite time of year—not because of the gifts but because it was a chance to spend time with those you loved, enjoying their company and having fun together.

It sounded as if fun hadn't been part of Antonio's Christmases, growing up. Everything had been so formal and stuffy. All the priceless and historic ornaments on the tree that couldn't be played with in case they were accidentally broken: things that had to be admired from afar. Receiving gifts from people he might never even have met, and gifts he probably didn't get a chance to play with. Standing to greet the citizens and doing his royal duties instead of playing games with his family.

His family.

How could they ever accept someone like her? Someone who didn't have blue blood; someone who didn't have the first clue about protocol and royal etiquette.

So she needed to keep a lid on the attraction she felt towards Antonio Valenti. She needed to ignore the impulse to wrap her arms round him and hold him close when she thought about how lonely his childhood must have been, because this really wasn't her place.

She'd promised him a couple of days to talk things over. She'd keep her promise. And then she'd depart quietly for London and leave all this behind her.

With her hands wrapped round the mug of tea, she walked into the conservatory and curled up in one of the big armchairs, enjoying the beautiful view. At least this was a memory she could share with her baby in years to come.

If only she could share it with Antonio, too.

But he didn't love her, and she wasn't prepared to commit to a life with him without love—for her or for her baby.

She'd promised him three days. Antonio really hoped that would be enough to talk her round to his point of view.

He decided to start by bringing Tia a cup of tea in bed, and then possibly bring her a breakfast tray. Then they'd go into the village and find a Christmas tree together, and choose some ornaments. They'd spend the afternoon decorating the tree. And he could drop hints that this was something they could do with their baby. They could follow her family traditions and there would be a new one from a shop every year, and a home-made one.

It was almost the total opposite of the Buschetta ornament tradition that he was used to. But if Tia wanted things handmade and personal, that was exactly what he'd give her. And, even though he couldn't ever remember sitting down with glitter and glue, he was quite prepared to do that. He'd do whatever it took to make her happy and believe in him. Because maybe, just maybe, Tia and the baby were going to change his life. Fill in the gaps. Just as he could fill in the gaps of her life. He'd thought that these three days were to persuade her, but his feelings towards her had already started to change. She wasn't just the unexpected mother of his baby, the woman he had a duty towards; he was starting to really enjoy the time he spent with her.

He showered and changed into a pair of black jeans and a cashmere sweater, then headed down to the kitchen.

Except, when he went to fill the kettle, he realised that it was still hot.

So did that mean Tia was already up and about? She'd liked the view from the conservatory yesterday, he remembered, so he went in search of her. And there she was, curled up in a chair, sipping tea and looking out at the mountains.

'Good morning,' he said.

And how weird it was that his pulse had leaped at the sight of her. She looked so cute sitting there in a half-dream, with her dark curls caught back at the nape of her neck. She didn't need make-up to emphasise those beautiful brown eyes, either.

This was more than attraction. Antonio kept circling round to the L-word in his head, but love wasn't something that he believed in or could even define. In royal circles, you didn't marry for love; you married for duty and for dynastic reasons. His father had made that mistake in his first marriage, falling in love with someone who couldn't cope with the Royal life that came with him.

Being with Tia, marrying her, was really going to put the cat among the pigeons, politically.

Or maybe this would take his life in a new direction. A better direction. Because being with her made him feel that there could be something more than duty and work in his life. Something he hadn't expected or looked for, but now he'd had a glimpse of it he wanted more. And he definitely wanted that for their baby.

'Good morning,' she said, smiling back at him. 'I hope it was OK for me to make myself some tea.'

'Of course. Please treat the house as your home,' he said.

'I was going to make you a mug, too, but I wasn't sure if you'd be awake yet.'

There was a shyness in her smile that really drew him.

And then he noticed the bump moving; he could see her silky top shimmering in the light. 'Is that…?' he asked.

'The baby kicking? Yes.' She looked at him, then held her hand out. 'Here. Feel it for yourself.'

He let her take his hand and rest it on the bump.

This felt oddly intimate. Strange. He could hardly breathe.

'Say hello to the baby,' she said.

'Hello, baby,' he whispered.

Immediately, there was a strong kick against his hand, as if the baby was saying hello back, and it blew him away. He really hadn't expected to feel that sudden rush of wonder.

'Our baby just kicked me!' He dragged in a breath. Now it felt real.

Of course it was real.

For pity's sake, anyone who looked at Tia could see that she was six months pregnant.

But for the first time Antonio felt as if he'd actually connected with the baby. A baby he hadn't expected, hadn't ever dreamed about—and now he discovered that he really, really wanted this baby. It was a sudden, unexpected, visceral longing, stronger than anything he'd known before.

And it made him look at Tia differently, too. She was the mother of his child. And although he'd been telling himself that they barely knew each other so they couldn't possibly feel anything for each other, now he realised that he'd been totally in denial. Because he did feel things for her. More than just physical attraction. This went deeper. He didn't have the words for it and it scared the hell out of him because he'd never felt anything like this before. All he knew was that he wanted her. Her and the baby.

That kick just now made him even more determined that this would work out.

'Can the baby hear me talking?' he asked.

She nodded. 'He likes being talked to. He really likes it when Mum sings to him.'

Singing to an unborn baby. He'd never thought of doing something like that. 'What, like a lullaby or something?'

She smiled. 'Pop songs. The Beatles, Take That, the Beach Boys. And we watched *Love Actually* again last weekend—Mum and I watch it every Christmas. He kicked like mad to "Catch a Falling Star" and "All I Want for Christmas is You".' She grinned. 'Probably because Mum and I were singing along, too.'

Singing to a baby.

He had so much to learn.

Would she have the patience to teach him?

'Does he—she—our baby,' he amended, 'kick at certain times?'

'He's usually quite lively first thing in the morning,' she said. 'And he's taken to doing somersaults at two in the morning. Mum says that's probably when he's going to wake up, wanting milk.'

'Our baby,' Antonio whispered.

* * *

Antonio's face was full of wonder. And was that a catch in his voice, a shimmer of tears in his eyes as he connected with their child?

For a moment, Tia was filled with hope.

Maybe he'd been right to bring her here. Maybe spending time together would help make the future clearer. Talking about their dreams, their hopes, what they wanted for the baby. Getting to know each other properly—their real selves—would help them find a way forward. Not in the daily grind of London, not in the unreal glamour of the palace, but here in the mountains—the place he'd loved since he was a child and came back to when he needed a breathing space. Here, where Antonio could be himself instead of being what he thought the world expected a prince to be.

'I never expected...' For a moment, his hand curved protectively over the bump. And then he grimaced and pulled his hand away. 'I apologise. That was intrusive of me.'

He was worried about touching her? Considering that they'd made a baby together... On the other hand, he'd been brought up with the strictest of protocols, and his job meant following rules and regulations, too. 'Most people like feeling a baby kick,' she said. 'Perfect strangers come up to me sometimes and ask if they can feel the baby kick.'

He looked surprised, as if it was something that had never occurred to him before.

'And this is your baby,' she added softly. 'It's absolutely fine for you to put your hand on my bump and feel him kick whenever you want to.'

He still didn't look comfortable with the idea. What would it take to make him unbend completely? she wondered.

'Can I get you some breakfast?' he asked.

'Toast would be lovely. Or fruit and yogurt. Whatever you have.'

'I'll call you when breakfast is ready,' he promised.

The toast was perfect, and there was a choice of local honey and jam.

'Would you like to go and choose a tree this morning?' he asked.

She wrinkled her nose at him. 'It seems a little bit extravagant, buying a tree for just a couple of days.'

'I'd like to give you a sort of Christmas in Casavalle,' he said.

Start some memories that they could share with the baby one day? Tia didn't say it out loud, in case she was wrong. But that moment when Antonio had first felt their baby kick, when his eyes had been full of joy and wonder, gave her hope that maybe he could break through the constriction of his upbringing. And if he could unbend, if he really was the man she was beginning to get to know, then maybe they really did have a future together. Maybe they really could be a team and have the kind of relationship her parents had had: the one thing she'd longed for so much but had thought would never happen. And the hope burned, so clear and so bright, in her heart.

'All right,' she said. 'Let's buy a tree. As long as it's a small one.'

Decorating the streets for Christmas seemed to be in full swing when they walked into the village together. There were nativity scenes in every shop window, each slightly different; there was a Christmas tree made out of wine bottles in the wine shop, a nativity scene with a backdrop of beautiful silk scarves in a boutique, another made from spun sugar in a confectionery store, and another made entirely from teddy bears in the toy shop.

'This is all amazing,' she said. 'So creative.'

'The shop windows are incredible,' he agreed. 'Displaying the nativity scene in shop windows has been a tradition here for many years, like it is in mainland Italy.'

Once they'd finished enjoying the displays, he said, 'Let's go and choose our tree. What would you like?'

Thinking of the scarily large tree at the palace, she said, 'Nothing taller than you.'

He grinned and pointed out the massive tree that had just been put up in the central square. 'Not like that, then? Because that might just fit.'

For a moment, remembering the double-height hallway in his house, she wondered if he was serious; then the glint in his eyes made her realise that he was teasing her. Something she hadn't expected, and which reinforced her hope for the future.

Not to mention how cute he was. That little quirk at the corner of his mouth. It made her want to stand on tiptoe, wrap her arms round his neck and steal a kiss.

What would he do if she did that?

Would it be too much, too soon? Would he push her away? Or would he wrap his arms tightly round her and kiss her all the way back?

She didn't dare take the risk. Not until she had a better idea of what he was thinking.

Instead, she kept the conversation light. Decorating was a safe subject. And she wasn't going to mention mistletoe.

'I'd prefer a little tree,' she said with a smile. 'Do you normally decorate the house here?'

'No,' he admitted. 'We're expected to be at the palace from the middle of November. It seems a bit pointless to decorate the house without anyone being here to enjoy it.'

'So do you actually have any decorations for the tree?'

'No. I thought maybe we could choose them together.'

Start a new tradition together, perhaps? But she suppressed the hope before it could take hold.

They headed for the pop-up Christmas stalls in the market place, and finally found the tree with the perfect shape and the perfect height. Antonio paid for it and arranged to have it delivered to the house later that morning.

The baby seemed to be kicking more at the sound of Antonio's voice. Recognising his father, perhaps?

At another of the stalls, Tia was really taken with a fir wreath that had seed pods of honesty sprayed with copper paint threaded through it. 'That's so pretty,' she said. 'I must remember to suggest that to Mum. She always makes the wreath for our front door. Maybe I can ask if they'd mind me taking a photograph.'

'I have a better solution. Would you like this one for the house?' he asked.

'I...' She looked at him. 'Would that be all right?'

'If it makes you happy, it makes me happy,' he said softly. 'And by buying here in the Christmas market I'm supporting the local economy, which is a good thing.'

So everybody won. 'Thank you. That would be really lovely,' she said.

Once they'd finished strolling around the stalls, Antonio steered her into a café. 'Until you've tried the hot chocolate here,' he said, 'you haven't tasted perfection.'

The hot chocolate was thick and rich, yet less sweet than the sort she'd drink back in England, and it was teamed perfectly with a slice of white chocolate and lemon *panettone*.

'Sorry, I'm afraid I need the ladies',' she said when she'd finished her hot chocolate.

'I've been reading up,' Antonio said. 'I gather it's a pregnant woman thing, especially in the third trimester.'

She nodded ruefully. 'I'm afraid so.'

On her way to the toilets, she saw a notice about the village children's Christmas party in the town hall. She didn't think anything of it until she was washing her hands and two women came in, both looking anxious and speaking in rapid Italian.

'I can't believe Mario went skiing yesterday and managed to break his leg. Whatever was my brother thinking? He was supposed to dress up as Father Christmas tomorrow afternoon for the children's party. He can't possibly do it now, not with his leg in plaster,' one of them said.

'Of course not. Poor man.'

'Oh, I don't pity him too much. He knew we were relying on him, but he had to go and show off on the slopes.' The first woman rolled her eyes. 'But now we have to find another Father Christmas, and everyone I've asked has a prior commitment they can't break.'

'We can't let the children down,' the second woman said.

'I'll keep going through my phone book, but I'm beginning to think we need some kind of Christmas miracle to find a new *Babbo Natale*,' the first woman said.

Or maybe they just needed an incognito prince, Tia thought. Antonio didn't have any prior commitments tomorrow at the palace; he'd arranged to spend a couple of days here with her, and she was perfectly happy for him to spend some of that time playing Father Christmas for the children. She almost opened her mouth and suggested it, but a kick from the baby stayed her.

Perhaps she really ought to check with Antonio first before she offered his services as *Babbo Natale*. Would he even be allowed to do something like that? And, if he was allowed to, would he want to, or was she expecting too much of him?

She looked at the poster again on her way back to the table, and took a photograph of it on her phone. If she could persuade Antonio into the Christmas spirit this afternoon, when they decorated his Christmas tree, then maybe he would agree to help save the children's Christmas party and arrange it with his security team.

Antonio had just had the perfect idea for the next stage of persuading Tia to give them a chance. What went with a Christmas tree better than a Christmas dinner?

A full-blown traditional Italian Christmas Eve dinner might be a little rich for a pregnant woman, he thought. But maybe he could cook her a traditional English dinner, the sort she'd shared with her family when she was young. The sort Nathan had told him about, with crispy roast potatoes, Brussels sprouts, sausages wrapped in bacon and, most of all, a huge roasted turkey.

And, with a little help, he could make this a nice surprise for her. He knew he could look up what he needed to know, but there was a quicker way to deal with this—and he needed to get this organised right now, before Tia came back to their table.

He grabbed his phone from his pocket and called Gina, the housekeeper who looked after the place when they weren't there.

'Good morning, Prince Antonio,' she answered. 'How are you?'

'I'm fine, thank you, Gina. And how are you?' he said politely.

'*Bene, grazie*,' she said, and he could hear the smile in her voice. 'Is there something you need me to do for you?'

'I was wondering… How long does it take to cook a traditional English roast turkey?'

'A turkey? It depends on the size.'

'For Christmas dinner, I was thinking a big one.'

'A six-kilogram turkey would take just under four hours to cook, plus half an hour to rest,' Gina mused.

He glanced at his watch. 'That would be perfect. Would you be able to source one for me and get it delivered to the house, please?'

'Of course, Prince Antonio.'

'And I need a few other things, too, please.' He rattled off the things he remembered Nathan talking about. 'And finally a Christmas pudding.'

'An English one?'

'An English one,' he confirmed.

'Now, that,' Gina said, 'will be a problem. A homemade one has to be made at least a month in advance so it can mature. And none of the shops in Picco Innevato is likely to stock an English Christmas pudding. Your best option for that, perhaps, is to have one flown in—either from Rome or from London.'

Which would be expensive. Money wasn't a problem for him but he knew it was a problem for Tia. Antonio was pretty sure she would react badly if he spent so much money on something as frivolous and extravagant as having a Christmas pudding flown in from London. And what if she didn't actually like Christmas pudding? 'What could I make as an alternative?'

'Perhaps a jelly, something that you can serve with fresh fruit and biscuits,' Gina said. 'Or perhaps some traditional Italian Christmas doughnuts.' She paused. 'Prince Antonio, I know I'm stepping outside the boundaries, but may I ask *why* you want to cook an English Christmas dinner?'

'I want to do something nice for my best friend's sister,' Antonio said. 'And I'd like to surprise her with it this evening.'

'Then why not make the meal a mixture of English and Casavallian traditions?' Gina suggested. 'So then you can have ravioli or gnocchi for a starter, the turkey and all the traditional English trimmings for the main, and then an Italian pudding and cheeses to finish?'

'That's a really good idea,' Antonio said. 'Thank you.'

'Your best friend's sister. Hmm. Would this be the same lady I bought the maternity clothes for?' Gina asked.

'Yes, and she loved them. Thank you again for your help,' Antonio said.

'It was my pleasure. And I will organise your turkey,' Gina said. 'Since you want to surprise her, you need to keep away from the house for long enough for me to get everything bought and delivered. Give me, say, two hours. Shall I prepare and cook everything for you?'

That would be the easy way out. He rather thought he needed to make the effort himself, if he was to impress Tia. 'Thank you, but I want to cook it myself. I'd appreciate a note about the turkey, though. I can handle everything else.' Or he could look it up online.

'*Bene.* I will arrange everything, and I will text you when I'm done,' Gina said.

'Thank you, Gina. I really appreciate your help,' he said.

He could see Tia walking back to their table, so he ended the call swiftly and pretended he'd simply been looking at something on his phone.

'Is everything all right?' he asked.

'Yes, thank you.'

Now all he had to do was to keep her away from the house for a couple of hours.

'Shall we go and look for decorations?' he asked.

'Of course. Do you want a particular colour scheme?'

Like the ones in the palace? He had a feeling that she'd

like something a lot more informal. 'This will be my first Christmas tree all of my own,' he said. 'So I'm happy to hear your suggestions.'

'Let's see what they have in the shops and what you like,' she suggested.

'What do you need for a tree?' he asked.

'Lights, maybe tinsel, something for the top of the tree and some ornaments,' she said promptly.

Lights turned out to be incredibly complicated.

'First of all, do you want white lights or coloured ones?' she asked when they were in the middle of one of the shops.

'Do you have a preference?' he asked.

'I like white ones,' she admitted. 'So they look like the stars.'

'Then we'll have white ones.'

But then it was about choosing string lights or LED lights; warm white or ice white; and did they want lights that twinkled, or glowed, or flashed, or moved in a pattern, or came with sound effects?

He didn't actually care, but he did need Tia out of the house so Gina could organise the ingredients for his surprise Christmas dinner, so he pretended to be much more interested in all the different functions than he really was. Ordering Tia about simply wouldn't work. He knew from his army days that if your team felt they had a stake in things and you were listening to them, they'd go above and beyond the call of duty for you.

They'd do this together. The personal way. So Tia would be sure he'd listened to her and wanted to work with her instead of imposing his Royal will. He'd prove to her that they were a good team. And then perhaps she would agree to marry him and the baby would have his protection.

Once they'd chosen the lights, they wandered into the

decorations department. Antonio paid close attention to the things she passed over and the things she seemed to like. In the end she chose silver and blue baubles, filigree silver stars, blue tinsel and a large silver star for the top of the tree.

She paused by the stand of glass baubles; there was a special one etched with a picture of the mountain and the words '*Picco Innevato 2019*'.

Hadn't she said that she, her parents and Nathan had chosen a new, special decoration together each year?

He was fairly sure from her expression that she really liked the glass bauble. He was also fairly sure that she thought it was way too much money for one little decoration.

'May I buy this for…?' He paused, getting the strongest feeling that she'd say no if he asked to buy it for her. But for the baby, perhaps… 'For our baby?' he said.

She nodded, and he thought he could see the sudden sparkle of tears in her eyes. Oh, no. He hadn't meant to upset her. 'Are you all right?' he asked.

'Yes. It's just…'

Part of her family tradition that would never be the same again, because her brother was no longer with them. He knew how that felt.

'It's a new beginning,' he said softly. 'We can't share this Christmas with Nathan or my father. But we can still share it with others. My new sister. Our baby.'

'Yes,' she said, and this time a single tear really did slide down her cheek.

He brushed it away with the pad of his thumb. Funny how such a light contact sent a shard of desire through him.

He needed to be more careful. This wasn't about his feelings. It was about doing the right thing. The honourable thing. His duty. He was beginning to think that they might just be in the same direction. Tia Phillips made him feel all kinds of things he'd never felt before. It was unsettling, yet at the same time it made him want to explore further, discover what it was about her that roused all his instincts: protectiveness, desire and...

He didn't quite have a name for the emotion, or at least he wasn't ready to admit it, even to himself. But he did know he wanted Tia around. And this wasn't like his past relationships, strictly for fun and only for now. He wanted more. He wanted all the warmth and the sweetness she could bring to his life.

When they'd finished in the decoration shop, he managed to stall her by insisting on having lunch out at one of the cafés in the village. Even though he'd made it very clear that this was his treat, he noticed that she picked the cheapest thing on the menu, and his heart bled for her.

If only she'd let him cherish her, the way she deserved.

But he was pretty sure she'd see it as an attack on her independence.

Finally, his phone buzzed to signal a message; he glanced at it surreptitiously, relieved to see that it was from Gina.

All done. Turkey in fridge, in roasting tin and foil, ready to go in oven.

She'd added cooking times and temperatures, too.

So Operation Persuade Tia could go full steam ahead.

As soon as Tia headed for the toilets, he texted Gina back.

Thank you.

He'd make very sure to arrange for a delivery of flowers this afternoon to show his gratitude properly. Even though it was Gina's job to look after the house and the family's needs when they were in residence, she was going the extra mile because he'd asked her to, and he wanted her to know he appreciated it.

Back at his house, he asked Tia, 'Where do you want to put the tree?'

'It's your family house, so it's your decision,' she reminded him.

'It's our Christmas,' he countered. 'So tell me what you want.'

'Could we put it in the conservatory?' she asked.

He'd half expected her to say that. He knew how much she loved the view from there. 'Of course,' he said.

While she set out the decorations, he put the Christmas tree up in the conservatory.

And maybe letting her be in charge of the decorating was the way forward, he thought. It would show her that he wouldn't insist on everything being done *his* way.

'So how do you want to do this?' he asked when she came to stand beside him.

'Start with the lights. Check they work, first.'

That was blatantly obvious—before you drove a car or flew a plane, you checked the lights worked—but he wasn't going to snap at her. She seemed to be enjoying the fact that he was deferring to her experience in Christmas-tree decorating. And he rather liked this confident side of her, so he just smiled and plugged them in. 'All present and correct.'

'So then we start at the top, weaving them in and out of the branches as we work our way down. It's probably easiest if we stand either side of the tree and feed the lights round to each other,' she said.

Antonio enjoyed that. Particularly when his fingers

brushed against hers when they transferred the lights to each other, and she blushed.

So she wasn't that indifferent to him, then…

Maybe, like him, she wasn't quite ready to put a name to what she was feeling. And maybe they'd find the courage to admit it—together.

Deliberately he let his fingers brush against hers again. And he held her gaze when she looked up at him. Her mouth was very slightly parted. Soft. Sweet. Tempting.

He remembered what it felt like to kiss her.

He wanted to kiss her again.

Yet, at the same time, he didn't want to push her too fast. These three days were supposed to be all about getting to know each other, spending time together, and talking. Kissing her meant that they wouldn't be talking. Not talking meant that they wouldn't be able to sort things out. So he resisted the urge. Though he noticed that she was staring at his mouth, too. Was she, too, remembering what it had felt like to kiss? To touch?

He nearly dropped a bauble at the thought, but he kept himself under control, the way he always did—both as a prince and as a soldier. Because he was going to do this the right way. Slowly. Well, as slowly as you could get in the three days she'd promised him.

When they'd finished, she turned on the lights and walked round the tree. 'That's great. No dark patches or gaps. Now we can put the star on the top.'

'Don't you do that last?' he asked.

She shook her head. 'Mum always said to work top down.' Her smile was wistful. 'Nathan and I used to take turns in putting the star on the top. Dad would lift us up, even when Nathan was twelve and getting really tall. But we were too big for Mum to lift us after Dad died, so then we used to stand on a chair.'

What would she do if he lifted her up? Would she back away? Or would she melt into his arms? Both options made him nervous. And, although he wanted to show her that they had a future, he didn't want her to feel that he was railroading her into things. He wanted her to want this, too.

He looked at her. 'Your choice. Chair or…?'

Was she going to choose him, or would she pick the safe option?

'Chair,' she said.

The safe option, then. He needed to back off. 'Chair,' he repeated, and fetched one. 'Though I'd prefer you to hold my shoulder for balance.'

She smiled, then. 'From the kick I just got, I think someone agrees with you.'

'Good. Our baby's sensible, then,' he said lightly.

Even though he knew she was only holding on to him for balance as she climbed up and he was careful not to breach any boundaries, his skin still tingled through his sweater where her hand rested on his shoulder. What he really wanted to do was to wrap his arms round her, kiss the bump, and then lift her down from the chair so he could kiss her… But still he kept himself in check. Just.

Once she'd climbed down again, he helped her add the tinsel garland, the baubles and the snowflakes, and then finally the special glass bauble for the baby. Again, his hands brushed against hers, and this time when he turned to her he noticed that her lips were slightly parted and her pupils were enormous.

All he had to do was lean forward and brush his mouth against hers.

She held his gaze for a moment, glanced at his mouth and then up again.

His heart skipped a beat as she closed her eyes.

Now…

He'd closed half the gap between them when the alarm on his phone shrilled.

Her eyes opened again and she stared at him in shock.

Talk about *timing*. 'Sorry,' he said. 'That's my schedule.'

'Schedule?'

'Uh-huh. I need to do something in the kitchen.'

So much for thinking that he was going to get away with this, because she followed him into the kitchen. 'You've got an alarm on your phone to tell you to do something in here?'

'Yes.' He sighed. 'Since you're clearly not going to budge until I tell you, I need to put the turkey in the oven.'

'What turkey?'

'The turkey we're eating tonight. I'm cooking you Christmas dinner.'

'You're cooking me Christmas dinner?' she echoed, blinking at him with surprise.

Oh, honestly. Just because he was a prince, it didn't mean he was incapable of doing anything. He could dress himself, too. The years of royals needing valets and lady's maids had gone long, long ago. And he'd made her dinner last night. 'I *can* cook, you know,' he said, slightly exasperated. 'Putting alarms on my phone means I know when to put things in the oven and when to check them or take them out.'

'You're cooking me Christmas dinner,' she repeated. And this time she smiled. 'I really didn't expect that.'

'It's not a completely traditional English Christmas dinner. It's a fusion,' he said. 'In Casavalle, traditionally we have fish on Christmas Eve. The meal can be eight or nine courses.'

She rubbed her bump. 'I'm not sure I'd be able to manage that much.'

'And some of it's spicy. So that's why I'm cooking a fusion meal,' he said. 'I remember Nathan talking about turkey and the trimmings, so I'm cooking that. I don't have time to soak the salt cod to make *baccalà* for a first course, so I'm doing traditional gnocchi with sage and butter sauce instead—well, I admit it's not home-made and comes from the deli—and an Italian pudding, because the only way I'd get a traditional English Christmas pudding here is to fly one in.'

She frowned. 'Fly one in? That's crazy—it's a total waste of money. You could use that to do something better.' She spread her hands. 'Say, something nice for the villagers here in Picco Innevato.'

'I thought you might react like that,' he said, 'so I'm not flying a pudding in. I'm making *frittelle*—fried Christmas doughnuts. But you're putting me off my schedule. Can you just—well—not talk for five minutes?' he asked plaintively.

She gave him a speaking look, but nodded.

He took the turkey out of the fridge.

'That's enormous!' Tia protested.

So much for her not speaking for five minutes. 'Isn't that the point of a Christmas turkey, to be enormous?' he asked, putting the bird into the oven.

'We'll never eat all that, even if you can talk Giacomo into eating with us this evening,' she said. 'And how did you get this anyway? It wasn't in the fridge when I got the milk out this morning.'

'I called Gina while we were in the café,' he admitted, 'and she organised this for us.'

'Then perhaps you can invite Gina to share Christmas dinner with us,' Tia suggested. 'Does she have a family?'

'Yes. She lives with her husband. Her children are grown up now, and they live in the capital rather than here.'

'That would make five of us for dinner, then,' she mused. 'Though that turkey's easily big enough for twelve people.'

'Isn't it also traditional to have turkey as leftovers?' he asked.

'Well, yes,' she admitted.

'Then it will be fine for five. I'll invite Giacomo, Gina and her husband.'

'So it'll be like a family Christmas.'

She looked wistful, and Antonio realised what was missing. Family. He wasn't asking his family to meet her, not until she'd agreed to marry him; but he could invite hers to join them. 'Yes. I can fly your mother over. Give me ten minutes to arrange it. I'll sort out a private plane so she won't have to wait for a flight, and a car to take her to the airport in London and another one this end.'

Tia bit her lip. 'That's kind of you, but I think the journey might take it out of her too much.'

'Help me here, Tia,' he said softly. 'What do you want?'

'What you planned. That was a really nice thought.'

'But with more people, so it's like a real family Christmas?'

She nodded. 'And I want to help you prepare dinner. Even if you have got a gazillion alarms on your phone telling you what to do.' Her lips quirked. 'Mind you, I should've expected that. Nathan did stuff with military precision, too.'

'It works,' he said.

She grinned. 'So what now—you're going to cut every vegetable exactly the same length, and to make sure of it there's a tape measure next to your knife rack?'

There was a slight twinkle in her eye and Antonio

couldn't help responding to it. 'Are you saying I need a tape measure?'

'Do you?' She lifted her chin.

Right then, she was near enough to kiss, and he almost, *almost* dipped his head to brush his mouth against hers. But then he could see the sudden panic in her eyes, as if the teasing had gone too far and had tipped into something else entirely, something she wasn't quite ready for.

This wasn't about putting pressure on her. It was about getting her to relax. About getting to know her. About letting her get to know him. So he pulled back. 'If we spend all this time talking about doing the veg instead of actually doing them,' he said, much more lightly than he felt, 'then our dinner guests are going to have to wait until tomorrow before we can feed them.'

'Good point,' she said.

'Let me call Gina and talk to Giacomo. And then we'll make dinner together.'

She really hadn't expected this. And she was seeing a completely different side to Antonio Valenti. He was trying to give her the family Christmas she missed so badly and longed for so much. And he wasn't standing on ceremony, insisting on asking the village's mayor and important personages to join them; he was perfectly happy to eat with her and his housekeeper and his security officer. He'd taken on board what she'd said about Christmas not being about money but about spending time together.

So, if she agreed to marry him and give the baby his name, maybe she wasn't going to be trapped in a completely loveless marriage. Maybe he was trying to show her that he could give her what she needed. That he could learn to love her and she could learn to love him.

Maybe, just maybe, this was going to work out.

Once Antonio had arranged for their dinner guests to join them, he brought out the vegetables, pans and sharp knives. 'OK. Crispy roast potatoes and parsnips, carrots, Brussels sprouts and red cabbage. I have chipolata sausages ready to be wrapped with bacon, and I have stuffing—which Gina says I should cook separately. What else?'

'That,' she said, 'is pretty comprehensive. Cranberry sauce?'

'Yes.' He grimaced. 'Though it's not home-made. It's in a jar.'

'A jar is fine. Gravy?'

'I think,' he said carefully, 'I might put you in charge of gravy.'

She smiled. 'So you're learning to delegate?'

He coughed. 'I believe your brother had a saying about pots and kettles.'

She laughed. 'OK. You have a point. I'm not very good at delegating, either.' But his mention of Nathan made her eyes prickle. 'I miss him. Nathan.'

'Me, too,' Antonio admitted.

'I was thinking. If our baby really is a boy, I'd like to call him Nathan—after my brother and my dad.' Though Nathan wasn't the only one Antonio had lost. 'And maybe his middle name could be Vincenzo, after your dad?'

'That,' Antonio said, 'would be perfect.'

Would the baby's last name be Valenti or Phillips? They still hadn't agreed on that bit. But this was a step in the right direction, she thought. They were starting to meet in the middle.

But Tia found herself enjoying the afternoon, preparing dinner together with Christmas music playing softly in the background. It really felt like the Christmases of her child-hood, memories that pierced her heart with their sweetness.

Before their guests arrived, she showered and changed into the pretty dress Gina had bought for her.

'You look lovely,' Antonio said.

'Thank you.' So did he, in a formal white shirt, beautifully cut dark suit and understated silk tie. And his shoes were polished the same way as she remembered Nathan and her father polishing theirs, to a military mirror finish.

But could the Soldier Prince allow himself to be ruffled just enough at the edges to deal with a baby?

She pushed the thought aside. Not now. He'd gone to a lot of effort for her, and she wasn't going to start complaining.

Their guests arrived, and Antonio introduced Tia to Gina and her husband Enrico.

'It's lovely to meet you,' Tia said, hugging Gina. 'And thank you so much for finding me such beautiful clothes. It was so kind of you.'

'My pleasure, *piccola*,' Gina said, hugging her back.

Once their guests were seated, Tia helped Antonio bring in the first course, and then the dishes for the main. He carved the turkey at the table, just as she remembered her father doing when she was small, and they all helped themselves to the sides.

Tia was surprised to find how much she was enjoying herself—and how relaxed Prince Antonio was.

Perhaps now was the right time to ask him...

'Do you have plans for tomorrow?' she asked.

'We can go exploring, if you like, take a drive deeper into the mountains,' he suggested.

'I have a better idea,' she said. 'When we were in the café this morning, I overheard someone talking about the village Christmas party for the children tomorrow afternoon.'

'They hold the party every year in the town hall,' Gina explained, 'for all the children in the villages who attend the *scuola elementary* and *asilo*—primary school and kindergarten. I used to help out, in the years when my Chiara and Matteo were young enough to go to the party.' Gina smiled. 'Basically the party's for children under the age of eleven, so there's dancing and games and party food and, of course, *Babbo Natale* to give each child a small gift.'

'Father Christmas,' Tia said. 'But the man who's supposed to be doing it this year can't do it now because he's just broken his leg skiing.'

Antonio looked puzzled. 'How do you know all this?'

'I overheard two of the organisers talking in the ladies' yesterday. They said they couldn't find a replacement Father Christmas.' And this was the thing. Would the Prince think of his own child-to-be and unbend enough to do something kind for the children in the village—something that wouldn't cost him at all financially, but would mean giving up his time and doing something in person? 'And I was wondering,' she continued, 'if maybe you might offer to step in and help?'

'Me?' He looked as shocked as if she'd just suggested that he should take off all his clothes in public to raise money for charity.

He might put his life at risk, the way her brother had, for his job; but putting his dignity at risk was clearly a very different thing. A step too far, perhaps?

But she pressed on. 'All you'd have to do is put on a costume and a beard, maybe tie a pillow round your middle so you look plump enough to be Father Christmas, say, "Ho, ho, ho," a lot, and give each child a present.'

Dress up as *Babbo Natale*.

Antonio tried to get his head round it. This just wasn't the sort of thing his family did. And he hadn't had much to do with children, despite being the patron of a charity for children from an armed forces background who'd been bereaved; he had no idea how they would respond to him.

Then again, in three months' time he would have a baby of his own. He probably ought to take every opportunity he could to have some practice at being around babies and children.

Tia, he thought, would be a natural at being a mother. He could easily imagine her calming a fractious toddler in the coffee shop with a story or crayons, or soothing a baby while its tired mum sat down for two minutes with a cup of tea. And he could understand the attraction of the children's party for her, given that she'd had to put her dreams of being a primary school teacher to one side.

She wanted him to do this.

And it would be another step forward in his campaign to prove to her that they'd be good together and he would learn to be a good husband and father.

He took a deep breath. 'All right. I'll do it. Gina, given that you know about the party, do you know who's organising it?'

'Actually, I have the answer to that one,' Tia said. 'Excuse me for being rude and using tech at the table.' She grabbed her phone and pulled up a photograph. 'There was a poster in the café. The organiser's number is here.'

'Signora Capelli.' Although most of the villagers would speak English for the tourists, the children's Christmas party was for the locals, so the conversation had probably been in Italian. 'Do you speak much Italian, Tia?' he asked, curious.

She nodded. 'Giovanni and Vittoria—my bosses at the café—are originally from Naples. So over the years I've gradually learned from them.'

So even though she hadn't been able to travel, she'd

at least had the pleasure of being able to learn another language.

He looked at her, then switched to Italian. 'If I play Father Christmas, will it make you happy?'

She paused for a bit, as if working out the correct phrases. '*Sì. Molto felice*,' she said.

He grinned. 'Then for you,' he said, switching back to English, 'I will do it. Giacomo, if I call and arrange it, would you…?'

'Sort out the security aspect? Of course,' his security officer said with a smile. 'Actually, sir, I think you would make a very good *Babbo Natale*.'

Antonio wasn't so sure, but he'd do it. 'Excuse me. As you said, Tia, tech at the table is rude, but let me make that call.'

A few minutes later, it was all arranged.

'They're delighted that I can help,' Antonio said. 'But I told them that you were the one who persuaded me to do it, so they'd like to invite you to come to the party as well.'

'I'd love to,' she said, and the sheer pleasure in her eyes made Antonio feel something odd in the region of his heart—as if something inside was cracking.

Once they'd eaten the fresh fruit and little Christmas fritters Antonio had prepared during the afternoon, he ushered everyone through to the sitting room.

'But surely we need to clear up first?' Tia asked.

'No. I'll sort it out later. Tonight is for having fun,' he said. 'Let's go through to the sitting room.'

They played a few rounds of charades, half in English and half in Italian. And then Antonio brought out a box that he'd had delivered earlier that day, containing a copy of the musical game with kazoos that Tia had told him about enjoying so much.

Tears glittered in her eyes as he placed the box on the table.

He went to stand next to her. 'I ordered it online for delivery today. Did I do the wrong thing?' he asked softly, taking her hand. 'Because we don't have to play the game if you'd rather not. I apologise for upsetting you. That wasn't my intention.'

'No, it's a really kind thought.' She swallowed hard. 'I have such lovely memories of playing this with Mum and Dad and Nathan. And now I'm going to have lovely memories of playing with you.'

He didn't want this to be just a memory. He wanted it to be the start of a whole new tradition. But he didn't know how to tell her. Instead, awkwardly, he squeezed her hand.

Several times during the game, Tia caught his eye and his heart felt as if it had done a backflip. And several times he could see the baby kicking. It blew him away. He'd never expected to feel anything like this, and he really wasn't sure how to deal with it. All he could do was be the polite, perfect host, the way he'd been brought up to be. And he wished he could let himself go as easily as Tia, Gina, Giacomo and Enrico seemed to be able to do. But nobody in his family ever let go like that. He'd just have to try harder.

Or maybe that was the point: this should be effortless, and he was trying too hard. And the crack he'd felt inside him earlier seemed to freeze up again.

'Time to make some tea,' Tia said, holding her sides. 'I need a break from laughing.'

'I'll help you,' Gina said. She followed Tia into the kitchen and stacked the dishwasher while Tia filled the kettle and put cups and a teapot on a tray. She winked at the younger woman. 'I know the Prince said he'd clear up tomorrow, but men never stack the dishwasher properly.'

'That's what Vittoria says about Giovanni at work,' Tia said with a smile. Gina reminded her very much of her boss, making her feel completely relaxed and at home.

'I've known Prince Antonio for many years, since he was tiny and his family first came here to this house,' Gina said. 'But this is the first time I've seen him look this relaxed, as an adult. It's not my place to ask questions, but…?' She looked pointedly at Tia's bump.

Tia knew the older woman had Antonio's best interests at heart. 'Yes, the baby is his.' She wrinkled her nose. 'But it's complicated.'

'Antonio needs love in his life,' Gina said softly. 'King Vincenzo was always very formal with both the boys. Queen Maria was a bit less so, but there was still always a little reserve and they never really had a proper childhood, even here. I think you and the baby might be good for Prince Antonio.' She flapped a hand. 'But I'm speaking out of turn.'

'Not at all,' Tia reassured her. 'And I won't say a word of what you said to the Prince.'

It hadn't occurred to her before that maybe the Prince didn't have everything in his life—that maybe her love and the baby would be a gift to him. But, the more she thought about it, the more she realised that he really was the 'poor little rich boy' and their positions were completely reversed. Although she was financially and socially much poorer than him, when it came to love and family she was so much richer.

But would she and the baby be enough for him?

Because, even though she felt she'd grown so much closer to Antonio today—that she was more than halfway to falling in love with the man behind the royal mask—she didn't think he felt the same about her. Antonio was all about duty, and she wasn't sure that she could live a life without love. If he married her purely because he thought it was the right thing to do, could he grow to love her and the baby? And did she really want to live in a world where everything they did or said was put under the microscope of public opinion?

She forced the thought away and took the tray of tea through, smiling at Antonio, Giacomo and Enrico. But her busy day started to catch up with her, and she found herself yawning.

'I'm so sorry,' she said. 'I don't mean to be rude.'

'Being pregnant is tiring, child,' Gina said. 'Go to bed. We understand.'

'Thank you. And thank you all for such a lovely evening. It really felt like a proper Christmas,' she said.

But by the time she climbed into bed, she was wide awake and worrying again.

Antonio had been very quiet after dinner. Was he having second thoughts about this? Could he grow to love her? Should she marry him, give the baby his protection? Or would she be better off going back to London and bringing up their baby in love and relative obscurity?

CHAPTER FIVE

ANTONIO HAD ALMOST finished clearing up in the kitchen when his phone pinged.

Who would message him this late at night? It must be something important, he thought, and picked up his phone to see a message from Luca.

I thought you should know about this before it hits the media tomorrow.

There was an attachment to the message: a PDF of a press release.

Antonio read it and blew out a breath. According to the press release, the DNA test proved beyond all doubt that Gabriella was the oldest child of King Vincenzo, and the palace would like to announce that she would accede to the throne rather than Luca. Luca would remain in his role as the Crown Prince and would support his older sister through the beginning of her reign.

As soon as this news reached the media, Antonio realised, it would be splashed over the front pages of the newspapers. And he would be expected back at the palace as soon as possible. Which meant time was running out for his impromptu getaway with Tia.

His duty meant that he ought to fly back first thing in the morning. Or even tonight.

But he'd promised to play *Babbo Natale* at the village children's Christmas party.

Although he knew the organisers would understand him having to duck out at the last minute, given the news, it would mean leaving them in a mess. And Antonio Valenti was a man who kept his promises. He didn't want to disappoint the children or the villagers—and he really didn't want to disappoint Tia.

But if he didn't go back to the palace first thing tomorrow, he would disappoint his family.

Whatever he did, he was going to let someone down.

Thinking about it logically, he knew that his brother, his mother and Gabriella had each other and all the resources of the palace to support them. Tia had nobody; although she would have emotional support from her mother, Grace Phillips wasn't well enough to deal with the inevitable media intrusion. The stress might even bring on a relapse of her medical condition.

Well, he wasn't going to abandon Tia for a third time.

He typed a message into his phone.

Thanks for update. Will be back in a couple of days. Things I need to do here first.

He was surprised when a message came back almost immediately.

Miles told me who Tia was, but he refused to tell me anything else. Though someone in the office told me she looks very pregnant. Assume congratulations are in order?

Oh. With Tia being so petite, her bump really showed. Of course people would gossip in the palace, even if Miles told them not to, about the pregnant woman who'd come to see the Prince, and Antonio's subsequent disappearance. He'd be naive to think otherwise.

Does Mamma know?

I haven't said anything. I think this needs to come from you.

Of course it did. He already knew that.

Hopefully the media will concentrate on events here. Wrap things up and come back as soon as you can.

Thanks. I will.

Antonio was pretty sure that Luca would leave it at that, but then his phone pinged again.

So do you have a view of snow?

Of course his brother would guess where he'd gone. Antonio had been fooling himself to think otherwise. Picco Innevato was where Antonio always went when he needed some space after a difficult mission.

Yes.

Christmassy. That's nice.

Antonio nearly typed back, *Who are you and what have you done with my older brother?* But, actually, it was nice to feel that for once his older brother wasn't as unbending as their father.

Yes, it is. I put a tree up in the house.

Though he wasn't entirely sure that Luca would understand about him playing *Babbo Natale* at the children's Christmas party. Not when a major announcement was being made and he really ought to be back at the palace, supporting his family.

I'll message you when I'm on my way back.

Good luck. I hope it works out with Tia. Finding someone who loves you—that's special.

And then the penny finally dropped.

Luca had changed. When he'd come back from meeting Gabriella at Crystal Lake, he'd been different. And Antonio was pretty sure that it had a lot to do with Imogen Albright, the woman he'd met out there and become engaged to.

His brother was in love; and that love had melted his habitual reserve.

Antonio couldn't quite get his head round the fact that his elder brother was actually wishing him luck in love.

Then again, he knew he needed luck. If he couldn't persuade Tia to love him, he needed at the very least a good working relationship with the mother of his baby—a child who was definitely going to be fourth in line to the throne.

Me, too, he typed, though this time he didn't send the message.

The next morning, Antonio checked the main news sites on his phone. They were full of the shock announcement about Gabriella, the long-lost Princess of Casavalle who was about to become the new Queen. And quite a few of them seemed to have noticed that Prince Antonio wasn't at the palace and were asking exactly where he was.

Thankfully the villagers at Picco Innevato had always been protective of his family, and he knew that none of them would sell him out to the media. Until he'd persuaded Tia to marry him and let him give her and the baby his protection, he wanted to stay well out of the limelight.

Today was their last full day in the village in any case, but he knew that time was running out. He needed to wrap things up here and go back to the palace.

He sent a holding message to his mother, Gabriella and Miles—all of whom had texted him that morning—saying that he'd be back tomorrow but had some things he needed to do first. He knew the message was vague, and it would no doubt infuriate them all, but he'd learned in the army that you needed to do the right things in the right order. Tia had to come first.

When she came downstairs, he made her breakfast. Now wasn't the time to worry her about palace politics. He wanted to concentrate on *her*. 'I was going to ask your advice.'

'My advice?' She looked surprised. 'About what?'

'The children's party. It's a little outside my usual sphere.' Which was an understatement. 'I've rarely had contact with children with my family duties, even as patron of the charity—I tend to work with the fundraisers rather than the children.'

'And you don't know what to do?'

'No,' he admitted. 'I'm guessing that your customers at the café include families with children.' Plus he knew she'd dreamed of being a primary school teacher. So she must have some idea of how to work with children.

'Just be yourself,' she said. 'After you've finished being *Babbo Natale*—and obviously make sure that none of them see you change out of the costume—I think just join in with the games.'

Could it really be that simple? 'OK.' But then there was the party. 'Maybe I ought to do more for the party. Perhaps I could pay for the presents?'

'Christmas really isn't about money and heaps of expensive presents,' she said softly, 'it's about spending time with people and making them feel good. When you were a child—I know things were a bit different for you, but wasn't the best part of Christmas playing games with your brother?'

He thought about it.

Just as last night hadn't been about presents—it had been about having fun, and that one game he'd bought had meant more to Tia than if he'd bought her the richest and most exclusive of jewels.

'Yes.'

'Well, then,' she said. 'And I'm sure the organisers have already sorted everything out. If you go in and say you're going to buy extra presents for the children, it's kind of like you telling them that whatever they've already done isn't good enough.'

'I hadn't really thought about it in that way.' He looked awkwardly at her. 'Just that with my family's background, I feel I ought to do more.'

'Time's so much more important than money. Anyone can buy gifts; it's the easy way out,' she said. 'And not just anyone's prepared to dress up as Santa and be patient with children who are shy or nervous. The people in the village will appreciate what you're doing so much more than if you call a shop and pay for a huge sackful of presents to be wrapped. You're giving something of *yourself*.

What the children want at the Christmas party is Father Christmas. And today that's going to be you.'

Tia Phillips looked like an ordinary woman. But Antonio was beginning to learn just how extraordinary she was.

'You're right,' he said. 'They want Father Christmas.'

He knew he really ought to tell her about what was going on in the palace, especially as it meant that they'd have to leave Picco Innevato tomorrow, but he knew she was looking forward to the party and he didn't want to spoil today for her. There was time enough for them to have to deal with the politics. He'd tell her tomorrow.

Half an hour before the party was due to start, he and Tia went into the village hall to meet the organisers.

'We're so grateful, Your Royal Highness,' Signora Capelli said.

'It's nice to be able to do something for the village,' Antonio said. 'So what exactly do I do?'

'Once in costume, *Babbo Natale* sits on the chair in the grotto,' Signora Capelli said, indicating the chair festooned with tinsel underneath an arch decorated with more tinsel and cut-out Christmas trees that had clearly been painted by the children. 'He greets each child, wishes them a merry Christmas and gives them a present.'

He could do that.

'We've put the presents into sacks, split by age group, and your helper will tell you the name and the age of each child just before they come to see you,' Signora Capelli continued.

'Thank you,' Antonio said. 'That's very clear. Who's my helper?' He looked at Tia. Given that he was dressing up as Father Christmas, would she be prepared to dress up as an elf?

Signora Capelli smiled. 'I would suggest Tia, but her condition is a little…distinctive.'

Her baby bump. Of course the children would notice that the guest at their party had the same bump as *Babbo Natale*'s helper.

'But perhaps you'd like to help us with the table, Tia?' Signora Capelli asked.

'Of course,' Tia said with a smile. She indicated the other helpers, who were wearing Santa hats or reindeer antlers. 'And I'm perfectly happy to wear a hat or reindeer antlers if you want me to.'

'Antlers. Of course.' Signora Capelli looked anxious. 'Sir, forgive me for being rude, but I assume you know the names of all the reindeer?'

'Rudolph,' he said. Then he stopped. He didn't actually know any others. It wasn't something they'd ever talked about at the palace or in the army.

Tia laughed. 'Don't worry—I do. Dasher and Dancer, Prancer and Vixen, Comet and Cupid, Donner and Blitzen.' She made him repeat the names until he was word-perfect, and it made him realise what a fabulous teacher she'd make.

He changed into the costume and beard. 'You're right. I need padding,' he said.

Signora Capelli found some cushions and Tia, wearing antlers and looking incredibly cute with her huge brown eyes and curly black hair, helped him put the final touches to his outfit.

Tia stood back with her hands on her hips and looked at him. 'Perfect.'

Never in a million years would he have expected to do something like this. Or that she'd have tears in her eyes.

'Are you all right?' he asked.

'Yes. It's just… Thank you for doing this, Antonio.

For making things right for the children.' Impulsively, she hugged him; and the feeling of something cracking in the middle of his chest intensified.

As soon as he was sitting on the tinsel 'throne' in his grotto—a million miles away from the real throne in their palace—the children streamed into the hall and a queue formed to meet him. He didn't have time to watch out for Tia, because he was too busy playing his role, and he found himself improvising when a child asked him about the North Pole and what the elves did there.

'They help me make gifts and wrap them up for the children who would like them,' he said, crossing his fingers mentally.

Another child asked him about the reindeer, and he was grateful that Tia had drilled him on the right names.

Every single child seemed thrilled with their gift from *Babbo Natale*, but it didn't take long for Antonio to realise that Tia had been right when she'd said that Christmas wasn't about the presents: today was all about the gifts of time and love and kindness.

The smiles on their faces warmed his heart. Then one little boy gave him a carrot. 'It's a present for Rudolph,' he said.

'Thank you very much,' Antonio said. 'Carrots are his favourite. He'll be delighted to share that with his friends for dinner.'

Another little girl who must've been about seven shyly handed him a Cellophane wrapper tied with a bow. 'You always bring us presents every year, *Babbo Natale*,' she said, 'but nobody brings you one and I think they should. My *mamma* helped me make this for you this morning and I put special sprinkles on it and I wrapped it just for you.'

There was a huge lump in his throat. A small, thoughtful gift that felt incredibly special. Over the years, as a child, he'd been given incredibly expensive and exclusive gifts; but this one was *personal*. One that taught him the real meaning of Christmas. 'That's so kind of you,' he said. 'It looks so pretty. I'll enjoy that with my glass of milk later today. Thank you so much.'

When he'd given the last child their present, he waved goodbye to everyone and wished everyone a merry Christmas, then headed out of the hall back to the room where he'd changed into the costume. He folded everything up neatly—Tia would no doubt tease him about doing it with military precision, just as she'd teased him about his schedule for cooking Christmas dinner—and then headed back towards the hall.

Tia was waiting for him just outside. 'Are you OK?' she asked.

'Yes. That was amazing—really humbling.' He blew out a breath and nodded through the open doorway. 'See that little girl over there with the curly black hair in the blue dress?'

'Yes.'

'She gave me a cookie, all prettily wrapped. She'd made it especially for me this morning with her mother's help and chose the sprinkles. She said nobody ever brings *Babbo Natale* a present and she...' Suddenly, he just couldn't say anything else.

She hugged him, clearly realising how deeply the gift had affected him. 'That's what Christmas is about,' she said. 'It's the thought behind the gift, how personal it is.'

Right then, he knew exactly what he wanted for Christmas.

Tia.

And their baby.

But he didn't know how to tell her. He couldn't get the

words out. They stuck in his throat. But he wanted her so much. Needed her. Needed both of them.

Why was it so hard to say it? Why couldn't he just open his mouth and say, 'Tia, the way I feel about you puts my head in a spin and I can't find the right words, but please stay with me'?

This wasn't the place, either. And it was too important for him to mess up by simply blurting out the jumble in his head.

'We'd better get back to the party,' she said.

The children insisted that the Prince and Tia should share their party tea—bruschetta, cherry tomatoes, carrot sticks, little cubes of cheese and ham and the traditional Italian *tronchetti di Natale*.

'I love chocolate Yule log,' Tia said with a smile, accepting a slice.

Both he and Tia danced with the children and joined in the games—sticking a carrot 'nose' on the outline of a snowman while their eyes were covered with a scarf, guessing the items in a stocking just by feeling them, using a paper straw to blow a cotton wool 'snowball' in a race to the finish line, and 'Christmas ornament' musical chairs, where the children danced round the cut-out ornaments as the music played and had to stand on an ornament when the music stopped.

It was way, way outside anything Antonio had ever done before, though he suspected from the way that Tia joined in that she'd maybe been involved with something similar at the café where she worked. And he was surprised by how much fun it was, everything from the games to the dancing. It made him feel different—part of the village, more so than he did even as a child, and he really felt connected with his people.

He realised then that the weird feeling in his chest was

happiness. Here in Picco Innevato at the children's party, he felt accepted for who he was, instead of being seen as a remote prince. He'd never even had that feeling in the army, where he had previously been at his happiest.

So much for persuading Tia; what he'd actually done was persuade himself. Because Tia had shown him how good life could be, how it felt to be part of a family—and that was what he wanted. To see her eyes sparkle and her face glow with happiness as she danced with the children, to see her glance over at him and smile with a warmth that made his own heart sing. He wanted to see her look like that while she danced with their own child in the middle of their kitchen. A private moment far from the formality of his day-to-day life.

Once the party was over, he and Tia helped to clear up, hugged all the organisers goodbye, and walked back through the village to his house.

'I believe you now about doing your fair share of the cleaning,' she said with a smile. 'Seeing you wielding that broom with military pr—'

'Tia,' he cut in, 'that particular joke is wearing just a little bit thin.'

'But it was,' she said, her smile broadening into a grin. 'Watching you sweep a floor was like watching a man with a mower making a stripy lawn.'

He thought about kissing her to stop her talking.

But that was too tempting—and too dangerous to his peace of mind. If he let himself give in to his feelings, if he said the wrong thing and scared her away… Plus they were in a public place. He'd wait until they were back at the house. And maybe the walk home would give him enough time to put his thoughts and his feelings back in order. Instead, he said, 'The Christmas market in the square looks really pretty, all lit up for night-time.'

Thankfully it distracted her, and she smiled at him. 'That'd be nice.'

And when she allowed him to take her arm—which was ostensibly for safety in case she slipped, but was really because he just wanted to be close to her—he was shocked to discover that it made him feel as if he'd just conquered the world.

'We have a Christmas market a bit like this on the South Bank in London,' she said. 'You can buy mulled wine, hot chocolate, various foods and gifts. And then you can cross the river over to Somerset House and go to the skating rink. But here it's different—the hot chocolate is much thicker, and there are those gorgeous nativity scenes everywhere.'

When they got to the stalls, she stopped by the little wooden shack offering snow globes for sale, and her eye seemed to be caught by one in particular—a crystalline star suspended inside the globe and set on a crystal base. She picked it up, and her dark eyes gleamed with pleasure. But then she examined the base, looked regretful and replaced it carefully.

Antonio had the strongest feeling that she loved the globe, but she'd just seen the price and it was outside her budget. He knew that Tia would be too proud to admit that she couldn't afford it, and if he insisted on buying it for her right now she'd be embarrassed and awkward. But there was a way around it: he'd buy it without her knowing and give it to her later, in private. A surprise gift. And he'd make it clear there were no strings. He stood behind her so she couldn't see his face, caught the stall-holder's eye and mimed to him to save the snow globe for him. The stall-holder glanced at Tia, clearly checking to make sure she couldn't see his reaction and guess what was going on, then winked at Antonio.

At the next stall, when Tia bought a scented candle decorated with pressed flowers for her mother, Antonio excused himself and went back to get the snow globe she'd liked. The stall-holder wrapped it in a box tied with a bright scarlet ribbon; Antonio slipped the box into his pocket so it wasn't visible. He'd give it to Tia later, when the time was right.

Antonio insisted on carrying Tia's purchase from the candle stall but, when he went to tuck her hand into his arm for balance, somehow they ended up holding hands.

At the party, Tia had seen a whole new side to the Prince.

Sure, he'd been a bit formal and over the top when he'd helped clear up, marching up and down with the broom as if he was on a military parade: but he *had* helped, as if he was just another one of the villagers and not the man who was third in line to the throne of Casavalle. And the way he'd been with the children… Even though she knew he'd had such a formal upbringing and he'd actually asked her advice about what to do at the party, he'd then done his best to fit in and make the afternoon fun for the children. She'd taken a sneaky snap of him on her phone while he'd been playing the snowball-blowing game, surrounded by children and laughing, and he'd really looked as if he belonged.

It gave her so much hope for the future. From what she'd seen, she really believed that Antonio could learn to be a warm, loving father. That maybe he could escape his upbringing and learn to be *himself*. And that maybe she was the one who could help him do that. To think that she might be the one to finally unlock his heart was amazing: it would be a real privilege, even though it scared her because she might not be up to the task. Though, for the sake of their baby—and for themselves—she'd make sure she was good enough.

As they walked up the steps to the porch leading to his front door, he paused.

'What?' she asked.

'What do you see?' he asked.

'Your front door. A Christmas wreath.' The one with copper-painted honesty seed pods that they'd bought together. 'Gorgeous sparkly lights on the trees on either side of the door.' Immaculately clipped cones of yew that were no doubt measured to get them that precise shape.

'And?' He glanced upwards, indicating where she should look.

'Mistletoe.' She caught her breath. Was he suggesting they should…? 'Do you have a tradition about mistletoe in Italy?' she asked, her voice hoarse.

He inclined his head. 'Here it tends to be New Year's Eve when you kiss under the mistletoe. But you're English, so I think perhaps we should use the English tradition.'

Which meant kissing under the mistletoe at Christmas…

Then again, they'd decorated the house for Christmas and he'd cooked them a proper Christmas dinner. This was a sort of early Christmas. It counted.

So she made no protest when he dipped his head and kissed her, his mouth warm and sweet and coaxing. She leaned into the kiss and slid her hands into his hair, drawing him closer. He wrapped his arms round her, holding her tightly, and kissed her until she was dizzy.

There was suddenly a volley of kicks in her stomach, and he broke the kiss, laughing. 'I think someone wants to tell us something.'

'That might be the baby equivalent of saying "Get a room",' she said ruefully.

He rested his hand on her bump. 'This blows my mind. Our baby.'

The expression on his face was a mixture of pride and tenderness and… No, Tia didn't dare let herself hope for anything else. But if he bonded with their baby, that would be a good thing—both for Antonio and for their baby.

She shivered, and he brushed his mouth against hers again. 'Sorry. I shouldn't keep you on the doorstep in the cold.' He unlocked the front door and ushered her inside.

Right at that moment it felt as if they were a proper couple. As if they were just coming home from an event in the village—leaving their coats on the bentwood stand in the hallway and ending up in the kitchen, where he put the kettle on while she got the mugs out.

'So did you enjoy the party?' she asked.

'More than I expected to,' he said.

She showed him the picture she'd taken on the phone. 'You looked as if you were having fun.'

'Something so simple. I never did things like that as a child,' he said. 'But our baby definitely will.'

And Tia felt as if her world had just exploded into colour.

'So, we have leftovers for dinner.' He smiled at her. 'What sort of thing did you do as a child?'

'Cold turkey, home-made chips or French bread, and salad,' she said promptly. 'And Mum used to make vegetable and turkey soup. We used to wrap up warm and go to the beach, the day after Boxing Day, and we'd take a flask of Mum's soup and have a picnic.'

He wrapped his arms round her. 'I know it won't be the same, but we have beaches here. I'd be happy to take you.'

Which sounded as if he saw a future for them.

Even though part of her wanted to be sensible and acknowledge that their lives were too far apart for them to be together, part of her was thrilled by the idea. Warmed by hope that maybe he wanted a future for them—and Antonio Valenti was the kind of man who'd make things happen. If he wanted her, really wanted her in his life, then he'd find a way through the traditions that bound him.

And she'd meet him halfway.

In the end, they made turkey salad sandwiches and ate them in the kitchen, then went into the conservatory to curl up on a sofa together and watch the stars and talk about anything and everything.

Tia was so easy to be with.

Antonio wished it could always be like this, but he knew they'd have to go back to the palace soon and face real life, the politics and the press. Eventually she fell asleep and he sat there just holding her.

He knew now that this was what he wanted: to be a family with her and their baby, to live out of the limelight of the palace and be part of the community of the village. He wanted her to be his wife, his partner in everything.

But he couldn't work out how to tell her. If he asked her to marry him now, would she believe him that he wanted her for herself, or would she still think he was asking her purely out of a sense of duty and honour?

'I want to be a family with you,' he whispered.

She didn't wake, so he gently eased her out of his arms, then fetched a blanket and tucked it round her. She looked so cute, curled up on the sofa. And so *right*. He resisted the temptation to kiss her awake, because there was something else he needed to do. A letter that he should've written a long time ago.

He fetched notepaper, an envelope and a pen from his

office—an impersonal typed letter was absolutely not good enough for this—and took a photograph from his wallet. And then he began to write.

When he'd finished, Tia was still asleep.

He knelt by her and stroked her cheek. 'Tia? Tia, wake up, *bella*,' he whispered.

She opened her eyes, looking lost and incredibly vulnerable.

'Time to go to bed,' he said, and gently helped her to her feet.

'Sorry. I didn't mean to fall asleep on you.' She bit her lip, looking guilty.

'You're six months pregnant and you've had a busy day. I think you're allowed to fall asleep,' he said, smiling.

He was so tempted to carry her up the stairs, though he knew that wouldn't be fair. But at the door to her room he couldn't resist kissing her goodnight.

Her eyes were huge as she stroked his face. 'Antonio.'

He kissed her again.

'Stay with me tonight?' she asked.

Fall asleep with her in his arms. Wake up with her in his arms.

How could he possibly resist?

And this time he did pick her up and carry her to bed.

Afterwards, it took him a long time to fall asleep, because he knew now that this was what he wanted more than anything else. To be with her. And for her to want to be with him.

Please let her want the same thing.

Please.

Later that night, Tia woke when the baby started somersaulting. Antonio's arms were wrapped round her, and she felt safe and warm and cherished.

Could this work out, or was it just a hopeless fantasy?

She and Antonio had come so far over the last couple of days; but she had no idea whether his family would accept her. She knew that her father's family had rejected her mother, and she knew how much the situation had hurt both her parents. What if this turned out to be the same sort of thing?

Then, whatever she did, she lost. She didn't want to make Antonio choose between his family and her, because that wasn't fair; yet leaving him and quietly taking the baby away to live anonymously in London was no longer an option. Not now she'd seen the joy in his eyes when he'd felt their baby kick inside her.

Please, please let this work out...

CHAPTER SIX

THE NEXT MORNING, Tia was woken by the sound of a phone shrilling. At first she was disoriented but then last night came rushing back to her. How she'd fallen asleep on the sofa in Antonio's arms. How he'd ushered her up to bed, and she'd asked him to stay. How tenderly he'd held her...

The shrilling was from Antonio's phone, and he was sitting up in bed, frowning and speaking rapidly in Italian.

He was speaking too quickly for her to follow what he was saying, but something was clearly wrong, because he ended the call and then appeared to be looking up something on his phone.

She sat up. 'What is it?'

'Ah, Tia. Good morning.'

'What's happened?'

He grimaced. 'That was Gina on the phone. Apparently the media have descended on the village. There's some stuff in the news.'

'What stuff?'

He handed her the phone in silence.

It was a newsfeed showing the front pages of various newspapers and headlines for their stories. Someone had clearly taken photographs last night when Antonio had kissed her on the doorstep.

One of the pages had mocked up a kind of photo love

story: in the first photograph he was kissing her, the second had her sliding her arms round his neck and kissing him back, and the third showed her smiling at him while he rested his hand on her bump, obviously feeling the baby kick.

The first one was captioned *Who's that girl?* The second bore the line *A kiss is just a kiss—or is it?* The third had a heart drawn round them and was captioned *Baby Love?*

She read through the actual article. It was asking who she was, and if this was Prince Antonio's secret baby.

Is this the third baby scandal to rock the kingdom of Casavalle in recent months? The oldest child of King Vincenzo, Gabriella, was kept secret for decades, Prince Luca's fiancée was pregnant with someone else's baby, and now it seems Vincenzo's youngest child isn't to be left out of the scandal...

Horrified, Tia realised that the story was going to cause huge waves in Casavalle and also in London. If the media started digging to find out who she was, then her mother was going to be dragged into this.

She skimmed over the speculation, and then came to the last paragraph.

Prince Luca has confirmed that his older half-sister Gabriella will be acceding to the throne instead of him, with the coronation due at the end of the year.

So Gabriella was definitely becoming Queen? Since when? Antonio hadn't mentioned anything about that to her. He'd said that they were waiting for DNA test results and Gabriella's decision. 'Gabriella's actually becoming Queen?' she asked.

'With the support of our family, yes,' he said.

She frowned. 'Did you know about this?'

'Yes. Luca sent me the press release.'

Her stomach felt tied in knots as she took in the coolness of his expression and his tone. She'd been so sure that he was thawing out. But now he'd gone all aloof on her again. He was reverting to being Antonio the Prince, and she realised that she had just been kidding herself. Antonio was a prince first and foremost. Even if he did thaw out with her again, it would never be for long.

'You didn't say anything to me.' The words came out before she could stop them. How stupid of her. Why would he feel he needed to tell her anything about Palace business?

And then a really nasty thought sneaked into her head.

If he'd known about the press release, known that the press would be asking about him... Suddenly his actions of yesterday took on a whole new meaning. 'So you must've known the media would want to know where you were, when it was obvious you weren't at the palace.'

'I didn't think they'd find me here,' he said.

How, when it was his family's house so it was an obvious place to look? 'But they did—and they took that photograph.' She swallowed hard. 'On your doorstep.'

'I didn't notice any flash.'

Neither had she. She didn't *think* he was lying. But she did feel manipulated, and she wasn't sure whether she was more angry with herself for not realising that of course he was a prince and the media would follow him relentlessly, or with him for bringing her here in the first place and not letting her go quietly back to London where nobody would know about her or the baby.

The phone shrilled again, and the palace secretary's name flashed up on the caller ID.

'For you,' she said, handing the phone back to him.

She couldn't hear what Miles was saying, and she could tell nothing at all from Antonio's side of the conversation. His face was completely impassive, and all he seemed to say was 'Yes', 'No' or 'I see'.

He ended the call and looked at her. 'Miles says the media knows who you are, that you live in London and you're a waitress.'

She looked at him in dismay. 'Does that mean they're going to go after my mum now?' And maybe her bosses. Her friends. Anyone who'd known her even vaguely in the last twenty years. The media wouldn't care, as long as they got their story.

'It's a strong possibility,' he admitted. 'I'm sorry you've been dragged into this.'

'Are you?' she asked, with the doubts still nagging at her. 'Or did you engineer it, knowing that you're the only one who could protect my mum so I'd have to agree to all your demands?'

He stared at her, saying nothing, and with a sick feeling she realised she hadn't just been hormonal and paranoid. This really was manipulation. She'd been fooling herself yesterday, thinking that he was getting closer to her and hoping that maybe, after all, this was going to work out. He didn't love her, but she was carrying his heir, the fourth in line to the throne, so he thought it was his duty to give the baby his name. She'd already refused to marry him, so he'd put her in a situation where she'd *have* to agree.

The cold, unemotional soldier was a master strategist.

He knew that Tia would do anything to protect her mother. If her mother was in danger from being hounded by the media, then Tia would agree to anything to stop that.

So he'd got close to her. Made her think that he cared. Put her in the perfect position for a photo opportunity.

And now...

This time her mobile phone was the one to ring.

Seeing their neighbour's name on the screen made her heart freeze for a second.

Was Becky ringing to tell her that her mother was ill—or worse? Please, no. She couldn't lose her last family member. Please. *Please*.

'Hello, Becky,' she said, trying to keep the panic from her voice. 'Is Mum all right?'

'Yes, love, she's fine. Don't worry,' her neighbour reassured her.

Which was when she started shivering, in reaction to the fear that had flooded through her.

Antonio moved to put his arm round her, but she didn't believe it was to warm her or comfort her. This was all about duty and control, and she'd been too stupid to see it.

She angled herself away from him, and thankfully he took the hint and backed off.

'But there's reporters and photographers everywhere,' Becky said. 'I went out to get a pint of milk and everyone kept asking me about you. I just told them you were a lovely girl and to leave you alone.'

'Thank you. I really appreciate that.' With neighbours like Becky on their side, at least Tia knew that her mother was going to be OK. She took a deep breath. 'I'll be home as soon as I can. I'll text you when I know the flight times. And I'll ring Mum in a second.'

'All right, love. Don't you worry. I'll keep an eye on her.' Becky paused. 'Your young man's very handsome.'

He wasn't exactly hers, though like a fool she'd let herself start to believe that he might be. And wasn't the old saying, 'Handsome is as handsome does'? But Becky was waiting for an answer. She didn't need to know what a mess this was. 'Yes,' Tia said. 'I'll see you soon. And thank you again.'

'Is your mother all right?' Antonio asked as soon as she ended the call.

No thanks to him. 'Yes,' she said, her voice cool. 'Don't worry. You win. I'll do what you want and marry you so you get your heir—but only on condition you take care of my mum and make sure the media doesn't hassle her.'

At least he didn't look full of triumph.

Then again, he wasn't showing any emotion at all.

How, just how, had her brother been friends with him? Or was he totally different at work?

Not that it mattered.

Nothing mattered any more.

She'd been very naive to think he was starting to care for her. Antonio the Automaton. He'd just been a very, very shrewd tactician.

Military precision.

How stupid she'd been to tease him about that. It was exactly what it had been. Who he was.

'I'll arrange for someone to handle things for your mother in London,' Antonio said. 'Although I think it would be best to fly her to Casavalle.'

'So she gets no say in it, either? Like the baby, she's going to be another royal pawn in a game?' she asked bitterly.

'Tia, it isn't like that.'

'Isn't it?' She looked levelly at him. 'If you'll excuse me, I'd like to shower and get dressed.' In clothes he'd arranged for her, because she'd been so carried away with the gorgeous Christmas he'd made for her that she hadn't done any laundry. Leaving her with no choice. Just as the rest of her life was going to be now.

Stupid, stupid, stupid.

Right at that second, she felt *bought*.

Tia had already made up her mind, so there was no point in arguing with her, Antonio thought. Right now it would only make matters worse. And if he upset her, it would be bad for the baby. He needed her to be calm. Maybe, if he didn't escalate things, when she'd had time to think logically about it she'd realise that he hadn't been trying to manipulate her. That he'd been caught unawares, too.

Instead, he said neutrally, 'I'll arrange for a flight back to the palace.'

'Thank you.'

'And for you to go back to London. Please call your mother and reassure her that I'll do everything in my power to protect her.'

'Of course, Your Royal Highness.'

That hurt. That she could be so formal with him after what they'd shared. That she could believe he'd engineered this whole thing.

Thankfully his upbringing meant that the hurt didn't show.

And he'd do this logically. Get the media spotlight off them, and then once they were in the palace he could start to sort things out with her.

'I'll leave a suitcase outside your door,' he said.

'Suitcase?' She looked surprised.

'For your clothes.' When it looked as if she was about to argue, he raked a hand through his hair. 'Tia. There were no strings to those clothes.'

'I suppose you can't have your bride-to-be wearing cheap chainstore clothes in public,' she said.

Did she really think he was such a snob, that he gave

a damn about money? The unfairness stung enough for him to say, 'Don't be so ridiculous.'

'Ridiculous?'

'I'm not a snob. It's nothing to do with money. I was trying to do something nice for you without rubbing your nose in the difference between our financial situations or making you feel beholden to me.'

She looked crestfallen then, and he felt guilty—because by saying that out loud he'd done precisely what he'd been trying not to do. He'd rubbed her nose in it. She'd been angry and hurt and snapping at him, but he shouldn't have snapped back and continued the fight. Time to back off. Not because he was in the wrong or afraid of a fight, but because she was out of sorts and he needed to think of the baby. 'I'm going to have a shower and go downstairs. I'll make breakfast when you're ready.'

She nodded, and looked away.

He left her room, showered and dressed swiftly, and sent holding texts to his brother, his mother and Gabriella, saying that he'd explain everything when he was back at the palace later that morning. He took the special glass bauble from the tree and wrapped it up, then added an addendum to the letter he'd written the previous night, and stowed them both in his bag along with the wrapped snow globe.

Tia was silent when she finally came downstairs. For a moment, he thought she was going to refuse breakfast. So he just said quietly, 'You need to eat. For you and the baby.'

There was a movement across her stomach. At least the baby agreed with him, he thought wryly.

She shrugged, still looking hurt and angry, but at least she ate her toast. Drank the mug of tea he'd prepared. Climbed into the back of the car—this time, Giacomo drove, and the windows were blacked out to avoid the press.

Tia stared out of the window all the way to the airport, and Antonio didn't push her to talk. She barely spoke to him on the flight back, either.

How could he even begin to fix this? Tia was going to marry him, which was what he'd wanted since she'd told him the news about the baby: but he could see now that it was only to save her mother from the press. Not because she wanted to be with him.

How ironic that he'd been trying to persuade her to fall for him, and what he'd managed to do instead was let himself fall for her. If he told her how he felt about her—if he could even find the right words—he didn't think she'd believe him. Not now the press were involved.

He'd been honest with her and told her how much he hated palace politics, so why did she believe he'd do something underhand? He really hadn't engineered that kiss. He'd *wanted* to kiss her. Wanted to be with her. He'd been so wrapped up in those unexpected emotions that he hadn't noticed the paparazzi hanging round, and he hadn't seen the flash from the camera.

If only he was good at saying what he really felt. But every time he opened his mouth to tell her, it was as if his throat was filled with sand and the words just wouldn't come out.

When they landed, he said, 'Would you prefer to go to the palace or to go straight back to London?'

'Do I have a choice?'

That really hurt. 'Yes. Of course you have a choice.'

'I want to see my mum,' she said. Before he could offer to go with her, she said, 'And I'll go on my own. I expect you have official duties.'

He needed to speak to his family and the palace secretary, yes, but he wanted to support her. He wanted to be with her; he wanted to make this work. And he rather thought he owed her mother an apology and a personal explanation.

He didn't get the chance to tell her, because she continued, 'And I need to see Giovanni and Vittoria, explain everything to them. They've been so good to me and I feel bad about letting them down. And my friend who was going to share childcare with me. I've let her down, too.'

Guilt flooded through him. She had a whole life without him, and he was ripping her from that support network and expecting her to be in Casavalle with him. She wasn't the only one whose life was changed by this mess. 'Look, I'll sort everything out.'

'That's my life, not yours. *I'll* organise it,' she cut in. Which told him exactly where he stood. She'd see any offer of help as throwing his money around, not a genuine desire to make things better.

'Will you at least let my pilot take you back to London?' he asked.

'Are you worried I might talk to someone in the airport while I'm waiting for my flight and say something I shouldn't?'

He remembered the conversation he'd had with her before, and sighed. 'No, Tia. The media will write what they like.' It hurt that she thought he was so underhand, and he had to draw on every ounce of the training he'd had over the years to remain cool and calm and collected. But he wanted her to know his real motivation, so he said, 'I'm asking if you'll let my pilot take you back because you're six months pregnant and the last thing you need is to wait for hours for connecting flights, perhaps without anywhere to sit if the airport's really busy.'

She turned away so he couldn't see her face, couldn't read her eyes. 'Whatever. I don't care any more.'

And how that hurt, to see her so flat and cold towards him, with all her bubbliness gone. Worse, to know that it was all because of him. That she didn't trust him. 'Let me have a word with the pilot.'

He went into the cockpit and arranged with the crew that they'd take her to London and look after her on the way. 'And can you please make sure that this letter's delivered, and these two parcels go to Tia's mum?'

'Of course, Your Royal Highness.'

'Thank you.' He returned to Tia. Although part of him wanted to take Tia back to the palace before she went to London and at least introduce her to his family, from the set look on her face he didn't think she'd be amenable to the suggestion. 'Please let me know when you're safely back in London.'

She huffed out a breath. 'I'm surprised you don't want to put some kind of tracking device on my phone.'

He winced. 'I'm not trying to trap you, Tia.'

'It feels like it.'

He would've done anything to rewind the last few hours—to go back to the children's Christmas party where he'd felt so happy, where he and Tia had worked as a team and he'd thought they were actually getting closer. And last night, when he'd kissed her under the mistletoe. When she'd fallen asleep on him on the sofa. When she'd shyly asked him to stay with her and he'd woken in the night to feel the baby kicking in her stomach. 'I'm sorry. It's not meant to be...' His throat closed. *A prison*. But hadn't he felt like that at the palace, too? Hemmed in and miserable and trapped by all the politics?

On the other hand, he couldn't just throw Tia to the

wolves. The media would make her life miserable without him.

'Safe journey,' he said, and walked to the door of the plane where the stewardess was waiting.

'Look after her for me, please,' he said.

And his misery must've shown in his eyes, because the stewardess forgot herself enough to pat his arm. 'It'll be all right, Prince Antonio.'

He rather didn't think it would.

And he couldn't bear to look back at Tia and see how much she loathed him.

Antonio strolled off the plane, as cool as a cucumber, and didn't even look back at her. He was clearly so secure in his triumph that he didn't need to make sure his new chattel was sitting exactly where he'd left her.

Tia felt sick.

Right at that moment, she wished she'd never met Antonio Valenti.

There was a volley of kicks, and she rested her hand on her bump. 'I don't regret *you*,' she whispered softly. 'But I thought he was different. That he felt something for me. That he cared. That over the last few days he'd shown her the real man behind the Prince, a man I could really love. But none of it was true. All along it was just to manipulate me into a situation where I'm forced to do what the palace wants.'

She'd let everyone down. Her mum, the memory of her dad and her brother, her bosses, her friends.

And life was never going to be the same again.

Antonio had everything planned in the official car back to the palace. First, he'd talk to his family; then to the palace secretary, to make sure that their plans for protecting Tia and Grace were completely in place; and then he'd organise Tia and her mother coming to the palace.

Back at the palace, he found his mother in her study, doing something on a computer. He knocked at the door and, when she looked up, bowed deeply, 'Good morning, Mamma.'

She inclined her head. 'Good morning, Antonio.'

'I'm sorry I've…' He took a deep breath. 'I'm sorry I've brought scandal to the family.'

This was her cue to tell him he was a disgrace, how disgusted his father would be, and how she expected better from him.

But to his surprise she stood up, walked over to him and took his hands, squeezing them. 'Welcome home. Where is Tia? Is she resting?'

'No. She's on a plane to London,' he said.

'I see.' Maria looked disappointed. 'I would have liked to meet her, talk with her a little.'

'It's not her fault, Mamma,' he said softly. 'I accept the blame fully.'

'For putting her on the plane?'

He nodded. 'And for the baby—' he choked '—for everything.'

She shocked him even more by touching his face. 'Antonio. A baby is something never to be sorry for. I'm going to be a grandmother. That's wonderful news.'

'Even though…?' He blinked. 'This baby wasn't planned, Mamma. And Tia and I are not married.'

Maria shrugged. 'She seems very sweet, very genuine. You don't know how glad I am that you and Luca have found someone to love, and that Luca's engaged. I know how much Imogen loves him—and, from the look of that photograph, Tia clearly loves you.'

Oh, no, she didn't. She might've started to feel something towards him over the last few days, but he'd managed to kill it. Right now, Antonio was pretty sure that she hated him.

'I've been worried about you,' his mother said. 'I know you took your father's death very hard.'

Antonio closed his eyes for a moment. All the regrets for things that might have been. 'I'll never be able to make him proud of me now.'

'He was always proud of you, Antonio. He just didn't know how to tell you.'

Antonio didn't believe her.

'Your father wasn't an easy man,' Maria said. 'He was a good king, a good man—but he found family life hard. Especially after Sophia walked away from him.'

This was a subject that was never, ever discussed in their family. But Luca had actually mentioned their father's past in public, after he'd got engaged, so maybe things were changing.

'He loved Sophia, but she was from a different world.'

So was Tia.

'She found it hard to deal with our way of life.'

Antonio rather thought that Tia, on the other hand, could deal with anything.

'Walk with me, my child,' Maria said. 'We'll talk in the garden.'

He helped his mother put her coat on—he hadn't had time to take his off—and went with her into the formal garden. Even though it was almost December, there were still a few roses in bloom.

'I love this garden,' she said. 'Your father did, too. He was the one who increased the collection of roses here. He used to enjoy talking to the gardener and looking over rose catalogues with him. I rather think, if he'd had the time, he would have liked to breed his own roses.'

Was she talking about the same man he'd grown up with? Antonio was amazed. 'I didn't think my father—' He stopped abruptly, knowing his words were tactless and not wanting to hurt his mother.

'What?' she asked gently.

He didn't think his father had been interested in anything else other than ruling. 'Being the King was his entire life,' he said eventually.

'It was a very big part, but not all,' his mother corrected. 'He was a husband and a father as well as the King.'

Antonio struggled to think of a time when his father had showed open affection to his wife or his children. They hadn't even had a pet dog or cat. Even at Picco Innevato, his father had never really switched off. He had been the King first, and everything else had come way down his list of priorities.

As if his mother guessed what he was thinking, she said, 'Vincenzo found it hard to open up about his feelings.'

Yeah. He knew how that felt. He struggled, too.

'And Sophia couldn't cope with royal life.'

'What about you, Mamma?' The question came out before he could stop it. He winced. 'I apologise. That's much too personal. Forget I asked.'

'No, it's a valid question, and you have a point. I should have done more when you were younger,' Maria said with a sigh. 'Your father could never open up because of the way he was raised. In the view of his parents, children should be seen and not heard. They were very closed off and they never told Vincenzo that they valued him for himself—and with hindsight I think he needed to hear that.'

Antonio had never considered it before, and it made him feel guilty. 'I never told him I valued him, either.'

'But he knew you did,' Maria said gently. 'And he valued you, even though he didn't tell you. *I* value you. And maybe I should've told you that more often.'

The lump in Antonio's throat was so huge, he couldn't answer her. But he wrapped his arms round her and hugged her.

Maria stroked his hair. 'Your father was raised to be a king and a statesman, and he made sure he was the very best King and statesman he could be. But he couldn't open up—even to me, sometimes. I think he wanted to try to be closer to you. It's why he suggested that we should buy the house in Picco Innevato.'

'That was my father's idea?' Antonio pulled back, surprised, and looked his mother straight in the eye.

'Yes. So you and Luca would have somewhere to be children, without being in the public eye all the time.'

'That's where I took Tia,' he admitted. 'Picco Innevato.'

'I guessed that,' Maria said gently.

'I asked Miles not to tell anyone anything about where I was going or who I was with.'

She smiled. 'I'm your mother, Antonio. I know things without having to be told. Picco Innevato is where you always go when you need time to think. Where you go to decompress after a bad mission. Luca said that Tia Phillips had been trying to get in touch with you. He assumed that she was someone trying it on and told Miles to ignore her, whereas if either of them had thought to say something to me I could've told them she was Nathan's sister—and I know you blame yourself for Nathan's death.'

Antonio blew out a breath. 'I should've been in that car along with him.'

'I'm very glad you weren't,' Maria said. 'I feel for his poor mother—of course I do, because it's the fear every soldier's mother has, the worry about getting that phone call. I tried never to stand in your way, but I hated you being in danger all the time, and I worried about you every second you were on a mission. So did your father,' she added wryly, 'but he said you needed to do things your own way.'

'He was right,' Antonio admitted. 'I did.'

'I wish he'd written you a letter or something like that, to tell you how he felt. But your father was your father. A different generation.'

'Does Luca know?'

'That your father loved you both and couldn't say it?' She nodded. 'And I think love has changed Luca, too. What happened with Meribel… That was hard for both of them. I feel guilty about that. I should've stepped in and said no, don't agree to marry the girl unless you really love her, because you shouldn't sacrifice yourself for your country.'

'But I thought you said Meribel was crazy to…' Antonio stopped.

'I think,' Maria said gently, 'she will be OK, and in the end she did Luca a favour.'

How would Tia's mother judge him? Would she see him as the man who seduced her daughter, abandoned her, and was now forcing her into a marriage she didn't want? Or would she judge him more kindly?

'So what will you do now, Antonio? About Tia?'

'I…' He sighed. 'I don't know, Mamma.'

'You look as if you're in love in that photograph. And you didn't know it was being taken.'

'She thinks I set it up, to force her to marry me and make the baby my heir,' Antonio said.

'Then you need to talk to her. Find out what she wants. Find out if you can come to some kind of compromise—

one where you both win rather than both lose,' Maria advised. 'Tell her how you feel.'

'I don't have the words,' Antonio said.

'Tell her that first. Tell her you find it hard,' Maria said. 'Ask her to help you. And be as honest as you can.'

Once he'd finished talking to his mother, Antonio went to find Luca, who clapped him on the shoulder. 'Congratulations, little brother.'

'Not yet,' Antonio said. 'I haven't quite followed in the footsteps of you and Imogen. I might have messed things up.'

'If you love her,' Luca said softly, 'go after her. Tell her you love her.'

'Is that what you did with Imogen?'

Luca nodded. 'And it was the best thing I ever did.'

Antonio looked at his elder brother. He'd never seen Luca so relaxed and happy. Was it because he was free of the burden of their father's expectations? Or was it love? And, if it was love, could that work out for him and Tia, too?

And how was he going to convince Tia that they had a future?

He still had no idea by the time he went to see Gabriella.

'Antonio. It's good to see you.' She smiled at him 'I saw all the stuff in the press,' she said. 'Are you OK?'

He grimaced. 'I think I might have been an idiot.'

'The girl you kissed under the mistletoe on your front doorstep?'

He nodded. 'I've acted like every other Valenti man—I've expected everyone to fall in with my wishes, and kept my feelings shut away.'

'But you can change that,' she said.

'Yes. It's time things changed in Casavalle,' he agreed.

And then it hit him. He didn't need to shut away his emotions, like he'd always done in the past. Not any more. He loved Tia. Although he knew she didn't love him back, he loved her enough to give her what she wanted. She didn't want to be stuck here in the palace; she wanted to be with her mother in London.

So he'd go to see her. He'd release her from her agreement to marry him, and he'd tell her that he would support her, the baby and her mother however they needed him—just as Tia had always supported her family. If she eventually came to love him, then maybe she would come and live with him. But he was going to put her first.

Before he could arrange a flight to London, Miles called up to see him. 'I was hoping to have a meeting with you and your mother,' he said.

'If it's about Tia, I'm not in a position to discuss anything just now,' Antonio warned.

'It's about Gabriella,' Miles said.

Antonio frowned. 'Surely Gabriella needs to be part of any discussions about her?'

'They're preliminary discussions so we don't need to bother her just yet,' Miles said.

'What about Luca?'

'Prince Luca,' Miles said, 'is otherwise engaged at the moment.'

Antonio sighed. 'I really need to be in London. When do you need the meetings?'

'If your mother is free, we could start now,' Miles suggested.

Maria was available, so Antonio joined her in Miles's office.

'We're having a presentation ball for Gabriella before the coronation, to welcome her to the country,' Maria said.

'That's nice,' Antonio said, wondering just why he was needed at this meeting. Surely they didn't need his input into a ball?

'And we need to think about possible marriages for her,' Miles added.

Oh. So *that* was it. Politics. Antonio folded his arms. 'If you want my honest opinion, I think we should call a halt to this discussion right now. Gabriella should choose her own groom. The last arranged marriage for this family didn't work out well for anyone.'

'That's true,' Maria said, 'and we do need to repair relations between our countries.'

Diplomacy and palace politics. The two things Antonio loathed most. 'I still think Gabriella should choose her own groom. It's the twenty-first century.'

'The word is that Prince Cesar has broken up with his girlfriend,' Miles said. 'And he will be attending Gabriella's presentation ball. He's been called home to welcome her.'

Antonio snorted. 'I hope you're not marking him out as a potential match, Miles. Cesar Asturias is a smooth operator, a playboy who doesn't take women seriously—and I'm not sure he's good enough for my sister.'

Maria said gently, 'Things aren't always what they seem. Remember, the media calls you a playboy as well. Your girlfriends don't exactly last a long time.'

'Because I never found the right one,' Antonio said, 'and I hope that's just about to change.' He looked pleadingly at his mother. 'Do you *really* need me in these discussions? I think you should talk to Gabriella, not to me.' He took a deep breath. Time to tell them how he felt. 'Mamma, Miles—right now, I don't want to be here discussing politics. I want to see Tia. I need to tell her...' The words stuck.

'Tell her what's in your heart,' Maria advised, and gave him a hug. 'Good luck.'

'Good luck, sir,' Miles said, shaking his hand.

To get Tia to really listen to him, Antonio thought, he was going to need more than luck.

And if his words froze on him again when he was talking to her, he was really going to be in trouble. Maybe he should write them down. Just to be sure.

CHAPTER SEVEN

LONDON FELT GREY, dull and dingy after the bright, open spaces of Picco Innevato.

But Tia's time in Casavalle had all been a lie. She knew she'd be very stupid to let herself believe otherwise.

She'd been such a fool. Fancy thinking that Prince Antonio might really care for her.

And now she was going to be trapped into marriage with a man who didn't love her. And was marrying her purely for the baby's sake. This was utterly ridiculous in the twenty-first century, but she supposed things were different when you were a Royal. If she said no, that would mean the press would hound her mother, and Tia couldn't let that happen. She'd do anything to protect her family.

She rested her hand on her bump. 'Why couldn't he have just let us disappear back here?' she whispered.

The baby didn't kick.

Yeah. She had no idea, either.

There was a gentle knock on her door. 'Tia?'

She forced herself to look all smiling and happy. No way was she going to let her mother know what an idiot she'd been. She didn't want Grace to worry. 'Hi, Mum.'

'I thought you might like to see these,' Grace said, coming into the room with a box that Tia recognised as being full of Nathan's things.

'I'm not sure I can face that,' she admitted.

'I think you need to see what's in here,' Grace said gently. 'I'll leave you to it.'

Tia sat staring at the box for a long, long time. Then she removed the lid.

Inside were books and papers. On the very top was a photograph of Nathan and Antonio in their fatigues, smiling, their arms round each other.

Her eyes prickled. How much she missed her brother.

And the man with him in the photograph—that was the man she'd let herself fall for. Except he didn't really exist, did he?

She turned the photograph over and recognised the handwriting on the back. Nathan's handwriting.

A—the dream team on a good day   N

Why was a photograph that had a message obviously addressed to Antonio in Nathan's belongings? Had her brother never sent it?

The next thing in the box was a letter. Except it wasn't to Nathan—or from Nathan. It was a letter to her mother.

She was about to fold it up again, rather than pry in her mother's things, when she noticed the address at the top of the page.

Picco Innevato.

Antonio's house.

Why would Antonio be writing to her mother?

Was this her mother's way of trying to tell her something?

Frowning, she read on.

Dear Mrs Phillips
  I would like to apologise sincerely to you for the way in which I broke the news of Nathan's death back in January. I should have told you back then

that Nathan was like a brother to me, and I miss him terribly. I should also have been there to support you and Tia in your grief.

My only excuse, such as it is, is that I find it very hard to show my feelings. I grew up knowing that duty should always come first. But I want that to be different for my child, whether the baby is a son or a daughter—I know the baby will be loved because Tia is his or her mother, and she's amazing.

I apologise, too, for the way in which I've behaved towards Tia. I truly didn't intend to abandon her, or you. It feels like a weak excuse, but we've had a lot of unexpected events in our family over the last few months and it's been a struggle to deal with them.

Your daughter is an amazing woman. She deserves more than I can ever give her. I have asked her to marry me, and I know she thinks my sole motivation is that the baby will be fourth in line to the throne of Casavalle. But I think a lot of your daughter and I want to be a full part of our baby's life.

I should have asked your permission before asking her to marry me, and I apologise for my forwardness. With your permission, I should like to ask Tia again if she will marry me. It has nothing to do with convention and everything to do with who she is and how she makes me feel.

I am trying to be more open about my emotions, and I hope that she and our baby will find it in their hearts to help me.

I thought that you might like this photograph, taken on the mission before Nathan's last one. It means a lot to me, but I think you should have it.
With kindest regards
Antonio Valenti

The date was yesterday.

The day of the children's Christmas party.

The day when she'd fallen asleep on the sofa; when he'd woken her later, she'd realised that he'd tucked a fleecy blanket round her.

And this letter, where he said that he thought a lot of her... Antonio wasn't one to talk about his feelings. He was aloof and formal and *royal*. So this was tantamount to saying that he loved her.

She couldn't quite take it in.

Did he love her?

Had she misjudged him?

Frowning, she went out into their kitchen, where her mother was sitting at the table.

'Are you all right, love?' Grace asked.

'Confused,' Tia admitted. 'When did you get that letter?'

'Today, when the car brought you back from the airport,' Grace said. 'And there were two parcels, too, with a note asking me to let you rest for a bit before giving them to you.'

'Parcels?'

Grace indicated the two boxes on the kitchen countertop, both perfectly wrapped.

Tia opened the smaller one first, and caught her breath. It was the etched glass bauble for the tree.

In silence, she handed it to her mother.

'That's beautiful. Is that where you were?' Grace asked.

Tia nodded. 'He said he bought it for the baby. For the tree.'

'Just like your father and I used to buy a new decoration every year for our tree,' Grace said softly.

With shaking hands, Tia undid the scarlet ribbon on the second box. And she had to bite back the tears when she saw the snow globe nestled among the packing peanuts that protected it: the beautiful filigree star suspended in a perfect orb, except she hadn't wanted to spend the money on herself.

When had he bought this?

Perhaps when she'd been browsing at the candle stall yesterday. He must have gone back and bought it especially for her.

Antonio Valenti might not say a lot, but he noticed things. He'd seen how much she'd liked it. He'd guessed that she didn't want to spend money on herself when she had the baby to think of, and he'd bought it because he'd wanted to do something nice for her, give her something that she'd denied herself.

Especially given what he'd written to her mother, that snow globe was a definite declaration of love. It wasn't the cost of the item; it was the thought behind it.

With horror, Tia realised that he really did love her. And he hadn't been able to tell her exactly how he felt because he'd been brought up in a formal, public world where he'd always felt forced to hide his emotions away. She hadn't made it easy for him to talk to her, either.

This year, he'd been emotionally swamped: he'd lost his best friend, actually been there when the land mine had exploded and seen Nathan killed; he'd lost his father; and then his life had been turned upside down with the revelations about his brother's fiancée cheating on him and the existence of his half-sister.

And then she'd come along, six months pregnant, and informed him that their one night together had had consequences and he was going to be a father.

No wonder Antonio had had trouble talking about it. It was an overwhelming amount for anyone to deal with, let alone someone who wasn't used to talking about his feelings.

She'd pushed him away because he couldn't tell her

how he felt. She'd made the assumption that he'd manipulated the situation with the media, so she'd be forced to
marry him and make the baby his heir. Yet had she been
fair to make that assumption? If she looked at what he'd
actually done... He'd taken her away from the public glare
of the palace to his family's private home, the place where
he'd spent the summers during his childhood.

He'd tried to make a proper family Christmas for her,
choosing a tree and decorations with her and then cooking her Christmas dinner. He'd agreed to fill in for the Father Christmas who'd broken his leg—the kind of role she
knew he'd never done before, simply because she'd asked
him to. He'd kissed her under the mistletoe, shown her
with actions rather than words how he really felt about her.

And, because he hadn't had the words to tell her, she'd
assumed the worst.

How could she have been so stupid—and so unfair?

And this was the last straw. For the last year, she'd tried
so hard to be strong, kept all her worries locked inside.
Now tears slid down her face. She cried not just for her
brother, but for the man she loved, for her mum, for her
dad, for her baby and for herself.

Grace wrapped her arms round Tia. 'It's going to be
all right, love.'

'How can it be? I've messed everything up. I've hurt
Antonio; and I just don't know what to do.'

'I do,' Grace said. 'Talk to him. Go back to Casavalle
and tell Antonio how you really feel about him.'

'I can't leave you in London, Mum.'

'Yes, you can. I'll be fine,' Grace said firmly. 'I'm
managing. Yes, I'm still going to have bad days, but I
have support here. And I've always felt terrible about you
putting your own life on hold because of me. I know you
love me and you worry about me—but that's how I feel

about you, too. And it's about time you started living your own life instead of trying to fit everything around me.'

'But, Mum—'

'But nothing,' Grace cut in. 'All I want is to see you happy. Go to Antonio and tell him how you feel about him.'

'What if he's changed his mind? What he said in that letter… I didn't give him a chance to tell me any of that.'

'Give him a chance now. It's not too late.'

'But…how can he be with me? How will his family ever accept me?'

'They'll love you as much as he does,' Grace said. 'I know your father's family didn't accept me, but not everyone is like them.'

'But he's a prince, Mum!'

'Think about how he was with you in Picco Innevato,' Grace counselled. 'That's the private man—the man he really is. One who cares. One who might not be very good at telling you how he feels, but look at that photograph.' She brought the newspaper over to Tia, showing her the front page. 'The look on his face when his hand's on your bump and he's feeling the baby kick. You're looking at him with exactly the same expression. You love each other, Tia. You just need to give him the chance to learn how to tell you.'

Tia hugged her mum and cried even more, letting out all the misery and loneliness she'd hidden away for the last year.

And then, once she'd washed her face, she started packing.

She was halfway through when their doorbell rang.

'I'll get it,' Grace called.

When her mother didn't call her, Tia continued packing, assuming that it was a courier wanting them to take in a parcel for their neighbour.

But then Grace knocked gently on her door. 'I'm just going next door to see Becky. And you have a visitor.'

'A visitor?'

'Remember what I said,' Grace said softly. 'Give him a chance.'

Tia's pulse leaped.

Had Antonio come for her?

'I've made you both a cup of tea. You need to talk,' Grace said.

Tia followed her mother into the kitchen. Antonio was sitting there as if he belonged—but how could a prince belong to her world?

'Good luck,' Grace said, patting his shoulder, then left the flat.

Oh, help.

What did she do now? What should she say?

In the end, she fell back on a simple, 'How was your flight?'

'Fine, thank you.'

His face was as impassive as ever. She didn't have a clue what was going on in his head. Was he here to follow up on the letter he'd written to her mother, to try to tell her how he felt? Or was he here because he'd had time to think about it and had changed his mind?

'Why are you here?' The words slipped out before she could stop them.

'I've come to release you from your agreement to marry me.'

It shocked her so much that she ended up sitting down at the table with him, knowing that her knees simply weren't going to support her.

He wasn't here to follow up on that letter. She was too late. He'd changed his mind.

'What I did was selfish,' Antonio said. 'I railroaded you

into agreeing to marry me. I didn't give you the choice and I was wrong. You're a strong, independent woman and you're amazing.'

Tia couldn't quite get her head round this. Was he breaking up with her, or was he trying to tell her something else?

'I'm not very good at showing my emotions,' he said. 'That's true of all the Valenti men—my father, my brother and me. But when you stayed with me at Picco Innevato, you taught me so much. You taught me how to feel—and that it was OK to admit I love someone.'

She stared at him, still not quite comprehending.

'I'm making a mess of this,' he said with a sigh. 'I'm trying to tell you that I…' He paused.

That he what?

That he loved her?

He pulled a piece of paper out of his pocket and looked at it. '"I love you, Tia. I want to marry you, but only if you want to marry me. I'm not asking you out of a sense of duty or of honour, just because you happen to be pregnant with my baby. I'm asking you because I want to be with you."'

She looked at him. 'Are you *reading* that to me?'

'Yes,' he said. 'Because I can't do the words otherwise. They freeze in my throat. I don't know how to say it. That's why I wrote everything down on the plane, in case I froze. So, yes, I'm reading from a script, because otherwise I can't do it and I don't want you to think…' He blew out a breath. 'I'm off script. I'm stuck.'

He loved her.

So much that he'd written it down to make sure, with his usual military precision, he got it right.

'Go back on script,' she said softly. Because she needed to hear what he had to say.

His face brightened, and he looked at the paper again.

'"I know you're strong enough to cope with just about anything on your own, and I admire your strength, but you don't *have* to be on your own. If you'll let me, I'll be right by your side, supporting you all the way. You might have to yell at me from time to time, and remind me to tell you what's in my head instead of assuming that you already know by some weird kind of osmosis, but I'll be there with you all the way. I'll be the best husband I can possibly be to you, and the most loving dad I can possibly be to our baby—and, if we're lucky, to our future babies.'" He lifted his chin and put the paper down. 'I'm going to do it without the script now. I love you.'

'You love me.' She still couldn't quite take that in he was actually saying it to her.

'If I'm really honest with you, I fell in love with you before I'd even met you,' Antonio said. 'The way Nathan described you, so full of courage and strength, I knew you were the kind of woman I wanted to be with. But when I finally met you everything had just gone horribly wrong. I felt guilty that Nathan died.'

'It wasn't your fault.'

'I still felt guilty,' Antonio said. 'Survivor guilt, maybe, but guilty all the same. Plus you were his little sister. You were off limits. I was all mixed up, wanting you and feeling guilty about that, too. I'd wanted to tell you and your mum how much Nathan was loved, how much everyone thought of him—and instead I just closed off and made a mess of it.' He grimaced. 'When I saw you again at the charity gala, I felt so bad that I hadn't stayed in touch.'

'Don't be so hard on yourself. Your father died, and you were needed at the palace,' she said gently. 'I understand.'

He took her hands. 'I still should've done more, and I'm sorry I let you down.'

'It's OK. You're here now—and you're not the only one

who shut your emotions away,' she told him. 'I couldn't cry for Nathan because I thought I had to be strong for Mum, and I was wrong, too.'

'You've been crying now.' He lifted one hand to stroke her face.

She nodded. 'For everything. For you, for Nathan, for both our dads, for my mum, for the baby…'

Antonio leaned over the table and kissed her lightly. 'You don't have to be strong all the time—just as I don't have to be strong and silent, either. We'll have each other's backs. And we can be ourselves with each other and with our baby.'

'I love you, too.' She swallowed hard. 'And I knew before you told me that you love me, because you bought me the snow globe. You noticed I liked it and guessed that I didn't want to spend the money on myself. It's the thought that counts more than the gift.'

'True. You've taught me that, too.' He looked at her. 'So, what now?'

'I told you about my mum—how my dad's family didn't like her.'

'And you worry that my family will feel that way about you?'

'I don't have a drop of blue blood in my veins. How am I going to fit in?'

'By being yourself,' he said. 'Just so you know, my mother told me to come and see you and tell you how I really felt. She said those photographs on the news made her feel better, made her feel that I'd found someone to love and who loved me all the way back. And she's thrilled about becoming a grandmother.'

'Really?'

'Really,' he confirmed. 'Luca told me to go after you and tell you how I feel about you. So did Gabriella. You'll be more than welcome in Casavalle, and so will your mother. I want to… I want to be a family with you, Tia. You come as a package, and that's fine by me—because I come as a package, too.'

Then, to her surprise, he slid off his chair and got down on one knee. 'I know I'm rushing you and you don't have to answer me now, but will you marry me? I'm not asking you because I think it's my duty or yours, but because I hope we both feel the same way about each other,' he clarified. 'Because we both love each other, and we want to make a family together.'

She knew that speech had been tough for him. Telling her how he really felt. Particularly as he'd done it without working out the words and writing them down first.

But it was how she felt about him, too.

'Because we both love each other, and we want to make a family together,' she repeated. 'Yes.'

He got to his feet in what looked like a nanosecond, and wrapped his arms round her. 'I love you, Tia. It feels weird saying it, but I'm hoping the more I tell you, the easier it'll be, and that you'll come to believe me.'

'I believe you now,' she said. 'I love you, too.'

He kissed her lingeringly, and there was a volley of kicks in her stomach.

He broke the kiss. 'Is that baby-speak for "Get a room"?' he asked wryly.

'No. I think it's baby-speak for "I approve",' she said with a smile.

'Good. Let's go and tell your mother the news. And then I'd like to take you, your mother and the baby home with me to Casavalle. Home to our future.'

'Our future,' she echoed.

EPILOGUE

Valentine's Day

TIA PEERED OVER the edge of the cot at the sleeping week-old baby. 'I can't believe we made someone so perfect,' she whispered.

'Nathan Vincenzo Valenti. The most beautiful baby in the world.' Antonio slid his arm round her shoulders. 'It doesn't get better than this, does it?'

'I didn't think I'd ever be this happy,' Tia said. 'But your family's wonderful and they've all made me feel so welcome—Mum, too.'

'Because you're part of us,' Antonio said simply. 'You have been, since the first moment you walked into the palace and gave my mother a hug. And definitely since you stood in our private chapel and said your wedding vows. You've got the Valenti name now. No escape for you.'

She twisted round and kissed him. 'I don't want to escape. I love you, Antonio.'

'Good. Because I love you, too.'

They were still gazing besottedly at their sleeping son when Grace walked into the room.

'Is he asleep?' she whispered.

'Yes,' Antonio said.

'Then I'll come back for a cuddle later,' Grace said.

They followed her out into the living room. 'Are you having lunch with us today, Mum?' Tia asked.

'It's lovely of you to ask, but I'm afraid I can't—I'm already going out,' Grace said.

'Anywhere nice?' Tia asked.

Grace blushed. 'Miles says it's a mystery tour.'

Tia exchanged a glance with Antonio. They'd both noticed that the palace secretary was spending a lot of time in Grace's company. Miles and Grace seemed to have bonded over organising Tia and Antonio's wedding in a private ceremony in the middle of December, and that blush just now made Tia pretty sure that her mother was going out on a date rather than simply doing a bit of sight-seeing.

'Have a wonderful time, Mum,' she said, hugging her mother. 'And don't overdo it.'

Grace smiled. 'I know better than to do that, love. Besides, Miles won't let me. I'll see you both later and I'll be back to cuddle my grandson.'

Antonio smiled at Tia as his mother-in-law left their apartment. 'I have a feeling there might be a little bit of romance in the air.'

'Me, too, and I'm glad,' Tia said. 'Mum's been on her own for much too long. And I like Miles. He's a nice guy. Kind.' She smiled back at him. 'Even if he did refuse to let me talk to you for weeks.'

'He was doing his job. Being diligent. And he'll look after Grace the same way,' Antonio said. 'And now it's my turn to look after you. Sit on that sofa and put your feet up, because a cheese toastie and a cup of tea are in your very near future.'

She grinned. 'Are you ordering me about, Your Royal Highness?'

'I can try,' Antonio said, laughing. 'But no. We're a

team. And I only made that suggestion because I know it's your favourite. You can have anything you like.' He kissed her lightly. 'If anything, I'm yours to command.'

She scoffed. 'I'm no general.'

'No. You're just gorgeous,' he said. 'I love you, Tia. I never thought I'd ever be this happy in Casavalle. But things have changed in the palace. Everywhere feels lighter and happier and less formal. You, Imogen, Gabi and Grace have kind of taken over the palace, and my mother's just blossomed, having daughters and a new best friend. And with you and our baby here with me… My world's complete.'

'Mine, too. I love you,' Tia said, kissing him. 'We don't have to have lunch, you know. We could just go and snuggle up under the covers.'

'That,' Antonio said, 'is an excellent idea.' He scooped her up and carried her into their bedroom.

But just as he was about to deposit Tia on the bed, they heard a wail.

'We,' he said, 'are going to have to wait. Because it sounds as if someone's hungry.' He settled Tia back against the pillows. 'I'll go and get him. And then I'll make you that cup of tea.'

'And join us, I hope,' Tia said. 'Because there's nothing more perfect than snuggling up with my gorgeous son and even more gorgeous husband.'

Antonio kissed her again. 'I agree. You're the wisest of women, Tia Valenti.'

Tia made herself comfortable, ready to feed the baby. The newest Valenti Prince had stolen everyone's heart, and he'd made a huge difference to life at the palace. Their baby was an unexpected gift who'd brought Antonio's family closer together, cracking the reserve and formality at the palace to let the warmth of love radiate through.

Love and tenderness that weren't kept just for private moments: Antonio was openly affectionate, holding her hand and sliding his arm round her and stealing kisses. He'd lost his cold, remote shell for good, and the real Antonio was definitely the man of her dreams.

'Penny for them?' he asked, walking in while rocking the baby on his shoulder.

'Just thinking how lucky I am,' she said.

'How lucky we are,' he corrected. 'And this is something I'll never take for granted. A happiness I always want to share with the world. Because love is the best gift of all.'

* * * * *

CLAIMING MY
HIDDEN SON

MAYA BLAKE

PROLOGUE

THE DRUMMING IN my ears was loud. So loud I had the fleeting thought that I was on the verge of suffering a stroke. Of doing myself irreparable harm and comprehensively ending this debacle once and for all.

But that would be too easy.

And the headline…

I could see it now.

> *Axios Xenakis Suffers Stroke Due to*
> *Family Pressures!*

They would have no clue as to the unreasonable part, of course. Despite the media outlets lauding the story of the Xenakis near-ruin to phenomenal rise on a regular basis these days, they would be swift to jump on past flaws. Old skeletons would be dragged out of closets. I would be deemed weak. Broken. Not quite up to the task of managing a global conglomerate.

Just like my father.

Just as my grandfather had been falsely labelled after that one risky move that had seen all his hard work whittled away to almost nothing.

He'd had to bear that one misfortune all the way to his grave.

Once a titan of his industry, a simple decision to align himself with the wrong partner had decimated him, leaving the Xenakis name with a stench of failure that had lingered long after his death, causing insidious damage.

Damage that had taken back-breaking hard work to reverse, with my refusal to allow my family name to sink without a trace spurring me to seek daring solutions.

The Xenakis name was no longer one to be ashamed of.

Now it was synonymous with success and innovation—a global conglomerate that *Fortune 500* companies vied to be associated with.

However, the solution being proposed to me now was one set to resurrect the unsavoury ghosts of the past, with their talons of barefaced greed—

'Ax, are you listening? Did you hear what Father said?' asked Neo, my brother.

'Of course I heard it. I'm not deaf,' I replied, with more than a snap to my voice.

'Thank God for that—although you do a great stone statue impression.'

I ignored Neo and fixed my gaze on the man seated behind the large antique desk. My father was studying me with a mixture of regret and apprehension. He knew my precise thoughts on the subject being discussed.

No, not *discussed*.

It was being *thrust* upon me.

'No,' I replied firmly. 'There has to be another way.'

The tension in the room elevated, but this was too serious for me to mince my words. Too serious to let the elephant that always loomed in the room on occasions like this cloud my judgement.

I simply couldn't allow the fact that my grandfather had chosen me as his successor instead of my father to get in the way of this discussion. Nor could I allow the resentment and guilt that had always tainted my relationship with my father to alter my view on what was being proposed.

What was done was done. I'd turned the tides and restored the fortunes of my family. For that even my father couldn't object.

Which was why I was a little surprised when he emphatically shook his head.

'There isn't. Your grandfather was of sound mind when he made the arrangement.'

'Even though he was judged otherwise in other areas?'

Barely fettered bitterness filtered through my voice. The injustices dealt to my grandfather and mentor, the man who taught me everything I know, still burned like acid all these years after his untimely death.

'Now is not the time to reopen old wounds, Axios,' my father said, jaw clenched.

My quiet fury burned even as I accepted his words. 'I agree. Now is the time to discuss ways to get me *out* of this nonsense.'

And it *was* nonsense to expect an arrangement like this to hold water.

'A sweeping agreement where the other party gets to call the shots whenever they like? How come the lawyers haven't ripped this to shreds?' I demanded, striving to keep a tighter rein on my ire.

My father's lips firmed. 'I've spent the last month discussing it with our counsel. We can fight it in court, and probably win, but it'll be a protracted affair. And is now really the time to draw adverse publicity to the company? Or drag your grandfather's name through the mud again for that matter?'

My own lips flattened as again I grimly accepted he was right. With Xenakis Aeronautics poised for its biggest global expansion yet, the timing was far from ideal.

Which was exactly what Yiannis Petras had banked on.

'You mentioned you'd offered him ten million euros and he refused? Let's double the offer,' I suggested.

Neo shook his head. 'I already tried. Petras is hell-bent on Option A or Option B.'

The breath left my lungs in a rush. 'Over my dead body will I go for Option A and hand over twenty-five percent of Xenakis Aeronautics,' I replied coldly. 'Not for the paltry quarter of a million his father bailed Grandpapa out with, while almost crippling him with steep interest repayments!'

The company I'd spent gruelling years saving was now worth several billion euros.

My brother shrugged. 'Then it's Option B. A full and final one hundred million euros, plus marriage to his daughter for minimum term of one year.'

A cold shudder tiptoed down my spine.

Marriage.

To a bride I didn't want and with a connection to a family that had brought mine nothing but misery, pain and near destitution.

During the formative years of my life I witnessed how a fall from grace could turn family members against each other. Clawing my own family out of that quagmire while other factions sneered and expected me to fail had opened my eyes to the true nature of relationships.

Outwardly, the Xenakis were deemed a strong unit now, but the backbiting had never gone away. The barely veiled expectation that everything I'd achieved would be brought down like a pile of loose bricks and that history would repeat itself was a silent challenge I rose to each morning.

While my extended family now enjoyed the fruits of my labour, and even tripped over themselves to remain in my good graces, deep down I knew a simple misstep was all it would take for their frivolous loyalties to falter.

I didn't even blame them.

How could I when my own personal interactions had repeatedly taken the same route? Each liaison I entered into eventually devolved into a disillusioning level of avarice and status-grabbing.

It was why my relationships now had a strict time limit of weeks. A few months, tops. Which made the thought of tying myself to one woman for twelve long months simply...*unthinkable.*

My chest tightened, and the urge to rail at my grandfather for putting me in this position seared me with shame before I suppressed it.

He'd been in an equally impossible position. I knew firsthand what the toll of keeping his family together had cost him—had watched deep grooves etch his grey face once vibrant with laughter and seen his shoulders slump under the heavy burden of loss.

Yes, he should have told me about this Sword of Damocles hanging over my head. But he was gone. Thanks to the ruthless greed of the Petras family. A family hell-bent on extracting another pound of flesh they didn't deserve.

'The hundred million I understand. But why insist on marriage to the daughter?' I asked my brother as his words pierced the fog of my thoughts.

Neo shrugged again. 'Who knows how men like Petras think? Maybe he just wants to offload her. The clout that comes from marrying into the Xenakis family isn't without its benefits,' he mused.

I shuddered, the reminder that, to most people, my family and I were nothing but meal tickets sending a shock of bitterness through me.

'And did you meet this woman I'm to tie myself to?'

He nodded. 'She's…' He stopped and smiled slyly. 'I'll let you judge for yourself.' His gaze left mine to travel over my grey pinstriped suit. 'But I'm thinking you two will hit it off.'

Before I could demand an explanation my father leaned forward. 'Enough, Neo.' My father's gaze swung to me, steel reflected in his eyes. 'We can't delay any longer. Yiannis Petras wants an answer by morning.'

The pressure gripping my nape escalated—the effect of the noose closing round it ramping up my discord. Marriage was the last thing I wanted. To anyone. But especially to a Petras. Both my grandparents and my parents had been strained to breaking point because of the Petras family's actions, with ill-health borne of worry taking my grandmother before her time too.

There had to be another way…

'What's her name?' I asked my father—not because I

cared but because I needed another moment to think. To wrap my head around this insanity.

'Calypso Athena Petras. But I believe she responds to Callie.'

Beside me, Neo smirked again. 'A dramatic name for a dramatic situation!'

I balled my fist and attempted to breathe through the churning in my gut. First they'd forced my grandfather's business into the ground, until he'd broken his family right down the middle by working himself into an early grave. Now this…

'Show me the agreement.' I needed to see it for myself, find a way to assimilate what I'd been committed to.

My father slid the document across the desk. I read it, my fingers clenching as with each paragraph the noose tightened.

Twelve months of my life, starting from the exchange of vows, after which either party would be free to divorce.

Twelve months during which the Petras family who, by a quirk of karma—if you believe in that sort of thing—had fallen on even harder times than they'd condemned my family to would be free to capitalise fully on their new status of wealth and privilege by association.

My lips twisted. I intended to have my lawyers draft divorce papers before I went anywhere near a church.

I exhaled, knowing my subconscious had already accepted the situation.

'Don't overthink it, brother. You're thirty-three next month. This will be over by your thirty-fourth birthday. If you bite the bullet,' Neo offered helpfully.

Slowly, I dragged myself back under control. 'I've worked too hard and too long to restore our family back to where it belongs to lose it to a greedy opportunist. If there's no other way…tell Petras we have a deal.'

My father nodded, relieved, before he sent me another

nervous glance. The kind that announced there was something more equally unsavoury to deliver.

'What now?' My patience was hanging by a thread.

'Besides paying for the wedding, we also need to present the family with a…a dowry of sorts. Petras has asked for Kosima.'

I surged to my feet, uncaring that my chair tipped over. '*Excuse* me?'

My father's face tightened. 'No one has stepped foot on the island since your grandfather passed—'

'That doesn't mean I want to hand it over to the son of the man who caused his death!'

A flash of pain dimmed his eyes. 'We don't know that to be strictly true.'

'Don't we? Did you not see for yourself the pressure he was under? He only started drinking after the problems with Petras started. Is it any wonder his heart failed?'

'Easy, brother,' Neo urged. 'Father is right. The house is rotting away and the land around it is nothing but a pile of weeds and stones.'

But I was beyond reason. Beyond furious at this last damning request.

'Grandpapa loved that island. It belongs to us. I'm not going to hand it over to Petras. Isn't it enough that he's imposing this bilious arrangement on us?'

'Is it enough for you to drag your heels on this last hurdle?' My father parried.

Unable to remain still, I strode to the window of the building that housed the headquarters of Xenakis Aeronautics, the global airline empire I'd headed for almost a decade. For a full minute I watched traffic move back and forth on the busy Athens streets while I grappled with this last condition.

I sensed my brother and father approach. I didn't acknowledge them as they positioned themselves on either side of me and waited.

Waited for the only response that I could conceivably give. The words burned in my throat. Left a trail of ash on my tongue. But it had to be done. I had to honour my grandfather's request, no matter my personal view on it. Or I'd risk everything he'd built. Risk mocking the sacrifice that had taken the ultimate toll.

'Tell Petras he has a deal.'

My father's hand arrived on my shoulder in silent gratitude, after which he exited quietly.

Neo chose more exuberant congratulations, but even then I barely felt him slap my shoulder.

'Think of it this way. For twelve months you'll be free of all the scheming socialites and supermodels who've been falling over themselves to extract a commitment from you. I'll happily carry that burden for you instead.'

'Unless you wish to date one of those supermodels whilst sporting a black eye, I suggest you leave my office immediately,' I growled.

My brother's laughter echoed in my ears long after he'd slammed the door behind him.

But long before the echo died I made another silent vow to myself. Petras and his kin would pay for what they'd done to my family. Before the stipulated year of marriage was out they'd regret tangling with the Xenakis family.

CHAPTER ONE

'Smile, Calypso. It's the happiest day of your life!'

'Here, let me put some more blusher on your cheeks... you're so pale. Perhaps a bit more shadow for your beautiful eyes...'

Beneath the endless layers of white tulle that some faceless stranger had deemed the perfect wedding gown material and gone to town with my fingers bunched into fists. When the tight clenches didn't help, I bit the tip of my tongue and fought the urge to scream.

But I was past hysteria. *That* unfortunate state had occurred two weeks prior, when my father had informed me just how he'd mapped out the rest of my life. How it was my turn to help restore our family's honour.

Or else.

The cold shivers racing up and down my spine had become familiar in the last month, after a few days spent in denial that my father would truly carry out his intentions.

I'd quickly accepted that he would.

Years of bitterness and humiliation and failure to emulate his ruthless father's dubious acclaim had pushed him over the edge once and for all.

The soft bristles of the blusher brush passed feverishly over my cheeks. The make-up artist determined to transform me into an eager, blushing, starry-eyed bride.

But I was far from eager and a million miles away from starry-eyed.

The only thing they'd got right in this miserable spectacle was the virginal white.

If I'd had a choice that too would have been a lie. At twenty-four I knew, even in my sheltered existence, that being a virgin was a rare phenomenon. At least now I realised why my father had been hell-bent on thwarting my every encounter with the opposite sex. Why he'd ruthlessly vetted my friendships, curtailed my freedom.

I'd believed my choices had been so abruptly limited since the moment my mother fell from grace. Since she returned home the broken prodigal wife and handed my father all the weapons he needed to transform himself from moderately intolerable to fearsome tyrant. I thought I'd been swept along by the merciless broom of wronged party justice, but he'd had a completely different purpose for me.

A purpose which had brought me to this moment.

My wedding day.

The next shudder coagulated in my chin, making it wobble like jelly before I could wrestle my composure back under control.

Luckily the trio of women who'd descended on our house twenty-four hours ago were clucking about pre-wedding nerves, then clucking some more about how understandable my fraught emotions were, considering who my prospective husband was.

Axios Xenakis.

A man I'd never met.

Sure, like everyone in Greece I knew who he was. A wildly successful airline magnate worth billions and head of the influential Xenakis family. A family whose ill fortune, unlike mine, had been reversed due the daring innovation of its young CEO.

It was rumoured that Axios Xenakis was the kind of individual whose projections could cause stock markets to rise or fall. The various articles I'd read about him had boggled my mind—the idea that any one person could wield such power and authority was bewildering. To top it off, Axios Xenakis was drop-dead gorgeous, if a little fierce-looking.

Everything about the man was way too visceral and invasive. Just a simple glance at his image online had evoked the notion that he could see into my soul, glean my deepest desires and use them against me. It was probably why he was often seen in the company of sophisticated heiresses and equally influential A-listers.

Which begged the question—why the Petras family? More specifically, why *me*?

What did a man who dated socialites and heiresses on a regular basis, as was thoroughly documented in the media, have to gain by shackling himself to me?

I knew it had something to do with the supreme smugness my father had been exhibiting in the last several weeks but he had refused to disclose. Somehow, behind the sneers and bitterness whenever the Xenakis name came up over the years, my father had been scheming. And that scheming had included me.

In all my daydreams about attaining my freedom, marriage hadn't featured anywhere. I wanted the freedom to dictate who I socialised with, what I ate, the pleasure to paint my watercolours without fear of recrimination, without judgement… The freedom to live life on *my* terms.

The hope of one day achieving those things had stopped me from succumbing to abject misery.

But not like *this*!

I forced my gaze to the mirror and promptly looked away again. My eyes were desolate pools, my cheeks artificially pink with excess rouge. My lips were turned down, reflecting my despair since learning that I was promised to a stranger. One who'd demanded a wedding within twenty-eight days.

My flat refusal had merely garnered a cold shrug from my father, before he had gone for the jugular—my one weakness.

My mother.

As if summoned by my inner turmoil, the electric whine of a wheelchair disturbed the excited chatter of the stylists. The moment they realised the mother of the bride had entered the bedroom, their attention shifted to her.

Taking advantage of the reprieve, I surreptitiously rubbed

at my cheeks with a tissue, removing a layer of blusher. The icy peach lipstick disappeared with the second swipe across my lips, leaving me even paler than before but thankfully looking less of a lost, wide-eyed freak. Quickly hanging the thick lace veil over my face to hide the alteration, I stood and turned, watching as the women fawned over my mother.

Iona Petras had been stunningly beautiful once upon a time. Growing up, I was in awe of her statuesque beauty, her vivacity and sheer joy for life. Her laughter had lit up my day, her intelligence and love of the arts fuelling my own appreciation for music and painting.

Now, greying and confined, she was still a beautiful woman. But along with her broken body had come a broken spirit no amount of pretending or smiling, or even gaining the elevated position as mother of the bride, soon to marry a man most deemed a demigod, could disguise.

She withstood the stylists' ministrations without complaint, her half-hearted smile only slipping when her eyes met mine. Within them I saw ravaging misery and the sort of unending despair that came with the life sentence she'd imposed on herself by returning when she should have fled.

But, just as I'd had to remain here because of her, I knew my mother had returned home because of me. And somewhere along the line Iona Petras had accepted her fate.

'Leave us, please,' she said to the stylists, her voice surprisingly steely.

The women withdrew. She wheeled herself closer, her face pinched with worry. For the longest minute she stared at me.

'Are you all right?'

I tensed, momentarily panicked that she'd learned what I'd hidden from her for the last few weeks. As much as I'd tried to ignore the ever-growing pain in my abdomen, I couldn't any more. Not only had it become a constant dull ache, it had become a reminder that even health-wise my life wasn't my own. That I might well be succumbing to the very real ailment that had taken my grandmother—

'Callie? Are you ready?'

Realising she was talking about the wedding ceremony, I felt the urge to succumb to hysteria pummel me once again. As did the fierce need to be selfish just this once…to simply flee and let the chips fall where they may.

'Is anyone ever ready to marry a man they've never met?' I asked. 'Please tell me you've found out why he's demanding I do this?' I pleaded.

Eyes a shade darker than my own lapis-lazuli-coloured ones turned mournful as she shook her head. 'No. Your father still refuses to tell me. My guess is that it has something to do with your grandfather and old man Xenakis.' Before I could ask what she meant, she continued, 'Anyway, Yiannis will be looking for me, so I need to be quick.'

She reached inside the stylish designer jacket that matched her lavender gown and produced a thick cream envelope, her fingers shaking as she stared at it.

'What's that?' I asked when she made no move to speak.

Within her gaze came a spark of determination I hadn't seen in years. My heart leapt into my throat as she caught my hand in hers and squeezed it tight.

'My sweet Callie, I know I've brought misery to your life with my actions—'

'No, Mama, you haven't. I promise,' I countered firmly.

She stared at me. 'I'm not sure whether to be proud or to admonish you for being such a good liar. But I know what I've done. My selfishness has locked you in this prison with me when you should be free to pursue what young girls your age ought to be doing.' Her fingers tightened on mine. 'I want you to make me a promise,' she pleaded, her voice husky with unshed tears.

I nodded because…what else could I do? 'Anything you want, Mama.'

She held out the envelope. 'Take this. Hide it in the safest place you can.'

I took it, frowning at the old-fashioned cursive lettering spelling out my name. 'What's this?'

'It's from your grandmother.'

'Yiayia Helena?' A tide of sorrow momentarily washed over me, my heart still missing the grandmother I'd lost a year ago.

My mother nodded. 'She said I'd know when you needed it. And even if I'm wrong...'

She paused, a faraway look in her eyes hinting that she was indulging in all those might-have-beens that sparked my own desperate imagination. When she refocused, her gaze moved dully over my wedding dress.

'Even if this...alliance turns out to be tolerable, it'll help to know you were loved by your grandmother. That should you need her she'll be there for you the way I wasn't.'

I held on tighter to her hand. 'I know you love me, Mama.'

She shook her head, tears brimming her eyes. 'Not the way a mother should love her child, without selfish intentions that end up harming her. I took the wrong turn with you. I left you alone with your father when I should have taken you with me. Maybe if I had—' She stopped, took a deep breath and dabbed at her tears before braving my worried stare again. 'All I ask is that you find a way to forgive me one day.'

'Mama—' I stopped when she gave a wrenching sob.

Her gaze dropped to the envelope in my hand. 'Hang on to that, Callie. And don't hesitate to use it when you need it. Promise me,' she insisted fervently.

'I… I promise.'

She sniffed, nodded, then abruptly turned the wheelchair and manoeuvred herself out of my bedroom.

Before I could process our conversation I was again surrounded by mindless chatter, unable to breathe or think. The only solid thing in my world became the envelope I clutched tightly in my hand. And when I found that within the endless folds of tulle the designer had fashioned a pocket, I nearly cried with relief as I slipped the envelope into it.

Even without knowing its contents, just knowing it came from my grandmother—the woman who'd helped me stand up to my father's wrath more times than I could count, who'd loved and reassured me on a daily basis during my mother's year-long absence when I was fifteen years old— kept me from crumbling as my father arrived and with a brisk nod offered his stiff arm, ordered me to straighten my spine…and escorted me to my fate.

The chapel was filled to the brim, according to the excited chatter of the household staff, and as my father led me out to a flower-bedecked horse-drawn carriage I got the first indication of what was to come.

Over the last three weeks I'd watched with a sense of surrealism as construction crews and landscapers descended on our little corner of the world to transform the church and surrounding area from a place of rundown dilapidation into its former whitewashed charming glory.

The usually quiet streets of Nicrete, a sleepy village in the south of the island of Skyros, the place generations of the Petras family had called home, buzzed with fashionably dressed strangers—all guests of Axios Xenakis. With the main means of getting on and off the island being by boat, the harbour had become a place of interest in the last few days.

Every hotel and guest house on the island was booked solid. Expensive speedboats and a handful of super-yachts had appeared on the horizon overnight, and now bobbed in the Aegean beneath resplendent sunshine.

Of course the man I was to marry chose to do things differently.

My carriage was halfway between home and the church when the loud, mechanical whine of powerful rotors churned the air. Children shouted in excitement and raced towards the hilltop as three sleek-looking helicopters flew overhead to settle on the newly manicured lawns of the park usually used as recreational grounds for families. Today the whole park had been cordoned off—evidently to receive these helicopters.

Beneath the veil I allowed myself a distasteful moue. But the barrier wasn't enough to hide my father's smug smile as he watched the helicopters. Or his nod of satisfaction as several distinguished-looking men and designer-clad women alighted from the craft.

I averted my face, hoping the ache in my heart and the pain in my belly wouldn't manifest itself in the hysteria I'd been trying to suppress for what seemed like for ever. But I couldn't prevent the words from tumbling from my lips.

'It's not too late, Papa. Whatever this is… Perhaps if you told me why, we can find a way—'

'I have already found a way, child.'

'Don't call me a child—I'm twenty-four years old!'

That pulse of rebellion, which I'd never quite been able to curb, eagerly fanned by Yiayia when she was alive, slipped its leash. She'd never got on well with my father, and in a way standing up to him now, despite the potential fallout for my mother, felt like honouring her memory.

His eyes narrowed. 'If you wanted to help then you should've taken that business degree at university, instead of the useless arts degree you're saddled with.'

'I told you—I'm not interested in a corporate career.'

Nor was I interested in being constantly reminded that I wasn't the son he'd yearned for. The one he'd hoped would help him save Petras Industries, the family company which now teetered on the brink of bankruptcy.

'*Ne*—and just like your mother you let me down. Once again it has fallen to *me* to find a way. And I have. So now you will smile and do your duty by this family. You will say your vows and marry Xenakis.'

I bit my lip at this reminder of yet another bone of contention between us. I'd fought hard for the right to leave the island to pursue my arts degree, only returning because of my mother. The small art gallery I worked at part-time on Nicrete was a way of keeping my sanity, even as I mourned my wasted degree.

'After that, what then?'

He shrugged. 'After that you will belong to him. But remember that regardless of the new name you're taking on you're still a Petras. If you do anything to bring the family into disrepute you will bear the consequences.'

My heart lurched, my fists balling in pain and frustration—because I knew exactly what my father meant.

The *consequences* being my father's ability to manipulate my mother's guilt and ensure maximum suffering. His constant threats to toss her out with only the clothes on her back, to abandon her to her fate the way she'd briefly abandoned her family. But while my mother had deserted her child and marriage in the name of a doomed love, my father was operating from a place of pure revenge. To him, his wife had humiliated and betrayed him, and he was determined to repay her by keeping her prisoner. Ensuring that at every waking moment she was reminded of her fall from grace and his power over her.

The reason that I'd been roped in as a means to that end was my love for my mother.

Eight years ago, when he'd returned home with my absentee mother after the doctors in Athens had called and informed him that she'd been in a crash, and that the man she'd run away with was dead, he'd laid out new family rules. My mother would stay married to him. She would become a dutiful wife and mother, doing everything in her power to not bring another speck of disgrace to the family. In return he would ensure her medical needs were met, and that she would be given the finest treatment to adjust to her new wheelchair-bound life.

For my part, I would act the devoted daughter…or my mother would suffer.

The horses whinnying as they came to a stop at the steps leading to the church doors dragged me to the present, pushing my heartache aside and replacing it with apprehension.

The last of the guests were entering while organ music piped portentously in the air. In less than an hour I would be married to a man I'd never exchanged a single word with. A man who had somehow fallen in league with my father for reasons I still didn't know.

I glanced at my father, desperate to ask why. His stony profile warned me not to push my luck. Like my heartache, I smothered my rebellion.

My father stepped out of the carriage and held out his hand. Mine shook, and again I was glad for the veil's cover to hide my tear-prickled eyes.

A small part of me was grateful that my father didn't seem in a hurry to march me down the aisle because he was basking in the limelight that momentarily banished the shadow of scandal and humiliation he'd lived under for the past eight years. For once people weren't talking about his wife's infidelity. Or the fact that the woman who'd deserted him had returned in a wheelchair. Or that he'd taken her back just so he could keep her firmly under his thumb in retribution.

Today he was simply the man who'd seemingly bagged one of the most eligible bachelors in the world for his daughter—not the once illustrious but now downtrodden businessman who'd lost the Petras fortune his father had left him.

The doors to the church yawned open, ready to receive their unwilling sacrifice. My footsteps faltered and my father sent me a sharp look. Unable to meet his eyes without setting off the spark of mutiny attempting to rekindle itself inside me, I kept my gaze straight.

I needed to do this for my mother.

I spotted her in the front row, her head held high despite

her fate, and it lent me the strength to put one foot in front of the other. The slight weight of my grandmother's envelope in my pocket helped me ignore the rabid curiosity and speculative whispers of three hundred strangers.

Unfortunately there was only one place left to look. At the towering figure of the man waiting in perfect stillness facing the altar.

He didn't twitch nor fidget. Didn't display any outward signs of being a nervous groom.

His broad back and wide shoulders seemed to go on for ever, and his proud head and unyielding stance announced his power and authority. He didn't speak to the equally tall, commanding figure next to him, as most grooms did with their best man. In fact both men stood as if to military attention, their stance unwavering.

My gaze flicked away from Axios Xenakis, my breath stalling in my throat the closer I approached. Even without seeing his face I sensed a formidable aura—one that forced me again to wonder why he was doing this. What did he have to gain with this alliance?

He could have any woman he wanted. So why me?

And why had several butterflies suddenly taken flight within my belly?

Wild instinct urged me to fan my rebellion to life. *Fight or flight*. Pick one and deal with the consequences later.

But even as the thoughts formed they were discarded.

I had no choice. None whatsoever.

But maybe this man I was marrying would be a little more malleable than my father. Maybe—

He turned. And the feeble little hope died a horrible death.

Eyes the colour of polished gunmetal bored into me as if they were with fierce, merciless hooks. They probed beneath the veil with such force that for a moment I imagined I was naked—that he could see my every weakness and flaw, see to the heart of my deepest desire for freedom.

His lips were pressed into a formidable line, his whole demeanour austere. Axios Xenakis could have been in a boardroom, preparing to strike a deal to make himself another billion euros, not poised before an altar, about to commit himself to a wife he'd never met.

I catalogued his breathtaking features. Wondered if that rugged boxer's jaw ever relaxed—whether the cut-glass sharpness of his cheekbones ever softened in a smile. Did he maintain constant control of those sleek eyebrows so they were permanently brooding? Did his nose ever wrinkle in laughter?

Why was I interested?

I was nothing but part of a transaction to him—one he didn't seem entirely thrilled about, judging by his icy regard. So it didn't matter that the olive vibrancy of his skin drew from me more than a fleeting look, or that he was without a doubt the most strikingly handsome man I'd ever seen.

He was a world removed from the boys I'd sneakily dated at university, before my father had found out and ruthlessly thwarted my chances with them before anything resembling a relationship could form.

Axios Xenakis belonged in a stratosphere of his own. One I was apprehensive about inhabiting.

My footsteps stalled and I heard my father's sharp intake of breath. It was swiftly followed by the tight grip of his hand in warning.

Don't disgrace the family.

Defiance sparked again.

But then I saw my mother's head turn. The ubiquitous misery filmed her eyes, but alongside it was a look so fierce it might have been a reflection from my grandmother's eyes.

It was a look that infused me with courage.

It's up to you, it said. *Do this...or don't.*

My heart thundered. The need to turn around and simply walk away was a wild cyclone churning through me.

At the altar, Axios's eyes never shifted from me, his

stance unchanging in the face of my clear reluctance. It was as if he knew what I'd decide and was simply waiting me out.

And, since I was playing in a game whose rules no one had bothered to apprise me of, there was only one move I could make.

I would play this round, then fight my corner later.

With that firm promise echoing inside me, I stepped up to the altar.

I saw a fleeting disappointment in his eyes before he masked his features. He was *disappointed*? Did that mean he didn't want this?

Wild hope flared within me even as bewilderment mounted. If he didn't want this then there might be room to negotiate. Room to get what I wanted out of this.

Realising I was staring, and that my father had been dispatched and I was now the sole focus of Axios Xenakis' eyes, I hurriedly averted my gaze. But not before acknowledging that up close he was even more electrifying. Perhaps it was the severity of his grey suit. Or the fact that the hand he held out to me screamed a silent command.

The last strains of the hymn trailed away, leaving behind a charged silence. With each second it weighed heavier, pressing down on me.

His hand extended another inch, and heavy expectation thickened the air.

With a deep breath, inevitably I slipped my hand into his—and joined the stranger who was to be my husband.

Almost immediately he released me. But the sensation of his touch lingered, and a sizzling chain reaction I was unprepared for travelled up my arm, flaring wide.

It was enough momentarily to drown out the intonation of the priest's voice as he began the ceremony.

I rallied long enough to murmur the words I'd reluctantly memorised and, when the time came, to pick up the larger of the two platinum wedding bands.

With fingers that still trembled I faced Axios. The impact of his eyes, his towering frame, the much too handsome face momentarily erased the words from my brain.

In silence he held out his left hand, his laser eyes boring into me as he simply...*waited.*

'I take thee...'

'For better or worse...'

'With my body...'

'Love, honour, cherish...'

'Till death...'

With each spoken vow my heart squeezed tighter, the mechanical delivery I'd expected to give morphing into a whispered outpouring wrapped in consternation.

The second I was done he reached for the other ring without taking his eyes off me, again holding out his hand for mine.

And then Axios Xenakis spoke for the first time.

'I, Axios Xenakis, take thee, Calypso Athena Petras...'

The rest of his words were lost to me as the deep, hypnotic cadence of his voice struck like Zeus's thunderbolt into a place I didn't even know existed until that moment.

His voice was...*sexy.* Alluring. Magnetic.

It seemed impossible that a voice could be all those things, and yet I felt every one.

The cold brush of platinum on my skin brought me back to myself just in time to hear the priest announce us as man and wife. To say that my new husband could now kiss me.

I started to turn away. Because this was a far cry from a normal wedding ceremony. And we were far removed from two people in love.

Large, firm hands cupped my shoulders, shocking me into stillness. Unable to stop a cascade of light shivers, I held my breath as he lifted the heavy veil and draped it behind me with unhurried movements. I watched his gaze take in my bound hair, the small headband made of tiny diamonds and pearls that had belonged to Yiayia Helena and the similar necklace adorning my throat.

Had he been anyone else I might have entertained the notion that Axios Xenakis was reluctant to look into the face of the woman he'd just committed himself to. Because when his piercing grey eyes finally settled on me, I caught a momentary confusion, then his eyes widened and his jaw slackened for a split second before he reasserted supreme control.

Any fleeting pleasure I'd felt at gaining some unknown upper hand fled as heat suffused my face at his intense, almost shocked scrutiny.

Admitting that I should have left the make-up artist's work alone didn't help my urge to squirm under his candid regard. But I forced myself to hold his gaze, ignore the consternation in his eyes and the humiliating thud of my heartbeat.

Just when I thought he intended to drag the torture out for ever he slid one finger beneath my chin to nudge my head upward. Caught in the mysterious hypnosis of his gaze, I watched his head descend, so close that heat from his skin singed mine.

I braced myself, my stomach churning with emotions I couldn't name.

I'd been kissed before. Those university colleagues I'd toyed with before my father's bitter reach had scared them away. None of them had elicited this level of shivery anticipation.

His kiss arrived, subtle as a butterfly's wing and powerful as a sledgehammer. Sensation rocked through me like an earthquake, dizzying and terrifying, leaving me with nothing to do but to brace my hands on his chest, anchor myself to reality somehow.

But all that did was compound my situation. Because the solid wall of his chest was like sculpted warm steel, inviting the kind of exploration that had no place in this time and space.

Pull away.

Before I could, he gave a sharp intake of breath. In the next moment I was free of him and he was turning away.

Back to earth with a shaky thud, I fought angry bewilderment even as I strove for composure before our three-hundred-strong audience.

The feeling lingered all through our walk down the aisle, through our stiff poses for pictures and then the ride back up the hill to the crumbling mansion overlooking the harbour—the only home I'd ever known.

The horse and carriage had been swapped for a sleek limousine with darkened windows and a partition that ensured privacy. Beside me Axios maintained a stony silence, one I wasn't inclined to break despite the dark, enigmatic looks he slanted me every now and then.

When it all became too much, I snatched in a breath and faced him. 'Is there something on your mind?'

One eyebrow quirked. 'As conversations go, that's not quite what I expected as our first. But then I'm making many surprising discoveries.'

He wasn't the only one! 'What's that supposed to mean?'

He didn't reply immediately. Then, 'You're not what I was led to expect.'

I couldn't help my lips twisting. 'You are aware of how absurd that sounds, aren't you?'

He stiffened, and I got the notion that once again something about me had surprised him. 'No. Enlighten me,' he replied dryly.

'Not what you were *led to expect*?' The slight screech in my voice warned me that hysteria might be winning but I couldn't stop. 'Let me guess—you thought you were getting some biddable wallflower who would tremble and trip over herself to please you?'

You were trembling minutes ago, when he kissed you.

I ignored the voice and met his gaze.

He'd turned into a pillar of stone. 'Considering the ink

isn't dry on our marriage certificate, perhaps we should strive not to have our first disagreement. Unless you wish to break some sort of record?' he rasped, gunmetal eyes boring into me.

Apart from our marriage, I still didn't know the precise details of the deal between my father and my new husband and it momentarily stalled my response. But the fire burning inside me wouldn't be doused.

'I get the feeling you're just as…*invested* in this thing as my father is, so it bears repeating that you're *not* getting a simpering lackey who will jump through hoops to amuse you.'

His eyes narrowed. 'Your *father*? Not you?'

Short of revealing my ignorance on the matter, I had to prevaricate. 'I'm a Petras—same as he.'

Something that looked very much like contempt flickered through his eyes. 'Consider me forewarned,' he replied cryptically.

Before I could query what he meant the limo was pulling up to the double doors of my family home. Liveried footmen hurried to throw our doors open.

Inside the rarely used but hastily refurbished ballroom guests drank champagne and feasted on canapés and my father gave a painfully false speech. I only managed to sit through it by reaching into my pocket and clutching the envelope within.

The moment the speeches were done Axios was swarmed upon by fawning acquaintances, eager to engage the great man in conversation. I told myself that my primary emotion was relief as the stylists, also roped into acting as my attendants, rushed to straighten my veil and train, twitching and tweaking until they were satisfied that I'd been restored to their vision of bridal beauty.

But just when I thought I'd have a moment's reprieve Axios's gaze zeroed in on me, his eyes falling to the barely touched food on the plate that lay next to my untouched glass of champagne.

One brow rose. 'Not in the mood for celebrating? Or are you trying to make some sort of point by not eating?'

I couldn't eat—not when the inkling was deepening that Axios Xenakis was far from a willing participant in this devilish deal. And if that was the case, what had I let myself in for?

I pushed the anxious thought away and let my gaze fall on his equally full plate. 'You should talk.'

He lifted his champagne and took a healthy gulp. 'Unlike you, this occasion isn't one I feel inclined to celebrate.'

My breath caught, but before I could ask him to elaborate, he continued.

'And in the interest of clarity let me warn you that neither you nor your father have any cards left to play. Should you feel inclined to make *more* demands.'

Christos, what exactly had my father done?

But even as the question burned fire boiled in my blood. 'Are you threatening my family? Because if you are, please know that I will fight you with everything I've got.'

His lips twisted at my fierce tone. 'What a fiery temper you have. I wonder what other surprises you're hiding beneath those unfortunate layers of… What *is* that material?'

As much as I hated my wedding dress, his remark sparked irritation. 'It's called tulle. And you should know. You paid for it, after all.'

The barest hint of a sardonic smile lifted his sensual lips. 'Writing a cheque for it doesn't mean I pay attention to every single detail of a woman's wardrobe. I have better things to do than concern myself with the name of the fabric that comprises a wedding gown.'

'But this is *your* wedding too,' I taunted, knowing my mockery would aggravate.

Something about this towering hunk of a man, who'd made it clear that this was the last place he wanted to be, riled me on a visceral level, firing up a need to dig beneath his formidable exterior.

'Isn't it supposed to be one of the momentous occasions of your life?'

Every trace of humour disappeared. Piercing grey eyes pinned me in place, and the tension vibrating from him was so thick I could almost touch it.

'Momentous occasions are highly anticipated and satisfactorily celebrated. You'd have to be delusional or deliberately blind to imagine I'm in such a state, Calypso Petras.'

The way he said my name, with drawling, mocking intonation, fired my blood. Along with other sensations I couldn't quite name.

'It's Calypso Xenakis now—or have you already forgotten?' I fired back, taking secret pleasure in seeing the irritated flare of his nostrils.

'I have not forgotten,' he answered with taut iciness.

'If this is such an ordeal for you, then why all this?' I waved my hand at the obscenely lavish banquet displayed along one long wall, the champagne tower brimming with expensive golden bubbles, the caviar-laden trays being circulated, and the designer-clad guests, shamelessly indulging their appetites.

'Because your father insisted,' he replied, his voice colder than an arctic vortex. 'As *you* well know.'

I opened my mouth to tell him for once and for all that none of this made sense to me because no one had bothered to consult me about my own wedding.

The sight of my mother's face, staring at me from one table away, pain and misery etched beneath her smile, dried the words in my throat.

For whatever reason fate had tangled the Xenakises and the Petrases in an acrimonious weave and my mother and I were caught in the middle. I could no more extricate myself than I could turn my back on her.

A tiny, tortured sound whistled through the air and I realised it came from my own throat—a manifestation of that hysteria that just wouldn't die down. I stood abruptly, knowing I had to get away before I did something regrettable.

Like climb on top of the lavishly decorated lonely high table, set apart from everyone else to showcase the newly married couple in all their glory, and scream at the top of my lungs.

That just wouldn't do. Because while I might have acquired a new surname, it was dawning on me that until I learned the true nature of what I was embroiled in I would be wise to keep a firm hold of my feelings.

And an even firmer hold of my wits.

CHAPTER TWO

MONEY MAKES THE world spin.

I swallowed my champagne, careful not to choke on it as I dispassionately observed the guests indulging in the revelry of my sham of a wedding.

Money had made this happen, and in the exact time frame I'd requested it.

Money had put that smug smile on Yiannis Petras's face.

Money had made the family, decimated by my grandfather's fall from grace, rally together for the sake of enjoying the rejuvenated fruits of my labour.

I'd seen first-hand how the lack of it could cause backbiting and untold strain. Ostensibly solid marriages crumbled under the threat of diminished wealth and influence. I'd seen it in my parents' marriage. It was why I'd never have freely chosen this route for myself.

My gaze shifted to my brand-new wife.

Had money influenced her agreement to this fiasco?

Was she getting a cut of the hundred million euros?

Of course she was. Had she not proclaimed herself a true Petras?

For those seconds as she'd hesitated at the altar I'd entertained the notion that she shared my reluctance, had imagined the merest hint of resistance in her eyes.

Her words had put me straight.

A cursory investigation had revealed that while she'd graduated from Skypos University with a major in Arts, she'd done nothing with her degree for the last two years. Her father's daughter through and through, sitting back and taking the easy route to riches.

So what if outwardly she wasn't what I expected?

I snorted under my breath at this colossal understatement. Calypso Petras...*ochi*, make that Calypso Xenakis...was be-

yond a surprise. She was a punch to my solar plexus, one it
was taking an irritatingly long time to wrestle under control.

Even now my senses still reeled from what I'd uncovered beneath her veil. She was far from the drab little mouse
I'd assumed.

'I believe there's a rule somewhere that states you
shouldn't scowl on your wedding day.'

I resisted the urge to grind my teeth and faced my
brother. 'You think this is funny?'

'This whole circus? No. I believe that ring on your finger
and the look on your face makes it all too real.' Neo affected
a mocking shudder intended to rile me further.

It worked.

'I'm talking about your implication that my... Calypso.'
Thee mou, why did her name sound so...erotic?

Neo's eyes widened before glinting with keen speculation. 'If I recall, I didn't give you any specifics.'

There was a reason Neo was president of marketing at
Xenakis Aeronautics. He could sell hay to a farmer.

My fingers tightened around my glass. 'You deliberately
let me to think she was...unremarkable.'

She was quite the opposite. Hers was the confounding
kind of beauty one couldn't place a finger on. The kind that
made you stare for much longer than was polite.

Neo shrugged. 'No, I didn't. And don't blame me for the
dire state of your mind, brother,' he answered.

The low heat burning through my blood intensified. And
while I wanted to attribute it to this conversation, I knew I
couldn't. Ever since I'd pulled that hideous veil off her face
and uncovered the woman I'd agreed to marry a different
irritation had lodged itself deep inside me. One I wasn't
quite ready to examine.

But that wasn't to say I was ready to let Neo off the
hook for...

For what?

Making obfuscating observations about Calypso Petras

that had made me dismiss her from my mind, only to be knocked off-kilter by her appearance?

Granted, she still wasn't my type. Her eyes were too large...much too *distracting*. They were the type of turquoise-blue that made you question their authenticity. Framed with long eyelashes that begged the same question. And then there were her lips. Full and sensual, with a natural bruised rose hue, and deeply alluring despite the absence of gloss.

The dichotomy of fully made-up eyes and bare lips had absorbed my attention for much too long at that altar. And it had irritated me even further that since our arrival at the reception those lips had been buried beneath a hideous layer of frosty peach.

But it hadn't stopped me puzzling over why the two aspects of her initial appearance had been so at odds with each other. Or why she'd seemed...startled by our very brief kiss on the altar.

False innocence wrapped around her true character? A character that contained more than a little fire.

My mind flicked to other hints I'd glimpsed over the last few hours. While I was yet to discover what lay beneath the layers of the wedding gown, there were more than enough hints to authenticate her voluptuousness.

Yet to discover...

The peculiar buzz that had been ignited during that fleeting kiss notched up a fraction, the fact that the brief contact still lingered on my lips drawing another frown.

'Your new wife is looking a little...unhappy. Perhaps you should see about fixing that?'

About to state that I had nothing to fix, that her happiness was none of my concern, I found my gaze flicked to the table. Despite the picture of poise she was trying to project she looked pale, her eyes flitting nervously. A quick scrutiny of our guests showed she was the object of several stares and blatant whispers.

A helpless prey in a jungle of predators.

My feet moved almost of their own accord, the niggling urge to reverse that look on her face irritating me even as I moved towards her, effectively silencing the whispers with quelling stares.

Regardless of how this union had come about, rumours couldn't be allowed to run rife. This was how undermining started.

As I neared, silence fell. Her gaze shifted, met mine. Her chin lifted, a wisp of bewilderment and skittishness evaporating and her eyes flashing with defiance.

For some absurd reason it sparked something to life inside me. Something I fully intended to ignore.

Defiance or bewilderment, the deed was done. She and her family had capitalised on an agreement made under duress and bagged themselves a windfall. She should be celebrating.

Instead I caught another trace of apprehension as I stopped beside her chair. Eyes growing wide, she looked up at me. The graceful line of her neck—another alluring feature that seemed to demand attention—rippled as she swallowed.

Thee mou, if this was an act then she was a good actress!

Aware of our audience, and a burning need to find out, I held out my hand to her. 'The traditional first dance is coming up, I believe.' The earlier we could get this spectacle out of the way, the quicker I could resume my life.

Her gaze darted to the dance floor, her reluctance clear. 'Is that…really necessary?'

Something about her reluctance and her whole demeanour grated. She was behaving as if I was contaminated!

'Enough with this pretence. That wide-eyed innocent thing will only work for so long. Give it up, Calypso.'

She offered me her hand, but the eyes that met mine as she stood sparkled with renewed fire. 'No one calls me Calypso. My name is Callie,' she stated firmly.

I attempted to ignore the slim fingers in mine, the smooth softness of her palm and the way it kicked to life something inside me as I led her to the middle of the dance floor.

'I'm your new husband—surely I don't fall under the category of *no one*?' I curled my arm around her waist, a singular need to press her close escalating inside me as the band struck up a waltz.

She stiffened. 'Are you insinuating that you're *special*?'

For some reason my lips quirked. 'By your tone, I'm guessing I'm not. Not even special enough for you to grant me the simple gift of addressing you as I please?'

Her lips firmed again, drawing my attention to their plumpness. Reminding me of that all too fleeting taste of them.

'And what am I to call *you*? Other than *stranger* or *husband*?'

For some reason the fiery huskiness of her voice drew another smile. A puzzle in itself, since humour was the last emotion I should have been experiencing. I was in this situation because of money and shameless greed.

'Call me Axios. Or Ax, as most people do. I doubt we will reach the stage of coining terms of endearment.'

'On that I think we're agreed,' she replied, her gaze fixed somewhere over my shoulder.

Another scrabble of irritation threatened to rise, but I suppressed it when I noticed that once again, beneath the show of sharp claws, she was trembling, her wide eyes a little too bright. As if she was holding on to her composure by a thread.

'Is something wrong?' I asked. Again I questioned my need to know. Or care.

'What could possibly be wrong?'

She didn't bother to meet my gaze. If anything, she attempted to detach herself, which ought to have been impossible, considering how close we were dancing. But I was learning that my new wife had several…interesting facets.

'It is polite to look at me when you address me.'

She maintained her stance for another few seconds, then her blue eyes rose to mine. The urge to stare into them, to commit every fleck and expression to memory, charged through me, this time bringing a wave of heat to my groin.

I inhaled slowly, forcing myself to ignore that unsettling sensation and address her as I would any acquaintance.

Even though she wasn't.

Even though she'd taken my name and we were effectively bound together for twelve long months.

'This thing will go smoother if we attempt to be civil with one another. Don't you agree?'

'I'm not a puppet. I cannot act a certain way on command.'

'But you *can* dispense with that little-girl-lost look. And I find it curious that you would choose to refer to puppets. Perhaps you're familiar with knowing exactly which strings to tug to get what you want?'

Unlike me, she didn't attempt to disguise her frown. 'What are you talking about?'

'This whole scheme, orchestrated by you and your family, has gone off without a hitch. Feel free to stop acting now.'

She inhaled sharply, her eyes darting to the guests dancing around us. 'Please keep your voice down.'

'Afraid you'll be found out? Are you really so blind to the fact that every single guest is speculating wildly about how two people who've never met are now married?'

Her plump lips pressed together for a moment. 'I can't control what other people think. But I do care about perpetuating unfounded rumours.'

'Do you, *yineka mou*?'

Her blue eyes shadowed and her gaze quickly flicked away. 'Can you not call me that, please?'

'Why not? Are you not my wife?'

The more the term fell from my lips the deeper it bored

into me, as if rooting for a place to settle. Of course the search would be futile, because this was far from what I wanted.

The strain and stress of trying to save his failing company while keeping his family and his marriage together had driven my grandfather into an early grave, his spirit broken long before the heart attack that had suddenly taken him. It was the same stress that had nearly broken my own father, forcing him to step down after a mere two years as CEO.

I didn't intend to weigh myself down with similar baggage.

I refocused on Calypso, attempting to ignore the effect of her soft curves against my body as she asked, 'So, what happens after this?'

'"This"?'

'After we're done here,' she elaborated.

Unbidden, my thoughts flew ahead. To when the evening would turn exclusive and intimate. When wedding euphoria traditionally took on another, more carnal dimension.

A traditions I *wouldn't* be indulging in.

'Do you plan on getting back into your helicopter and leaving me here?'

The carefully disguised hope in her voice threw me back to that day in my father's office a month ago, when an agreement that bore all the hallmarks of blackmail had crashlanded into my life and threatened the Xenakis name and business. Did she really think she and her family could take financial advantage and then sail off into the sunset?

The silent vow I'd taken that day to ensure neither Calypso nor her father escaped unscathed resurged as I looked down into her face. A face struggling for composure and a body twitching nervously beneath my hand.

I pulled her closer, steadied her at her slight stumble, and lowered my lips to her ear.

'It's our wedding night, *matia mou*. How would it look if we didn't stay under the same roof? Sleep in the same bed?'

My lips brushed the delicate shell of her ear and she shivered. A moment later wide, alluring eyes sought mine.

'Sleep in the same bed? But you don't even know me. What…what's the rush?'

I opened my mouth to tell her there was no rush. That giving her my name was the final payment she and her family would extract from me. Instead I shrugged, noting absently that a part of me was enjoying this a little too much.

'Other than ensuring there will be nothing to be held over my head when the whim takes your father? Are you suggesting a period of getting to know one another before we decide if we must consummate this marriage?'

She gave a little start. '*If?* Don't you mean *when*?' she whispered fiercely, her eyes wider, searching.

Again the words to answer, to state that this dance was as close as we would get for the duration of our agreement, remained unsaid on the tip of my tongue. If she believed I would further compound this debacle by gracing her bed, so be it. She would discover differently later.

Absurdly, the pleasure in that thought of delivering disappointment never arrived. Instead I was unarmed by a disturbing throbbing in my groin, by the temptation to take a different approach. To gather her closer, breathe in the alluring perfume that clung to her silken skin.

I did just that, nudging her close with a firm clasp on her lower back. And heard her sharp intake of breath.

Pulling back, I glanced at her pale face. 'Are you all right?'

Her swift nod assured me that she was lying, and the wild darting of her gaze confirmed that belief.

'Calypso?'

'I… I'm fine. Just a little headache. That's all.'

I frowned. 'Then why are you touching your stomach?'

Her hand quickly relocated from her midriff to my shoulder, her smile little more than a grimace. 'It's nothing, I assure you.'

About to refute that assurance, I was forestalled by the end of the music and the applause that followed. And then by the arrival of Iona Petras.

My introduction to Calypso's mother, along with everyone else in the Petras clan, had been stiff and perfunctory, with no disguising exactly what this bloodless transaction was.

Everyone except Calypso.

'May I have a private moment with my daughter?' the older woman asked, although I got the feeling it was more an order than a request, giving me a momentary glimpse of where Calypso had inherited her quiet fire.

My fingers started to tighten on Calypso's waist, as a peculiar reluctance to let her go assailed me. I strenuously denied it and released her. 'By all means.'

A silent conversation passed between mother and daughter before Calypso held out her hand. Without so much as a glance my way, they exited the ballroom.

A fine irritant, like a tiny pebble in my shoe, stayed with me throughout all my inane conversations with people I didn't know and another five-minute ribbing from Neo. By the time my father approached I had the notion that my jaw would crack from being ground so tight.

'Am I mistaken or do you two seem to be getting along?' my father asked.

'You are mistaken,' I quipped, unwilling to admit how that dance and the feel of Calypso in my arms had fired up my blood.

He grimaced. 'I was hoping this would be less of an ordeal for you if you got along.'

'I said I'd do what needs to be done. And I will.'

Despite that small, startling flame of anticipation burning inside me.

Despite the fact that I'd completely dismissed any occurrence of a wedding night until exactly five minutes ago.

That sensation of her slender back beneath my hand...

that pulse beating at her throat… The shivers she couldn't control.

The fire of anticipation flared higher, resisting every attempt to dampen it down.

But did I need to?

This abhorrent agreement hadn't, thankfully, included a stipulation for consummation. But would it be a true marriage without it?

Enough!

Wrestling with myself over this was beneath me. Everything Yiannis Petras had asked for had been delivered. They would get nothing more from me.

That declaration lasted until my new wife walked back into the room and attempted to dismiss me with a vacant smile, even while her eyes challenged me.

Something locked into place inside me.

A challenge that needed answering.

Without stopping to question the wisdom of doing it, I crossed the wide room to where she stood. Took the hand loosely fisted by her side and brushed my lips over her knuckles.

Satisfaction sizzled through me when her breath caught. 'Say your goodbyes, Calypso. It's time to leave.'

'So what now?' I cringed inwardly at the nerves in my voice.

The helicopter ride—my first—from Nicrete to Agistros, the large island apparently owned entirely by Axios, had been breathtaking and exhilarating, and thankfully had not required much conversation. Largely because Axios had piloted the aircraft and I'd felt too nervous to disturb him, even if there'd been anything to talk about.

My mind was still a jumble after our charged snippets of conversation and that little slip on the dance floor, when he pulled me close and the ache in my belly manifested itself, and my last unsettling conversation with my mother.

But most of all it was the look in Axios's eyes before he'd

whisked me away from the reception and down to the waiting helicopter that kept my heart banging against my ribs.

That look was far too unsettling and electrifying for me to rest easy.

Especially not after landing on a dedicated cliff-side helipad on this island that boasted its own dormant volcano and a jaw-dropping villa that seemed almost too beautiful to be real.

I thought it was the setting sun that leant it that fairy tale look and made the unevenly staggered storeys seem to go on for ever. But every single facet of it turned out to be real, from the blush-hued stone, the towering arched windows, the rooftop infinity pool that seemed to blend into the sky and the endless reception rooms and bedroom suites, each holding priceless ancient works of art interspersed with the work of new cutting-edge artists whose work I loved.

Every jaw-dropping fact I'd read about Axios Xenakis had seemed amplified the moment he'd stepped out of the helicopter, and his aura was intensifying with each second as he walked me around Villa Almyra, exuding flawless power and authority.

Now, standing in the luxury sitting room adjoining what I assumed to be the master bedroom, I couldn't hold my words back.

He didn't answer for the longest time. He shrugged off the bespoke jacket he'd worn for the wedding ceremony. Then strolled over to the extensive drinks cabinet.

'Would you like a drink?' he asked.

About to refuse, I stopped. It would buy me time to ease my nerves. 'Mineral water, thanks.'

He poured my drink, then a single malt whisky into a crystal glass, handing mine to me before taking his time to savour his first sip.

The feeling that he was waiting, biding his time for… *something* threatened to overwhelm me, even while my senses skittered with alien excitement. Slowly it grew hotter, more dangerous.

His gaze raked over my wedding dress for a charged few seconds. 'Now we do whatever you want. It's *your* wedding night after all,' he drawled.

I got the feeling he was testing me. For what, I didn't know. And I wasn't sure I was ready to find out.

'The modern art pieces all over the house. Did you pick them yourself?'

His eyes widened fractionally, as if I'd surprised him. 'Yes,' he bit out. Then, on a softer note, 'Good art rarely loses its value.'

A layer of my nerves eased as I nodded. 'And pieces from emerging talent only appreciate with time.'

He strolled to the massive fireplace in the living room and leaned one muscular shoulder against the mantel. 'Masterpieces from the greats are all well and good, but modern art has its place too. They should be appreciated side by side.'

Just as he had placed them all over the house. I took a sip of water, settling deeper into my seat. 'I agree. Does that theme echo in all your properties?'

'Yes, it does.'

Before I could express pleasure in the thought, the gleam in his eyes arrested me.

'Is this how you wish to spend your wedding night, Calypso? Discussing art?'

The nerves rushed back and my hand trembled. 'What if it is?'

'Then I suggest you might want to be in more comfortable attire than that gown?'

Again, his eyes raked me, sending heat spiralling through me.

'Is this a ploy that usually works for you?'

One corner of his mouth lifted before his eyes darkened. 'Like you, I've never been married, so we both find ourselves in strange waters. Either way, the dress is going to have to come off one way or the other.'

'And if you don't like what is underneath…?' I dared. 'Will you send me back?'

His eyes narrowed. 'Is that what you're hoping for?'

Was it? I could have sworn my answer would be yes until actually faced with the question. But the word stuck in my throat, refusing to emerge as he sauntered towards me, taking a moment to discard the crystal tumbler so both his hands were free to capture my shoulders when he stopped in front of me.

'What I'm hoping for is that you will stop dishing out those enigmatic smiles and tell me what you meant earlier,' I said.

He frowned. 'You've lost me,' he drawled.

'When you said *if* we were to consummate this marriage? Are you incapable of doing so? If so perhaps you should get one of your staff to show me where I'm to sleep.'

His eyebrows rose. 'If I didn't know better I'd think you just issued me a challenge,' he drawled, in a voice that ruffled the tight nerves beneath my skin.

His scent filled my nostrils, his calm breathing propelling my attention to his sculpted chest, to the pulse beating steadily at his throat. To the magnificent vitality of his skin and the sheer animalistic aura breaching my tightly controlled space. Screaming at me to notice his masculinity. And not just to notice. He drew me with a power I'd never known before. I didn't just want to breathe him in. I wanted to touch. Explore. Taste.

That sensation was so strong I stepped back, eager to diffuse it.

The hands that held me stemmed my movement, and hard on the heels of my immobility came the realisation that I wanted to stay right where I was. But I didn't want him to know that.

'Well? *Are* you?' I taunted.

A mysterious smile tilted one corner of his lips before his hands slid down to my elbows. 'It should be easy enough to prove, *matia mou*.'

Just like that I was hit with the reality that this was my wedding night. That I was all but taunting him into...*possessing* me.

The thought sent a shiver through me. Coupled with something else. Something way too close to the forbidden desire that had coursed through me when I'd allowed myself to dream of this day some time in the dim and distant future, when I was out from under my father's thumb and free to have a boyfriend. A lover. A *husband*.

But how could that be? The man I'd imagined bore no resemblance to this formidable man, who wore arrogance and power as if it were a second skin. *Theos*, even his frown was attention-absorbing.

'Are you cold?' he asked.

I shook my head. Like everything else in this stunning villa, the temperature was perfect, blending with the early summer breeze.

'Then what's wrong?' he rasped, his eyes turning speculative again, as they had when I almost gave myself away on the dance floor.

The pain had thankfully receded, but other questions loomed just as large. The subject of my virginity and how that would factor into things, for one.

I pushed it away, seizing on another pressing need. 'I want you to tell me exactly what your agreement with my father is.'

One eyebrow rose. 'Isn't that a case of shutting the barn door after the horse has bolted? What's the point of rehashing the subject?'

It was time to come clean. 'I... I may have let you operate under the assumption that I know what's going on.'

Surprise flickered through his eyes before they narrowed. 'Are you saying you don't?'

'Not the exact details, no.'

Scepticism flared. 'You expect me to believe that? When you walked willingly by his side up the aisle?'

'Tell me you've never done something against your will and I'll call you a liar,' I replied.

The flare of his nostrils confirmed what I suspected—that this marriage was as much without his approval as it was without mine.

'Assuming it was solely your father who pushed for this, what steps did you take to stop him?'

None. Because my protests, like everything else, had fallen on deaf ears. I didn't say the words out loud, his timely reminder that, despite the promise I'd made, my mother's fate was in my father's hands, stilling my tongue. My hesitation gave Axios the answer he needed.

'I didn't, and the details don't matter. We are where we are. But I know there's an agreement between you. I simply want you to spell it out for me so I know what I'm dealing with.'

He stared at me, his measuring gaze weighted. I shouldn't have been relieved, even a little pleased to see the cynicism fade a little, but I was.

'Maybe he didn't tell you. How very like Petras to want to keep the spoils all for himself,' he muttered almost absently, before dropping his hands from my arms to say abruptly, 'Under an agreement signed between your grandfather and mine, Yiannis Petras, or any appointed representative after his death, can collect on a debt owed by my family. Your father wanted twenty-five percent of my company or the cash equivalent. We settled on one hundred million euros. And you.'

I couldn't hide my gasp at the confirmation that I'd been sold like a chattel.

Again, his cynicism receded. 'He really didn't tell you? Are you saying you're a victim in this?' he breathed.

The label smarted. 'I'm not a victim. But, no, he didn't tell me.'

Jaw gritted, he shoved a hand through his hair. 'So you don't know that under the terms of the agreement he'll also receive the deeds to Kosima?'

'What is Kosima?'

A bleak expression darkened his face. Whatever Kosima was, it held an emotional attachment for him.

'It's the private island where my grandfather was born. It was his favourite place on earth. Your grandfather knew that when he and my grandfather struck their unholy agreement. I assume he passed the information on to your father.'

My heart lurched with guilt, and for a wild moment I wanted to ease his pain. 'And my father demanded it as part of the agreement?'

Again his lips twisted, before his gaze slanted over me from head to toe. 'Of course. Just as he demanded that I marry *you*.'

This time my heart lurched for a different reason. He truly hadn't wanted this marriage—was entangled in it against his will just as I was.

About to stress that I had known absolutely nothing about this, that my father's avaricious demands were nothing to do with me, I heard that stern warning from my father slam into my brain. I didn't doubt that he would make my mother's life even more of a living hell than it was now.

The realisation that nothing had changed, that nothing *would* change, settled on me like a heavy, claustrophobic cloak.

'Why did you go through with it?' I asked. When he frowned, I hurried to add, 'You obviously hate what my family has done to you, so why…?'

My disjointed thoughts rumbled to a halt, my insides twisting with dread. A caged lion was an unpredictable creature, and from the first moment I'd set eyes on him I'd felt his banked fury.

Now I knew why.

His eyes blazed grey fire at me. 'You think I didn't try to find a way that didn't involve tying myself down for twelve months or handing over a multi-million-euro pay-out your father has done *nothing* to earn?' he sliced at me.

My breath caught. 'Why twelve months? Why not three…or even six?'

His mouth tightened. 'Ask your father. He had the power to nullify some or all aspects of this agreement. He chose not to. And he counted on me not fighting this in court because adverse publicity is the last thing my company needs right now. Your grandfather was an unreasonable man who my own grandfather had the misfortune of partnering with.'

'I know they started the airline business together, but—'

'Your grandfather wasn't interested in an airline business. He wanted to invest in boats, despite knowing next to nothing about them,' he spat out the words. 'But because they were tied together my grandfather was forced to work twice as hard to maintain both arms of the business. The only way Petras would agree to dissolve the partnership was to leave without taking his quarter-of-a-million-dollar share of the business immediately. If he had done so he would've bankrupted the company. But that didn't stop him from demanding crippling interest on the loan, and an agreement promising a percentage of Xenakis Aeronautics should he or any other Petras need a future bail-out. But even then, it was too late. My grandfather had spread himself too thin, trying to maintain two suffering businesses, but he was too proud to declare bankruptcy. The strain broke his marriage and his family, and after my grandmother died his heart just…gave up.'

My heart twisted at the anguish in his voice. 'I…'

What could I say? *I'm sorry*? Would Axios even believe me? What did it matter? My father had cunningly used the past against him. Against both of us.

'I didn't know any of this.'

His jaw rippled. 'My grandfather was my mentor. He taught me everything I know. But he withheld the extent of how bad things were until it was too late. Until I had to watch him wither away.'

After an age of losing himself in the bleak past, his eyes zeroed in on me.

'Why? If you didn't know all this, why present yourself to me at that altar like a sacrificial lamb?'

The cynicism was back full force. 'I'm not a lamb!'

One corner of his mouth lifted. 'No, I'm learning that my initial impression was mistaken. But I still want to know why,' he pressed with quiet force.

How could I tell him without speaking of the very thing I'd done all this to avoid? If my father had managed to pressure a powerful man like Axios Xenakis to do his will, what would he do to my mother if he found out I'd been divulging family secrets?

'Perhaps I had something to gain too,' I responded truthfully, knowing how it would be viewed.

True to form, his eyes slowly hardened, and that disappointment I'd briefly spotted at the altar flashed across his face.

As one of his hands slowly rose to cup my face, it seemed he wanted to delve deeper, perhaps even attempt to understand how we had become caught in this tangled web. But then he slowly withdrew, his demeanour resigned, even a little weary.

An urge to soothe him spiked through me. I managed to curb it, barely managing not to fidget under his piercing scrutiny.

'Did the agreement stipulate that we needed to…to consummate the marriage?' I asked.

He froze, and a sizzling, electrifying look entered his eyes. I got the feeling that he'd been waiting for this…that somehow coming to this point was what that sense of heightened expectancy had been all about.

'Not specifically, no.'

'But you don't know that it won't be held against you… against us…further down the line?'

He gave an indolent shrug even while his eyes continued to pin me in place. 'He's *your* father, Calypso. You tell me.'

I couldn't rule it out. And I suspected Axios knew that.

'Maybe he will. Maybe he won't. But I can't take the risk.'

With my mother's words echoing in my heart, my hunger for freedom grew with every second.

He took a slow, steady step towards me. His hands at his sides, he simply stared down at me, his only movement the deep rise and fall of his chest.

'What does that mean, Calypso?' he queried softly.

'It means I want there to be no room for misunderstanding later.'

Slowly, his hand rose again, his knuckles grazing my cheek. My shiver made his eyes darken.

'I need to hear the words, so there's no misunderstanding now.'

Heat suffused my face, as if chasing his touch. But his gaze wouldn't release me. Not until the words trembling on my lips fell free.

'I want to consummate this agreement. I want you to… take me.'

The full force of the words powered through me, shaking me from head to foot. Dear God, this wasn't how I'd imagined losing my virginity. None of this was how I'd dreamed it. So why did my insides twist themselves with… *excitement*?

For the longest time he simply stared at me, a myriad of emotions crossing his face. Eventually that dark gleam returned in full force, his presence filling the room as he turned his hand and brushed a thumb over my lips.

'Are you sure you don't wish to discuss…art?'

The thickness of his voice displaced any levity his words

attempted. And it drove home that this was happening. My wedding night. No, it wasn't the one I'd dreamed about, but really, if life was fair, would my father have tossed me in as part of a hundred-million-euro deal?

That thought was buried beneath the turbulent need climbing through me as he dragged his digit back and forth over my lip.

'I'm sure,' I answered, in a voice that sounded nothing like mine.

He tilted my gaze to his, making a gruff sound at whatever it was he saw on my face. His head started to lower—just as the other delicate subject raced to the forefront of my mind.

Tell him. He's going to find out soon enough.

'There's something you should know.'

One eyebrow rose in silent question.

'I'm a virgin.'

His fingers froze beneath my chin, his whole body turning to marble. 'What did you say?'

I swallowed the knot in my throat, praying the shivers would stop coursing through my body. 'I've never done… never been with a—'

A curse fell from his lips, raw and stunned. 'Why?'

Finally—*finally*—that burst of hysteria filtered through. 'You're asking why your wife is a virgin? Isn't that an odd question?'

'*Ne*—and it is precisely why I want to know why a twenty-four-year-old who looks the way you do is still untouched.'

Heat flowed through me. 'Looks the way I do…?'

The faintest colour washed his cheekbones. 'You must be aware of your beauty, Calypso,' he rasped, and his deep, husky voice set fire to my belly.

I blushed at the raw intensity in his words that reached into a secret part of me and took control of it. Hot tingles raced over my skin, warming me from the inside, tightening low in my belly and hardening my nipples. A gasp tore from my throat. His gaze dropped to my parted lips, his eyes darkening with each charged second that ticked by.

Then his eyes narrowed. 'Surely Petras didn't keep you under lock and key simply for this possibility?' Incredulity racked his voice.

Pain lashed through me, because the same thought had occurred to me. My father might not have visited the ultimate indignity upon me by spelling it out in black and white, but by thwarting all my previous attempts at a relationship he'd ensured his deal would be sweetened with my virginity. Another indication as to how little he cared for me.

Despite the anguish racking me, I raised my chin, pride insisting I did not confirm his suspicion. 'Does it not occur to you that I've simply not met anyone interesting enough?'

Shrewd grey eyes conducted a slow scrutiny. 'Your pulse is racing. Your face is flushed. I don't need a crystal ball to tell me you're excited. It is safe to say that, regardless of why you've remained untouched before, you're definitely interested now, Calypso.'

I silently cursed my body for betraying me but I wasn't ready to be cowed yet. 'You want me to bolster your ego by admitting I find you attractive?'

His head went back, as if he was surprised by the question. Of course he did. Good looks. Power. Influence. All attributes that made him irresistible to women. The stunning parade of women he'd purportedly dated was evidence that his effect on the opposite sex was woven into his DNA.

A sexy, arrogant smile curved his lips. 'I don't need you to *tell* me, *matia mou*. I *know* you do.'

My gasp was swallowed by the simple act of his head swooping down and his mouth sealing mine in a hot, savage possession that snatched the breath from my lungs. If that kiss in the church had been spine-tingling, this complete mastery was nothing short of earth-shattering.

The bold sweep of his tongue over my sensitive lower lip

fired electricity in every cell. When he followed that with the lightest graze of his teeth, in another clever tasting, a tiny hunger-filled sound left my throat.

Axios muttered something beneath his breath before the fingers capturing my chin moved to my lower back, tugging me closer, until the hard column of his body was plastered against mine and the wide stance of his powerful legs cradled me. Until the hot brand of his manhood was unmistakably imprinted against my belly, in a searing promise of what was in store.

His lips devoured mine with unapologetic hunger. And when one hand grasped mine and redirected it to his chest I gave in to the heady desire and explored him. Tensile muscle overlaid by his expensive cotton shirt was warm and inviting, and after a tentative caress, I sighed and gave in to *more*. The ultra-masculine line of his shoulder and neck drew my fingers, and that mysterious hunger built up into something that both terrified and thrilled me.

He made a gruff sound when my fingers brushed his warm, supple throat. It was enough to startle me. Enough to remind me that I didn't really know what I was doing. That, while I understood the mechanics of sex, I wasn't well-versed in its nuances.

Nerves dulled by the fire of arousal resurged, breaking free by way of a helpless whimper.

He raised his head and stared at me for the longest time before catching my hand in his. 'Come,' he commanded huskily.

I snatched in a much-needed breath. We both knew where we stood—that we were products of my father's machinations—surely we were going into this with our eyes open, in the knowledge that this was a one-time thing…weren't we?

Molten grey eyes watched me. When I slid my hand into his, he led me to some wide, imposing double doors. With casual strength he pushed them open to reveal the most magnificent bedroom I'd ever seen. While it bore unashamed signs of masculinity, the Mediterranean blue hues of the furniture blended with solid wood and gold-trimmed furnishings in the kind of design afforded only to the rich and influential.

But of course the centrepiece of the huge space was the bed. Emperor-sized, with four solid posts, its only softening effect was the muslin curtains currently tied back with neat ribbons.

Axios released me long enough to toss away extraneous pillows and pull back the luxury spread before he recaptured me. This time both hands went to my waist, his gaze dropping down to where he held me. He muttered something under his breath that I couldn't quite catch and when our gazes reconnected flames danced in the dark grey depths.

My knees weakened and I lifted my hands to rest them on his shoulders. He drew me closer while his hands searched along my spine, located the zip to my dress and firmly drew it down.

The dress gaped and he drew in a harsh breath, his gaze trailing over my exposed skin to linger on my barely covered breasts. Through the silk his hands branded my skin, making me squirm with a need to feel them without any barrier. As if he heard my silent wish, he took hold of the straps and eased them down my arms. The material pooled at my feet, leaving me in the scrap of lace panties and matching strapless bra.

One expert flick and the bra was loosened. Instinctively, I moved to catch it. Moved to delay this exquisite madness unfurling inside me.

Axios caught my hand, drew it firmly back to his shoulder. 'I want to see you, Calypso. I want to see everything.'

Unable to stand the raw fire in his eyes, I fixed my eyes on his chest. On the buttons hiding that steel and muscle from me. Again he read my wants with ease.

'Take my shirt off, *yineka mou*.'

Yineka mou. My wife.

Why did my insides dance giddily each time he called me that? Especially when we both knew this was an enforced, transient thing?

'Don't keep me waiting.'

The husky nudge brought me back to him. With fingers that had given up being anywhere near steady, I reached for his sleekly knotted tie, tugged it free and released his top shirt button. It was simpler to avoid his eyes as I concentrated on my task, but halfway down, when my fingers brushed his abs, he hissed under his breath.

Impatience etched on his face, he took hold of the expensive cotton and pulled the shirt apart. That raw display of strength tossed another log onto the flames building inside me. By the time he lifted me free of my wedding gown and took the few steps to the bed I'd lost the ability to breathe.

Riveted, I watched him shrug off the shirt, followed by his other clothing, before prowling to the bed. With the ease of a maestro he caught me to him, his fingers sliding up my nape and into my hair to release the three pins that secured the thick strands. His eyes raked my body as he slowly trailed his fingers through my hair. The effect was hot and hypnotising, the need to melt into him surging high.

So when he settled his expert lips over mine all I could do was moan and hold on, shudder in shocking delight when his chest grazed my hardened nipples.

But soon even that grew insufficient. Tentatively I parted my lips, in anticipation of the next decadent sweep of his tongue. When it grazed mine the zap of electricity convulsed my whole body.

Axios tore his lips from mine, incredulous eyes burning into me. 'You truly *are* innocent…' he muttered.

Mercifully, he didn't require an answer, or he was too impatient. After another searing kiss, in which his tongue breached my lips and brazenly slicked over mine, he trailed his lips over my throat.

Each pathway he claimed over my skin sent a pulse

straight between my legs, plumping and heating my core
until I thought I would explode. Large hands moulded my
breasts, his fingers torturing the peaks. I cried out, my
senses threatening to splinter.

The feeling of delving into another dimension, one where
only pure pleasure existed, swelled through me, drawing
me into a place of wonder. A place where I could give expression to what I was experiencing.

'That's…so amazing. How is this feeling possible?'

Had I said that out loud? Axios momentarily froze, but
I was too caught up in bliss to find out why. Then his caresses continued, his mouth pressing kisses on my midriff,
my belly, along the line of my panties.

When he tugged them down, my breath stalled.

He parted my thighs, trailed kisses up one inner thigh,
then another.

'Your stubble feels…incredible.'

Again I felt him still.

'Am I doing something wrong? Please…'

Long fingers grazed the swollen nub, sending feverish
pleasure racing through my body. Without him close to anchor me I grabbed hold of the sheets. Anything to keep me
from disintegrating beneath the force of pleasure ramping
through me.

Except that force tripled when his mouth settled with
fierce intent on my feminine core. Brazenly, he tasted me
with a connoisseur's expertise, teasing and torturing and
dragging me to the brink of madness.

Until a new tightness took hold of me.

'Ah…it's too much… I… I can't take it…'

'Yes, you can,' he declared huskily.

His lips went back to wreaking their magic, to piling on
that enchantment, until I simply…blew apart.

Bliss such as I'd never known suffused my body, convulsions rippling over me before sucking me under. I was
aware of the cries falling from my lips, was aware that

Axios had returned to my side, and I gripped him blindly, needing something solid to hang on to.

When he moved away I started to protest before I could stop myself. His kiss settled me for the few moments while he left the bed. The sound of foil ripping barely impinged upon my enchanted calm, my senses only sparking to life when he resumed his overwhelming presence between my thighs.

The intensity of the eyes locked on mine was almost too much to bear. I sought relief elsewhere. But there was none to be found in the wide expanse of his shoulders, the ripped contours of the chest I suddenly yearned to explore with my mouth, or… *Theos mou*…the fearsomely impressive evidence of his maleness.

The tiniest whimper slipped free. And while it brought an arrogant little twitch to his lips, there was also a slight softening of his fierce regard.

'Look at me, Calypso.'

The low command brought my gaze back to his. To the lock of hair grazing his eyebrow that I yearned to brush back. The slightly swollen sensual lips I wanted to kiss.

'Do you want this?' he asked.

The thought of stopping now was unthinkable. 'Yes,' I answered.

He gripped one thigh, parting me with unwavering intent.

The first shallow thrust stilled my breath. The second threw me back to that dimension where only sensation reigned.

Apprehensively, I exhaled. Axios moved his powerful body, withdrawing before penetrating me. Once. Twice.

On the third glide the sting was replaced by a different, jaw-dropping sensation, one that dragged me deeper into that dimension.

'You're…so deep. It feels…incredible.'

Above me, Axios hissed, his fingers digging into my

thigh as he held himself, still and throbbing, inside me. The sensation was indescribable. But…

'Why aren't you moving? Do *I* need to? Maybe if I roll my hips…'

Tentatively I experimented, then cried out as pleasure rained over me.

'That was…sensational. I want to… Would you mind if I did it again?'

'No. I wouldn't,' he said thickly, then met my next thrust with an even more powerful one.

What the hell was happening?

I stared down at Calypso. Her eyes were shut in unbound pleasure.

My fraying control took another hit, the feeling that this little witch with her wide streak of innocence that had turned out not to be a clever trick was responsible for my curious state driving confusion through me.

The giving and taking of carnal pleasure was far from new to me but this…

I wanted to tell her to open her eyes. To centre her to me. To—

'Why are you stopping? Please don't stop. I want more.'

Her husky, innocent plea ramped up my arousal, the enormity of what was happening lending a savage edge to my hunger I'd never experienced before.

But just to be sure she was right there with me I leaned closer, flicked my tongue over her nipple. 'Do you like this, Calypso?'

Short blunt nails dug into my back. 'Yes!'

'And this?' I pulled the tight bud into my mouth, suckling her sweet flesh with fervour.

'*Ne.* That… You do that so well. I never want it to end.'

Theos. Did she not know what she was doing? That this kind of uncensored commentary could drive a man over the edge?

But she wasn't doing it with another man. She was doing it with *me*. The man she was bound to for the next twelve months.

Her husband.

Knowing I was her first shouldn't be sending such primitive satisfaction through my blood. And yet it was, settling deep inside me with such definitive force it threw up a shock of bewilderment.

I was thankful to avoid examining it in that moment. Because the utter nirvana of taking her, hearing her unfettered pleasure, was creating an unstoppable chain reaction inside me. One that kept me thrusting into her snug heat, my pulse racing to dangerous levels as her delicious lips parted and another torrent of words ran freely.

'*Glykó ouranó...* I'm on fire... What you're doing to me... Please... I need... I *need...*'

My teeth gritted as I hung on to control with my fingertips. As her sweet body arched beneath mine and her head thrashed on the pillow.

'You need to let go, Calypso.' I sounded barely coherent to my own ears.

With a sharp cry she gave herself over to her bliss, her sweet convulsions triggering mine. The depth of my climax left me gasping, the stars exploding across my vision unending.

Leached of all power and control, I collapsed onto the pillows, stunned by the sorcery I'd just experienced. A unique experience I wanted to relive again. Immediately.

Soft arms curved around my waist and I reached for her before I could stop myself—before I could question the wisdom of lingering when I normally exited. Pulling her into me when I normally distanced myself.

I will. In a moment.

Once I'd gathered myself. Once this experience had been dissected and slotted into its proper place.

I would have fought any future attempt by Yiannis Petras to further line his pocket, but Calypso's way of sealing all avenues had been…better. Pleasurable, even.

Or foolish?

I tensed, unwilling to accept that perhaps I could have found another way. Not succumbed to this bewitchment so readily.

So draw a line under it. Leave!

Her soft breathing feathered over my jaw. Sleep was stealing over her slightly flushed face. The urge to join her whispered over me—another wave of temptation that lingered for far too long, making me close my eyes for several minutes before common sense prevailed.

So what if the sex was sublime? It was just sex. Come tomorrow my life would resume its normal course. This whole day would be behind me.

I'd done my duty. Had ensured Petras would no longer be a threat to my family. For now the night was still young. There was no rush to go anywhere…

Except temptation was ten times stronger when I woke in the early hours of the morning. In the murky light of dawn I caught the faintest glimpse of the slippery slope my grandfather had been led down by another Petras.

A road I couldn't risk.

I put words to definitive action by rising and leaving the bed, gathering my clothes and walking out of the master bedroom.

Because my business with my wife was over.

CHAPTER THREE

MY TRANSITION FROM sleep to wakefulness was abrupt, bracing in the way that fundamental change manifested itself. Confirmation that I hadn't dreamt any of it registered in unknown muscles throbbing with new vigour. The sheets also bore evidence of what had happened, and confirmed that Axios had left some time in the night.

Had he chosen to sleep somewhere else? Or had his helicopter taken off during one of the brief stretches of time when I'd fallen asleep?

Although my agitated thoughts wanted to latch on to the fact that it was the sex that had driven him away, intuition suggested otherwise. Axios might not have wanted to experience the depth of chemistry that blazed between us but he'd been caught up too. Maybe a little bit too much?

Because I was reeling from the wildness of our coming together, the sheer abandonment that still rocked me to my core. The sheets might have cooled in his absence but his possession still remained. As did my growing consternation.

Last night my decision had seemed so clear-cut. Close all avenues by which my father could further interfere in my life. But the experience had been nothing like clear-cut. The experience of sleeping with Axios had been...unparalleled.

And now he was gone.

I refused to allow the dull thudding of my heart to dictate my disappointment. Whatever my future held, it was time for action.

About to get out of bed, I paused as my last conversation with my mother replayed one more time.

'You will know very quickly if this is the right choice for you. If it isn't, don't be like me. Don't accept it as inevitable. Do what is right for you.'

'What are you talking about, Mama?'

'Find your own happiness, Callie. Don't let your father's

*actions dictate the rest of your life. Your grandmother said
the same thing to me on my wedding day and I didn't listen.'*

'*I don't think I have a choice. You... Papa—'*

'*Forget about me! There's nothing your father can do
that will hurt me any more. Knowing you're unhappy because of me will break my heart. Promise me you'll put
yourself first.'*

'*Mama—'*

'*Promise me, Callie!'*

My promise weighed heavy on my heart as I rose from
the bed. For a moment I swayed in place, my limbs weak
with recollection and my body heating after every little
wanton act of last night.

But, lips firmed, I approached what I hoped was the bathroom. There, further signs that this was Axios's domain
were everywhere—from the luxury male products to the
thick dark robe hanging next to the shower.

Trying not to let the intimacy of his belongings get to me,
I quickly showered. Thankful for the voluminous towel that
covered me from chest to ankle, I was contemplating the
less than palatable thought of wearing my wedding dress
again when a soft knock broke into my thoughts.

I cleared my throat. 'Come in.'

One of the younger staff members who helped manage
the villa entered with a shy smile. She'd been introduced
to me last night, when my senses had been grappling with
unfolding events.

With a strained smile, I pulled the robe closer around me
and returned her greeting.

Her gaze passed quickly over my towel. 'May I assist
you with anything, *kyria*?'

'If you could direct me to where my belongings are, I'd
appreciate it.'

'Of course. This way, please.'

Expecting her to leave the room, I was surprised when
she crossed to the opposite side and opened another door.

I followed her through a short hallway into another impressive suite, complete with living room, bathroom and dressing room.

An adjoining suite.

'I came to ask if you would like some breakfast, Kyria Xenakis?'

The title added another layer of shock to my system and it took me a few seconds to answer with a question of my own. 'Um…is Kyrios Xenakis still here?'

She nodded. 'Yes. But he will be leaving soon. So if you wish to—'

'Yes, I would very much like to. Can you wait for me to get dressed?'

Her eyes widened a touch, probably at the request. But I didn't care. I needed answers. Needed to know how he intended the next twelve months to proceed. And, if necessary, insist on taking back control of my life.

My father had shown me that he cared nothing about me except as a pawn to further his needs. Regardless of my commitment to Axios, I didn't intend to be pushed around any more.

That affirmation anchored deep as I concentrated on getting dressed.

The small suitcase that had accompanied me when I left Nicrete was empty, its contents sitting on a lonely shelf in the vast dressing room. But those weren't the only contents of the large, opulent space. Rack upon rack of clothes were displayed in fashion seasons, with matching shoes arranged by colour, height and style.

Awestruck, I stared. It was by far the most extensive collection I'd seen outside a clothes store. Simply because I didn't know who the clothes in the closets belonged to, I fished out a simple shirt dress from my own belongings, added comfortable flats and caught my hair in a ponytail.

The maid led me down the stairs and through several halls before stopping at a set of double doors.

'He's in there,' she said softly. Then melted away.

The faint sound of clinking cutlery reached my ears as I paused to take a fortifying breath. But, aware that no amount of deep breathing could prepare me for the morning after last night, I pushed the door open.

He was seated at the head of a long, exquisitely laid table. Impeccably dressed in formal business attire, minus the jacket, with the sun streaming down on him.

I almost lost my footing at the sheer visceral impact of his masculinity. It really was unfair how attractive Axios Xenakis was. How the simple act of caressing his bottom lip with his forefinger, his brow furrowed in concentration, could spark fire low in my belly.

You're not here to ogle him.

Fists tightening at the reminder, I approached where he sat. 'We need to talk.'

He took his time to look up from the tablet propped up neatly next to his plate, to power it down with a flick of his finger before cool grey eyes tracked over me from head to toe and back again.

'*Kalimera*, Calypso. Sit down—have something to eat.'

His even tones threw me. He wasn't behaving like a man who'd left his marriage bed after bedding his virgin wife. In fact, he seemed far too confident. Far too...*together* for my liking.

When I didn't immediately obey he rose, his gaze resting on me as he pulled out a chair and...waited.

I sat, because hysteria would achieve nothing. What I intended to say to him could be said standing or sitting. Besides, this close, the potent mix of his warm body and his aftershave was making my head swim. Reminding me of what it had been like to stroke that warm body, to cling to it as fevered bliss overtook me.

'What's on your mind?' he enquired as he poured exquisite-smelling coffee into my cup, then nudged platters containing sliced meats, toast and cheeses towards me.

Cool. He was far too cool.

Something was going on here. I probed his face and saw the slight tension in his jaw. The banked emotion in his eyes. I might have known Axios for less than twenty-four hours, but I'd quickly deciphered that his eyes gave him away. Right now, they were far too shrewd.

My heart jumped into my throat.

'My father may have put us both in this position, but there's no reason why we should remain like this.' Relief welled as my voice emerged strong and steady.

His nod of agreement stunned me. 'You're right,' he said.

'I am?'

He shrugged. 'The agreement states that we should be married for a year minimum—not that we need to be in each other's pocket. Of course that's not to say it's cart blanche for you to do as you please.'

'What does *that* mean?'

'It means that for the time being Agistros is yours to enjoy. We will revisit our circumstances again when I return in a few weeks.'

His announcement was still resonating inside me when he rose from the table and strode, his head proud, shoulders stiff, towards the door.

'When you return? Where will you be?'

He paused, his tall, imposing body swivelling towards where I sat, frozen. 'In Athens, where my business is, and where I intend to stay for the foreseeable future.'

Despite sensing this had been coming, I found the announcement took me by surprise. 'You're leaving me here on my own?'

Theos—could I sound any more alarmed?

He gave a curt, unfeeling nod. 'It is the best decision.'

I pushed my chair back and stood, feeling a yearning spiralling inside that wouldn't be silenced. A yearning to know that his condemnation of my father meant that he was different. That, despite tarring me with the same brush as my parent, he wouldn't punish me too.

'Why can't I live in Athens too?' *With you.*

It would be the perfect place finally to put my art degree to good use. To start a career.

His hardening features broadcasted his displeasure at that question even before he spoke. 'Why force us to endure one another when we don't have to?'

'I'm perfectly happy living on my own. I can rent a flat, get a job in an art gallery—'

The twist of his lips reminded me again of how hot his kisses could be. 'What's the point of staging an elaborate wedding to fool the world if my wife immediately moves into an apartment?'

'Then why did you do it?' I challenged.

'Your father timed his strike to perfection—because my company needs stability now more than ever.'

Invisible walls closed in on me. 'So this is a *business* decision?'

His jaw clenched. '*Everything* that has transpired between us has been based on a business decision.'

Even last night?

My heart lurched and I was glad I was sitting down. 'There has to be another way.'

'There is. You stay here, in our purportedly happy home. You'll want for nothing. Your every wish will be catered for. Buy as much art as you wish to—or even make it if you want.'

Yesterday the promise of freedom from this nightmare would have brought boundless relief. Today, all I felt was… trapped.

'I can't. I can't live like that.'

The words were uttered more for myself than for him. Born from my deep desire never to fall under another's command the way my father had forced me to live under his.

'How long am I to stay in this gilded *prison*?'

His eyes darkened. 'If this is a prison, *yineka mou*, it is not of my making. I tried for months to make your father listen to reason. *He* caused this situation, not me. If you want a way out of this, then find one.'

With that, he walked out, leaving my insides cold as ice.

Axios's words echoed through the long days and nights that followed his departure from Agistros. Long after the days in the luxurious paradise had begun to stretch in brain-numbing monotony.

My new husband, having made his feelings clear about our forced marriage, didn't bother to come home. The stunning villa had indeed become my prison, and its elegant walls and priceless furnishings closed in on me more with every day that dragged by.

And the more my world became narrow, the louder my mother's words and the contents of my grandmother's letter clamoured.

By the end of the second week dejection had me in a constricting hold. But alongside it was the discomfort in my abdomen, which wouldn't let up. Telling myself it was a psychosomatic reaction to my current situation began to feel hollow when I knew my grandmother had felt similar symptoms in the year before her death.

Then the housekeeper informed me one sun-drenched morning that Axios had left a message to say that he would be away on business in New York for another ten days. It seemed like the ominous catalyst I needed.

In the privacy of my suite, I quickly considered and discarded the things I wouldn't need. My large hobo bag was big enough to hold the most crucial essentials, and the small stash of cash I'd saved from my allowance was more than enough to see me through the first few days of my unknown adventure.

After that...

My heart lurched as I attempted to hold down my breakfast the next morning. I took my time, ensuring I was well-sustained before I left the table. Aware of the housekeeper's keen eye, I calmly drank another cup of tea, then helped myself to fruit before drawing back my chair.

'Agatha, I'm thinking of visiting friends. I'm not sure how long I'll be. A few days—maybe longer.'

Surprise lit the housekeeper's eyes. 'But Kyrios Xenakis said you were to stay here—'

'Kyrios Xenakis isn't here. And he's not coming back for ten days. I seriously doubt he'll miss my absence in the meantime.' I slapped on a smile to take the sting out of my words.

She gave a wary nod. 'When do you wish to leave? I'll tell Spiros to ready the boat.'

'Don't bother. I'll grab a water taxi from the harbour. The walk down will do me good.'

Disapproval filmed her eyes. '*Kyria*, I don't think that's a good idea.'

One of the few facts I'd learned about my absent husband was that he was far wealthier than I'd imagined. The members of the Xenakis dynasty basked in the sort of wealth that required bodyguards and well-orchestrated security for them to travel. Exactly the sort of attention I didn't need.

'I appreciate your concern, but it's not necessary, Agatha. Thank you.'

I walked away before she could respond. And, since I wasn't entirely sure she wouldn't alert Axios at the very first opportunity, I rushed up to my suite, grabbed my bag and hurried back down.

Two hours later I stepped up to the sales counter at the airport on the mainland. 'One-way ticket to Switzerland, please.'

The attendant eyed me for what seemed like for ever before issuing my ticket. But if I thought that was nerve-racking, discovering what my grandmother had left for me once I arrived at the Swiss bank left me shamelessly sobbing in a cold and grey bank vault.

And then everything that had gone before paled in comparison to the fear that gripped my heart when I sat before a Swiss doctor three days later.

Dr Trudeau, a short, grey-haired physician with kind eyes, peered at me over his rimless glasses, gentle fingers tapping the file in front of him before he sighed.

'Miss Petras, I have good news and bad news. Although I'm not entirely sure how welcome the good news will be once I explain what I believe is happening with you. I'm so sorry.'

CHAPTER FOUR

One year later

THE TURQUOISE WATERS of the Pacific were so blindingly beautiful they brought tears to my eyes. Or perhaps it was the stinging salt from the spray.

It definitely wasn't because today was my first wedding anniversary.

No. Most certainly not that.

On the list of the most forgettable things to happen to me in the last year, my hastily arranged wedding and the shockingly cold ceremony was right at the top. Not to mention the trapped groom who couldn't wait to walk away from me. The man I now had the dubious pleasure of calling my husband.

My heart leapt into my throat even as I pushed Axios's image away. He would need to be dealt with soon.

But not just yet.

I lifted my face to the blazing sun, willed it to pierce through my desolation and touch my wounded soul. I needed brightness and mirth, sunshine and positivity. If only for a little while longer… It might all be gone soon, slipping through my fingers like mercury.

Gripping the railing of the sleek sailboat transporting me from an exclusive Bora Bora resort to the adjoining uninhabited island where I'd ordered my picnic, I mentally went through my list from bottom to top.

Number five: Take control of my life. *Check.*

Contrary to my fears, walking away hadn't doomed me or my mother. My monthly phone calls reassured me that she was fine. My father, now a hundred million euros richer, was engrossed in yet another business venture. Better still, he hadn't challenged any of the terms of the contract he'd made with Axios.

Number four: Do something worthwhile with my painting. *Check*.

The past year had been frightening in some ways but immensely fulfilling in the exploration of my talent. I was still basking in the knowledge that I could have had a career if fate hadn't pushed me down a different path.

Number three: Accept that my condition might not have a happy ending and that my prognosis might follow my grandmother's. *Check*.

It had been a difficult acceptance, often pitted with tears and heartache and grief for all the things I might never have. For what this would do to those I love.

Number two: Cherish my precious gift for as long as I can. *Check. Check. Check.*

The last item on my list filled me with equal parts desolation and trepidation. But it needed to be done.

Number one: Hand over my precious gift to Axios Xenakis.

As if that gift knew he was in my thoughts, a soft cry rippled through the sun-drenched breeze, followed by a sharper one, demanding attention.

Smiling, I turned from the railing and crossed the deck to the shaded lounge. There, lying amongst the cushions, was the reason for my heartbeat. The reason I needed to keep fighting for my unknown future.

'Are you awake, my precious boy?'

At the sound of my voice Andreos Xenakis kicked his plump legs, his arms joining in his giddy response as his searching eyes found mine. For an instant my breath caught. The similarity between the piercing grey eyes of father and son was so visceral, I froze.

Another insistent cry had me reaching for him. His warm, solid weight in my arms quieted the worst of my trepidation, and soon even that evaporated beneath the sheer joy of cradling him, feeding him, doing such mundane things as changing his nappy and handing him his favourite toy, basking in his sweet babbling while I enjoyed the stunning view and just...*being*.

Pushing away the terrifying news the doctor had given me that day in Switzerland and the choice I'd had to make, I breathed in relief when the boat slowed and a staff member approached with a courteous smile.

'We're here, miss. Your picnic is set up for you on the shore.'

Whatever the future held, I would deal with it.

After all, I'd dealt with so much this past year.

Except the future had found me before I was ready. And it came in the form of a solitary figure with furious gunmetal eyes and a gladiator stance, waiting with crossed arms on the jetty as the sailboat returned to the exclusive resort.

My heart leapt into my throat, my breath strangled to nothing as I watched the figure grow larger, more broody, more formidable.

More everything.

He'd grown harder. Edgier. Or perhaps that was all imagined. A product of those feverishly erotic dreams that frequently plagued me.

Whatever... The man who watched me in silent condemnation as the boat gently butted the wooden planks on the jetty had zero mercy in him. And when his gaze shifted to Andreos and widened with chilled shock I had the distinct notion that I'd played this wrong.

I'd been too selfish.

Taken too much time for myself.

Too much time with my son.

'Axios.'

He didn't respond to my whispered utterance of his name. He couldn't take his eyes off Andreos. His strong throat moved in a swallow and his pallor increased as several expressions charged through his eyes.

Shock. Amazement. Utter fury.

'What are you doing here?' I asked.

Finally eyes the colour of a dark arctic night clashed with mine. 'What am I *doing* here?' he asked with icy incredulity. 'This is what you have to say to me after the stunt you have pulled?'

My insides shook but I forced myself to hold his gaze. 'You'll want to discuss this, I'm sure, but can it wait till—?'

'I'll *want to discuss this*? Are you for real?'

A drowsy Andreos stirred in my arms, his senses picking up on the frenetic emotions charging through the air.

'Miss, would you like us to—?'

'Leave us.' Axios's tone was deep. Implacable.

I wasn't in the least bit surprised when the staff hurried away.

'How did you find me?'

It seemed a monumental feat for him to drag his gaze from Andreos.

'Through an act of sheer coincidence. The owner of this resort happens to be a business acquaintance of mine. He was on a rare tour of his property when he spotted you. Had he not chosen to take his yearly tour this last week…' He stopped, shaking his head as if grappling with the sheer serendipity of the occurrence that had led him to me.

My chalet was on the beach, and I made the short walk to the gorgeous timber-clad structure aware of his every step behind me.

'I intended to come back—I promise.'

'You *promise*? Why should I take your word on anything? You told the staff you were visiting friends when all along you intended to abscond from our marriage. And now you're hiding in a resort on the other side of the world under a false name. Not to mention you seem to have had a child during that time. I am assuming the child is yours?'

'Of course he his. Who else's would he be?'

He went as rigid as an ice statue, and what little colour

had flowed back into his face on the walk from jetty to chalet receded momentarily before fury reddened his haughty cheekbones once more.

'So I can add infidelity to your sins?'

'Infid—? What are you talking about?' Shock made my voice screech.

Andreos whimpered as I laid him down in his cot, and then went back to sound sleep.

'We used contraception on our wedding night, as I recall,' he rasped with icy condemnation.

'Well, I wasn't on birth control. I never have been. And, while I'm not an expert, I'm sure there's a caution that states that condoms aren't one hundred percent foolproof.'

'And I'm suddenly to accept that the protection that has never failed me before suddenly malfunctioned with *you*?'

I wasn't sure why the reference to other lovers drilled such angst through me. His lovers, past or present, were of no consequence to me. I had no hold over him, nor did he over me, when it came right down to it. All that had brought us together was my father's greed and manipulation.

'I don't know what to say to make you believe me but I know the truth, Axios. Andreos is yours.'

Piercing eyes locked on mine for the better part of a minute. 'If he's mine, why have you hidden him from me for the better part of a year?'

His voice had changed, turned grittier, and he even looked a little shaken as his gaze swung again to Andreos. He started to walk towards the cot as if compelled, then stopped, shook his head.

'Why is he here on the other side of the world when he should be in Greece, with his family?'

It would have been so easy to blurt out everything that had happened to me since that dreaded visit to the doctor in Switzerland. and the urgent summons to hear my diagnosis three gut-churning days later, when it had been confirmed that there was indeed a growth in my cervix.

But I was also told I was pregnant, and that any further exploration, even an initial biopsy to ascertain its malignancy or benignity, would jeopardise my baby.

I could have told him about the latest scans I had in my suitcase, taken by Dr Trudeau in Switzerland, and his recommendation to take action.

But if Axios's presence here wasn't warning enough that the time I'd bought for myself was over, the look in his eyes said I wouldn't escape scot-free.

Nevertheless, I wasn't the same woman he'd married. Harrowing decisions made in the cold grip of fear had a way of changing a person.

'Why does it matter to you, anyway? I thought you would be glad to see the back of me for ever.'

A ferocious light glinted in his eyes for a heart-stopping second before he took a step towards me. 'You married a Xenakis, Calypso. You think simply packing your bag and walking out through the door is the end of it? That you simply had to hightail it to the other end of the world for your marriage vows to cease to have meaning?'

I stemmed my panic as his words rankled. 'Our vows had *meaning*? I could've sworn you challenged me to find a way to make them *stop* having meaning.'

His eyes narrowed. 'You think *this* was the answer?'

'It was *my* way!'

'Perhaps I should've added an addendum that finding a way needed to involve discretion and consideration. Nothing that would throw a spotlight on me or my family. My mistake. Tell me, Calypso, do you think disappearing off the face of the earth for over a year screams discretion or consideration?'

I shrugged with a carelessness I didn't feel. 'You didn't stick around long enough to hash out another course of action. I did what was best.'

'What was best for *you*, you mean?'

My senses wanted to scream *yes!* Caution warned me to

remain calm. To talk this through as rationally as the tower of formidable fury in front of me would allow.

'You still haven't told me why you're here.'

He made another sound of incredulity. 'Because you're my wife! Because the whispers need to cease. Because you will not jeopardise everything I've worked for. And that's just for starters.'

'Ah, *now* we're getting to the bottom of it. You're here because of what my absence is doing to your business? Is that it, Axios?'

With lightning speed warm fingers curled over my nape. His hold wasn't threatening, simply holding me in place so that whatever point he needed to make would be accurately delivered.

'While no one would dare say it to my face, rumours of my wife fleeing our marital home has caused ripples in my life. The kind I can do without. So make no mistake: I intend to remedy that. Whatever point you intended to make, it ends now.'

Each word contained a deadly promise—an intention to have his way that stoked the rebellion that had gone dormant in the last year back to life.

'Believe it or not, my walking out had absolutely nothing to do with you.'

'Enlighten me, then, *matia mou*. What was it all about?'

The soft cadence of his voice didn't fool me.

'What could possibly have driven you from the life of luxury and abundance your father battled for so cunningly?'

The mention of my father brought my goals back into focus. Reminded me why I hadn't been able to stomach staying under Axios's roof for one more day. That feeling of a loss of control. Of suffocation. Of not being able to live my life on my own terms. My choices being taken away from me without so much as a by your leave…

'I'm not my father,' I stressed, with every cell in my body.

'No, you're not. But while I was prepared to give you

the benefit of the doubt before, your actions have led me to form a different opinion about you. So whatever your reasons were, tell me now.'

'Or what?'

He didn't speak for the longest moment. Then his attention shifted to the cot where Andreos slept, lost in baby dreams. My heart tripped over itself as I watched Axios's face. Watched him speculate with that clever mind financial analysts rhapsodised over.

'Is he the reason?'

'What do you mean?'

His jaw rippled. 'If there was an indiscretion, I urge you to confess it now rather than later.'

His words shouldn't have scraped my emotions. Considering what my mother had done, and the fall-out and gossip that had followed, I knew all too well how assumptions were made, judgements passed without verification. But the reality that he suspected Andreos wasn't his lanced a soft spot in my heart.

A fierce need to protect my child's honour ploughed through me. 'We may not have known each other before we met at the altar, but you should know that I would rather cut off my own arm before attempting to lie about my child's parentage. Whether you're willing to accept it or not, he's yours.'

If I'd expected my fervour to melt his coldness, I was sorely disappointed.

'Your vigorous defence of your child is admirable. But, as you said, we were virtual strangers before we came together. If you want me to believe you, tell me where you've been. Every single thing you've done in the past year. Then perhaps I'll consider believing you.'

The list reeled through my head.

Finding the bank account in Switzerland my grandmother had left in my name.

Seeing the private doctor who'd treated me.

Getting the results and feeling the soul-wrecking fear that my fate would echo my grandmother's.

Making the choice I had to make.

Andreos's arrival.

Saying the fervent prayers for *more*. One more day. One week. One month.

One year.

I couldn't tell Axios any of that. Even the simple joy of rediscovering my love of painting and finding the shops and galleries I'd sold my watercolours to seemed too sacred, too private to share with the man who looked at me with rancour and suspicion. Whose every breath seemed like a silent pledge to uncover my secrets.

My life. Lived on my terms.

That was what I'd sworn to myself that rainy afternoon in my hotel room after leaving Dr Trudeau's office. For the most part, it had been.

Axios's arrival had simply shortened the time I'd given myself before checking off the last item on my list.

'You'll consider believing me after you've triple-checked everything I say?'

The unapologetic gleam in his eyes told me he intended to do exactly that. Tear through every new, unconditional friendship I'd formed along the way, every haven I'd sought refuge in.

My stomach churned at the thought of Axios finding out the true state of my health and exploiting it the way my father had done with my mother. It was that terrible thought more than anything else that cemented my decision to keep my secret.

If he found out my condition, he would wonder if the state of my health affected my suitability as a mother. Unlike my mother, my flaws weren't outward. For the precious time being, I could hang on to that.

As for when I couldn't…

'All you need to know is that Andreos is yours and I'm prepared to return to Greece. If that's what you want?'

His nostrils flared and his gaze raked my face for long sizzling seconds before his lips twisted. 'Oh, yes, wife. The time has most definitely come for that. And whatever it is that you're keeping from me, rest assured, I'll find out.'

With that he stepped back.

Thinking he was going to leave me to grapple with the turmoil his unexpected arrival had caused, I watched, my heart speeding like a freight train, as he headed to the cot where Andreos slept.

Silence disturbed only by the slow stirring of the ceiling fan throbbed in the room as Axios stared down at the son he hadn't accepted was his. His jaw clenched tight and his throat moved convulsively as he watched the rise and fall of the baby's chest.

He remained frozen for so long I feared he'd take root there. When he turned abruptly and tugged a sleek phone from his pocket my senses tripped.

'What are you doing?'

Eyes the colour of a stormy sky met mine as he hit a number and lifted the handset to his ear. 'Getting the answers I need.'

The sharp orders he gave in Greek when the phone was answered didn't surprise me. The irony that the one truth I'd told him was the one he was having a hard time accepting wasn't lost on me. But, conversely, I understood. I too had wondered why fate would choose to lay both joy and sorrow on me in one fell swoop, leaving me with a choice that had seemed both simple and terrifying.

After all, my actions pointed to behaviour that would've left *me* suspicious too. And, considering what my own mother had done for the sake of freedom and love—an act that was an open secret in Nicrete—I didn't blame Axios for wanting to verify that the baby he'd helped create was truly his.

When he was done making an appointment for his private doctor to visit his home in Athens the moment he returned, to take DNA samples for a paternity test, he hung up, his piercing regard staying on me as he tucked his phone away.

I ignored the blatant challenge and asked the question more important to me. 'Is it going to hurt him?'

For the most fleeting second the charged look in his eyes dissipated. 'No. I'm told all it requires is a swab from his cheek.'

I nodded. 'Very well, then.'

He frowned, my easy acquiescence seemingly throwing him. But his face returned to its formidable hauteur in moments, and his strides were purposeful as he strode to the house phone and picked it up.

Before he dialled he turned to me. 'Is the child okay to travel on a plane?'

'The *child's* name is Andreos. And I'd thank you not to make any plans without discussing them with me first.'

A muscle ticked in his jaw. 'Why? Did you not tell me that you intended to return to Greece?'

'Yes, I did.'

'When exactly were you proposing to do that? When he was a year old? When he was five or perhaps ten?' he grated out.

The cold embrace of knowing that time wasn't on my side stalled my answer for several seconds. 'I was thinking days—not months or years. My booking at this resort is only for a week. I was going to fly back to Athens from here.'

His lips flattened. 'I don't plan on leaving you behind, Calypso. My good faith where you're concerned is gone. When I fly out of here in three hours you and the child will be by my side. And that state will continue until such time as you choose to come completely clean about your actions for the past year or I furnish myself with the information.'

After that, there really wasn't much more to say.

Moments after Axios left my suite the head concierge arrived with instructions to get as many staff as I needed to help me pack. I almost laughed, considering my meagre belongings and everything Andreos needed could fit in one small suitcase.

I dismissed the staff and was done with my packing in twenty minutes. The rest of the time I spent sitting beside Andreos's cot, hoping against hope that my time with him going forward would be just as peaceful as the past precious months had been. Because I didn't intend to be separated from him for a second. Time was too precious. Too special. And I would fight for every moment.

As if aware he was at the centre of my thoughts, he stirred and woke, his face remaining solemn for a few seconds before a toothless smile creased his chubby face. Blinking back the tears of joy that just looking at him prompted, I scooped him up and cradled him close.

By the time Axios knocked on the door we were both ready.

After another taut spell of staring at Andreos with turbulent eyes, he eyed the single suitcase with grating consternation. 'This is all you have?'

'I believe in travelling light.'

His expression darkened. 'What about safety equipment for the baby? A car seat?'

'I find it easier to hire what I require as and when I need it. And, before you disparage my methods, I research and make sure everything I use is of the highest safety standard.'

His gaze remained on me for another second before he nodded at the porter.

My suitcase was quickly stowed on a sleek private boat. Within minutes my last sanctuary had become a dot on the horizon.

I'd forgotten just how ruthlessly efficient Axios Xenakis could be. I received another rude reminder when, upon our arrival at the jetty, a smiling courier presented me with a gleaming state-of-the-art buggy and car seat combo, already assembled.

I braced my hand on Andreos's back, tugged him closer to where he nestled snugly in his papoose. 'That won't be necessary. The airline I'm flying with will have all the equipment I need.'

Axios stepped forward and took hold of the pushchair. 'You think I'm going to let you out of my sight now I've found you?'

'But I have a ticket—'

'And I have a private jet.'

Of course he did.

I'd blocked so many things out of my mind for the sake of pure survival. But the world had kept on turning. Axios had remained a powerful mogul with looks that weakened women's knees. And, as a billionaire who commanded an airline empire, didn't it stand to reason he'd possess his own plane?

A short SUV ride later we arrived at the private area of the airport, where an obscenely large aircraft bearing the unique Xenakis family logo stood gleaming resplendently beneath the French Polynesian sun.

'So what's it to be? Athens or Agistros?' he asked silkily.

I stared at him in surprise. 'You're giving me a *choice*?' It was more than he had the last time. More than my father ever had. Not that I planned on reading anything into it.

He shrugged. 'The location doesn't matter. Whichever you choose will be home. *For all of us*,' he added succinctly.

I chose Athens.

A mere twenty-four hours later we drove through the imposing gates of Axios's jaw-dropping villa. A different set of staff greeted us, and an even more opulent set of adjoining master suites had been readied for the prodigal wife's return.

I was standing in the middle of cream and gold opulence when I felt his presence behind me. Not wanting to look into those hypnotising eyes, I kept still, my precious bundle safely tucked in my arms.

My skin beginning to tingle wildly, I snatched in a breath and held it when his mouth brushed over the shell of my ear and he said, in a low, deep whisper, 'Welcome home, *yineka mou*. And rest assured that this time you will not get away from me that easily.'

CHAPTER FIVE

My son.

I have a son.

My chest squeezed tight. The emotions tumbling through me were…indescribable.

Back on Bora Bora everything inside me had prompted me to accept Calypso at her word—accept that the child was mine. Only I'd made the mistake before of thinking I could manage her, that she was a victim when she was anything but. She was cunning. Intelligent and resourceful enough to disappear without a trace for a whole year.

And apparently to take what is mine with her.

The result of the paternity test spelled out in stark indelible ink confirmed that, in this at least, Calypso had spoken the truth. But swiftly on the heels of that knowledge came a mystifying mix of searing fury and heady delight—the former for what I'd been deprived of and the latter for the astounding gift I hadn't even realised I wanted.

My son.

She kept him from me. Deliberately. Chose to leave my home and have my baby on her own, with no care as to what my feelings were in the matter. Why? Because I'd left her on Agistros? In the lap of the kind of luxury most people only dreamed about?

But did you give her any choice?

I swallowed the bite of guilt as my eyes locked on the paper.

Andreos.

Even as a part of my brain tested the name out and accepted that it fitted him my fingers were shaking with the enormity of everything I'd missed. Things I'd never have thought would matter suddenly assumed colossal importance.

His first cry.

His first smile.

His first laugh…

Did babies his age laugh? I'd been robbed of the opportunity to find out for myself.

I tossed the document away and stood. Sudden weakness in my legs stopped me from moving. One hand braced on the polished wood surface, I sucked in a deep breath, attempted to bring myself under control.

Control was essential. Over my erratic emotions. Over my wayward wife and over the belief that she should take such actions without consequence. To deprive me of my own flesh and blood…

Why?

The deeply visceral need to know straightened my spine.

I found her in the smallest living room—the room farthest from my study and the one she seemed to have commandeered for herself and Andreos since her return. He lay on a mat on the floor, his fists and legs pumping with abandon as Calypso crouched over him. A few toys were strewn nearby, momentarily forgotten as mother and son indulged in a staring game of some sort. One that amused Andreos…*my son.*

So babies his age did smile. They also returned their mother's stare with rapt attention until they were tickled, then dissolved into heaps of laughter.

Something stirred raw and powerful within me as I stared into the eyes that had seemed familiar to me from the start, even as I cautioned myself against full acceptance. The feeling intensified as I watched Calypso's utter devotion, saw the bond between mother and son, the unit I'd been excluded from.

The unit I wanted to belong to—

Sensing my presence, Calypso's gaze flew to mine, then immediately shadowed.

Theos mou, was I really that frightful?

'You can be.'

I dismissed the uncanny sound of Neo's voice in my head.

Too bad. I'd given her four days to settle in. Four days of swimming in the uncharted waters of her re-entry into my life with a son...*my son*...in tow.

It took me but a moment to summon Sophia, one of several household staff who'd been infatuated with Andreos since his arrival.

To Calypso, I said, 'We need to talk. Come with me. Sophia will look after Andreos.'

Her clear reluctance lasted for the moment it took for her to spot the piece of paper clutched in my fist. Then she slowly rose.

About to head back to my study, I changed my mind and headed up the stairs.

'Where are we going?'

The hint of nervousness in her voice rankled further.

'Where we won't be disturbed,' I replied as evenly as I could manage.

'But...'

I stopped and turned. 'Do you have a problem with being alone with me?'

The faintest flush crept into her cheeks, but her head remained high, her gaze bold. 'Of course not.'

Truth be told, perhaps my suite wasn't the best choice. Amongst everything I'd imagined might happen when I finally located my wayward wife, discovering that the chemistry that had set us aflame on our wedding night still blazed with unrelenting power was the last thing I'd expected.

The fact that I couldn't look at the curve of her delicate jaw without imagining trailing my lips over her smooth skin, tasting the vitality of the pulse that beat at her throat or palming her now even more ample breasts was an unwelcome annoyance that nevertheless didn't stop my mind from wandering where it shouldn't.

Did unfettered pleasure still overtake her in that sizzling, unique way it had during our one coming together? Did she go out of her head with unbridled passion at the merest touch? If so, just who had been stoking that particular flame in her year-long absence?

It took every ounce of control I had to contain my searing jealousy at the thought. Answers to those questions would come later. *This* was too important.

Without stopping to further examine the wisdom of the venue, I made my way into the room.

She followed, making a point to avoid looking at the bed as she passed through into the private living room. From my position before the fireplace I watched her take a seat and neatly fold her hands in her lap. Had her pulse not been racing in her throat I would have been fooled by her complete serenity.

'He's mine.'

Just saying the words dragged earth-shaking emotion through me, robbing me of my next breath. That a small bundle could do that—

'I told you he was.'

There was a new defiance in her demeanour, a quiet, fiery strength that had been there a year ago but had matured now.

'I've never lied to you.'

'Then what do you call *this*?' I tossed the report on the coffee table.

She paled a little, her throat moving in another swallow. And why did I find that simple evidence that she felt *something* so riveting?

'You were always going to know your son, Axios. I simply took a little time before informing you.'

Rejection seared deep. 'No. I should've been informed the moment you found out you were carrying my child.'

'Why? So we could discuss it like a *loving married couple*? Or so you could treat it as another *business* transaction, like our arranged marriage? I'm sure you'll forgive me for choosing neither option, since the former was a farce and the latter was unpalatable.'

The accusation scored a direct hit, making my neck heat with another trace of guilt. Over the last year I'd gone over everything that had happened in those twenty-four hours. Accepted that perhaps I could've handled things differently. But was this the price I had to pay for it?

'I had a right to know, Calypso.' My voice emerged much gruffer than I'd intended. And deep inside me something like sorrow turned over.

Her lashes swept down, but not before I spotted the sea of turmoil swelling in the blue depths. My nape tightened and my instincts blared with the notion that she was hiding something.

'What if I told you that I didn't know what I wanted?' she asked.

A white-hot knife sliced through me at the thought that it would have decimated me had she taken a different route than bearing my son.

'Calypso…'

Her name sounded thick on my tongue. I waited until she raised her gaze to mine.

'Yes?'

'Regardless of this…disagreement between us, you will have my gratitude for choosing to carry our son for ever.'

Her eyes widened in stunned surprise. 'Um…you're welcome,' she murmured.

Once again her gaze swept away from mine—a small gesture that disturbed and confounded me. And then that defiant bolt of blue clashed with mine and absurd anticipation simmered in my gut.

'He's here now. Can we not put what has gone on in the past behind us and move on?'

'Certainly we can. As soon as you tell me what I want to know I'll take great strides to put it all behind me.'

Again that mutinous look took her over, sparking my own need to tangle with it. To stoke her fire until we both burned.

'Are you prepared to do that, Calypso?'

For several moments she held my gaze. Breath stalled, I awaited an answer…*one* answer…to quell the questions teeming inside me. But then that unnerving serenity settled on her face again.

'It's not important—'

'*Not important?* You leave my home under cover of a blatant falsehood, then you disappear for a year, during which time you bear my son, and you think your absence isn't *important*?'

'Careful, Axios, or I'll be inclined to wonder whether you actually missed the wife you bothered with for less than a day before walking away.'

I sucked in a stunned breath. A year ago she'd warned me that she wouldn't be biddable. Discovering she was innocent had clouded that warning. But this kitten had well and truly developed claws. Sharp ones. I was tempted to test them. Intellectually and…yes…*physically.*

Unbidden, heat throbbed deep in my groin, stirring desires I'd believed were long dead until one glimpse of my wayward wife from a jetty in Bora Bora had fiercely reawakened them.

That unholy union of sexual tension and unanswered questions propelled me to where she sat, cloaked in secrets that mocked me.

Her slight tensing when I crouched in front of her unsettled me further, despite the fact that I should've been satisfied to see that she wasn't wholly indifferent to me.

'You want to know about the inconvenience your absence caused, Calypso?'

She remained silent.

'Some newspaper hack got wind that my wife wasn't in Agistros, enjoying her first weeks of marital bliss. Nor was she with friends, as she'd led everyone to believe. To all intents and purposes she seemed to have fallen off the face of the earth.'

A delicate frown creased her brows. 'Why would that be of interest to anyone? Especially when you intended to banish me to Agistros for the duration of our arrangement anyway?'

'You're my wife. Everything you do is news. And appearing to have deserted your marriage was definitely newsworthy.'

She blinked. '*Appearing* to have?'

'I have an outstanding PR team who've had to work tirelessly to put a lid on this.'

There was no hint of remorse on her sun-kissed face. Instead she looked irritated. 'If you've managed to somehow spin my absence to suit our narrative then there's no problem, is there?'

I allowed myself a small smile, one her gaze clung to with wary eyes. 'You would like that, wouldn't you? To escape every unpleasant fall-out from your actions?'

'You don't have the first idea of what I want, Axios.'

My name on her lips sent a punch of heat through me. Thinking back, I couldn't recollect her ever saying it before Bora Bora. Not when she'd spat fire at me, not when she'd confessed her untouched state, and not when she'd been in the complete grip of passion. Certainly not when she'd asked me to take her with me to Athens.

There had been far too many times over the last year when I'd regretted not doing so—not because of that infernal hunger that had long outstayed its welcome, but simply because it would have curtailed her actions.

But the past was the past. There was still the future to deal with. And my new reality.

My son.

'For the sake of probability, and if I were in the mood to grant wishes, what exactly would you want, *matia mou*?'

Wariness made her hesitate, but slowly defiance laced

with something else pushed through. 'I'd want a divorce. As soon as possible.'

Stunned disbelief rose in me like a monumental wave I'd once ridden on the North Shore, and then just as swiftly crashed on the beach of her sheer audacity and shock. It was all so very dramatic.

I couldn't help it. I laughed.

Her pert little nose quivered as she inhaled sharply. 'What's so funny?'

Affront and defiance flushed her skin a sweet pink, drawing my attention to her alluring features. My wife was now all woman. An arrestingly feminine woman who'd just demanded…*a divorce*.

'Why you, my dear, and your continued ability to surprise me.'

'I'm glad you're amused. But I'm deadly serious. I want a divorce.'

Humour evaporated as abruptly as it had arrived. Leaning forward, I grasped her upper arms and fought not to be distracted by her smooth supple skin or the need to caress her and reacquaint myself with her.

My once sound argument about staying away from her had backfired spectacularly. I'd left her on Agistros thinking that she'd be safe and I'd be saved from temptation. Look how that had turned out.

Even with sex off the table I should have kept her close. I could have prevented her fleeing. Instead I'd borne the subtle snipes of those who had been quick to point out my failure. Quick to compare me to my grandfather and test me to see whether I'd crack under the same pressure.

With Calypso gone I'd experienced a taste of what he'd gone through—sometimes even with members of my own family.

Now she was back…and asking for a divorce.

'We seem to have veered a little off-track to be indulging in hypotheticals. You'll recall that, according to the agreement, this marriage needs to last at least twelve months.'

'Yes, I remember.'

'Twelve *ongoing* months. Not twelve absentee months.'

She swallowed and my fingers moved, some compulsion driving me to glide my fingers up her neck, trace the colour flowing back into her cheeks. She made a sound under her breath, bearing a hint of those she'd made on our wedding night.

Before I could revel in it she pulled back abruptly. My hands dropped back to her arms.

'My father hasn't contested the agreement,' she said.

'So you took the time to check on his activities?' Disgruntlement rumbled through me at the thought.

Her flush gave me my answer. 'What are you saying, Axios?'

'I'm saying the clock stopped the moment you walked out. But, fortunately for you, your father is no longer in the picture. For one thing he can't prove that you've been an absentee wife—unless you apprised him of your intentions?'

'No, I didn't,' she muttered, her eyes not quite meeting mine.

I'd long suspected that while she might have avoided contact with her father, her mother was a different story. But Iona Petras had remained resolutely closed-lipped about the whereabouts of her daughter.

'Good—then the ball, as they say, is in my court.'

She met my gaze boldly, read my clear intent and gasped. 'You mean you have the power to give me a divorce but…?' Her voice dried up, a telling little shiver racing through her body.

'But I won't, sweet Calypso. Not until a few things are set straight.'

'What things?'

'For starters, my PR company didn't make *all* the problems go away. While I frustrated the news media enough to make them chase other headlines, my competitors and my business partners were another story. Your absence fuelled enough rumours about instability to stall my latest deal.'

A peculiar expression that resembled hurt crossed her face. 'So this is about stocks and shares again?'

The disparaging note in her voice grated. 'Why? Did you want it to be something more?'

She stiffened. 'No.'

Her firm, swift denial rankled, but again I dismissed it. 'There will be no divorce. Not until I'm completely satisfied that there will be no permanent fall-out from your actions. And not until we've thoroughly discussed the impact this will have on Andreos.'

She stiffened. 'Does it occur to you that I might be doing this for him? That this arrangement might not be the best environment for him?'

'Then we will strive to make it so. You'll get your divorce, if you wish it. It could be as early as a month from now or it could be the year you were supposed to give me. In that time, wherever I go, you and my son will go also. He will be your priority. But when called upon you will be at my side at public functions and you will play the role of a devoted wife. And you will do all of that without the smallest hint that there's dissent between us.'

Her sweet, stubborn chin lifted in a clear defiance. 'And if I don't? What's to stop me giving the newspapers what they want? Telling them the true state of this so-called marriage?'

Why did her rebellion fire me up so readily? In truth, very few people got to display such attitude towards me. Neo tried me at the best of times, but even he knew when to back down. The rest of my family fell in line, because ultimately I held the purse strings.

But it seemed my errant wife's fiery spirit turned me on. Made me want to burn in the fire of it.

I caught her chin in my hand, my thumb moving almost

of its own volition to slide over the dark rose swell of her lower lip. She shivered, this time unable to disguise her arousal. I intensified the caress, a little too eager to see how far she was truly affected. Blue eyes held mine for another handful of seconds before they dropped. But her breathing grew more erratic, her pulse hammering against the silken skin of her throat.

I held still, my groin rudely awakening as the little eddy of lust whipped faster, threatened to turn into a cyclone.

'You really wish to defy me? You think that now you and your family have received what they want they can simply sit back and enjoy the spoils of their ill-gotten gains? Do you think that I will let you get away with it?'

She glared blue fire at me. 'I won't be ordered about, Axios. I won't be dictated to like one of your minions!'

'I would never mistake you for a minion. But a little hell-cat, intent on sinking her claws into me? Definitely.'

For a charged moment she returned my stare. Then her gaze dropped to my lips.

A sort of madness took over. A breathless second later our lips met in a fiery clash, the hot little gasp she gave granting me access to the sharp tongue that seemed intent on creating havoc with my mood and my libido.

Caught in the grip of hunger, I slicked my tongue against hers, took hold of one hip to hold her in place. She attempted to smother her moan, attempted not to squirm with the arousal I could already sense. I needed more. Needed confirmation of...*something*. Something that bore a hint of the torrid dreams that had plagued me almost nightly for a solid year. Something to take away the disarming hollowness that had resided in me since I'd got the call in New York that my wife had fled Agistros.

My teeth grazed the tip of her tongue when it attempted to issue a challenge. This time she couldn't hold back her moan. Couldn't stop herself from straining against me, from gasping her need.

And when she did I took. Savoured. Then devoured.

Her moans fuelled my desire, and the scramble of her hands over my chest, then around to my back facilitated the urgent need to lay her on the sofa so I could slide over her, to once again experience the heady sensation of having Calypso beneath me.

Her nails dug in deeper as I lowered myself over her, felt the heavy swell of her breasts press again my chest. The recollection that she'd borne my child, that she still nurtured him, was a powerful aphrodisiac that charged through me and hardened me in the most profoundly carnal way.

Could I get any more primitive?

Yes, my senses screamed.

The deepening urge to claim and keep what was mine thundered harder through me, drawing me away from the naked temptation of her lips to the seductive smoothness of her throat, her vibrant pulse, the exquisite valley between her breasts.

It took but a moment to slide the thin sleeve of her sundress off her shoulder, to release the front clasp and nudge aside the cup of her bra to bare her delicious flesh to my ravenous gaze. To mould the plump mound in anticipation of drawing that stiff, rosy peak into my mouth.

Beneath me, Calypso's breath caught. Her eyes turned a dark blue with the same fiery lust that was causing carnage wit in me, then snapped to mine and stayed there.

Slowly, with an ultra-feminine arching of her back that held me deeply enthralled, she offered herself to me, somehow turning the tables on me. Because for all that this was supposed to be a punitive lesson, a way to remind her who held the power now, after her actions had swung the tide to my advantage, I was caught in a vortex of desire so voracious I couldn't have stopped even if I'd wanted to.

So I lowered my head and with a powerless groan sucked the bud into my mouth.

Savage hunger exploded inside me, all my senses lost as

her fingers locked in my hair and held me to my delight-ful task.

'Oh... *Theos mou*,' she gasped.

The memory of our one night together, of her unreserved responsiveness and the unique way she'd expressed her plea-sure, sharpened my hunger, sparking a desire to relive that experience. I slid one hand beneath her body, urged her even closer. She answered by arching higher, offering more of herself to me.

'Tell me what you're feeling,' I urged thickly, aware that my voice was hoarse, barely intelligible.

She froze, the eyes that had rolled shut mere seconds ago flying open.

Watching her, I lazily caught that peak between my teeth, felt a carnal shudder unravel through her. 'You taste ex-quisite.'

Arousal and denial warred in her face, and then her fin-gers flew from my hair as small but effective hands pushed at my shoulders. 'No! Stop!'

For a moment I considered a different tactic. Negotia-tion. Talking her round to my way of thinking. Satisfying this need that dogged us both. But hadn't my family and I given the Petrases enough in this lifetime? This was sup-posed to be the time to extract *my* pound of flesh after what they'd done to my grandfather. Besides, sex was what had led us here in the first place. Was I really going to fall into the well of temptation I'd counselled myself against a year ago when I should be dealing with the reality of my son?

The reminder was enough to propel me off her and across the room. Even then it took several control-gathering breaths to master my raging libido. It didn't help that her reflection in the window showed her naked breasts for another hand-ful of seconds before she righted her clothes.

When she was done, she rose. She didn't approach— which was a good thing, because I wasn't sure I wouldn't have given in to the urge to finish what we'd started.

'Axios…'

I gritted my teeth, the discovery that my name on her lips was its own special brand of hell driving my fingers through my hair.

This had gone on long enough. 'This is no longer purely business, Calypso. I want to know my son.'

I caught another expression on her face—one that sent a different type of emotion charging through me.

I turned around, wanting to verify it more accurately, but whatever it was had gone, her face a composed mask.

'Of course. I won't stand in the way of that.'

Why didn't that agreement satisfy me?

Why did that hollowness still remain?

'Good. Then we shelve discussion of divorce until further notice.'

That gruff, shaken tone was gone. It was almost as if that little display of emotion over his son had never happened. As if the wild little tumble on the sofa less than five minutes ago was already a distant memory.

But, no…there were tell-tale signs. Signs I didn't want to notice. Like how deliciously tousled his dark, luxuriously wavy hair was now, courtesy of my restless fingers. How colour still rose in his chiselled cheekbones.

And that definitive bulge behind his fly—

With a willpower that threatened to sap the last of my composure I averted my gaze from the pillar of temptation he represented, and reminded myself why we were here in the first place. Dear heaven. I needed to be done with this before the desire I'd believed eroded by distance and absence made a complete fool of me.

'I need your word, Calypso.'

The implacable demand centred my thoughts. Reminded me that this wasn't over. Contrary to what I'd believed, twelve months of living apart from him had done nothing to lessen my sentence. I was back to square one, with a child to think about.

A child Axios fully intended to claim.

'Where exactly does Andreos feature in your grand plan?' I asked, belatedly focusing on the most precious thing in my life. On safeguarding his welfare before I embarked on fighting for my survival.

Axios's head went back, as if the question offended him. 'He is my son. He will be brought up under our care with the full benefit of the Xenakis name at his disposal for as long as he needs it.'

Through all of this I'd held on to the secret fear that Andreos might suffer. Over the past year I'd meticulously researched the Xenakis dynasty, with Andreos's needs at the forefront of my mind.

Outwardly, they appeared a close unit—but, as with most super-wealthy and influential families, rumours of acrimony abounded. Once or twice it had been rumoured that Axios's status as CEO had been challenged by a daring cousin or uncle. None had succeeded, of course.

'You give me your word that you'll protect Andreos, no matter what?'

'Of course. I vow it.' His voice was deep and solemn and immediate.

Relief weakened my knees, and for some absurd reason I wanted to throw my arms around him. 'Thank you.'

His frown deepened, speculation narrowing his eyes. I turned away before he could read my anxiety. Now wasn't the time to think about my precarious health…about the tough road ahead. About the battle my grandmother had fought against cervical cancer and eventually lost.

And it certainly wasn't the time to dwell on the fact that the pain in my abdomen remained, its presence edging into my consciousness with each passing day.

'Possible cancer… Prognosis uncertain if you choose to keep your baby…'

Dr Trudeau's words broke free from the vault I'd kept them in. Along with the frighteningly easy decision I'd made to keep my baby for as long as I could instead of chasing risky surgery. The tearful gratitude for every day Andreos had nestled in my womb, growing despite the unknown threat to his life and mine.

And his sweet cry the moment he was born.

I'd learned quickly that for my son's sake I needed to compartmentalise. His keen intelligence and sensitivity, even at such a tender age, had focused me on giving him my very best—always. But giving him my best included fighting to remain in his life. Even if I had to temporarily entrust him to Axios in order to do so.

'Do you agree?' Axios pressed, his gaze probing mercilessly.

'I'll give you what you want on one condition. Take it or leave it.'

After a moment he jerked his head in command for me to continue.

'I'll stay until your precious deal is done. On condition that you don't attempt to interfere in my relationship with my son.'

'What gives you the impression that I'd wish to do anything of the sort?'

My shrug fell short of full efficiency under his heavy frown. 'It's been known to happen.'

'Who? Your father?'

I could have denied it, kept up the years-long pretence. But time was too precious to waste on falsehoods. So I nodded. 'Yes.'

Axios moved towards me, his frown a dark cloud. 'What did he do to you?'

I hesitated now, because on the flipside I didn't want to bare my all to him. The desire to continue living on my own terms hadn't diminished an iota since my return to Greece. And even if I intended to agree to Axios's demands

I would always keep one small corner of my life free from his interference.

'He manipulated every relationship I ever had in some way. I don't want that to happen with Andreos.'

The grey gaze boring into mine stated blatantly that he wanted more. Mine declared I'd given him all I intended to.

'I've seen you with Andreos. He thrives under your care. I'd be a fool to jeopardise that.'

Before I could breathe my relief he stepped closer, bringing that bristling magnificence into touching distance. I balled fingers that tingled with the need to feel his vibrant skin under my touch again.

'You have my word I will not interfere. Will you give me yours?'

Again I was mildly stunned that it was a question rather than a declaration. But the searing reminder that giving in to one emotion around Axios was simply the gateway to a flood of other sensations I needed to keep a tight leash on, had me swallowing the desire.

'I will stay for as long as it takes to give you what you need,' I offered.

He accepted it with a simple nod, as if it was nothing to celebrate. And perhaps in the grand scheme of things it wasn't. We were picking up where we'd left off with the added inconvenience of needing to put out more fires than he'd initially anticipated.

After several skin-tingling moments during which he simply stared at me, as if probing beneath my defences to read my secrets, I twisted away, eager to escape those all-seeing eyes.

'I need to get back to Andreos.'

'We're not quite done, Calypso.'

About to ask what else we needed to talk about, I felt my tight throat close even further when he stepped closer. His scent curled around me, reminding me of what had happened on the sofa a short while ago. Had things really got out of hand so quickly? My body still hummed with unspent energy, and my heart hadn't quite settled into its steady cadence.

'I'll come with you to visit my son.'

The throb of possessiveness in his voice sent my senses flaring wide with warning. What exactly that warning was refused to surface as we left his suite.

As it turned out it wasn't necessary to return to the ground floor. Sophia was carefully navigating the stairs, with a sleepy Andreos in her arms. We followed her as she entered the opposite wing of the villa, where a nursery had been set up by a team of designers on the first day of my return.

Seeing us, she smiled. 'We played for a while, but I think he's ready for his nap, *kyria*,' she said softly.

The sight of Andreos fighting a losing battle to stay awake drew a smile from my heart. Handing him over to Sophia even for such a short while had made my heart ache. I knew it would be a million times worse when I had to leave, but somehow I trusted Axios with his care. Sophia's clear devotion to him was an added bonus.

I reached out for him but Axios stepped forward.

'Do you mind?' The demand was gruff but gentle.

In stunned surprise I nodded. Still smiling, Sophia handed son over to father and discreetly melted away.

The sight of Axios holding his son for the first time shouldn't have brought a thick lump to my throat. The sight of his strong, powerful arms carefully cradling my baby, his throat moving in a convulsive swallow, shouldn't have fired a soul-deep yearning through my body. A yearning for things to be different. For fate not to be so cruel.

Why? Did I wish for things to be different between Axios and I?

Absolutely not.

As for other yearnings—hadn't I already been granted more than enough? I'd prayed for a healthy son and been given the child of my heart. I'd prayed for a little more time and had enjoyed almost four beautiful months.

But the thought of leaving him, even to fight for my health—

'What's wrong?'

I jumped, my gaze rising to see Axios watching me.

'Am I holding him wrong?'

The touch of uncertainty in his voice caught a warm spot inside me and loosened another smile from me as I approached, unable to stop myself from reaching out, kissing Andreos's forehead and cheek, breathing in his sweet and innocent scent.

'No, you're not doing anything wrong.'

Grey eyes so very similar to his son's dropped to the now sleeping Andreos, and his chest slowly expanded in a long breath before he headed over to the brand-new, state-of-the-art cot set out for our baby.

With the utmost care he transferred Andreos from his arms to the cot, barely eliciting any protest from him. Arms thrown up beside his head in angelic abandon, Andreos slept on as his father draped a soft cotton blanket over him, drew a gentle finger down his cheek and straightened.

Still smiling, I glanced over at Axios—and my heart leapt into my throat. Gone was the gentle look he'd bestowed on his son. In its place was a bleak visage full of loss and yearning that made me gasp. Made that pulse of guilt rise again.

The sound drew his attention to me. When he took hold of my arm and steered me out of earshot I tried to think past the naked tingles his touch brought. To think how I could contain the relentless waves of turbulent emotion bent on consuming us.

'I'd like answers to a few questions, Calypso. If you feel so inclined?' he rasped.

Seeing no way to avoid it without collapsing the agreement I'd struck, I nodded.

His hand dropped to my wrist. 'We'll discuss this further over lunch.'

Lunch was an extensive selection of *meze* fit for a small banquet—not the intimate setting for two laid out on one of the three sun-splashed terraces.

Axios must have spotted my surprise as he pulled out my chair because he shrugged. 'I didn't know your preferences so I instructed the chef to prepare a large selection.'

'Oh...thank you.'

His gaze rested on me as he lowered himself into his own chair. 'Again, you sound surprised. Believe it or not I want things to go as smoothly as possible for both of us.'

The knowledge that this included simple things such as what I ate widened the warm pool swelling inside me. Even cautioning myself that it was foolish to entertain such a sensation didn't do anything to stem it as I helped myself to pitta bread and tzatziki, feta cheese and chickpea salad and succulent vine leaves stuffed with lamb and cucumber.

'Where was Andreos born?'

His deep voice throbbed with one simple emotion—a hunger to know. And for the very first time since my decision to live life on my terms, twelve long months ago, I experienced a deep stirring of guilt.

But along with that came a timely warning not to divulge everything. Knowledge was power to men like Axios. Men like my father. And every precious uninterrupted moment with my son was as vital to me as the breath in my lungs.

Although in the past four days since my return, Axios had seemed a little more...malleable. While the man who'd laid down the law and walked away from me in Agistros still lurked in there somewhere, this Axios tended to ask more and command less.

But still I carefully selected the bits of information that wouldn't connect too many dots for him and replied, 'He was born in a small clinic in Kenya, where I was volunteering. He came a week early, but there were no complications and the birth was relatively easy.'

He didn't answer. Not immediately. The glass of red wine he was drinking with his meal remained cradled in his hand and his expression reflective and almost…yearning as he stared into the middle distance.

'I would've liked to be there,' he rasped. 'Very much.'

The warm pool inside me grew hotter, turning into a jet of feeling spiralling high with emotions I needed to wrestle under control before they got out of hand.

But even as the warning hit hard I was opening my mouth, uttering words I shouldn't. 'One of the nurses filmed the birth…if you'd like to see it?'

What are you doing sharing your most precious moments with him?

He's Andreos's father.

Axios inhaled sharply, the glass discarded as he stared fiercely at me. 'You have a video?'

I jerked out a nod. 'Yes. Would you—?'

'Yes.' The word was bullet-sharp, and the cadence of his breathing altered as his gaze bored into me. 'Yes. Very much,' he repeated.

For the longest time we remained frozen, our gazes locked in a silent exchange I didn't want to examine or define. Soon it morphed into something else. Something equally intimate. Twice as dangerous.

Perhaps it was in the molten depths of his eyes, or in the not so secret wish to relive what had happened upstairs ramping up that ever-present chemistry. Whatever it was, we'd brought it alive on that sofa and now it sat between us, a writhing wire ready to sizzle and electrify and burn at the smallest hint of weakening.

Forcing my brain back on track didn't help. Hadn't we been discussing childbirth? The product of what had happened in a bedroom the last time we were both present in one.

'I'll let you have the recording after lunch,' I blurted, then picked up my water glass and drank simply to distract myself.

From the corner of my eye I watched him lounge back in his seat, although his body still held that coil of tension that never dissipated.

After a moment he picked up his glass and drained it. '*Efkharisto*,' he murmured. 'Now, on to other things. Arrangements are being made to equip you with a new wardrobe. My mother tells me the things you left behind are hopelessly out of date.'

I frowned, the change of subject from the soul-stirring miracle of Andreos's birth to the mundanity of high fashion throwing me for a few seconds. 'I don't need a new wardrobe.'

'Perhaps not—but might I suggest you let the stylists come anyway? Who knows? You might find something you like for our first engagement on Saturday,' he replied.

The last tendrils of yearning had left his voice, to be replaced by the cadence I knew best. One of powerful mogul. Master of all he surveyed. Despite the pleasant heat of the sun a cool breeze whispered over my skin, bringing me harshly back to earth.

'What's happening on Saturday?'

'It's been four days since you returned. It's time we presented you properly to the world. My mother has organised a party in your honour. She was unwell when we married last year, and couldn't make it to the ceremony. She's anxious to meet you. And, of course, she's yet to meet her grandson. Call this a belated welcome, if you will, but several business acquaintances will be there, so it's imperative that everything goes smoothly.'

'Is it really necessary to parade me before your friends and family?'

'I think it's best to put the rumours to rest once and for all. Then we can concentrate on our son.'

While his attention to Andreos warmed my heart, the prospect of being paraded before his family and business didn't. 'And how do you propose we do that? Is there a storyline I need to follow, chapter and verse?'

He smiled as if the thought of playing out a role so publicly was water off his back. 'Leave that to me,' he stated cryptically. 'All I require from you is to present a picture-perfect image of loving wife and mother. I trust I can count on you to do that?'

For the sake of uninterrupted bonding with my son I would go to hell and back. 'Yes.'

Perhaps my agreement was too quick. Perhaps the depth of feeling behind it was too revealing. Whatever, his gaze grew contemplative, stayed fixed on me.

And when he walked away, moments after the meal was done, I got the distinct feeling there were more bumps and curves on this peculiar road I'd taken than I'd initially realised.

CHAPTER SIX

A PRE-PARTY FAMILY MIXER.

A harmless-sounding statement until you were confronted by the full might of the formidable Xenakis clan.

The gathering had been deceptive. Over the course of two hours they'd trickled in—some by car, others by boat. And Axios's formidable-looking brother Neo, looking a little distracted and a lot harassed, had come by sleek helicopter, with the iconic Xenakis Aeronautics logo emblazoned on its side.

Inexorably the trickle became a stream, and then a torrent. By four p.m. the largest salon in the villa, the surrounding terrace and the perfectly manicured lawn were overflowing with aunts, uncles, cousins and distant offshoots—some from as far afield as Australia and New Zealand.

Fascinatingly, despite the low buzz of tension surrounding their interactions, there were no overt signs of dissent.

Perhaps because I was their main focus.

I didn't want to admit it, but the six-hour makeover session I'd endured earlier in the day boosted my confidence now, as impeccably dressed men and couture-clad women approached the place where I stood next to Axios, with a wide-eyed Andreos nestled in my arms.

My hair had been brought back to shoulder-length, layered and trimmed into loose stylish waves that gleamed with new vitality. And the rails upon rails of new clothes hanging in the closets of my vast dressing room, complete with matching accessories and priceless jewellery, were the *pièce de résistance*.

After months of wearing flats and tie-dye sundresses, and ponytailing my hair, the transformation took a little getting used to. While the teardrop diamond necklace glittering just as bright as the pristine white linen shift dress and tan platform shoes were making me feel intensely aware of the kind of circles I'd married into.

The most striking of the women within those intimidating circles was Electra Xenakis—Axios's mother.

Her hair was a distinctive grey, which had been used to enhance her beauty rather than been dyed away, and it framed an angular face, highlighting superb cheekbones and the striking grey eyes she'd passed on to her sons. Tall and slender, with a ramrod-straight posture, she was formidable—until she gave a rare smile. Then warmth radiated from her every pore, and the icy grey palazzo pants and matching top she wore were suddenly not so severe.

On meeting Andreos she dissolved into hearty tears. And that unfettered display of love for her grandchild thawed the cold knot of apprehension inside me, easing my anguish at the thought of a permanent separation from my child.

The distance I'd needed to get my composure back after handing Andreos over to his grandmother lasted mere minutes before I sensed a presence beside me. It wasn't as visceral and all-encompassing as Axios's, but it demanded attention nevertheless.

I glanced up to find Neo Xenakis standing before me.

'I never quite got the chance to welcome you into the family last year.' His tone was measured, his eyes just as probing as his brother's.

'I guess the circumstances weren't exactly…conducive,' I replied.

'Ochi, they weren't. But your disappearing act didn't help matters, I expect?'

I stiffened. 'I had my reasons,' I replied.

Without answering, he dropped his gaze to the contents of the crystal tumbler he clutched. 'Whatever they were, I hope it was worth keeping a father from his child?'

Again his tone was more appraising than censorious, as if he was attempting to understand my motives. Again my guilt resurfaced. And this time brushing it away wasn't easy.

Before I could formulate a response, a deeper and more visceral voice asked, 'Is everything all right?'

For me not to have sensed his arrival spoke volumes of the kind of magnetism the Xenakis men possessed. And now Axios had arrived next to me the force of their presence had doubled. Their sole focus was on me, but one set of grey eyes was vastly more potent than the other, sending my composure into free fall.

I took a long, steadying breath to reply, 'We're fine.'

Axios's gaze slid from mine to his brother, a clear question in his eyes.

Neo's expression clouded for a moment, then he shrugged. 'Like your wife said, we're fine. No need to go Neanderthal on me.'

Before either of us could enquire what he meant, he excused himself and struck out for the large gazebo on the south side of the garden, currently decked out with fairy lights and free of guests.

'Is he okay?' I felt compelled to ask.

Axios's gaze stayed on him long enough to see his brother lift a phone to his ear before he turned to me. 'His issues aren't mine to disclose, but Neo is touchy on the subject of babies. Like the rest of the family, news about his nephew's existence surprised him. But, since Andreos is single-handedly winning everyone over, I suspect the circumstances of his arrival will be forgiven soon.'

Had he deliberately excluded himself from that statement? Unwilling for him to see the bite of anguish that distinction brought, I turned my gaze to where the majority of the Xenakis clan had now gathered, choosing to see the bright side.

Andreos was indeed holding centre stage, tucked into his favourite blanket and nestled lovingly within his grandmother's arms. The absolute devotion on the older woman's face eased my heartache, but in the next moment the sudden thought that my own mother hadn't met my son hit me with tornado-strength force.

'What is it?' Axios asked, the eyes that hadn't left my face since his brother's disappearance narrowing.

The fleeting thought to shrug off his question came and went, and I couldn't help the small shaft of pain that came with it. 'My parents haven't met him yet.'

His face tightened, the mention of Yiannis Petras drawing a reaction I would have preferred to leave out of the already fraught atmosphere. I held my breath, ready to fight my corner.

'We can arrange a visit for your mother later…if you wish?'

Surprised by that response, I blinked. 'I do. Thank you.'

After another minute of assessing scrutiny he nodded. 'Whatever your reasons for fleeing Agistros, I accept that I could've handled our last meeting a little better,' he said, his voice a deep rasp.

My lips were parted in shock when another wave of Xenakises wandered over. Axios's droll look and almost-smile told me he'd seen my shock at his apology.

I managed to get my emotions under control beneath his family's probing glances, watching their silent musing as to what had transpired with Axios's stray wife. I was grateful for their circumspection because, as baptisms of fire went, it could have been worse.

It was with far more trepidation that I contemplated my extensive closet three hours after everyone had disappeared into their various guest rooms and private homes to get ready for the main event. The knock on the door barely snagged my attention. Absent-mindedly I responded, my fingers toying with the tie of my bathrobe as I contemplated the stunning array of clothes.

'As much as you seem to enjoy simply staring at them, you do actually have to pick an outfit to wear for the party, you know?' Ax drawled, his deep tone more amused than I'd ever heard him.

I jumped and turned around, barely able to hold back a gasp at the sight of him, standing a few feet away, wearing half of a bespoke tuxedo. His pristine snow-white shirt was half buttoned, but neatly tucked into his tailored trousers, and his bowtie was strung around his neck.

The intimate knowledge of what resided beneath his clothes dried my mouth as I stared, slack-jawed, several superlatives crowding my brain.

Debonair. Breathtaking. Insanely gorgeous.

Slowly the silence thickened and he raised one sleek eyebrow. 'Can I help with anything?'

The hand I waved over my shoulder at the closet was irritatingly fluttery. 'I can't decide what to wear. Meeting your family was one thing… This is a different ballgame.'

His gaze travelled from the top of my hair, which still held its earlier style, thanks to the expertise of the stylist, then lingered at the belt holding my robe closed, before moving to my bare feet. Each spot his eyes touched triggered fiery awareness.

'You handled my family admirably and won them over with Andreos. Even Neo—and he's a handful at the best of times,' he added dryly. 'You'll excel just as well tonight.'

The deeply spoken reassurance made my heart lurch. To hide its effect I scrambled for something else to concentrate on, and spotted his dangling sleeves and the cufflinks in his hand.

'Do you need help with those?' I asked, even though assisting him would involve stepping closer, breathing in the intoxicating scent that clung to him and never failed to send my senses haywire.

He held out his arms. 'If you wouldn't mind?'

Breath held, in the hope that it would mitigate the erotic chaos stirring to life inside me, I reached for the two halves of his shirtsleeve in one hand and held out the other for the cufflinks. The tips of his fingers brushed my palm as he handed them over, and every inch of my skin responded as if set alight.

Intensely aware that my nipples were hardening, and that a pulse had started throbbing between my thighs, I hurried to finish my task, my own fingers brushing the inside of his wrist in the process.

Axios inhaled sharply, an incoherent sound rumbling from his chest.

Could we not even exchange a common courtesy without feeling as if the world was about to burst into flames? *Evidently not.*

Which was probably all the warning I needed to keep my distance. Never to repeat what had happened on his sofa.

'*Efkharisto*,' he murmured, his voice deep and thick.

His eyes were molten, as heated as that needy place between my legs. Unable to withstand his gaze, for fear I'd give myself away, I turned to face the rack of clothes. Of course my senses leaped high when he stepped next to me, then took another step closer to the open closet.

To my shaky memory this was perhaps the first time I'd been this close without having his laser eyes on me. The opportunity to give in to the urge to stare was too hard to resist.

The breadth and packed strength of his shoulders.

The vibrancy of his lustrous hair.

The sharp, mouthwatering angle of his freshly shaved jaw.

Too busy fighting the way every inch of Axios triggered this unwanted but unstoppable reaction, I didn't notice he'd made a selection until he pivoted, the momentary gaping of his shirt delivering one final punch of his sheer magnetism before he drawled, 'You'll look beautiful in any one of these gowns. But this one will do, I think.'

Heat engulfed my face as I reached out and snatched the gown from his hand, hastily stepping back. 'I...thanks.'

'You need help with the zip?' he asked, in a voice thicker than before.

Aware of the dangerous waters I was treading, I shook my head. 'I think I'll manage. Thanks.'

He hesitated for a stomach-churning moment, then nodded. 'I'll return in fifteen minutes. We will go downstairs together, if you wish.'

I nodded my thanks.

Contrary to his stealthy arrival, I was conscious of Ax's departure for the simple reason that he seemed to take the very air out of the room with him, leaving me breathless as I shrugged off the robe and slipped the gown over my head.

Barely paying attention to the design, I zipped it up and stepped into the heels that had been helpfully paired with the dress, spritzed perfume on my neck and wrists, and was adding the finishing touches to my make-up when his knock came.

Very much aware of the silk clinging to my hips and breasts, I prayed my body wouldn't give me away as I opened the door.

For the longest time he simply stared at me. 'Beautiful,' he finally stated, and the sizzling gleam in his eyes only lent him a more dangerous air, rendering all my efforts for composure useless as I accepted there was no level this man couldn't reach in the drop-dead gorgeous stakes.

'Thank you,' I replied, my voice a husky mess.

He held out his arm. I took it, and was still in a semi-daze when we exited the limo at the entrance to the six-star luxury hotel in the middle of Athens where the party was being held.

The moment Ax and I stepped into the ballroom silence fell over the guests, every eye fixed on me.

'I don't know whether to smile or scowl. What's *de rigueur* these days?' I murmured.

'Just ignore them. That's what I do when I feel out of place.'

I laughed, mostly to hide his unabated effect on me. Besides, I couldn't help it, because picturing Axios as a fish out of water was like attempting to imagine what the landscape inside a black hole looked like.

'Something funny?'

'You wouldn't look out of place amongst a clutch of nuns in a prayer circle.'

He smiled, and just like that my body went into free fall, breaking one tension while ratcheting up another. And as I was crashing down, towards some unknown destination, it struck me that this was the first time I'd seen any semblance of a smile from the man I called my husband.

'An unusual compliment, I think, but thank you all the same,' he said.

'You should've told me the whole of Athens would be here tonight,' I said, a little desperate to maintain a disgruntled distance from him.

He lowered his head even closer to murmur in my ear, 'Put your claws away, *pethi mou*. You look much too beautiful to pick a fight.'

'I'm sure we can find something to fight about if we look hard enough.'

Was I really that desperate to start a fight? Simply to stop this unruly attraction in its tracks?

His amusement disappeared, to be replaced with the unwavering regard that never failed to trigger mini-earthquakes inside me. My breath snagged in my throat as he stepped closer, until there was nothing but a whisper of space between us. To anyone observing us we'd look as if we were sharing an intimate moment. But I knew what was coming even before he spoke.

'Keep tossing those little challenges at me, Calypso, and I'll delight in picking you up on one.'

The electric promise in those words sent a bolt through me. It lingered through all the introductions to influential individuals, A-list celebrities and even more of the Xenakis clan and it slowly began to re-energise, that spark of rebellion re-ignited.

For some reason I *wanted* to challenge him.

So when I found a moment's reprieve I looked up from my untouched glass of champagne into his face. 'Do you know what I think, Axios?'

A simple but effective hitch of his brow commanded me to continue.

'I don't think you will pick me up on any challenge. I don't think you'll do anything to risk this reputation you're bent on protecting.'

'Are you brave enough to test your theory, I wonder?' he asked, and something untamed pulsed beneath his civil exterior. Something that made the glass in my hand tremble wildly.

His gaze dropped to it before returning to my face. With a wicked smile he raised one imperious hand and traced his knuckles down my heated cheek.

'Pick your battles with care, Calypso. You look stunning in this dress—every eye in the room keeps returning to you time and again, and I'm the envy of every man here. You should be celebrating that, not picking a fight with your husband.'

With that, he leaned even closer, replaced his hand with his mouth for the briefest of moments…

And then he walked off.

Leaving me shaking with a cascade of emotions.

The only reason I felt out of sorts was because that little incident in my dressing room had thrown me—shown me a different side to Axios that had intensified the illicit yearning inside me. And while standing next to Axios wreaked havoc with my equilibrium, watching him, the most prominent man in the room, walking away left me with a yawing hollow in the pit of my stomach.

Did I really want him? Or was I just terrified by the knowledge that the only eyes I wanted on me were his, not the guests' who kept coming up to me, some blatantly questioning why the great Axios Xenakis had tied himself down to *me*.

I shook my head, hoping to clear it of these confusing thoughts.

'I hope you're not shaking your head because you wish to deny me your company?'

I attempted to control my bewildering thoughts before turning towards another one of Ax's cousins.

At my blank look he said, 'I'm Stavros. We met earlier.'

I nodded, attempted to smile. 'Hello.'

His smile was reserved, but genuine. I found myself wishing for another smile. One that was edged in sizzling grey. I was really losing it.

'Having fun?'

I shrugged. 'I'm in a room full of some of the most powerful people on earth, sipping champagne and enjoying the status of hostess with the mostest. What's not to love?'

As with most of the Xenakis clan, his expression grew speculative. 'You sound...distressed. Is everything all right?'

About to answer, I looked across the room to where Ax had been talking to the trade minister moments ago. He was staring directly at me, as if he could see to the heart of my jumbled emotions.

That he could do that from across the room panicked me and irked me. Nevertheless, I had to hold on to what was important. And that was Andreos. Regardless of my personal situation, I couldn't afford for anything to jeopardise my time with my child.

With a deep breath, I forced a smile and turned to Stavros. 'I'm absolutely fine, Stavros. Sorry if I sounded a little off. Chalk it up to missing my baby.'

'Ah, a little separation anxiety, *ne*? As the father of young children, I remember that state well, too.'

'Yes… Speaking of which, would you mind excusing me? I'd like to call and check on him.'

This time Stavros's smile was a little tight. 'Of course. But I hope you'll honour me with a dance when you return?'

For some reason his request made me glance at Ax. He was once again engrossed in conversation with a clutch of men who were no doubt hanging on his every word.

That spark of rebellion returned and I answered Stavros's smile. 'Maybe. We'll see…'

Excusing myself, I wove through the crowd, my pinned-on smile beginning to fray a little more at the edges every time I was stopped by a well-meaning guest wishing to very *belatedly* congratulate me on my marriage and Andreos's birth, while subtly probing for cracks in my demeanour.

True to his word, Axios had taken care of all the speculation and chosen the most direct explanation for my absence.

'My wife wished to have a peaceful pregnancy and took the time she needed to safely deliver our son.'

Only the most daring would choose to probe my absence after that.

All evening I'd watched him hold court, effortlessly exuding power and charm over hardcore businessmen and moguls I'd only read about in the newspapers.

And while the wedding last year and the family gathering earlier had already shown me his authority and charisma, watching him speak to and mingle with some of the most influential people in the world truly rammed home to me the almost frightening power he wielded.

He was a powerful man whom my father had managed to bend to his will. A man whose reputation I'd put in jeopardy with my disappearing act.

Had I been fooling myself by striking a deal with him?

Enough! Running rings around my decisions was futile.

I stepped out onto the thankfully empty terrace of the grand hotel ballroom and called Sophia. Reassured that all was well, my thoughts flew as they often did when I thought of Andreos to the battle that awaited me. To the fear that my time with him would be cut short.

My hand dropped to linger over my stomach, to the dull ache residing deep inside…

'Are you all right?' Axios demanded with a gravel-rough voice.

I jumped and whirled around, hastily dropping my hand when his gaze moved to it. 'You're spying on me now?'

He sauntered towards me. 'I came to check on you because I didn't want you to feel neglected. And I haven't forgotten that you fled your marriage after one day and didn't return for a year,' he returned with sizzling fire.

'Because you were happy to leave me alone on your island without a care for what *I* wanted. Have you forgotten that? Did it even occur to you that I might want a different life for myself other than what *you* chose for me?'

For the longest time he didn't reply. Then, 'That was an error in judgement. One I regret,' he intoned solemnly.

The unequivocal apology had the same effect as the one earlier. My jaw dropped. 'You…do?'

'*Ne*,' he drawled.

For another charged moment he stared at me. Then his gaze dropped to my phone.

Almost dazedly I stared at it. 'You can stand down your spies. I was simply calling Sophia to check on my son.'

A deeply possessive look glinted in his eyes. 'He's *our* son, *pethi mou*. Yours and mine and no one else's.'

The very idea of Andreos being anyone else's child but Axios's was so profoundly impossible I almost laughed out loud. And then that notion faded under the weight of the electrified atmosphere crackling between us. The feeling of being caught on the edge of a lightning storm that never quite went away.

It didn't take a genius to see that Axios was in an equally edgy mood.

Attempting to dissipate it, I waved the phone at him.

'He's fine, by the way. According to Sophia, he went down without a fuss.'

Axios shrugged. 'He's almost four months old. I believe that as long as he's warm and well fed he has very little to worry about.'

'It's a little more complicated than that. He needs love and laughter. He's also at the stage where he'll really start recognising his mother's absence.'

Bleakness flashed across his face, momentarily slashing my insides. 'What about his father's? And whose fault is it that I'm not fully equipped with that information, Calypso?' His voice throbbed with raw emotion.

'Axios—'

His hand slashed through the air a split-second before he closed the gap between us and settled his hands on my shoulders. 'I want to move on from this. But there are questions you still haven't answered.'

My heart dipped. 'Like what?'

'What's the big secret about your whereabouts? I hunted for you high and low. My investigators visited Nicrete—discreetly, of course, since I had to protect my family from untoward gossip. The general consensus there was that Calypso Petras was far too level-headed, far too considerate to have made such a selfish move. At least without assistance or coercion of some sort. Perhaps from a source no one had considered.'

'What source?'

His tension heightened, his whole body seemingly caught in a live electric feed. 'You tell me.'

'Maybe a secret admirer? Perhaps even another man?' I taunted.

A fierce little muscle ticked in his jaw. 'Was it? Considering you were a virgin, I wasn't inclined to think you would jump into another man's bed that easily. Tell me I wasn't wrong,' he bit out.

He hadn't thought the worst of me.

The idea of it left me nonplussed for several seconds, considering he still had no idea of my whereabouts for the past year. Considering he had to have overheard some of the blatant whispers at the party.

'Why the interrogation? I thought you were all about keeping up appearances? Convincing the world that my absence was a well-orchestrated plan?'

'That's been taken care of. The results will be evident soon enough. Let's discuss us,' he said, then immediately frowned as if he hadn't expected to say that.

Perhaps he hadn't. After all, wasn't he the man who'd never engaged in a relationship that lasted more than a few weeks?

'*Us?* Are you sure? You seem as surprised by that word falling from your lips as I am to hear it.'

For the longest time he stared at me. Then he shrugged. 'Only a fool stays on a course that's doomed. Perhaps I'm embracing new changes. Attempting to be…different.'

My heart lurched, even as I tamped down fruitless hope. All this meant nothing. Not if my prognosis was as dire as my senses screamed that they were. Not if this marriage was ticking down to dissolution.

'Can we not do this here? I'd like to go back in.'

'Why? So Stavros can succeed at working his angle?'

I blinked in surprise. 'What are you talking about?'

He edged me back a step, following me so we were wedged against the stone balustrade. 'Just a heads-up. His marriage is on the rocks. He's attempting to raise his stature by undermining my authority every chance he gets—chances which, unfortunately for him, haven't been readily available. I'd rather not see you be his pawn,' he breathed, his voice absolutely lethal while being so soft.

Too late, I accepted that the fire inside me was building out of control. His body surged closer, reminding me in vivid detail of the hard-packed, streamlined definition of muscle beneath his bespoke suit. And the fact that his body could render me speechless with very little effort.

'You can stand down. I can take care of myself.'

'*Ne*, I'm beginning to see that,' he murmured, and again there was the barest hint of grudging acceptance in his eyes.

But I didn't get the chance to explore the discovery because his head slowly lowered.

Hot, sensual and commanding, his lips slanted over mine. With a gasp that was way too husky and way too revealing I threw up my hands. Somewhere in the back of my head I was aware that I'd dropped my phone. But it didn't seem to matter, because his tongue was delving between my lips, seeking entrance I was helpless to deny.

He tasted me with a brazenness that struck a match to the desire that had been straining to be freed after that episode on his sofa. With effortless ease he set it ablaze between one snatched breath and the next.

His tongue stroked mine with a possessiveness that took control of my whole body, so that when one hand slid from my shoulder and down my back to draw me into sizzling contact it felt as if I was made of warm, pliant dough, ready to mould myself to any shape of his bidding.

When his other hand angled my head to deepen the kiss it was all I could do to slide my own hands around his neck. To hold on tightly as the dizzying journey zipped like a rollercoaster ride I never wanted to end.

With a helpless moan, I parted my lips wider, strained onto my toes the better to absorb more of the experience.

Ax made a gruff sound that disintegrated beneath our frenzied kiss. His hold intensified until we were plastered together from chest to thigh. Until the unmistakable imprint of his thick, aroused manhood blazed hot and potent against my belly.

My fingers convulsed in his hair as the memory of him inside me, possessing me, surged into life. Feverish need pooled between my thighs, hunger prising another moan from my throat.

Before it could be anywhere near sated Ax was pulling away, his gaze searingly possessive as it moved from my damp and tingling mouth to my eyes.

'Now that we've shown the world how hot we still are for each other, will you come inside with me and dance with your husband?' he asked, his tone husky but firm.

Did he really want to dance with me or had he kissed me just for show?

The eyes burning into mine seemed to be attempting to read me just as hard as I was trying to reading him.

What was he looking for?

What was *I* looking for?

My scrambling senses flailed, and I was aghast at how easily and completely he'd overtaken my senses. How even now, with a few snatched breaths, I still couldn't think beyond the need to experience that kiss all over again. Yearning for more than just a kiss.

Realising he was awaiting a response, I scrambled the appropriate words together. 'Yes. If I must.'

He swooped down to pick up my discarded phone, then linked his fingers with mine before tugging me after him.

The crowd parted at our re-entrance, and some of the gazes I met were alight with the knowledge of what we'd been doing out on the balcony.

Being mired in my confused emotions saved me feeling embarrassment at those looks. It also made me pliant enough to survive half of the slow waltz with Axios before my senses began to return.

The reality of finding myself plastered to my husband once more, with the effects of that kiss still lingering in the form of my peaked nipples and erratic breathing, made me glance wildly around, avoiding his gaze as I tried to gather my shredded composure.

'Look at me, Calypso,' he instructed gruffly.

Almost helplessly I met his gaze.

His expression was studiously neutral but his eyes glinted with residual emotion. 'What just happened is nothing to be ashamed of,' he said gruffly. 'In fact, some might think it…fortunate that we're compatible in some ways.'

I wanted to laugh, because he was oh, so savvy about such things. While I continued to flounder.

'Don't you think it's a touch…*needy* to feel you have to be the centre of everyone's attention?' I asked.

The arrogant smile he slanted down at me said he didn't care one way or the other what people thought.

'I don't wish to be the centre of everyone's attention. Just yours,' he drawled.

For the sake of our audience, I sternly reminded myself, even as my insides lurched and jumped with misguided giddiness.

To mitigate that sensation I pressed my lips together and swayed in his arms, hoping the music would soothe my ragged nerves and spirit the rest of this infernal night away.

But, as fate had shown me time and again, hopes and dreams belonged in fairy tales. Axios danced me through three more tunes before conceding the fourth to the mayor.

Thereafter, quickly reclaimed by my so-called doting husband, we moved from group to group, his hand firm on my waist and his piercing grey eyes smiling down at me through each introduction.

His acting skills were exceptional. Our guests lapped up every soft caress, indulgently smiling at my every recounting of why I'd been away as if it was a true Greek love story.

We stopped within every circle long enough to project an image of cordiality before moving on. And I regurgitated the practised story of my absence until I feared I was blue in the face. Until I was ready to scream the truth to the whole world.

Perhaps his shark-like instincts sensed my frazzling composure. Because Ax turned to me as I impatiently waved away another offer of champagne and started to open my clutch.

'What is it?' he asked.

Remembering he had possession of my phone, I looked at him. 'Can I have my phone back? I want to check on Andreos.'

His gaze rested on my face for several beats. Thinking he wasn't going to answer, I was surprised when he turned to the business acquaintances he'd been talking to.

'It's time for us to take our leave. My beloved cannot bear to be away from our son for long, and I find that I'm not far behind her in that sentiment.'

Indulgent laughter followed, quick goodbyes were said, and before I knew it we were heading out to the waiting limo.

Settled into the back seat, I found my senses once again crowded with the sight and sound of Axios. My inability to dismiss him.

'I could've gone home on my own. You didn't need to leave with me.'

One sleek eyebrow spiked. 'You wanted me to stay there and reverse the effect of everything we've achieved this evening?' he replied.

'You seem to be a master at convincing everyone that the moon is made of caviar. I'm sure they'll believe whatever you tell them.'

He gave a low, deep laugh. Which drained away as his eyes latched to my face. 'Perhaps I do have this unique gift you speak of, but I also meant what I said. I've missed months of my son's life. I don't intend to miss any more.'

'For how long?'

His whole body froze. 'Excuse me?'

'How long do you think this phase of yours will last?'

'You have lost me…'

A thought that had been niggling me despite his assertion rose to the fore. 'You didn't want this marriage and we never got around to discussing children. We're only here because a condom failed at the crucial juncture.'

'And you think those circumstances beyond my control preclude me from assuming my mantle of responsibility towards my son? Did it you?'

'I… It's different.'

'How?' he challenged.

'I love him! I would do anything for him. While you…'

'What? Speak your mind, *glikia mou*.'

'You just want to show off your virility.'

After several tense seconds he settled back in his seat. 'You're right. I do want to show him off. He is my son, after all. As for showing off my virility—again, the evidence is there for all to see. But, while you're wrong if you think you're the only one invested in Andreos's existence, I'm aware that only time will prove what I say to you. So I guess the ball's in your court on that one.'

'How so?'

'You're the one who's in a hurry to leave. You say you were always going to come back? I'm choosing to believe you. If you want to ensure my devotion to my son is as strong as yours, then you need to rethink the urgency of your divorce demands, do you not, *pethi mou*?'

Despite his silky tone his eyes bored into mine in the dark interior of the car, and the notion that he was attempting to see right into my soul assailed me.

The thick lump wedged in my throat stalled my answer. Because *time* was the one commodity I might not have.

CHAPTER SEVEN

THE LIMO SWEEPING through the gates of his Athens mansion drew from me a breath of relief. But I soon realised I wasn't going to be set free from Ax's presence when he trailed me up the stairs to the door of Andreos's room.

I hesitated before the doors—partly because I didn't want to bring charged tension into Andreos's presence and partly because a tiny part of me wanted space to dissect everything that had happened this evening. But the greater part of me wanted to keep my son all to myself. Just for a little while.

A sharp cry from within dissipated every thought.

As Ax held the door open for me I entered the room in time to see Sophia lifting Andreos from his changing mat.

She stopped and smiled when she saw us. 'Good evening, Kyria Xenakis. You're just in time for Andreos's midnight feed. Would you like me to warm the bottle for you?'

I waved her away and Ax strode forward to take Andreos from her arms. 'Go to bed, Sophia. I'll take care of it.'

With a smiling nod, the young girl retreated to the adjoining bedroom, shutting the door behind her.

Ax adjusted his hold on Andreos, his strong hands lifting him aloft so they were face to face. My breath caught and, recalling his words in the car, I watched father and son stare at each other, one expression showing unabashed curiosity while the other probed with raw intensity as Axios absorbed his son's every expression as if hoarding it for his memory.

A little ashamed at questioning his motives in the car, I bit my lip as something settled inside me. No matter our personal angst, Axios cared for his son. Perhaps in time he'd love him almost as much as I did.

In that moment I wanted to tell him he would have years of special moments like this if I didn't manage to defuse the time bomb ticking inside me, but the words remained locked tight in my throat, the need not to have this time diluted with unwelcome outside influence stilling my tongue as I joined them.

Sensing another presence, Andreos turned towards me, his chubby arms windmilling as he babbled in delight. Then delight turned into familiar irritation as hunger kicked in and he whimpered his displeasure.

'Someone is impatient for his feed,' Ax mused, before his gaze dropped pointedly to my chest.

A fierce blush suffused my face. My breasts had been growing heavier in the last couple of hours. Even without the need to feed him myself I would have needed to express some milk before going to bed.

Expecting Ax to hand him over, I watched in surprise when he headed to the antique rocking chair I used for feeding Andreos. 'You're staying?'

'Unless you have an objection?' he asked, and I realised it was a genuine query.

About to say yes, I stunned myself by shaking my head.

A look flitted across his face faster than I could decipher it before he nodded. Once I was seated in the chair, which I'd discovered had been in his family for generations, Ax handed Andreos over. Then he started to move towards the adjacent sofa.

'Um...' I said.

He turned immediately. 'What is it?'

'Can you help me with my dress?'

Piercing grey eyes darkened a fraction as they moved to the halter neck of my dress. He gave a brisk nod, and in one deft move freed the fastening.

I caught the front before I was completely exposed, but there was no hiding from Ax's focused attention as I positioned Andreos on my lap.

He latched on with greedy enthusiasm, one fist planted firmly on my breast while both chubby legs jerked up to wrap around the forearm of the hand I'd laid on his plump belly to steady him.

The familiar action tugged at my heartstrings and drew a smile.

'Does he always do that?' Ax rasped, his voice gruff with emotion.

For a precious few seconds I'd forgotten he was there, watching my every move, absorbing his son's routine. Now my gaze met his and I nodded shakily, strangely overcome to be sharing this little snippet of time with the man who'd helped create my precious son.

'Since he was two and a half months old. I think it's his way of telling me to stay put. He'll let me go when he's satisfied.'

Ax lounged back in his seat and crossed his legs, a curious, heart-stopping little smile playing at his sensuous lips. 'He's a Xenakis. He knows what he wants.'

That display of unabashed male pride would have been unbecoming from any other man. From Ax it was a solid statement acknowledging his progeny. Progeny that would be completely his if I lost my fight.

The lance of pain to my heart made my breath catch.

'What is it?' Ax asked sharply. 'Does it cause you pain?'

My gaze flew to his and I had to swallow before I could answer. 'The breastfeeding? No, it doesn't.'

His narrowed gaze moved from Andreos and back to me. 'Then what is it?'

I flailed internally as I tried to find a plausible response. 'I was just remembering our conversation in the car. Perhaps I was...a little harsh.'

One brow quirked, but it was minus the mockery I'd become used to. *'Perhaps?'*

'Okay, I was. I... I don't want us to butt heads over Andreos.'

His hands spread in a manner that suggested a truce. 'Neither do I, Calypso.'

As milestones went, this was another sizeable one in an evening filled with small earthquakes of surprise. My breath caught. Andreos whimpered. I looked down to find eyes so much his father's wide and curious upon me. Reading my every expression just as intently as his father probed beneath my skin.

'Maybe we should discuss this further later?'

'I agree,' Ax responded, then proceeded to watch me with hawk-like intensity all through the feed.

When I transferred Andreos to my other breast Ax's gaze tracked my blush after dropping once to my nipple. But this time my self-consciousness was reduced. The natural act of providing sustenance for my baby was one I realised I didn't mind sharing with his father.

Just as abruptly as he'd wrapped his sweet limbs around my arm Andreos dropped his legs and he detached with a loud plop.

Ax rose and sauntered over, wordlessly securing my dress as I sat Andreos on my lap and rubbed his back. I was rewarded with a loud burp three minutes later.

With a gentle caress of his son's head, Ax stepped away. 'I have a few phone calls to make. I'll meet you in my suite when you're done here.'

The reminder that our suites were interconnecting and the memory of what had happened in his sent a pulse of electricity through me as I watched him walk away.

His icy indifference had receded. Something had happened on that balcony tonight. The realisation that Ax didn't tar me with the same brush as my father had eased something in me.

I was pondering the new path this might lead to as I laid a sleepy Andreos back in his cot and then entered the suite forty-five minutes later.

Both the living room and bedroom in Ax's suite were empty. Entering my own suite, I crossed to the dressing room, quickly undressed, then slid on my night slip before throwing a matching silk gown over it.

I was brushing my hair at my dressing table when Ax walked in, both hands in his pockets.

He paused in the doorway, his eyes holding a skin-tingling expression and resting on me for a long moment before he prowled forward. He stopped behind me and I waited, my breath locked in my throat as one hand reached out, tugged the brush from me and slowly dragged it through my hair.

For a full minute he said nothing, and the hypnotic sensation of his movements flooded my system with torrid lust.

'You'll be pleased to know our strategy worked,' he drawled eventually. 'My family and friends believe we are happily reunited. I expect my business partners to fall in line by morning.'

Something shook inside me. The easy way he laid his hand on me was a stronger warning that things were shifting. That the conversation on the balcony had indeed sparked much more than a rebellion and the need to answer it in both of us.

Before I could heed the warning he nudged me to my feet, slid his hand down my arm to link with my fingers. 'Come with me.'

Even the imperious tone had altered, become less...autocratic.

I followed him into his living room.

There, on a wide screen, he'd set up the video I'd given him. 'Ax...?'

'I haven't had a chance to watch this yet. Or perhaps I was putting it off,' he said, with a hint of vulnerability in his voice that stunned me enough to take the seat next to him when he settled on the plush sofa.

'You want to watch it now?' I asked.

His eyes met mine, held me in place. 'Yes,' he stated simply.

With a flick of his finger on the remote the video came to life. The simple but clean walls of the hospital room in Kenya came into view before the camera swung over the machines to rest on my heavily pregnant form.

My breath strangled into nothing as the uniquely intimate and life-changing event unfolded on the screen, tugging at the very heart of me.

Beside me Ax caught his breath audibly as he watched a contraction hit me, and the hand that still held mine tightened. This footage had been taken about ten minutes before Andreos's birth. Ax watched every frame without taking his gaze off the screen, his whole body rapt as Andreos was laid in my arms for the first time. He watched me kiss his wrinkled forehead, heard me murmur, 'My little miracle,' as tears of joy spilled down my face.

His throat moved in a swallow when the video ended, and he immediately hit 'rewind' and watched it all over again.

Then his gaze shifted to me.

'Ax...'

He shook his head, raised my hand to his mouth, gently kissed the back of it. 'It was a magnificent birth.'

Deep inside me something *essential* melted, pulling me into a dangerous spell I wasn't entirely certain I wanted to fight. Emotion clogging my throat, I smiled.

'He's a beautiful boy,' he rasped, a throb of deep pride in his voice.

I blinked unbidden tears away. 'Yes. He is.'

'As beautiful as his mother.'

As my breath caught all over again, his thumb rubbed across my knuckles.

'Again you have my thanks—especially since you had to go through that alone.'

'I'd do anything for him,' I replied, and I knew the fervent well of my emotion had registered with him.

For the longest time he simply stared, then his gaze returned to the screen, his vision going a little hazy. 'The reality of him—' He stopped. 'He may be an unexpected arrival in my life, but I want the chance to do right by him. To do things differently—'

Again he stopped, prompting questions I couldn't halt.

'Differently from what? Your father? I noticed your stiff interaction at the wedding, then again at the family mixer, and assumed *I* was to blame.'

He shook his head. 'Our issues go back a little further. I was still a teenager when my grandfather announced that I was to be his successor. In his eyes my father didn't have what it took to make the tougher decisions.' A muscle ticked in his jaw as his lips firmed. 'My father disagreed. He attempted to prove my grandfather wrong.'

I frowned. 'How?'

'My grandfather temporarily handed him the reins of the company. Six months later my father suffered a breakdown brought on by extreme stress. He didn't take the prognosis well.'

'What did he do?'

'He believed my grandfather had humiliated him. And when my grandfather made it known that he'd seen me as his successor all along, my father…didn't take it well. His resentment festered irreparably.' His lips twisted. 'Which, in a nutshell, is the story of my whole family.'

'But you all seem so…*united*—give or take the odd vibe or two.'

He shrugged cynically. 'Self-interest, especially where wealth is concerned, has a way of binding even the most dissenting individuals. My father may not like the status quo but he's had to accept it.'

'Is there no way to repair your relationship?'

A hint of bleakness came and went in his eyes within a heartbeat. 'We've accepted our strengths and our weaknesses. My father may resent me for seemingly usurping him, but he doesn't want the role.'

'You offered it to him?'

His lips thinned. 'A few years ago I suggested a partnership. He refused.'

'He wanted all or nothing?'

His lips twisted. 'Don't we all?'

Pain lashed me. 'Not all of us. Our fathers, maybe.'

Grey eyes met mine and a moment of affinity lingered between us, threatening to burrow into vulnerable places.

I cleared my throat. 'Is that why you're determined to try with Andreos?'

He'd said on the balcony that he was attempting to be different. The part of me that wasn't terrified of what the future held desperately craved to see that difference.

The question took him aback, and a naked yearning blanketed his features before he mastered it. 'Is it wrong to wish for a better outcome with my son than that between my father and I?' he rasped.

Again, a deep, sacred sensation pulled at me. Harder. Stronger. Making it impossible to breathe.

Despite the danger of falling under the silken spell he was weaving, I laid my hand on his arm. 'No, it's not.'

His gaze dropped to my hand. Silence charged with electricity filled the room as something flashed in his eyes. Primal and fierce. The video and our conversation had done something to him. Shifted the dynamic.

I was tempted to run. To hide from it. But I was just as determined not to regress.

'So…where do we go from here? After tonight, I mean?'

His eyes dropped to my lips, then moved back up to seize mine.

'Now we consolidate on what we've started,' he murmured huskily.

I wanted to ask for clarity. Wanted to ask whether he meant us or the larger world. But his fingers wound tighter around mine, his free hand rising to slide into my hair, dragging over my scalp in a wickedly evocative move that snatched the air from my lungs and hardened my nipples into aroused peaks.

Those penetrating eyes tracked my every reaction, his nostrils flaring when he caught the visible signs of my agitated state.

'And how do you propose to do that?' I asked.

'By making things real both inside and outside of the marriage bed,' he stated, his voice deep and sure.

Lightning-hot excitement charged through me, the need to experience this altered Axios overwhelming me. Would the change he wanted with his son manifest itself with me too, even in the short time I might have?

Only one way to find out.

I tugged myself free and stood to my feet.

Mutiny flashed in his eyes.

When he started to reach for me, I held up a hand. 'If you want me to change my mind convince me that you're worth it,' I said.

Then I fled.

I went after her like a beast possessed.

She was mine.

My wife.

All evening I'd caught tantalising glimpses of her. The way she moved, the thoughtful way she responded to strangers' rabid curiosity, even accommodating Stavros…

I'd run the gamut from telling myself I didn't care about all the facets of herself she was revealing to feeling a determination to pin her down and extract every last secret from her.

But that video…

Her father was in possession of a hundred million euros. My name could have commanded an entire wing in a plush private hospital. And yet Calypso had chosen to deliver our son in a state-run hospital in Kenya with third-rate equipment. And, not only that, she'd done all that with an inner strength that shone through the footage, surrounded by people who had clearly held her in high regard.

She'd spent some of the past year volunteering. I couldn't name a single member of my family who would devote their time to charity unless it came with a tax write-off or a star-studded gala where they could show off their diamonds.

And besides the awe-inspiring act of giving birth, the most striking thing about Calypso Xenakis was the determination I'd seen on her face in that video.

It had sparked something inside me. A need for...*more*.

That intoxicating little incident on the sofa this afternoon, compounded by the kiss on the balcony this evening and watching her nurse our son, was what had finally fully awakened the primitive beast inside me. The video was evidence of her strength and resilience, despite my less than stellar behaviour last year.

Even confessing the true relationship between myself and my father—a subject I'd never discussed with another living soul—had felt...liberating. That we were both products of our circumstances had triggered an affinity in us that had in turn laid out a different way to approach what had been thrust on us.

Perhaps it didn't need to be finite.

That admission to do things differently this time had surprisingly settled deep inside me.

The Calypso I'd married had possessed a banked fire.

The woman who'd returned from her mysterious absence was flame and grit.

Heat I was unashamedly drawn to. Grit I wanted to explore.

Both characteristics drove me after her.

I arrived in the suite just as she was entering her own bedroom. I stopped her with the simple act of capturing her delicate wrist. The electricity of contact simply reaffirmed my decision.

She waited, one eyebrow elevated.

Theos mou, did she know how alluring she was, with her blue eyes daring me even as her agitated breathing announced that she wasn't unaffected by this insane chemistry?

'I want you, Calypso. And unless I'm wildly off-base you want me too.'

'That's it? Surely you have better negotiating skills than that, Axios?' she taunted.

The breathless sound of my name on her lips escalated the heat pounding through my bloodstream. I wanted to kiss her. To prove with deeds instead of words how combustible this thing between us was.

'You're not the same woman I left on Agistros last year. I see that now.'

More than that, she had the power to walk away again if she chose.

The strange sensation of being on slippery ground forced me into further speech, even as I questioned the wisdom of the route I was taking.

'Come to my bed—not because of our agreement or because of your ultimatum. Do it because you want to. Because we can make each other feel things we've never experienced before.'

Her lips parted in a soft gasp. 'You… I do that to you?'

I couldn't help the hoarse laughter that was ejected from my throat. I dropped her wrist and removed myself several mind-clearing paces away.

'Barely two hours ago, I was close to saying to hell with propriety and taking you on that balcony. What do *you* think?'

Despite the heat flaming up her face her shoulders went back, accepting her power over me. It was all I could do to remain standing where I was and not stride across the room to demonstrate just how much the hunger inside me lashed through her too.

But this was too important.

I wasn't an animal, and she needed to grant me clear acknowledgement of her desire before it would work. But it *was* going to work. There were no viable alternatives to allay this…this insane *craving* inside me save for the highly unsatisfactory avenue of self-pleasure, which I wasn't willing to consider any more.

'I'm a man with healthy appetites, Calypso. And I haven't had sex since our wedding night. Do you know that?'

She gave another gasp, this time a heated one that went straight to my groin. She backed against the door, as if putting distance between herself and the live wire of desire lashing us would work.

Eyes wide, she lifted her chin in further challenge. 'How do I know that's true?'

Frustration threatened to erupt. I tamped it down. 'I don't make a habit of lying, *yineka mou*. Regardless of how we came together, I took a vow I intend to honour until I'm no longer bound by it. But if you don't believe me I can give you the number of a top investigator and you can discover the truth for yourself.'

'Even if I believe you, maybe you didn't seek another woman's bed because you didn't want to jeopardise your precious deal.'

She was really good at pushing my buttons. And the curious thing was that I preferred this version of Calypso to the one who'd glided down the aisle a little over a year ago.

I shrugged off my tuxedo, watched her gaze cling to my torso before another blush pinkened her smooth skin. 'Whatever my reason for staying celibate, I wish it to end now.'

'Because you decree it?'

'Because you're woman enough to admit you want me too. Because *when* you come to my bed it'll be because your needs are as strong as mine and you're not ashamed to give in to them.'

Tossing the jacket aside, I gave in to the urge and returned to her, my senses jumping at the promise of decadent friction when she swallowed but stayed her ground. And then, because I wasn't above playing dirty to get my way, I unbuttoned one shirt stud. Then another.

Brazenly, I revelled in the tremor that went through her lush frame as her eyes followed my undressing with abashed appreciation. A layer of femininity which might have been there all along or I might have missed called to the beast in me.

'I want to lay you on my bed…make you cry out my name in climax.'

Her eyelashes fluttered before sweeping down. That telltale sign that she was hiding something nearly derailed me. It certainly froze me in place, congealing my insides with the knowledge that, far from being a forward-thinking man, some things were sacred to me.

'Tell me what you're thinking.'

She remained silent for far too long. In real time it was probably a handful of seconds. But it was enough to unnerve me. Enough that when she deigned to lift those hypnotising eyes to mine all that remained in me was a frenzied roar.

I watched her lips move but didn't hear the words she uttered. Her eyes grew wider, possibly at my expression. She started to step back.

I closed the gap between us and tugged her to me. With her heavy magnificent breasts pressed against my chest all I wanted was to lose myself in her. To slay this terrible *need*.

Her nostrils quivered as she inhaled rapidly. Against my chest her hands fluttered, and a trembling I wanted to believe had nothing to do with sex seized her.

'Axios…'

'I said I want to be different, Calypso. Take this leap with me?'

But even as her eyes widened at my words she hesitated, her lower lip caught between her teeth, taunting me with the prospect of unaccustomed denial.

And all the while my insides churned with emotions I didn't want to examine.

All the while delicate tremors filtered through her body and her breathing grew more erratic with her undeniable arousal.

I was on the very edge of my sanity when Calypso's fingers whispered over the button above my navel, toyed with the stud for a second before fluttering away again. Eyes that refused to meet mine remained fixed on my chest.

She released her lip and I fought the urge to lean down and bite the plump, wet curve.

Before her wicked hands could further wreck me, I caught them in one hand. 'Calypso, look at me.'

After an eternity her lashes lifted. Dark blue hypnotic pools pulled me in, threatening to drown me.

'Say the words. I want to hear them,' I pressed, aware that my voice was a gravel-rough mess.

She inhaled. 'I'll take the leap with you. For now.'

I had to hand it to her—she knew how to time her negotiations to maximum effect. But I'd given my word and I wouldn't go back on it. Besides, the earlier we excised this fever from our systems the earlier we could start the extrication process.

The earlier I could return to my life as I knew and preferred it.

The punch of satisfaction I expected never arrived.

More...

'For now?' I repeated, dismissing the hollow echo of the words.

I steeped myself deeper in the moment. Revelled in the fingers gripping my shirt as if the small scrap of cotton would ground her. She swallowed again, then gave a nod.

I crooked a finger under her chin and nudged her head upward. 'Tell me, *pethi mou*,' I insisted.

'I want you,' she whispered.

The breathy little sound washed over my chin and throat,

making something frenzied and untamed leap inside me, filling me with the prospect of what 'more' could mean.

'More…' I pressed, wanting irrevocable confirmation that she wanted this.

Her chin lifted, her eyes gleaming boldly. 'I want to be in your bed. I want you to take me.'

I slid my hand up her delicate spine to tangle in her hair. To grip it and keep her attention on me. 'I want to make you mine again. Tell me you want that.'

Her fists bunched, a breathy little sound escaping her throat as she swayed closer. 'I want to be yours.'

Like over a breached dam, a torrent swelled inside me. Removing her silk dress was as simple as catching the fragile material and ripping it off her body.

She gasped, staring down at the tattered fabric at her feet before attempting to glare at me. 'I don't believe you did that.'

A smile caught me unawares. 'I didn't think you were that attached to it. If so, I'll buy you a dozen more,' I vowed thickly. Because the sight of her body, displaying changes after bearing my son in the form of slightly thicker hips, a rounded softness in her belly and, best of all, the heaviness of her breasts, had intensified the throbbing in my groin.

I was barely aware of sinking to my knees, framing her lush hips and pulling her to me. I welcomed the fingers clenching tight into my hair as my lips found the sensitive flesh below her navel and brazenly tasted her creamy skin. When she sagged against the door I went lower, removing her panties before catching one leg and throwing it over my shoulder so I could find the heart of her, the true feminine core that called to me with the strength of a dozen sirens.

'Ax!'

Her sweet cry urged me on, her taste a drug surging with unstoppable force through my bloodstream. I didn't relent until she was splintering in my arms, her moans music to my ears. Only then did I scoop her up and carry her to my bed to begin all over again.

Her head rolled on the pillow, her hair fanning out in a dark silken halo as her lips parted on hot little gasps as I rediscovered every delightful inch of her body.

'*Omorfi*…'

The word tumbled unbidden from my lips as I caught one pearled nipple in my mouth. And she *was* beautiful, with a certain indefinable layer of femininity and strength adding to her allure.

'When you glided up that aisle like an obedient wraith I had no idea you were hiding this…this steel and sensuality beneath that frothy gown.'

Her eyes widened in dazed surprise. 'Was that why you left the next morning? Because I wasn't what you expected?'

It was my turn to be stunned. To ponder how events had unfolded through her eyes. But now wasn't the time to admit I'd been unnerved then too. Just as I was now.

'No. My delivery wasn't great, but I believed leaving was best. However, *this*…' I slid a hand down her ribcage, revelled in her unfettered response '…was certainly a surprise.'

And the fact that she was even more responsive now threatened to annihilate my self-control completely.

Before I was entirely consumed I reached for a condom, donned it and accepted the enthralling welcome of her parted thighs. I slanted my lips over hers, unwilling to leave any feast unsatisfied as I entered her in one deep, glorifying thrust.

Pleasure detonated in a shower of fireworks as I seated myself deep within her. Felt her tighten around me, drawing me deeper. When she sought to shatter me further with needy whimpers and greedy hands I tore my lips from hers, gritted my teeth in an effort to make this last.

But of course the next layer of sweet torture waited in the wings. With her mouth free, and the nirvana of a higher plane of pleasure waiting, I watched her slide into that unique dimension, that place where her unfiltered pleasure rippled from her alluring lips.

'My God, you're so big. *So* deep. I feel every inch of you…'

A muted roar rumbled up my throat as her words threatened to completely unravel me.

Her nails sank into my back, ripping away another layer of control. And just like on that night I'd never been able to put out of my mind I realised she was unaware of herself, that pleasure had transported her into another dimension.

'Shall I roll my hips like that first time? That was incredible.'

'Calypso…' I wasn't sure whether saying her name was warning or encouragement. Either way, she didn't respond. She continued her mind-altering commentary. Commentary that fired a white-hot blaze inside me alongside the fiery one already raging from possessing her.

I stared down into her stunning, unguarded face as I pushed in and out of her, racing both of us towards that special peak.

Another man would have taken advantage of the situation, prised secrets from her subconscious while she was in this state. But that was an invasion my conscience wouldn't let me stomach for longer than a nanosecond.

So I refocused on the words tumbling from her lips, revelled in them for another reason altogether. Because they turned me on. Because no other woman had brought this unique, exquisite surprise to my bed. Because hearing her vocalise her pleasure charged mine in a way I'd never thought possible.

Increasing the tempo of my thrusts, I lowered my body to hers, drew her tighter against me. 'Wrap your legs around my waist, *omorfia mou*.'

With gratifying speed, she complied.

'Now, tell me more,' I growled in her ear. 'Tell me everything you're feeling.'

Whether she heard me or not, I didn't know, but the words spilled out.

Unmanned by her unfiltered longing, I kissed the corner of her luscious mouth and groaned when she chased mine when I withdrew.

'Kiss me. Please kiss me.'

'Say my name, *matia mou*. Say my name and I'll kiss you.'

'Axios,' she moaned. 'Kiss me, *please*, Axios.'

Unable to resist the sultry demand, I kissed her again. Felt her tighten around me in response and gritted my teeth to keep myself on that dizzying plateau for one more second. She was eroding every ounce of my willpower, pushing me towards the zenith long before I was ready.

And there was little I could do to stop it.

Especially not when my mind was already flying to the next time, to the next position.

She would be on top. Yes, she would ride me, her heavy breasts high and proud, while those unfettered words fell from her lips. The image was so potent, so vivid, I lost the ability to think straight.

My unguarded growl in response to that scenario pushed her higher. Her nails dug into my shoulders, her head thrashing on the pillow.

'Let go, Calypso. Now!'

The command set her free. With a sharp, sweet cry, she dissolved into uncontrollable convulsions, her body writhing beneath mine in innocently uncoordinated movements that finally shattered my control.

With a roar torn from deep within I succumbed to exquisite, untrammelled bliss. Time ceased to matter. I was aware I'd collapsed on top of her, one propped arm the only thing stopping me from crushing her. But her own arms were wrapped tight around me, as if holding me together.

The singular, searing thought that I wanted to remain

here *indefinitely* charged through my daze, forcing me to move. Forcing sanity back into this madness.

But even as I gathered her to me after my return from the bathroom she was unravelling me again, the hand on my chest reaching deeper as she turned her face to me.

'Ax?'

'Hmm?' Unfamiliar dread clenched my gut, escalating the notion that somewhere along the line I'd fallen under her mercy and her whim.

Her breath fluttered out in an almost reverent exhalation as her eyes lifted to mine. 'You're the only man I've ever been with. I just thought you should know.'

That gift, freely given when it could have been withheld in light of our circumstances, punched and winded me. The notion that opening up to her had possibly earned me this unsettled me even more.

Questions and wants and needs surged higher than before, racing to the tip of my tongue before circumspection halted them. I wanted more from her. But did I have more to give to her and to Andreos?

I pushed back the dismaying sensation.

She was staying…for now.

That unsettling little addendum would be tackled later. After much-needed regrouping.

'*Efkharisto.*'

The word emerged deeper, graver than I'd expected. I did nothing to offset it. Nothing but accept that things *had* to be different.

Nothing I'd seen of the marriages around me had fuelled a need to embroil myself in one—not when they strained so easily and threatened to break at the smallest hint of adversity.

But, in the hypothetical scenarios where marriage *had* crossed my mind, I'd known that unshaken faithfulness and stalwart support would be the cornerstone of its success. Not the kind of marriage held together by financial worth—the kind my grandfather had struggled to hold on to and ended up paying dearly for.

That reminder cooled my jets long enough to let in rational thought. Long enough to know that Calypso and I needed a base of trust from which to operate.

Which meant getting her to open up about her secrets…

I decided to come at it from a different angle. 'Are you ready to tell me why you chose to leave Greece?'

Her eyes shadowed and her lashes swept down. But before I could catch her chin and redirect her attention on me she lifted her gaze, her eyes boldly meeting mine with a resolution I wasn't sure whether to welcome or battle.

'Okay.'

Relief stunned me. 'Okay?'

She nodded. 'I want whatever time we have remaining to be peaceful.'

I forced my teeth not to grit at the reminder of a timescale. 'Good.'

A touch of nerves edged her features. When she went to move out of my arms, I caught her back. 'It would please me if you stayed right here for this.'

CHAPTER EIGHT

HE WAS UNRAVELLING ME with his low-voiced requests. With this side of him that hinted at the kind of man I'd dreamed of calling husband and father to my child. The kind of man who asked me to take a leap even when I knew that ultimately my path might lie elsewhere.

Tell him.

Maybe this could all turn out differently.

You could have more nights like this, far into the future.

But what if the worst happened? I couldn't put Andreos through that.

Besides, while Ax had readily agreed to my stipulation… for now…he'd given me no insight as to what would happen beyond that.

But I'd bought myself a little more time—and, *Theos mou*, I wanted to experience this again. And again. Without angst or acrimony.

Even now, with my limbs weak from their physical and emotional expenditure, hunger was slowly gathering force, anticipation adding fuel to a fire which didn't seem in a hurry to burn itself out. And if all it took was a simple recounting of my year, where was the harm?

I pushed away the voice urging caution and when I opened my mouth the words that tumbled out surprised even me.

'My grandmother was a feminists' feminist. She hated every aspect of a patriarchy that dictated what she could and couldn't do. She especially hated it when my grandfather died and everyone expected her to remarry because she had a young daughter to care for.'

I caught the edge of Ax's puzzled frown and couldn't help the smile that tugged at my lips.

'She never did remarry, but after she lost her house she was forced to live with my parents. I grew up in the shadows of her rebellion. She urged me to stand my ground. To question everything.'

His frown cleared, a droll look entering his grey eyes. 'Ah. I see.'

'Needless to say she butted heads with my father almost on a daily basis.'

Ax tensed. Not wanting the mood tarnished, I passed my hand over his chest—a soothing gesture that worked with Andreos but might not work with his father. My breath caught when he exhaled after a handful of seconds.

'Anyway, I found out on my wedding day that she'd left me an envelope. My mother was to give it to me when she thought I needed it.'

A trace of regret flashed across his face. 'She thought you'd need it the day you married me.'

It wasn't a question, more of an acceptance of how things had turned out.

I shrugged. 'Besides my father, none of us knew much about you. What little I knew before we met at the altar I found out online,' I said, recognising but unable to stop the hint of censure in my tone.

The regret in his eyes deepened as he nodded. 'I accept that. So your father really kept you in the dark about everything?'

'Yes. And it wasn't anything new. He did that most of my life.'

'Why?'

The whisper of family shame slithered over my skin. 'Surely you've heard the rumours?'

'I prefer facts to rumours,' he stated.

I didn't bother to ask what he'd heard. I wanted this discussion over as quickly as possible.

'My mother left home when I was fifteen. She'd met another man and was planning on leaving my father. But they were involved in an accident. The man died. My mother survived—obviously—but she suffered a spine injury and… Well, you've seen her. My father brought her back home and promised to take care of her—under certain conditions.'

The hand that had been lazily trailing through my hair froze. 'It seems your father makes a habit of using people's misfortunes against them.'

I couldn't deny that truth. And when Ax used his hold to gently propel my gaze up to his I couldn't hide it from him.

Whatever he saw in my face made him exhale again. 'I used to think that was an encompassing Petras family trait,' he murmured.

'*Used* to?' Did that mean he'd changed his mind? That he *wasn't* tarring me with the same brush as my father any more?

He continued to stare at me for a long stretch. 'You're nothing like him. You have a formidable inner strength that he doesn't—clearly inherited from your grandmother,' he said.

The low, gruff words opened up a fountain of emotion inside me that stopped my breath, especially when he brushed his lips over mine, as if wanting to seal the words in.

Getting carried away would have been so easy, but I forced myself to pull back. 'Anyway, I moved from under my father's thumb to under yours without any intermission—'

He stiffened, his face growing a shade paler. 'Under my thumb? I made you feel like that?'

I shrugged. 'You dictated where I would live. How I would live. Without giving me a say. So when you told me to find a way… I did.'

His jaw tightened and after a moment he nodded. 'I don't blame you for staging a rebellion. I would have in your shoes too. Perhaps not with anonymity but…that's understandable considering my reaction to our marriage.'

Tears prickled my eyes, threatening to spill at the thought that he was seeing things from my side. 'Anyway, my grandmother's letter left details of a Swiss bank account in my name. I went to Switzerland to see what it was all about. She'd left me the means to live under a new identity if I chose. There was also a box with some of her things in it.'

'That's how you were able to live without detection for a year?' he said.

I nodded. 'I think she meant me to use it more as a way to rebel against my father than a way—'

'For you to escape your new husband?' he finished with terse amusement.

'Either way, it seemed like a sign.'

A touch of hardness entered his eyes. 'Leaving your husband tearing his hair out for a year.'

'You weren't my husband. You especially weren't interested in being one the morning after the wedding. You married me to save your precious company, so don't pretend my absence caused you any personal slight or even—heaven forbid—any *anxiety*!'

'You carried my name. You were supposed to be under my care. Believe me, your disappearance was punishment enough—especially when I was left imagining the worst,' he rasped in a raw tone.

Plastered to him as I was, I felt the shudder that shook his frame, and his set jaw and the flash of bleakness in his eyes spoke to a vulnerability I'd never have imagined him capable of until tonight.

I stopped breathing, because… No, I hadn't quite thought about it. 'It wasn't just our forced marriage, Axios. My father was threatening my mother too.'

Fury flashed in his eyes. 'What?'

'He wanted to keep me in line through her. But she made me promise I wouldn't stay if I was unhappy. It all got a bit too much.'

'Did he carry out his threat?'

I shook my head. 'I'm guessing he was too busy playing with his windfall.'

The monthly phone calls with my mother had assured me she was okay, and had been all the wind beneath my wings I'd needed to stay away.

He bit out a tight curse and threw an arm over his forehead. 'Your father has a lot to answer for, but he's saved himself a trouncing by leaving your mother alone,' he growled. After a moment, his gaze pierced mine again. 'My investigators eventually traced your flight from Greece to Switzerland and assured me that my wife had simply chosen to run away of her own accord. At least now I know how you managed to avoid detection after you left Geneva, but perhaps you'd be so kind as to finish telling me where you went?'

The pulse of anguish still underlined his anger, but knowing it wasn't directed at me made it easier to finish my retelling.

'I took a train to Strasbourg and then wandered through Europe for a time before heading to South-East Asia. After that I made my way through Africa.'

All the while keeping in touch with Dr Trudeau and praying for my baby's continued health.

'When did you know you were pregnant with Andreos?' he rasped.

My stomach hollowed out in remembrance, and it took every ounce of self-control not to show how that fateful day still affected me. How the possibility that I would never meet my child had left me broken and sobbing for one day straight, until the fervent prayers had begun.

'I found out early. In Switzerland.'

He waited, his gaze imploring me for more. But I had nothing more to give. Nothing that wouldn't see the precious time I had left with Andreos compromised.

And it would be. It was clear Axios was deeply possessive and protective of his son. Over the past few days I'd learned just how meticulous and all-powerful he could be. I couldn't afford for the time I had with my baby to be compromised.

Or, on the flipside, he simply wouldn't care.

Pain snaked through me, dulling my heartbeat. No, he was better off not knowing.

'Why Kenya?' he asked, tugging me back to the present.

'Because I was seven months pregnant when I got there. Because I loved it there and knew I wouldn't be able to travel. I chose to stay and have Andreos there.'

Again, he lapsed into contemplative silence, those piercing grey eyes pinning me to the bed. Then, 'Thank you for telling me,' he said simply. Gruffly.

Tears prickled. To hide them, I lowered my head until our lips were a whisper apart. He didn't protest. His eyes simply went molten and his hard body stirred beneath mine as I closed the gap and helped myself to the magic of his kiss.

He allowed my exploration for a minute. Allowed the tentative probe and the slide of my tongue against his in a deeper kiss while the hand around my waist moved in a slow caress up and down my back, until he boldly cupped my bottom and brought me into brazen contact with his impressive arousal.

Then he flipped me over and took complete control, effectively emptying my brain of everything but the naked desire snaking through my body, setting me alight with a need so acute all I could do was let it wholly consume me.

Nevertheless, his warning ricocheted in my head long after our bodies had cooled. Long after his deep, steady breathing indicated sleep.

Because telling myself I didn't care what my actions had caused Axios after I took up the fight for my health, that I wasn't important enough to cause a ripple in his existence, didn't quite ring true in my head. I cared. Even if marrying him and taking his name had been a transaction dictated by my father for financial gain, our coming together had produced a son. And that mattered. Whether I liked it or not, Axios mattered to me. More than perhaps was wise.

The intensifying ache inside that reminded me I might have less time than I imagined added to the turmoil churning inside me, keeping me awake as dawn approached. Eventually mental exhaustion won out, and I fell into a sleep fuelled with pleasure and pain, blissful happiness and acute sadness.

Thankfully I was in a state of happiness when I resurfaced from sleep to the sound of a cooing baby.

'*Kalimera*, my angel,' I murmured, my drowsy awakening made all the better by my sweet baby's enthusiastic babble and the innocent smell of his freshly bathed body.

Eyes still closed, I felt my heart bursting with a joy that widened my smile.

'He's been very patient as he waited for his mama to wake, but I fear that state is about to be over,' drawled the deep, masculine voice of my baby's father.

My eyes flew open, the reminder of where I was and what had transpired last night fracturing my smile as I encountered the arresting image of a rudely vibrant Axios, one hand propping up his head and the other resting lightly on his son's stomach.

Andreos, his curious gaze switching between his father's face, mine, and just about every bright object it could touch upon, wriggled with impatience and babbled some more before letting out a cry that signalled he was well and truly done with waiting to be fed.

My lungs flattened with surprise and an unexpectedly sharp yearning as Ax shifted onto his back, lifted his son and held him aloft, a drop-dead gorgeous smile breaking out on his face as father and son stared at each other.

'You've made it this far, *o moro mou*. Give it another half-minute and you will be rewarded, hmm?' he teased.

I sat up, unable to help my blush and self-consciousness at the reminder that I was naked under the sheets.

After anointing his son's forehead with a gentle kiss, Axios turned to watch me sit up and arrange the pillows around me in preparation to feed an increasingly impatient Andreos.

When I was settled, Axios handed him over. And, just like last night, he didn't seem in a hurry to leave. In fact, he settled back on his pillow, his gaze unashamedly fixed on me as I settled our son at my breast.

Sunlight streamed through the partially opened curtain, bathing the parts of Axios I could see in mouthwatering relief—mainly his very naked, very chiselled torso. The effort it took to drag my gaze away and avoid the incisive eyes was depressingly monumental.

'I… What time is it?'

'It's a little after nine,' he answered, reaching out to caress his son's bare, plump foot. 'You were out of it when the monitor signalled that Andreos was awake. Sophia was about to give him a bottle, but I thought I'd bring him to you instead.'

I nodded, my throat clogging at the picture of togetherness and domestic bliss his words painted. Before I could stop myself, might-have-beens crowded my heart and I stared down at Andreos, painfully aware of Ax's presence in the pictures that filled my mind.

A little desperately, I reminded myself that this was all temporary. A short stretch of time to enjoy with my son before—

'Calypso?'

I blinked, unable to stop myself from being compelled to meet his gaze.

His eyes narrowed and he waited a beat before asking, 'What's wrong?'

I shook my head. 'It's nothing. I'm just a little tired, that's all.'

His shuttered gaze said he knew I was being evasive.

But he let it go. 'Not too tired to spend a few hours out of the city, I hope?'

Surprised, I stared at him. 'Out of the city?'

He nodded. 'I thought we could fly to Agistros for the afternoon. Agatha will organise a picnic for us and we'll spend a little time by the water.'

'Why?' I blurted.

He tensed slightly. 'On the rare occasion that I find myself with free time, I wish to spend it with our son. With you. I thought you might enjoy it. Am I wrong?'

I flushed. 'I... No.'

I'd planned nothing except spending a lazy day with Andreos. But the thought that Axios had plans, that he wanted to include us, kicked a wild little thrill into my bloodstream. A *dangerous* thrill. One I needed to nip in the bud sooner rather than later.

'I was planning on heading down to the beach here, but one beach is as good as any other, I suppose.'

A sly smile tilted one corner of his lip. 'I beg to differ. The beaches on Agistros rival the best in the world.'

My cheeky need to tease grew irresistible. 'According to *you*.'

His smile widened. 'Since I own it, my opinion is the only one that counts.'

The statement was so unapologetically arrogant I laughed. The sound seemed to arrest him, his eyes turning that molten shade that sent heat pulsing through my blood as we stared at each other.

'I believe this is the first time I've heard you laugh,' he rasped, his gaze raking over my face to settle brazenly on my mouth, almost effortlessly calling up another blush that suffused my face. 'I like it.'

Without warning his hand rose, his fingers trailing down one hot cheek and along my jaw before dropping down to recapture his son's foot.

Something heavy and urgent and profound shifted inside me. The thought that I didn't know this facet of the man I'd married and that I wanted to hit me square in the midriff, before flaring a deep yearning towards all the dark corners of my heart.

My smile felt frayed around the edges as I fought to maintain my composure, fought not to blurt out another prayer for things I didn't deserve.

I'd been given so much already.

Gloom wormed through my heart, the fear of what lay ahead and of fighting an uphill battle I might not win casting shadows over the gift of another day.

I was still struggling to banish it when a knock came on the door.

'Ah, right on time,' he murmured.

With another heart-stopping smile Axios launched himself out of bed. Naked and gladiator-like in all his glory, he walked across the suite, stopping long enough to pull on a dark dressing robe before heading for the door.

He returned a minute later, wheeling a solid silver trolley loaded with breakfast dishes. Bypassing his side of the bed, he stopped the trolley close to me before hitching up a thigh and settling himself next to me.

I tried and failed not to watch him pour coffee for himself, tea for me, and lift a large, succulent bowl of ripe strawberries.

He waited until I'd put Andreos over my shoulder and begun rubbing his back to elicit a burp before he shifted closer. Dipping one end of a strawberry into a bowl of rich cream, he leaned forward and then held the plump fruit against my lip.

'Taste.' His voice was deep, low. Hypnotising.

I leaned forward, parted my lips and took the offering. He watched me chew with the kind of rapt attention that could wreak havoc with a woman's sensibilities. Only after I'd swallowed did he help himself to a piece—minus the cream.

He alternated between feeding me and himself until the

bowl was empty, and then he set about piling more food on a plate.

'I can't eat all that,' I protested as I laid a very satisfied Andreos down beside me.

Axios shrugged, setting the tray in my lap. 'Our son is very demanding. And I get the feeling that state is only going to get more challenging. You'll need all the advantages you can get.'

About to tell him there was nothing I was anticipating more, the words stuck in my throat, and a bolt of heartache clenched my heart in a merciless vice.

Thankfully Axios was in the process of lifting a newspaper from a side pocket of the trolley, granting me a scant few seconds to get my emotions under control before he straightened and flicked the paper open.

Then a different sort of tension assailed me.

Seeing the pictures gracing the front page, I felt my gut twist. While I'd known we'd be under scrutiny last night, it hadn't occurred to me that we'd actually make front-page news.

The first picture had been taken when we'd first entered the ballroom. With our heads close together, Ax's masculine cheek almost touching mine, it hinted at an edgy intimacy between us that was almost too private.

From the look on Axios's face, he didn't feel the same.

He turned the page and my insides churned faster. There were more pictures, including some of us on the balcony, his hand splayed on my back, right before he pulled me in for that toe-curling kiss.

Axios stared at the pictures with something close to smug satisfaction.

'Did you know we were being photographed?' I asked, biting into a piece of ham-layered toast and concentrating on stirring my tea so I wouldn't have to look at the picture. At how the sight of Axios in a tuxedo continued to wreak havoc with my equilibrium. Nor face the fact that a very large part of me was wondering what true intimacy with this man whose name I'd taken would feel like.

He shrugged. 'I suspected we might be.'

That he was very much okay with it—had perhaps even wanted us to be photographed—was evident.

'And has it achieved what you meant it to?' I needed the reminder that this was all for a reason. For a definitive purpose which *didn't* include getting carried away with fairy tales.

With a flick of his fingers he folded the paper and picked up his coffee. 'If you mean are my business partners back on board, then, yes. But let's not rest on our laurels just yet,' he said.

Did that mean more socialising? More moments like those on the balcony? And why didn't that fill me with horror? Why was my belly tingling with thrilling anticipation?

Questions and sensations stayed with me through a quick shower and lingered while I chose a bikini set, pulled a floaty spaghetti-strap sundress over it and slipped my feet into stylish wedge shoes.

Stepping out to join Axios and Andreos two hours later, on the landscaped lawn that led to the helipad, I noticed we were flying in a different, larger chopper.

Axios caught my questioning look. 'This one is more insulated. To better protect Andreos's delicate eardrums,' he said, casting an indulgent glance at the baby nestled high in the crook of his arm.

Of course he *would* have a special helicopter that catered for babies!

With the sensation of having woken up in an alternative universe from which I couldn't escape, I walked beside him to the aircraft.

The trip, unlike last time, flew by, and before I knew it we were skimming the beaches of Agistros, the azure waters of the island sparkling in the sunlight.

The villa was just as breathtaking as it had been a year

ago, and this time, without deep trepidation blinding me, I was better able to appreciate it. Granted, there were other equally precarious emotions simmering beneath my skin, but just for today I let the dazed dream wash over me, revelling in simply *being* as Axios stepped out of the helicopter, reached to help me out and took control of Andreos's travel seat.

Expecting tension, in light of the way I'd departed the villa the last time, I breathed a sigh of relief when the staff, headed by Agatha, spilled out with welcoming smiles. It was obvious that news of Andreos had travelled as they cooed over him.

When Agatha carried him off to the kitchen to supervise the picnic preparation, I drifted into the living room with Axios.

Dressed in the most casual attire I'd seen him in so far— high-spec cargo trousers and a navy rugby shirt—he nevertheless still looked as if he'd stepped straight off the cover of a magazine.

To keep myself from shamelessly ogling him, I drifted over to the set of framed photos on one of the many antique cabinets gracing the room. There was a slightly faded one of an old man, his distinguished and distinctive features announcing him as Theodore Xenakis. Ax's grandfather. The man who'd been forced under duress to make an agreement that had changed lives—including mine.

Perhaps it wasn't the best choice of subject matter to bring up on what was meant to be a lazy day by the beach. But after hearing Axios open up about his father, I wanted to know more. Yearned to learn what had formed the man whose name I bore.

Once we'd made our way down to a private beach, tucked into the most stunning bay I'd ever seen in my life, I found myself asking, 'Did your grandfather ever live here on Agistros?'

He stiffened, but his tension eased almost immediately. 'In the latter part of his life, yes.'

There was more to that statement. 'Why? I mean, I've seen your family. I know you're dispersed all over Athens, and on several family-owned islands. I also know that Agistros belongs to you. So why did he live here? Did he need care?'

For the longest time I thought he wouldn't answer. When he did reply, his tone was low. Deep. As if remembering was painful.

'Before his company fell on hard times my grandfather invested in real estate and gifted islands to every family member. Neo has an island twenty miles from here.'

At the mention of his brother it was my turn to stiffen. 'I don't think Neo likes me.'

Ax's eyes glinted, a hard kind of amusement shifting in their depths. 'He's going through a...a situation.'

'A "situation"?'

'Something's been taken from him that he wasn't quite ready to part with,' he said cryptically.

I frowned. 'Someone's stolen from him?'

'In a manner of speaking.'

Recalling our conversation, I frowned. 'A woman?'

Again, dark amusement twisted Ax's lips. 'Yes. And a formidable one, I hear.'

Realising he wasn't going to elaborate, I pressed gently, 'So...about your grandfather...?'

A trace of bleakness whispered across his face. 'He left Kosima, his favourite island, for many reasons. But mainly because the strain of trying to save his company took a toll on his family, especially my grandmother. After she died we didn't deem it wise for him to remain on Kosima by himself. So he came to stay here.'

I wanted to probe deeper, find out why the once booming Xenakis empire had swan-dived to the brink of bankruptcy three years before his grandfather had died. But I held my tongue because I suspected my own family had had a hand in the Xenakis family's misfortune. Also, that flash of bleakness resonated inside me, his pain echoing mine.

Not wanting the day ruined by revisiting the animosity between our families, I stared at the stunning horizon, a different urge overtaking me. 'I wish I could paint this,' I murmured, almost to myself.

Ax turned to me. 'When was the last time you painted?'

Unsurprised that he knew of my passion, I answered, 'All through my pregnancy, and a short while after Andreos was born.'

'Why didn't you pursue your painting before?'

I shrugged. 'There wasn't much call for it on Nicrete.'

His silence was contemplative. 'You wanted to do something with it in Athens. Do you still want to?' he asked, a trace of guilt in his voice.

Not if I don't have much time left.

'Perhaps not full-time but…yes.'

'I would like to see you paint.'

Something melted inside me and I couldn't help my gasp. 'You would?'

He gave an abrupt nod. 'If you would allow it…very much.'

Again something tugged inside me, harder this time—a feeling of my world tilting, making me sway towards him.

To counteract it before I did something supremely unwise, I tugged my dress over my head. 'I'm going for a swim.'

With every step from sand to sea I felt his gaze burn into my skin, heating me up from the inside out. Thigh-deep, I dived into the cool, exquisite water, hoping it would wash away the discordant emotions zinging through me.

This really shouldn't be difficult. All we had to do was exist in the same space until I was absolutely certain Andreos would be safe and cared for, before I returned to Dr Trudeau in Switzerland to face my fate.

All I had to do was prevent myself from falling under Ax's spell. Surely it wasn't that hard?

Yes, it is. I feel more for him with every passing minute!

The weight of that verdict was so disturbing I didn't sense his presence until the second before he wrapped a strong arm around my waist.

His hair was slicked back, throwing the sharp, majestic angles of his face into stunning relief. Droplets of water sparkled on his face, a particularly tempting one clinging to his upper lip, evoking in me a wild need to lick it off.

'Andreos!' I protested.

'He's fine,' he said with hard gruffness as he pulled me closer, tangled my legs with his.

I looked over and sure enough our son was well-insulated by plump pillows, shaded by a large umbrella, happily playing with his rattle.

'Calypso…'

My name was a thick demand I couldn't resist. And when he pulled me into his arms and slanted his sensual lips across mine I gave in, my conflicting thoughts melting away under the heat of mounting passion.

Afterwards we returned and spread out on the blankets. A trace of trepidation returned, tingeing the closeness wrapping itself around us, a closeness I wanted to hang on to despite the uncertainty lurking in the future.

Because this version of Axios, who wanted to see me paint, who had opened up about his grandfather, was a version who could so easily worm his way into my heart.

On the Monday morning after our first trip to Agistros I arrived downstairs to find six high-spec easels and an assortment of expensive paints and brushes. Stunned, I blinked away tears as Axios presented them to me.

'You…you shouldn't have.'

He shook his head. 'You've denied your passion long

enough,' he said. 'A year longer than necessary because of me,' he added heavily.

Next he organised special transportation for my mother to visit. Having not seen each other for a year, our reunion was tearful, her joy over her grandson boundless.

Seeing her, reassuring myself that she was all right despite the pain still clouding her eyes, lifted a weight off my shoulders. And that melting sensation returned full force when Axios set out to charm her—a ploy that worked to dissipate the lingering tension between them once and for all.

From my father I heard nothing. And, frankly, it didn't overly bother me.

After that our lives fell into a pattern.

Weekdays were spent at the villa in Athens, with at least three evenings of the week spent at one social engagement or another, which inevitably made front-page news, while Saturday and Sunday were spent on Agistros.

It was almost idyllic—the only fly in the ointment Dr Trudeau's increasingly urgent emails and the knowledge that now I was assured of Ax's complete devotion to our son I had no cause to put my health issues on hold.

It was on one weekend a few weeks later, in the place we'd now designated our picnic spot, when he glanced over at me as he reclined on a shaded lounger with a sleepy Andreos dozing on his bare chest. Father and son were besotted with each other, the growing bond between them a source of untold joy to me.

'I'm flying to Bangkok on Tuesday for business.'

Since he never discussed his business arrangements with me I met his gaze in surprise, unwilling to expose the sharp sting that had arrived and lodged in my midriff. 'Okay...'

'You and Andreos can come with me.'

The swiftness with which the sting eased was dismaying—and a little terrifying. Enough to trigger a waspish response. 'Is that a question or a command?'

The flash of flint in his eyes stunned me. Hard on its

heels came the realisation that I much preferred his blinding smiles. The sexy growls when he was aroused. Even his sometimes mocking tones.

Theos, I'd fallen into a highly dangerous state of lust, complacency, and a host of other things I didn't want to name. One in particular had been gaining momentum, clamouring for attention I was too afraid to give it. It was there when I woke. It blanketed me before I fell asleep and teased my dreams. It was there now, pulsing beneath my skin as Ax's gaze locked on mine and another blinding smile made an appearance.

'It's whichever you find easiest to comply with.'

For some absurd reason my heart flipped over even as I wondered whether he was asking me along because the thought of being separated from us for any length of time was disagreeable to him or because of appearances.

His expression was mostly unreadable, but there was something there. A touch of apprehension I'd never seen before. And, though it was highly unwise to latch on to it, I found myself leaning towards it, indulging myself in the idea that he *cared* whether I agreed or not.

'How long is this trip going to last?'

'It's to finalise a new airline deal I've been working on for a year. It's been challenging at times, so I expect both sides will want to celebrate after the deed is done. Prepare to stay for the better part of a week. Did you travel to Thailand on your trip?' he asked, but his almost flippant query didn't fool me for one second.

Axios was a master at subtle inquisition. Over the past weeks he'd dropped several questions unexpectedly.

'No. My coin-flip landed in favour of Indonesia instead of Thailand, so I went to Bali.'

'Then this will be your chance to explore another country,' he replied smoothly, despite the trace of tension in the air.

Andreos chose that moment to make his displeasure at

the charged atmosphere known. Axios absently soothed a hand down his small back, but his eyes remained fixed on me.

When I reached for him Ax handed him over. Then he stayed sitting, his elbows resting on his knees.

'Will you come with me?' he asked, his eyes boring into mine.

And because that undeniable yearning for *more* wouldn't stop—because I craved this…*togetherness* more than I craved my next breath—I answered, 'Yes.'

CHAPTER NINE

TIME IS RUNNING OUT...

The unnerving sensation that time was slipping through my fingers had arrived like a thief in the night and stayed like an unwanted guest, permeating my every interaction with Calypso. I couldn't put my finger on *why* and nor did I have a clear-cut solution.

The sensation left me off-kilter and scowling as I climbed the steps into my plane two days later.

A lot of things I'd believed to be cut and dried had become nebulous in the past few weeks. The idea of marriage...of *staying* married, for instance...didn't evoke the same amount of resistance it had done a year or even a month ago. As for being a father...

Thoughts of Andreos immediately soothed a fraction of the chaos inside me. My son's existence had brought a deeper purpose to my life I wouldn't have believed possible had I not experienced it for myself. The chance to pass on my heritage to him, to teach him about the sacrifices his grandfather had made filled a bleak corner of my soul.

As for his mother...

The warmth I'd enjoyed with her over the past few weeks, watching her joy in painting and simply basking in the unit she and Andreos presented had subtly altered, leaving me with more questions than answers. Even more acute was the feeling of exposure after revealing so much of myself and the anguish her family's actions had caused mine.

Yes, but only one member of her family...not all of them...

My chest twinged with another sting of guilt. I'd learned from my grandfather's mistakes, applied his good mentoring to my life and avoided the bad. Shouldn't the same apply to Calypso? Especially when she'd been caught in the same web of greed as I had?

The urge to hash this out with her grew stronger. And

yet the fear of repeating the mistakes of last year, driving her away, stopped me.

It didn't help that over the last day or so she'd seemed under the weather, thereby curtailing any serious conversation I'd felt inclined to have or my reaching for that final resort of last resorts—tugging her into my arms in the dark of night and letting the mindless bliss of having her melt every fractious thought away.

Harmony and unstinting passion—it was a combination I would never have associated with her a few weeks ago, but I now craved to have it back.

My gaze fell on her as I entered the living area of the plane. She was chatting to one of the attendants, her alluring smile sparking heat in my bloodstream as she nodded to whatever was being said.

Unable to help myself, I let my gaze trail over her. The cream form-fitting jumpsuit caressed her luscious body from shoulder to ankle, its emphasis of her supple behind and lush breasts drying my mouth and reminding me that it had been three long days since I'd had the pleasure of her body.

The attendant departed, and as Calypso turned to sit I noticed the top buttons securing the front were left undone to reveal her impressive cleavage. My groin stirred harder and it was all I could do not to give a bad-tempered, frustrated groan.

I approached, dropping into the seat opposite her. She held Andreos like a buffer, her gaze stubbornly avoiding mine even though she was aware of my presence.

'The silent treatment isn't going to work where we're headed. You do know that, don't you?'

The blue eyes that finally deigned to meet mine were shadowed, her face still showing a hint of the paleness that raised an entirely new set of ruffled emotions inside me.

'Don't worry, Axios. I'll put on the appropriate performance when needed.'

Even her voice had lost a trace of that passionate lustre that fired up my blood.

'Are you all right?' The words were pulled from a deep, *needy* part of me.

Her eyes widened, then she nodded abruptly and her gaze dropped to Andreos. 'I'm fine. Just a slight…stomach ache.'

The unsettling sensation deepened, the niggling feeling that I was missing something escalating. 'Did you take anything for it? I'll get the attendant to bring you—'

She shook her head hastily when I reached for the intercom button, but I didn't miss the shadow that crossed her face, the knuckles that whitened in her lap.

'It's… I'm fine, Ax. I think I'll go and lie down with Andreos for a while after we take off.'

True to her word, the moment we reached cruising altitude she unbuckled herself, rose, and headed to the back of the plane with Andreos.

The urge to follow, to demand answers to the teeming questions ricocheting in my brain, was so strong I clenched my gut against the power of it.

I stayed put, forcing rationality over impulse. I had business to take care of, conference calls to make. And yet somewhere on that endless to-do list the looming issue of our agreement ticked louder.

An agreement I'd lately found myself re-examining with growing dissatisfaction.

Restlessness drove me to my feet. At the bar, I poured myself a cognac and tossed it back, hoping the bracing heat would knock some sense into me. All it did was emphasise the expanding hollow inside me and quicken this alien need demanding satisfaction.

Setting the glass down, I started to walk back to my seat—and then, unsurprised, I found myself moving towards the back of the plane.

After my soft knock elicited no response I turned the

door handle. Lamps were dimmed, the window shades drawn, but still I saw them. Both asleep.

One with small, chubby arms thrown above his head in innocent abandon.

My son. My world.

The other curled on her side with one arm braced protectively over Andreos and the other draped over her belly.

My wife.

But not for much longer. Unless I took steps to do something about it.

Resolution slid home like a key in a lock I didn't even realise needed opening. Now I did—now the possibility of *more* beckoned with a promise I didn't want to deny.

Shaking out a light throw, I tucked it over both of them, then stepped back.

Calypso made a distressed sound in her sleep, an anxious twitch marring her brow for a second before it smoothed out and her breathing grew steady.

Was her stomach still bothering her? I frowned as that niggling returned.

My hand clenched over the door handle.

Were her secrets disturbing her sleep? Could that be the last stumbling block I needed to overcome to make this marriage real? If so, could I live with it?

The breath locked in my lungs was released, along with the bracing realisation that, regardless of what the secret was, it needn't get in our way. If she was prepared not to let it.

Very much aware that several things hung in the balance, I stepped out, shut the door behind me and returned to the living room. But through all my strategising and counter-strategising my resolution simply deepened.

My grandfather had sacrificed and nearly lost everything in his dealings with one Petras.

But perhaps it was time to draw a line underneath all that, let acrimony stay in the past where it belonged.

Perhaps it was time to strike yet another bargain.

A more permanent one.

Thailand was magical.

Or as magical as a place could be when I knew that dark shadows crept ever closer. Knew that my stolen time was rapidly dwindling away.

It marred my ability to enjoy fully the sheer magnificence of our tropical paradise except on canvas, with the paints Axios had supplied me with, which conversely helped in keeping my true state under wraps for a little longer.

The discomfort in my abdomen which he had erroneously assumed was my period kept him from the jaw-droppingly stunning master suite of our Bangkok villa at night. And when we were required to make an appearance together at one of the many events marking the successful merger of Xenakis Aeronautics and a major Thai-owned airline he was painfully solicitous, showering me with the kind of attention that made the tabloid headlines screech with joy.

The kind that made my heart swell with a foolish longing that I knew would make the inevitable break all the more agonising.

The kind he'd showered me with over the last few weeks but that now came with a speculative look in his eyes. As if he was trying to solve a puzzle. As if he was trying to make our situation *work*.

But my guilt at the subterfuge was nothing compared to the grief tearing my heart to shreds at the thought of leaving Andreos.

When, after four days in Bangkok, Axios announced that we were relocating to Kamala in Phuket for the remaining three days, for a delayed honeymoon, I knew I couldn't hide from my feelings any longer.

I was in love with Axios.

Even knowing he didn't feel the same couldn't diminish the knowledge that I'd been falling since that night on the balcony. Since I'd agreed to *for now*. But, contrarily, accepting my true feelings meant I couldn't in good conscience burden him or my precious baby with the battle ahead.

I was in love with my husband. And to spare him our marriage had to end.

Tucked inside the bamboo shelter of a rainforest shower, I gave in to the silent sobs tearing my heart to pieces, letting the warm spray wash my tears away. When I was wrung out, I carefully disguised the tell-tale signs of my distress with subtle make-up before leaving the suite.

In bare feet and a floaty white dress that whispered softly around my body, I approached the sound of infant giggles, a deep, sexy voice and the playful splash of water.

Axios was enjoying a lazy swim with Andreos. And, as much as I wanted to stop and frame the beautiful picture father and son made, so I could carry it in my heart, I knew my emotions were far too close to the surface to risk detection.

Instead I made my way past the pool and through the glass hallway that led to another stunning wing of the multitiered luxury villa. To the special place I'd discovered on our arrival.

The suspended treehouse was accessed by a heavy plank and rope bridge from the second level of the villa and a broad ladder from the level below. I took the walkway, enjoying the swaying movement that made me feel as if I was dancing on air, and entered the wide space laid out with polished wooden floors, wide rectangular windows and a roped-off platform that gave magnificent views of the Andaman Sea and the Bay of Bengal.

A riot of vivid colour brush-stroked the horizon, signalling the approach of night. Silently awed, and my breath held, I watched the colours settle into breathtaking layers of a purple and orange sunset.

I wasn't sure how long I stood there, lost in my turbulent thoughts, selfishly praying for things I couldn't have. And even when I sensed Axios's approach I didn't turn around, didn't give in to the raw need to fill my senses with the sight and sound of him.

Instead I gripped the rope barrier until my knuckles shrieked with just a fraction of the pain shredding my insides.

Whether he sensed my mood or not, Axios didn't speak either. But when he stopped behind me I felt the intensity of his presence. And when he slid an arm around my waist and engulfed me in the poignant scents of father and son I couldn't help the scalding tears that prickled my eyes.

With a soft moan I sagged into his hold, and the three of us stood on the platform, staring at the horizon as the bright orange ball of the sun dipped into the sea and a blanket of stars started to fill the sky.

'Come,' he said eventually, his voice low and deep. 'The chef is almost done preparing dinner. Let's go put our son to bed, hmm?'

Throat tight with locked emotion, I nodded, making sure to avoid his probing gaze as we made our back into the villa. After putting a dozing Andreos in his cot, we retraced our steps to the open terrace, where a candlelit dinner had been laid out.

There, Axios pulled out a chair and I sat, my stomach in knots and my heart bleeding, as I looked at the face of the man I was hopelessly in love with.

The man I could never have.

Theos mou, she was gorgeous.

The breath that had stalled in my lungs fought to emerge as I watched candlelight dance over her face and throat. Even the veil of melancholy shrouding her didn't detract from the captivating mix of fire and calm I wanted to experience for a very long time.

For ever.

Our three-course dinner had passed in stilted conversation, and our appetites had been non-existent. She'd refused dessert and I'd downed my aromatic espresso in one go.

But it was time.

Business pressures had forced this conversation to the back burner for the last four days. It was time to lay my cards on the table.

'About the divorce you requested: I would like to renegotiate…'

A vice tightened my sternum when wild panic flared in her eyes. The hand resting on the table began to tremble and she snatched it away, tucking it into her lap as she exhaled sharply. 'What do you mean, "renegotiate"? You gave me your word!'

For the first time I felt a visceral need to take it all back, to smash it to pieces and rebuild something new, something lasting from the rubble created from greed and blind lust. Because there was something more here. This…*distance* between us had cemented my belief that this wasn't just sex. That I'd fallen deeper, farther than even my imagination could fathom. Perhaps even into that dimension where Calypso could exist.

The thought of that ending…of never experiencing it or her at some point in the future…twisted in something close to agony inside me.

The state was further evidenced by the quiet panic this very argument was fuelling inside me—the fine trembles coursing through my body, taunting me with the possibility that this might be the one deal that eluded me. That my actions last year and since finding her on Bora Bora might have doomed me in her eyes. The very thought that I might fail where I'd succeeded at everything else. Everything that mattered…

No.

'I know what I promised, but I no longer think it's—'

'No!'

She surged to her feet, and the trembling in her hand

seemed transmitted to her body as eyes steeped in turmoil centred on mine. But when she spoke her voice was firm, the most resolute I'd ever heard her. And that only twisted the knife in deeper. Because I sensed a dynamic shift in her the like of which I'd never experienced before.

She seemed to falter for a moment, her hand sliding to her stomach, before she shook her head. 'You made a promise, Axios, and I'm going to have to insist you deliver on that promise.'

That gesture…

'Tell me why, Calypso. Give me a reason why you won't even hear me out,' I challenged, feeling the ground slip away beneath my feet even as I rose and faced her across the dinner table.

'Why?' he grated again when words failed to emerge from my strangled throat in time to answer his question.

His features were changing from a determined sort of cajoling to frighteningly resolute.

'Are you pregnant?' he added hoarsely, and there was a blaze of what looked like hope in his eyes as they dropped to my stomach.

'What? No, I'm not pregnant,' I blurted, dropping my hand.

Was that disappointment on his face?

'Can we take a breath and discuss this rationally?' he asked.

The desire to do just that—to let him talk me into dreaming about an impossible future—was so heart-wrenchingly tempting it took the sharp bite of my nails into my palm to stop agreement spilling from my lips.

'No. I'm all talked out, Axios. All I want now is action. For you to stick to your word and…and let me go.'

His grey eyes went molten for a handful of seconds before his jaw clenched tight. 'Why? We've proved in the last few weeks that we're completely compatible. As parents to Andreos. And in the bedroom.'

Desperately, I shook my head. 'We…we can love Andreos as much together as apart. As for the bedroom…it's just sex. Basing a marriage on it is delusional.'

'I beg to differ. The kind of compatibility we have is unique. Don't be so dismissive of it. Besides, how would you know? I'm the only lover you've ever had,' he tossed in arrogantly.

And he would be the only one for me. 'That still doesn't mean I want to give up everything for the sake of—'

A throat clearing on the edge of the terrace interrupted me. Sophia, now Andreos's official nanny, had travelled with us to Thailand, and she looked supremely nervous.

'What is it?' Axios demanded.

'There's a call from Switzerland for Kyria Xenakis. They say they've been trying to reach you.'

I felt the blood draining from my face as Axios frowned. *Dr Trudeau, tired of waiting for me to contact him.*

'Tell them I'll call back tomorrow,' I said hastily.

The second Sophia hurried away, Axios's gaze sharpened on me. 'Why are you getting a call from Switzerland?'

'I still have business there,' I replied, hoping he'd let it go.

For a terse moment I thought he'd push, but then he sighed. 'What were you going to say before? For the sake of what, Calypso?'

For the sake of unrequited love.

Mercifully, the words remained locked deep inside me, the only hint spilling out in my strained voice as I fought to remain upright, to fight for this vital chance to do this on my own terms.

'I can't—I don't *want* anything long-term. I want to be free.'

To fight for the chance to return whole. Even to dream of starting again with a clean slate.

Hope dried up as Ax's face turned ashen, his eyes darkening with something raw and potent. Something I wasn't sure I wanted to decipher, because it resembled the helpless yearning inside me.

But that couldn't be. Axios not only hated what my father had done to him, he despised what my family had done to his grandfather. I was the last person he could be contemplating hitching himself to for the long term. Which meant that whatever his proposal was it still had an end date. That even if Dr Trudeau had a sliver of hope for me I might not have a chance with Ax.

Nonetheless, temptation buffeted me until I had to hold on to the edge of the table to keep from falling into it.

'Free to live your life? What about our *son*, Calypso?' he demanded scathingly, his voice ragged. 'Do you intend to drag him along on another freedom jaunt? Are you so blinkered to his needs that you would rip him from me to satisfy your own needs?'

'Of course not!'

The searing denial was the final thread holding my emotions together. I felt the hot slide of tears and could do nothing to stop it. So I stood there, my world going into one final free fall, and set the words I despised but *needed* to say spilling free.

'He…he's happy in Athens. He's a Xenakis. You love him. He belongs with you. You can…' *Keep him. Love him. The way I might not be able to.*

The final words dried in my throat, the final selfless act of handing over my precious son unwilling to be given voice. But still he *knew*.

Knew and condemned me absolutely for it.

Brows clamped in horror, he stared at me. 'Are you—?' He stopped, shook his head in abject disbelief. 'You're leaving him behind? Your quest for freedom is so great that you intend to completely abandon your son?'

His voice was bleak, his eyes pools of bewilderment.

'Or it is something else, Calypso? Is it me? Have I

not proved I can be a good husband, provide for you and our son?'

There was my chance. Say no and this would be over. Tell him he'd failed me and it would be done. But I couldn't. Because even if he didn't love me, he hadn't failed me.

'Please, Axios—'

'Please what?' he asked urgently, stalking around the table towards me. 'Make it easier for you to walk away from your child? From me?'

His chest rose and fell in uncharacteristic agitation, his eyes dark, dismal.

'I watched my grandfather's world crumble around him. You want me to let you do the same to mine?' he rasped jaggedly.

I squeezed my eyes shut. 'Please don't say that.'

'Why not?' he demanded, his expression hardening. 'You want easy? Let me make it simple for you. Take one step out through the front door and you will never set eyes on Andreos again. I will make it my mission to erase your name from his life. It will be as if you never even existed.'

Choked tears clogged my throat and my world turned inside out with sorrow.

'You would do that? Really?'

He hesitated, one hand rising to glide roughly over his mouth and jaw before he shook his head. 'Make me understand, Calypso. What could possibly be out there that you won't get with me? What could be more important to you than to care for our child? To watch him grow and thrive under our care?'

I pressed my lips together, the agony of keeping the naked truth locked inside me so it wouldn't stain Andreos killing me. 'My...my freedom. I want what I've wanted for as long as I can remember, Axios. I want to be free.'

For the longest time he simply stared in stark disbelief. Then his breath shuddered out. And with it the last of the bewilderment in his eyes. Now he saw how set I was on bringing this to an end, his jaw clenched in tight resolution.

'Is that your final decision?' he grated.

My balled fist rose from the table, rested on my abdomen and the possible time bomb ticking inside me. 'Yes. It is.'

'Very well. You'll hear from my lawyers before the week is out.'

My breath strangled to nothing. *It was over. Just like that?*

'Axios—'

'No!' His hand slashed through the air. 'There's no room for bargaining.'

And in that moment, presented with his bleak verdict, I felt the words simply tumble out. 'I'm sick, Axios. I have a lump...in my cervix.'

He froze, his eyes widening with shock as he stumbled back a step. 'What?' he whispered, his face ashen.

'I suspected it last year—a few weeks before we married. The doctor in Switzerland who confirmed I was pregnant also confirmed the presence of the lump. My...my grandmother died of cervical cancer—'

'Why have you waited this long for treatment?' he railed.

'Andreos. I wanted to make sure he was safe. And loved.'

He went even paler, his eyes growing pools of horror and disbelief. 'You've known this...you've carried this for a year...and you didn't tell me?' he rasped, almost to himself as he gripped his nape with a shaky hand. 'Why? Because you were testing me? Because I let you down? Because you don't trust me?'

No! Because I love you. Because I can't let you both watch me die.

'Because I didn't want to put Andreos through what might happen. He was a miracle, Ax. I couldn't...didn't know if I could carry him to term, but once I knew I was pregnant I knew I had to *try*.'

'You found out about the lump the same day you found out you were carrying Andreos?' he asked, his voice still stark.

I nodded. 'I just… I couldn't lose him, Ax. I couldn't risk a biopsy to find out whether my prognosis was the same as my grandmother's. But I agreed to frequent scans that wouldn't harm the baby. When the first one showed that the pregnancy was stopping the lump from growing—'

'You chose to stay pregnant,' he finished, awed disbelief in his voice.

I sniffed back tears and nodded again. 'You see, Andreos was a miracle in so many ways. Conceiving him bought me time, and once he was born… I just couldn't let him go.'

'But the lump is still there. It's causing you pain, isn't it?' he asked, even though the knowledge blazed in his eyes. 'That's why you touch your stomach. That's why you were unwell on the plane. And the timing of your return… That was your plan all along—to hand over Andreos and go off and fight this on your own?'

'Yes,' I answered simply. 'I've had one scan since Andreos was born. It showed a small growth rate. But it's… it's time for further tests. Axios, I watched my grandmother suffer in the last months of her life. I can't…*won't* put Andreos through that if that's what I'm facing. I *have* to leave. I would prefer it if you didn't fight me. But…what you said… about erasing me from his life—'

Axios cursed and shoved both hands through his hair. 'That was an idle threat. You'll always be his mother and he'll know you as such. He'll know your courage and what you did for him,' he intoned in a low, solemn voice.

At my sob of relief his lips firmed and he stared at me for an age. 'Andreos,' he said heavily, with a finality that struck real fear into me. 'He's the only reason you're doing this.'

It was a statement—as if he already knew the answer. He took a step back. Then another. Until an unpassable chasm yawned between us.

'Very well. If you've made your choice then so be it.'

I'd expected this to come, but still I stood in utter shock as Axios blazed one last searing look at me, then turned and stalked away.

Shock turned into numbing self-protection when, upon waking up alone in the master suite the next day, I learned from Sophia that Ax had left. That he'd left instructions for Andreos and I to return to Athens alone.

As if the staff knew things had changed drastically, from the moment we walked through the front door of the Athens villa the atmosphere seemed altered. The only one who thankfully remained oblivious was Andreos. Having mastered the art of rolling over, he was now determined to conquer sitting up in record time, and thus provided the only source of delight in the house.

In a bid to make the most of whatever time I had with him, before Ax returned, I all but banished poor Sophia as I greedily devoured every precious second.

Two days turned to three.

Then four.

And then came the news from the housekeeper that Ax was expected mid-afternoon.

The urge to delay my exit, to see his face one last time, pummelled me. But, knowing I couldn't delay the inevitable, I booked my flight to Switzerland. The bag I'd hastily packed while Andreos napped stood like a silent omen at the foot of my bed.

'The car's waiting, *kyria*,' Sophia informed me, her face wreathed in worry.

Unchecked tears streamed down my face as I leaned down and brushed my lips over Andreos' plump cheek. 'Promise me you'll look after him?' I managed through a clogged throat.

Sophia's anxious gaze searched mine. 'I... I promise. But, *kyria*—'

I shook my head, knowing I'd break down if this was prolonged. 'That's good enough for me. Thank you, Sophia.'

Bag in hand, I hurried out, flew down the stairs to the waiting car. Blind with tears, I didn't register his presence until the car was pulling away.

'I will allow those tears for now, *pethi mou*. But for what comes next I'll need that formidable resilience I've come to know and adore.'

CHAPTER TEN

'Axios! What...what are you doing here?'

His face was as gaunt and ashen as the last time I'd seen it. But in his eyes purpose and determination blazed in place of horrified anguish.

Even so, the sight of him shook me, his presence unearthing a cascade of emotions through me.

When he didn't answer, when all he seemed to want was to absorb every inch of my face, I tried again. 'I thought you'd gone...that I'd never see you again.'

His chest heaved in a mighty exhalation. 'I had to go,' he replied gruffly.

Despair and disappointment slashed me wide open. 'Oh. I understand.'

He gave a grating self-deprecating laugh that was chopped off halfway through. '*Do* you? Do you understand how utterly useless and powerless I felt? How I had to walk away because I knew I'd failed you again?'

'What? Why would you—?'

'We will dissect that later. But for now...' my breath caught as his thumb brushed away my tears, '...it's tearing me apart to see these tears,' he grated roughly.

Which only made them fall harder.

'Andreos... Leaving him...that's tearing *me* apart.'

'Just Andreos?'

The question was deep and low. But heavy with unspoken emotions.

I lifted my gaze to find him watching me with hawk-like intensity, his eyes burning with a new light. One that made my insides leap.

'Ax...'

Before I could answer his hand seized mine, his eyes steadfast on me.

'Will you give me the chance to make things right, Calypso? Trust me just for a little while?' he demanded with a hoarse plea.

About to answer, I paused as we pulled up at the private airstrip and stopped next to his plane. 'Axios, where are we going?'

He alighted and held out his hand. I slid out of the car, still in a daze, and didn't resist when he pulled me close.

'You've lived in fear for over a year, while bearing and caring for our son. You've loved him unconditionally when you could've taken a different option without judgement. But you don't need to be alone in this. You never need to be alone again,' he vowed.

The depth of his words made my heart pound with tentative hope. That hope turned to shock when I spotted the middle-aged man standing at the door of the plane.

'Dr Trudeau…what are you…? What's he doing here?' I asked Ax.

'He's here to help. As are the others.'

Taking my hand, he led me onto the plane. And my shock tripled.

'Mama?' Seated amongst three other distinguished-looking men was my mother. When she smiled tremulously and held out her arms a broken sob ripped through me as I rushed forward and threw myself into her embrace.

'Your husband rightly felt that you should be surrounded by those you love in your time of need.'

Did that include him?

Fearing I'd give myself away if I looked his way, I kept my gaze on my mother.

'You should've told us, Callie.'

I shook my head. 'I couldn't risk not having Andreos.'

And that seemed to settle the matter with her. She nodded, then looked over my head. I didn't need the signal to know that Ax was approaching.

'Let me introduce you, Calypso.'

Swiping my hand across my cheek, I composed myself

and stood. Besides Dr Trudeau, the three men were all doctors too, specialising in everything to do with the cervix.

'Your mother has been instrumental in providing details about your grandmother's condition. With your permission, we'll head to Dr Trudeau's clinic and start the tests.'

I gasped, my gaze finding Ax's. 'That's what you've been doing the last three days? Rounding up specialists?'

He nodded, that blaze burning brighter in his eyes. 'You are far too important, *yineka mou*. I'm leaving nothing to chance.'

I swayed. He caught me, held me tight.

After pinning me with his gaze for several seconds, he glanced around. 'We're about to take off,' he said. 'I would like to talk to my wife in private, so I trust you can all amuse yourselves?' At their agreement, he turned to me. 'Calypso?'

I nodded, a million hopes and dreams cascading through my brain as I followed him into the master suite.

He waited long enough for me to be seated and buckled in before stalking over to the drinks cabinet. Dazedly, I watched him pour a glass of cognac, grimace, and pour a thimbleful into a second glass. Walking over, he handed the smaller drink to me.

'A small sip won't hurt,' he stated gruffly, almost pleadingly.

With another befuddled nod I accepted it, took the tiniest sip and shuddered my way through swallowing it down. As the spirit warmed my insides, another sensation filtered through. But the joy bubbling beneath my skin fizzled out when Axios sank onto his knees before me.

'Was it just about Andreos?' he asked starkly. 'Were you leaving only because of him or did I feature anywhere in your thoughts?'

'Ax—'

'I know I didn't give you the wedding of your dreams, or make the time after that palatable. But did I drive you away completely, Calypso?'

There was a layer of self-loathing in his voice that propelled me to grip his hand. 'I just didn't want to burden you—'

'Burden me? You're my *wife*!'

'One who was a stranger when we exchanged vows! I didn't know how…what you would do…'

'What I would *do*? What other option was there besides seeking medical—' His curse ranged through the room. 'Did you think I'd exploit you the way your father did your mother?'

'I didn't know then.'

For an eternity he simply stared at me. '*Then?* Does that mean you know different now?' he asked, his voice awash with hope and his eyes alight with a peculiar kind of desperation that tore through me.

I didn't realise my nails were digging into the sofa until he set his hand on mine, stilling my agitation. I wanted to cling to him. *Theos* did I want to. But the fear of fanning false hope, triggering another torrent of might-have-beens that would further shatter my heart, stopped me.

Discarding his drink, he took both my hands in his. 'Tell me, please, if I have a chance with you. No matter what happens I intend to stay and fight this thing along with you. But after that—'

I pressed a hand to his lips. 'We might not have a future,' I whispered. 'It wasn't just about Andreos. I didn't want to put *you* through that.'

His fingers tightened around mine, and when his eyes fused with mine, I felt the live wire of his desperation.

'That's why you tried to leave me again this time?'

Suspecting I wouldn't be able to speak around the lump in my throat, I nodded.

A hoarse breath shuddered out of him. 'I never thought I'd be so relieved at such a reason for being dumped.'

He stopped abruptly, caught my face between his hands and blazed me a look so intense my insides melted.

'I love you, Calypso. I fell in love with your defiance in Bora Bora. Fell in love with you when I saw your love for our son. I adored your strength when I watched that video. Watching you paint, seeing your talent…awed me. Despite the odds, you have fought and continue to fight for what you want. One day our son will grow up to learn what an inspiration you are. He'll watch you and know he has the best mother in the world.'

The tears came free and unchecked. 'Oh, Ax…'

'Getting the call that you'd gone the morning after our wedding altered something inside me. I wasn't ready to admit it, but I knew I'd failed you. That I'd failed myself. Your agreeing to take a leap with me felt like a second chance. And with every breath I vow to make it worth your while.'

'Was…was this what you were going to tell me in Thailand?'

'Yes. I knew I was in love with you. I planned on begging you to give our marriage a chance. But—'

'But I chopped you off at the knees before you could lay out everything my own heart and soul wanted to tell you. That I loved you and would've given anything to remain your wife.'

He froze. 'Say that again, please?' he begged.

'I love you, too, Ax. Even before the possibility of Andreos and the possibility of love I was drawn to you. Something inside me made me put *you* at the top of my bucket list. I was always going to come back, even if only for a short time, because my heart knew I belonged to you. And these last few weeks have felt like a heaven I didn't want to leave. I may have been devastated when you left me the morning after our wedding, but watching you leave me in Thailand…'

He closed his eyes for a single moment. 'I knew I was making a mistake even before I got on the helicopter after our wedding night. But when I left this time I knew I was coming straight back. That nothing would stop me. Because you're my heart, *pethi mou*. My very soul.'

To cement that vow he slanted his lips over mine, kissed me until we were both breathless.

'Tell me again,' I commanded.

His eyes burned with feeling. 'I love you. With all that I am and everything in between.'

He kissed me again as the plane sped down the runway and soared into the sky.

When I broke away to look out of the window, he gently caught my chin in his hand. 'What is it?'

'Andreos.'

A warm smile split Ax's face. 'He has Sophia and a dozen other staff curled around his plump little fingers. They will take care of him until we send for him in the morning. He's our little miracle and we will fight this thing together. All three of us. For now, you will let me take care of you. You will allow me the privilege of helping to make you better. Please, my love?'

I nodded, but still hesitated. 'What if it's too late? What if they can't…?'

He slid his thumb across my lips, silencing my doubts. 'Whatever happens we face it together. For better or worse, you have me for life. I will never leave your side and I will never fail you again.'

His words unfurled my joy. This time I wasn't alone. I had my precious baby and the husband of my heart. I intended to fight with everything I had for the chance to ensure my days were blessed with nothing but love, health and happiness.

At cruising altitude, Axios swung me into his arms and strolled to the bed. I curled my arms around his neck and looked into molten eyes blazing with love.

'I love you, Calypso,' he said again, as if saying the words filled him with as much happiness as it filled my heart.

'*Se agapo*, Axios.

EPILOGUE

A year later

'WHAT ARE YOU DOING?'

'Starting on your payback,' Axios drawled, striding across the master bedroom in Agistros to lay me down on the king-sized bed before trailing his lips over my shoulder to the sensitive area beneath my earlobe.

'What?' I gasped, delightful shivers running through me at the wickedness he evoked.

'You owe me a full pregnancy experience. I can't think of a better time to start than now. I want to experience it all—from morning sickness to the moment our baby enters the world.'

I made a face. 'Morning sickness isn't very sexy.'

He dropped a kiss on the corner of my mouth. 'Perhaps not. But I made you a promise to be here for the good as well as the bad, *eros mou*. So I will be on hand to hold your hair when you throw up. To massage your feet when the weight of our child tires you. And everything you need in between. If that's what you want too?' he asked, hope brimming in his voice.

I curled my arms around his neck. 'More than anything in the world.'

The operation to remove what had turned out to be a benign lump in my cervix six months ago had been a resounding success, with every trace of it gone and quarterly scans showing it hadn't returned.

Today Dr Trudeau had given us the all-clear to try for another baby—a statement Axios seemed determined to capitalise on immediately. And with a doting grandmother to help care for Andreos, in the form of my mother, life couldn't have been better. Her decision to leave my father hadn't been easy, but I'd supported her. Yiannis Petras hadn't resisted for long, busy as he was with frittering away his millions on one bad investment after another.

Ax groaned. 'Don't cry. It rips me up when you do.'

I laughed tremulously. 'Oh, God, then prepare yourself. Because I'm very hormonal during pregnancy.'

'Hmm, I will have to think of ways to counteract that.'

'What did you have in mind?'

'Why, endless seduction, of course. I can think of nothing better than making love to my beautiful wife while she nurtures our baby in her womb.'

More tears flowed. With another groan, he sealed his lips to mine—most likely to distract me. It worked. Within minutes I was naked and gasping, lost in the arms of my true love.

And when, at the height of feeling, he looked deep into my eyes and whispered, 'I love you, Calypso,' he went one better and kissed my tears away.

The power of him moving inside me, possibly planting his seed inside me, triggered fresh tears.

I was still emotional when our breaths cooled. When he pulled me close and whispered in my ear.

'Our adventure is only just beginning, *eros mou*. And I couldn't have wished for a better partner at my side to experience it all but you, Calypso Xenakis.'

'Nor I, you, my love,' I returned, with every ounce of the love I held in my heart.

* * * * *

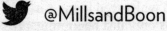

MILLS & BOON

THE HEART OF ROMANCE

A ROMANCE FOR EVERY READER

MODERN

Prepare to be swept off your feet by sophisticated, sexy and seductive heroes, in some of the world's most glamourous and romantic locations, where power and passion collide.

HISTORICAL

Escape with historical heroes from time gone by. Whether your passion is for wicked Regency Rakes, muscled Vikings or rugged Highlanders, awaken the romance of the past.

MEDICAL

Set your pulse racing with dedicated, delectable doctors in the high-pressure world of medicine, where emotions run high and passion, comfort and love are the best medicine.

True Love

Celebrate true love with tender stories of heartfelt romance, from the rush of falling in love to the joy a new baby can bring, and a focus on the emotional heart of a relationship.

Desire

Indulge in secrets and scandal, intense drama and sizzling hot action with heroes who have it all: wealth, status, good looks…everything but the right woman.

HEROES

The excitement of a gripping thriller, with intense romance at its heart. Resourceful, true-to-life women and strong, fearless men face danger and desire - a killer combination!

To see which titles are coming soon, please visit

millsandboon.co.uk/nextmonth

JOIN US ON SOCIAL MEDIA!

Stay up to date with our latest releases, author news
and gossip, special offers and discounts, and all the
behind-the-scenes action from Mills & Boon...

 @millsandboon

 @millsandboonuk

 facebook.com/millsandboon

 @millsandboonuk

It might just be true love...

GET YOUR ROMANCE FIX!

Get the latest romance news, exclusive author interviews, story extracts and much more!

blog.millsandboon.co.uk

MILLS & BOON
MODERN
Power and Passion

Prepare to be swept off your feet by sophisticated, sexy and seductive heroes, in some of the world's most glamourous and romantic locations, where power and passion collide.

MILLS & BOON
Desire

Indulge in secrets and scandal, intense drama and plenty of sizzling hot action with powerful and passionate heroes who have it all: wealth, status, good looks…everything but the right woman.